Lynne Graham was born in Northern Ireland and has been a keen romance reader since her teens. She is very happily married, to an understanding husband who has learned to cook since she started to write! Her five children keep her on her toes. She has a very large dog, who knocks everything over, a very small terrier, who barks a lot, and two cats. When time allows, Lynne is a keen gardener.

Clare Connelly was raised in small-town Australia among a family of avid readers. She spent much of her childhood up a tree, Mills & Boon book in hand. Clare is married to her own real-life hero, and they live in a bungalow near the sea with their two children. She is frequently found staring into space—a surefire sign that she's in the world of her characters. She has a penchant for French food and ice-cold champagne, and Mills & Boon novels continue to be her favourite ever books. Writing for Modern is a long-held dream. Clare can be contacted via clareconnelly.com or at her Facebook page.

THE RING
THE SPANIARD
GAVE HER

LYNNE GRAHAM

CINDERELLA'S
NIGHT IN VENICE

CLARE CONNELLY

MILLS & BOON

First Published in Great Britain 2021
by Mills & Boon, an imprint of HarperCollins*Publishers*
1 London Bridge Street, London, SE1 9GF

The Ring the Spaniard Gave Her © 2021 Lynne Graham

Cinderella's Night in Venice © 2021 Harlequin Books S.A.

Special thanks and acknowledgement are given to Clare Connelly
for her contribution to the Signed, Sealed…Seduced miniseries.

ISBN: 978-0-263-28241-2

MIX
Paper from
responsible sources
FSC™ C007454

This book is produced from independently certified FSC™ paper
to ensure responsible forest management.
For more information visit www.harpercollins.co.uk/green.

Printed and bound in Spain
by CPI, Barcelona

THE RING
THE SPANIARD
GAVE HER

LYNNE GRAHAM

CHAPTER ONE

RUY VALIENTE, THE reclusive billionaire owner of Valiente Capital, one of the world's largest and most successful hedge funds, didn't immediately answer his mobile when it pulsed in his pocket.

Why? He was in a great mood, happily contemplating a few weeks off finance and the opportunity to indulge in his secret passion. Those breaks were both rare and precious in his life because he had been brought up to be enormously disciplined and do his duty. He was also in transit to his rural English home, which he planned to make his very private bolt-hole. When he finally grudgingly drew out the phone, bearing in mind that a call to his personal number—known to few—could be an emergency, he was reassured when he saw his half-sister, Cecile's name flash up.

In his rigorously conservative, judgemental circle of relations, Cecile was just about the only one he could stomach, and it was to her that he owed the discovery of his new home, he reminded himself as he answered.

'I need your help,' Cecile told him without any preamble. 'And I know it's a dreadful imposition and that when you're moving into a house only a couple of miles away from Charles and me you will now suspect that we're going to be a nuisance—'

Ruy smiled. 'That thought would never occur to me.'

'Where are you?' she asked.

'Ten minutes from my new house.'

'Oh, good. Charles and I are stuck in a jam on the motorway. We were on our way home early to see the girls perform in their spring concert,' she told him. 'But we're not going to make it in time.'

'That's unfortunate.' Ruy was sympathetic because his sister and her husband were medics, whom he knew often struggled to combine work and family commitments. 'How can I help?'

'Lola and Lucia will be devastated when we don't turn up. They've been rehearsing their performance for weeks,' Cecile told him tautly. 'I know it's a very big ask, Ruy, because it's not your sort of thing, but if you could show up in our stead it would mean a lot to the girls. In fact, your appearance would be much more exciting than ours. Tio Ruy is hugely popular with them. The concert is in the village hall and it's already started. Luckily, the girls are in the very last act. Can you make it?'

Ruy swallowed every one of the objections brimming on his lips and murmured, 'Of course I can,' because it was the very *first* time his half-sister had asked him for anything.

All the rest of his relatives maintained a constant barrage of requests for money, jobs, help with legal and family problems—indeed every bump in the road of their lives from disease to divorce inspired their urgent pleas for assistance. Of course, his late father, Armando, had encouraged that dependency on the head of the Valiente family because it had fed his love of power and a subservient audience, but Ruy found that same steady stream of demands exasperating and was gradually doing what he could to discourage his relations from the habit.

'You…*will*?' Cecile could hide neither the relief nor the surprise in her response. 'You won't need to take the girls home or anything. Their nanny is with them. All you have to do is show your face and give them a hug afterwards and obviously *lie* when Lola asks how she did because she's like a baby elephant on stage…bless her! It shouldn't take more than an hour of your time.'

'It's fine, Cecile.'

'But this is your first visit to your new home and I'm totally invading your privacy,' she protested guiltily.

'I'm not that inflexible,' he assured her soothingly, although he knew that he was lying out of courtesy. He had learned the hard way over his thirty years that if he didn't ruthlessly carve out the time for his art from his incredibly demanding schedule in the world of investment, he didn't get *any* time to do what he most enjoyed. 'It will be good to see the girls.'

'If you would only agree to visit us more often… sorry, in a moany mood here,' Cecile mumbled apologetically, knowing that she was crossing his boundaries.

Ruy was very much a loner who cherished his privacy, a privilege he saw little of in the real world where he was invariably surrounded by staff. Employees waited on him hand and foot and hung on his every word and, all credit to him, he *was* aware that his lifestyle was far from normal. He was also rather more painfully aware that his twin brother, Rodrigo, his junior only by a matter of minutes, was consumed by envy, resentment and bitterness that he had not been the firstborn son, on whom all Armando Valiente's brightest hopes and expectations rested. It was a terrible ironic truth that Ruy would have very much preferred the far less demanding role of younger son and brother. And it struck him as even worse that his brother had asked him to his wedding to take place in a fortnight and that he was dreading the event, unable to unquestioningly accept that the invitation could be an olive branch.

The community hall beside the church was an old shabby building in need of a facelift, Ruy registered. He would consider making an anonymous donation. Philanthropic gestures came naturally to a man who had never in his life had to consider the cost of anything. It would also be the first time that Ruy actually set foot in the village near the property he had bought. There wasn't much to the place: a garage, a little supermarket and, opposite the church, a pub with a big flashy sign that said it had pretensions to be something more. On his one previous visit, he had driven through the village without stopping because it didn't interest him. He had no plans to get to know anyone in the neighbourhood, a decision that would protect the anonymity he treasured.

There were no empty seats available in the packed hall, which suited Ruy fine. He stationed himself by the back wall, his height of six feet four granting him an excellent view of the small stage, which was currently in darkness. Strange plinky-plonky music notes filtered out, the kind of New Age stuff that made Ruy, who liked rock ballads, wince. A low light came on above the silhouette of a woman kneeling with her head bent. Unexpected interest fired in him as the music swelled and the woman began to unfold. Like a flower in one of those sped up nature documentaries, he thought abstractedly.

As her arms lifted in a fluid shimmy, she leant back, seemingly as flexible as rubber, her long hair fluttering, her small full breasts jutting up, her body bending back in a natural curve. Ruy was riveted to the spot, only dimly aware of the children, crouched like little mushrooms awaiting their moment in the darkness, to either side of her. It was modern dance, again something he had no interest in, but the innocent sensuality of her every move captured him as both a man and an artist. She slowly rose upright, hands moving like silent poetry, her grace phenomenal and that fast he knew he had to find out who she was, knew he *had* to paint her.

'She's a firecracker,' a male voice commented next to him. 'A beauty.'

'Who is she?' Ruy didn't know whether or not she was a beauty because her entire performance had taken place in shadow; as if she were part of the backdrop and not the centre of the show, which would definitely be wishful thinking on her part if that had been the intention, he reflected with wry amusement, considering that she was the most eye-catching sight he had enjoyed in a very long time.

'Suzy Madderton, publican's daughter, well and truly off the market if you're interested.'

'I wasn't,' Ruy asserted, unusual colour slashing his high cheekbones because he was shamed by the throb at his groin in a place where children were present, even though in the darkness nobody could have seen or noticed his condition.

'Heard she's getting hitched soon and to a golden oldie, *not* a young chap like yourself…know what I mean,' the older man imparted. 'Local businessman, owns half the village…a crying shame *her* ending up with *him*!'

Ruy said nothing, too cynical after the life he had led to think it even remotely strange that a young and apparently beautiful woman would marry an older man for his money. His only concern was whether or not he could get her to model for him, and if money were a magnet that would be his 'in'.

He wouldn't touch a gold-digger with a bargepole, not that he had any personal interest in the dancer. A natural male response to a sensual performance was no proof of attraction, he assured himself. After all, sex was no big deal to Ruy and hadn't been in a long time. Casual sex was easily available to him and he hadn't been on a date in longer than he could recall. Love was anathema to him because he had witnessed and experienced how warped and damaged love could become. Someone like his former sister-in-law, Liliana, could get badly burned by that seemingly desirable emotion of love that so many foolish beings chased. Old unforgotten guilt burned in Ruy's gut as he watched his nieces dance across the stage as very cute little mushrooms. Lucia was sylph-like in comparison to poor little Lola, who stomped like a water buffalo. Slowly, almost painfully, Ruy smiled, reflecting that if it didn't entail getting married, he would have enjoyed having a child of his own...

'Reckon you raised a dad temperature or two out there!' Flora, the concert organiser, teased Suzy as she hurriedly pulled on her clothes at the back of the stage. 'The men can't take their eyes off you.'

'Nonsense, they're just keen to spot their kids,' Suzy declared, a little nauseous at the prospect of being the target of lust in public. Wasn't it bad enough that she had had to recently cope with it in private?

She squashed that self-pitying thought as soon as it popped up in the back of her brain. Hadn't she chosen her own path? Hadn't she decided to put her dad first? Her dad, the man who had loved her enough for two parents after her mother died in a car crash when she was a toddler. Roger Madderton was a great father, just not quite farsighted enough to see when a trap was being sprung in front of him. And Percy Brenton had caught both father and daughter in a hellish financial trap and there was no escaping the consequences of that miscalculation. Either she let her father go bankrupt through no fault of his own, and watched him lose his home and business, or she married Percy. And as she was marrying Percy in less than forty-eight hours, she had best settle down and accept the inevitable, she told herself irritably. By the weekend, she would be in Barbados on her honeymoon with Percy, and she cringed at the prospect.

The concert was over. People were already starting to leave as Suzy descended the stage steps. In her haste her rich auburn hair bounced against her spine in a flyaway mop of curls. Lola and Lucia came running across the floor to greet her, full of excitement after their performance. They were the cutest little girls, one seven, one four, and they were in the dance class that Suzy taught every week. Even though she was keen to escape the hall before Percy could put in an appearance, she couldn't resist the little hands grabbing hold of hers and pulling her forward. Laughing, green eyes sparkling with mirth at their enthusiasm, Suzy found herself looking, not at the parents she expected or even the nanny, but at a tall, dark total stranger.

A tall, dark, quite magnificent stranger, she adjusted, her tongue sticking to the roof of her mouth, because he was breathtakingly handsome. Olive-tinted skin stretched taut over a superb bone structure that formed the perfect backdrop to spare, flaring cheekbones, a sculpted jawline shadowed with a blue-black hint of stubble, a classic nose and wide, sensual lips. Add in his height and lean, powerful build and he came as close to a fantasy male as Suzy had ever seen in reality.

Beautiful wasn't an expressive enough word to describe Suzy Madderton, Ruy conceded, taken aback by her sheer visual impact. She glowed like a spectacular sunset with her vibrant copper-red spirals of hair, porcelain-pale skin, a scattering of freckles across the bridge of her small nose and green eyes brighter than polished emeralds. Spirit and energy bubbled out of her. All his defensive antennae came into play, snapping up his reserve like a safety barrier because Ruy instantly loathed the strength of his response to her. Even worse, he was deeply uneasy around any woman he sensed to be volatile in the emotional field.

'Tio Ruy!' Lola proclaimed importantly. '*Our* Tio Ruy!'

'Their mother's brother, their uncle,' Ruy interpreted smoothly.

Suzy was ensnared by eyes as dark as Hades and full of sardonic superiority. She didn't know why or how she read that message in his stunningly dark gaze, but she did, and her chin came up at an angle, her eyes sparkling with animosity. 'Thanks for the translation but I didn't need it. My mother was Spanish. I have a few words,' she murmured, thinking it was *very* few words, even after the evening classes she had attended for years, because lack of practice had killed her hope of becoming fluent in her mother's language.

Everything that was masculine and proud in Ruy thrilled to that unexpected challenge and he had all the pride of his *hidalgo* forebears. A firecracker, yes, he could *see* that in the aggressive lift of her delicate chin, the toss of her shamelessly untidy hair. She wouldn't suit his needs at all in the sex department, he acknowledged without hesitation. He preferred his women neat, meek and mild and unlikely to cause waves, but that didn't mean that he didn't *still* want her as a model. After all, he had barely spoken to his last model, now world-famous thanks to the exposure of his previous year's exhibition because his portraits of beautiful women sold for millions. He didn't do involvement in any part of his life and that was how he avoided the messy chaos of emotions that had once engulfed him in family disaster.

He spoke to Suzy in Spanish too fast for her to follow in detail and she only got the gist of what he was saying. He was offering her a job as a model. An artist's model. *Her?* Suzy couldn't believe her ears and marvelled that the girls' friendly outgoing mother, Cecile, hadn't mentioned the fact that her brother was an artist or that he had come to stay with her.

'Name your price,' he said to conclude in English, wanting to be sure she got that message. 'It would only take a couple of weeks of your time.'

A heavy arm fell round Suzy's shoulders and her heart sank instantly to the soles of her biker boots: Percy had arrived. 'Price for what?' he demanded.

'I was asking Miss Madderton if she would consider acting as an artist's model for me.' Ruy extended his hand politely to Percy. 'Ruy Rivera,' he murmured, borrowing his illegitimate half-sister's maiden name to assure his anonymity. When he was in artist mode and he wanted to be anonymous, he generally used Rivera as a name to cover his tracks.

'That is absolutely out of the question, Mr Rivera,' Percy announced with crushing contempt as he ignored Ruy's extended hand. 'Suzy and I are getting married the day after tomorrow. She'll be far too busy!'

'You could have been nicer to him. He didn't mean any offence,' Suzy whispered in sheer embarrassment as Percy herded her domineeringly towards the exit, affecting not to hear the sallies aimed at her from other people.

Angry fingers bit into her upper arm. 'Don't tell *me* how to behave!' her fiancé snapped in her ear as he thrust her bodily in the direction of his car. 'And that'll be the end of all this dance nonsense now. I'm not having my wife up on a stage showing herself off to all and sundry like some stripper!' he practically spat at her.

Pale and shivering in the cold air, shaken by his anger, Suzy stepped away from him in the direction of the street while rubbing at her arm. 'You hurt me,' she muttered unevenly. 'I haven't done anything. Why are you so annoyed?'

'Stop making a fuss, Suzy. Get in the car,' Percy told her impatiently. 'You'll come home with me and get some supper.'

'I'm sorry. I'm really tired after all that...er...dancing,' Suzy lied, screening a fake yawn with a slender hand, her wary gaze pinned to the older man's flushed and still furious face. Supper was merely a euphemism for groping in Percy's parlance and he had agreed months ago to her demand that theirs would be a marriage in name only. Whether or not he had believed he could change her mind on that score, she had no idea, but she had no plans to engage in an additional war of words and resentment on his sofa after the roughness with which he had handled her. 'As you said, I have a lot to do for the wedding, so I'll just head home now. Thanks,' she completed stiffly, wondering what she was thanking him for but dismayed by the rage in his bloodshot blue eyes and knowing that she was trying to placate him.

'Suzy!' Her father's wonderfully familiar voice hailed her, and she turned in relief to greet him.

Percy took a step back, a forced smile settling on his florid face. 'Roger,' he said quietly, all hint of the rage wiped from his expression.

'Where did you come from?'

'I ran over to see your dance and stood at the exit watching,' her father confided. 'I wouldn't miss you for the world.'

'But who's been watching the bar?' she asked.

'Old Man Morgan was left in charge,' he said with a smile as he named an elderly local who was practically a fixture in the bar and guided her across the road to the pub. 'Everything all right between you and Percy?'

Suzy stiffened. 'Yes…why are you asking?'

'From a distance it looked like you were having a quarrel,' the older man admitted, looking anxious. 'I reckon I'm being ridiculous but, for an instant there, I honestly thought he was about to *hit* you!'

Suzy was pale as milk as she stepped into the familiar heat of the pub where a log fire burned in the stone fireplace and where only one customer propped up the bar. 'Yes, that is ridiculous,' she told him firmly. 'Percy wouldn't do anything like that.'

'He looked like he'd been drinking as well and he must be drinking at home or at his hotel because he doesn't do any drinking here,' he pointed out worriedly. 'Are you sure about this marriage?'

'Yes... I can't wait to see Barbados!' she teased, hoping to take him off the subject.

Roger Madderton groaned and brushed a straying strand of red hair off her pale brow. 'It doesn't feel right to me...me owing him money, you marrying him, him saying I don't need to repay it now, like it's nothing, when he's known to be as tight as a drum with his cash!'

'Well, Percy's right that you shouldn't have money owing between family members, and after the wedding it *will* feel more normal,' she assured her father confidently.

'I still feel that he's too old for you,' Roger admitted. 'He's almost as old as I am, for goodness' sake, no spring chicken, and you wouldn't catch me chasing a woman half my age!'

'Everyone's different and Percy will give me a good life.'

Roger grimaced. 'If I taught you that a good life had to encompass a big house and foreign holidays, I failed somewhere along the line.'

'Dad...' Reluctant to tell him any more cover-up lies, Suzy hugged the older man. 'Stop being silly. You are the very best father any woman could ever want.'

'I'm sorry. All I want is to see you happy and I'm not convinced Percy can give you that.'

'You'll be convinced eventually!' Suzy quipped as she headed for the rear door that led into the apartment where they lived, not entirely convinced that Old Man Morgan was as deaf as he seemed. At the end of the day all that she cared about was her father's happiness and security and marrying Percy would ensure that.

Suzy went upstairs to bed, thinking about all the sacrifices her father had made to raise her alone. There hadn't ever been any other woman in his life because he had been afraid that he might give her one of those wicked stepmothers straight out of fiction. He had always worked very long hours striving to make the bar a success and it genuinely wasn't his fault that he was deep in debt.

His problems had begun years ago, after he had borrowed from the bank to renovate the pub in the forlorn hope that it would encourage more customers. When the loan payments had become too much, and he had fallen behind, the bank had threatened to foreclose on him. That was when Percy had come in, softly, softly like a thief in the night, she reflected with a faint shudder of recollection. Back then she had only been eighteen, incapable of seeing that Percy had undoubtedly always intended to take her father's business from him and that it was possible that she had only been an afterthought. Percy had been Roger's hero then, taking on the debt and offering lower repayments.

And then one day six months ago, just before her twenty-first birthday, Percy had stopped to give her a lift in the village and he had laid out the facts for her without an ounce of shame. He had threatened to repossess the pub and evict them unless Suzy agreed to marry him. When she had accused him of blackmail, he had made much of the fact that he was offering her the respectability of matrimony and an infinitely more comfortable life than she currently enjoyed, working all hours in the pub as she did, cleaning, cooking and

tending the bar. To balance the scales, Suzy had agreed
to marry him but she had also insisted that, while she
would act as a wife in every other field, she wanted her
own bedroom and their union would not include sex. At
the time, Percy had agreed, but more recently she had
begun to suspect that he regretted that pact and resented
her for her refusal to share a bed with him.

Suzy curled up in a tight ball in her bed, burning
tears of regret forcing a passage from beneath her eyelids. Had she realised six months ago just how difficult
it would be to marry a man she didn't love and whom
she wasn't remotely attracted to? No, back then, she'd
had no real idea of what she was signing up for and now
it was too late. She felt trapped but she had *agreed* to
be trapped. Either she told her father the truth and they
ended up homeless and broke or she married Percy.
Percy, who was suddenly getting rough with her, which
frightened her more than she wanted to admit.

Having parted from his nieces, Ruy climbed back
into his vehicle, a purely practical choice that would not
attract the particular notice that a fancier car or limousine and driver would. He was still marvelling that
a young woman as striking as Suzy Madderton could
choose to marry an ignorant loudmouth of a bully such
as the man he had met. But it was none of his business
and had he not still desired to paint her he was convinced he would have thought no more of her. As it
was, however, he was unaccustomed to meeting with
the word no and running into an obstacle only made
him all the more obstinately determined to get what
he wanted. Once he was settled into his new property,

he would call into the pub and speak to Suzy alone, he
decided with satisfaction. Women who said no to Ruy
were so rare as to be non-existent.

For the two days before the wedding, Suzy was run
off her feet. There was a final fitting for her gown. She
was not having any attendants, no bridal party as such,
having decided that the fewer people dragged into her
masquerade of being a happy bride, the easier it would
be. In any case, all her school friends had long since
disappeared to go to college or look for jobs unavailable in a rural village, options that had never really
been a possibility for Suzy. Besides the dress fitting,
which entailed a long drive into the nearest town and
took up the entire morning, she had to call into Percy's
country house hotel, which lay several miles outside
the village and where the reception was being held, to
check arrangements, and she also had to pick up the
cake and deliver it. She was doing the flowers in the
church with the florist that evening. All else completed,
she returned to the pub and was taken aback to see Ruy
Rivera lounging by the fire there with a whisky and a
broadsheet newspaper.

The first time she had seen him he had been wearing
a beautifully tailored suit and she had wondered vaguely
if he had been at a wedding or some similar event, but
on this occasion he was casually clad in jeans and a knit
sweater the colour of oatmeal. His hair, blue black as a
raven's wing and equally glossy and thick, was ruffled
back from his bronzed brow, a little longer in length
than was strictly conservative. In that first glance she
registered afresh that he was so gorgeous he literally

stole the breath from her lungs and made her mouth run dry. Fierce embarrassment claimed her as she glanced down at the sparkling solitaire on her engagement finger. Whatever else she owed Percy, she firmly believed that she owed him her loyalty and respect, and looking with interest at another man, no matter how hot he was, felt entirely wrong.

Her fair skin deeply flushed by guilty pink, she stepped behind the bar to give her father a break.

'I thought you were at the church doing the flowers,' Roger Madderton said in surprise.

'The florist changed the time. She has another booking to cover first,' Suzy explained. 'Go and get your tea.'

'Yes, your bossiness.' Her father chuckled and sped off through the door into their living quarters.

Ruy folded his newspaper and vaulted upright to approach the bar. 'I was hoping that you would appear.'

Crystalline green eyes glimmered over him as though reluctant to land or linger. 'What can I get you? Another whisky?'

'No, thank you. I'm driving,' Ruy murmured with perfect diction, his Spanish accent purring along the syllables like an expensive sports car, she heard herself think foolishly of his dark, deep, oh-so-masculine drawl. 'Would it be rude for me to ask about your Spanish mother?'

Disconcerted, Suzy stilled, her eyes reflective. 'No, not at all. I don't remember her because she died in a car crash when I was two. She was from Madrid and she lost her parents when she was quite young. She came to the UK as an au pair and met my father. They were married within months. I took Spanish classes because I wanted to feel closer to her, but it doesn't really work if you don't get to practise speaking the language.' She sighed.

'You could practise on me,' Ruy suggested. 'How long have you been giving dance lessons to the local kids?'

'A couple of years now, first as an assistant until the teacher, who taught me for years, retired because of her arthritis. Dancing was my only hobby growing up,' Suzy admitted.

'I'm still hoping that you'll act as a model for me. I really *would* like to paint you.'

'I'm sorry but it's not possible. I'm getting married tomorrow and then I'll be away on my honeymoon for a couple of weeks and, in any case, Percy wouldn't agree to it.'

'You don't strike me as a young woman who always does as she's told. I'm willing to wait a few weeks to paint you,' Ruy volunteered.

'I can't do it and that's that. Will you please drop the subject now?' Suzy shot back at him in exasperation. 'Don't you know how to take no for an answer?'

A slashing smile slanted Ruy's wide mobile lips. 'No,' he dared.

Suzy's teeth gritted. 'Well, it's a very annoying trait… yes, sir…what can I get you?' she asked another man who had wandered up to the bar and went to serve him.

Ruy was unused to being left to kick his heels; it was his turn to grit teeth. Just at that moment faking being a more ordinary mortal wasn't working well for him. The usual awe, flattery and flirtation that women gave him would have been remarkably welcome just then. *Hombre!* A barmaid was giving him lip! His half-sister's voice sounded in his conscience and he knew she would have told him that he was being both snobbish and unjust. Cecile, ignored and hidden by their father as the daughter of his mistress, had had a much rougher ride through life than Ruy had ever had, and he had a sneaking suspicion that his opinionated and down-to-earth sibling would have laughed at seeing him being ignored and cold-shouldered by a woman.

'One last word on the subject?' Ruy breathed softly as she moved closer to him while wiping the bar top.

'Name your price for being my model and I will pay it,' he murmured in sibilant conclusion.

'You're just inviting me to pluck some sum of money out of the air? I haven't a clue what artists' models charge!' Suzy objected.

'I want you, nobody else, which gives you a truly rare and special value,' Ruy told her. 'I will pay a *huge* sum for you to model for me.'

Suzy dealt him a frowning glance of reluctant fascination. 'That's crazy. There *has* to be a limit.'

'Not with me, there's not,' Ruy assured her stubbornly, forgetting in that instant that he was not in his own world of gilded exclusivity where nothing cost too much and nothing he desired was ever out of his reach.

Suzy wondered what it was about her that made men try to buy her. Percy had already done it, she reminded herself wretchedly. She could only think of the horrific sum her father had been told he owed after Percy had added on the interest charges that her poor father had misunderstood how to calculate. 'Fifty thousand pounds,' she said mockingly. 'I'll do it for—'

'That's a deal, then,' Ruy declared with intense satisfaction, relieved that money was the lure he had assumed it would be because it made him more conscious of the barrier between them, a barrier he was determined to maintain.

Suzy's brows rose at that response and she surveyed him in complete stupefaction. 'You expect me to *believe* that you can pay me fifty thousand pounds to act as your model? Like you're some Mr Rockefeller or something? Do I look like I still believe in Santa Claus and the tooth fairy?' She gulped with a sudden helpless giggle of appreciation. 'Oh, thank you, *thank you* for winding me up like that! I needed something to laugh about tonight and that offer was, not only tasteless, but also absolutely priceless!'

Ruy stared back at her in angry astonishment, never before having met anyone who failed to take him very seriously indeed. It was an instant when he surprised himself, learning that he was, in spite of all the many times he had assured himself he was not, a Valiente down to the backbone, proud of his blue-blooded heritage, his power and influence and arrogant as all get-out. He wouldn't let himself notice how laughter transformed her face from pure Madonna perfection to girlish natural amusement, eyes lighting up like stars, pale slender throat extending, that full pink cupid's bow mouth that tantalised him pouting in a delicious pillowy curve.

Percy stalked through the door, his mouth tightening when he saw his fiancée laughing behind the bar with Ruy leaning on it.

Unable to judge his mood as he stood in the shadows by the door, Suzy smiled at her fiancé and said, 'I thought I wasn't to see you tonight. I'm going over to do the flowers as soon as Dad comes back.'

'I'll see you there,' Percy declared curtly and swung on his heel to leave again.

Suzy breathed in deep and slow to soothe herself, recognising that she was in an anxious, volatile mood because she couldn't stop thinking about her wedding the next day and her nerves and regrets were really beginning to eat her alive. Making a sacrifice, even for someone that you loved as she loved her father, was much harder than she had thought it would be months earlier...

CHAPTER TWO

THE FLORIST, NOT PERCY, was waiting for Suzy when she crossed the road to walk into the picturesque little church. It was unusually cold for a spring evening and she shivered, wishing she had thought to put on a coat. The florist was in a hurry and had already positioned her arrangements by the time that Suzy arrived, leaving the bride to do nothing more than make her own few personal touches.

'It looks wonderful,' she told the older woman as she left, contriving a generous smile because it wasn't the woman's fault that Suzy was a less than happy bride-to-be. She hurried about tying small floral beribboned tokens to the ends of the pews. Her bridegroom had paid for everything and had spared no expense, although Suzy had not made a single extravagant choice for an event that she had feared taking place. Way back at the beginning, after his blackmailing start, though, Percy had been polite and reasonably pleasant but in recent months, as they got closer to the wedding, he had become terse and more difficult to deal with.

Sadly, however, her father's debt would not be written off until she became Percy's legally wedded wife. Could she honestly trust the older man to continue to respect the terms they had agreed, though? Right now, she was getting a little nervous about being alone with Percy behind closed doors, forced to tolerate his moods and hope for the best. Perhaps if she had been more sexually experienced she might have been less nervous of the older man, she reasoned uncertainly. Then she might have been more confident that she could accurately read his behaviour. But Suzy was a virgin, less from choice than from lack of opportunity, living in a small place where she met few single men.

Hearing a noise in the church porch, she grabbed her bag and went to switch off the lights, assuming it was Percy and wondering what on earth he wanted to see her about so late in the day. As she walked out into the dim porch, she was grabbed by both shoulders and flung back against the hard stone wall like a doll and a stifled shriek of fear erupted from her. She thought she was being attacked and then she saw Percy squaring up to her with a pugnacious face of fury.

'What the heck?' she began in disbelief.

Percy clamped a silencing hand to her mouth. 'Standing there at the bar flirting with another man...making a fool of me, were you?' he growled at her.

'No, we weren't flirting... I swear,' she declared shakily, sincerely afraid of the way he was behaving and eager to placate him so that he would free her. 'The silly man was still trying to persuade me to model for him—'

'You're lying, just like Barb did!' he thundered down at her, unimpressed.

'Who's Barb?' Suzy whispered, her spine and her head still stinging from that first rough meeting with the wall.

'My first wife and I'm not having another one like her, running after all the men, making a mockery of me round the neighbourhood!' he spat down at her, his eyes locked on her with what looked very like hatred to her frightened gaze.

'Please let me go, Percy,' Suzy whispered because, while Percy might not be a very tall man, he was built like an ox, square and stocky and strong. 'This has got out of hand.'

'Shut up...you don't tell me what to do...*ever*!' he launched down at her, slapping her across the face in a glancing blow that caused her head to strike the wall behind her again and extracted a gasp of pain from her pale lips. 'Not so cheeky now, are you? I've been too soft with you.'

'Let me go,' Suzy urged between clenched teeth. 'This is assault, Percy, and I won't stand for it!'

And he laughed as though she had said the funniest thing he had ever heard.

'What are you planning to do about it? Report me to the police when I can throw you and your dad out of this village any time I like? I own you just as I own all the businesses round here and don't you forget it!' Percy lifted his hands off her with an exaggerated flourish. 'I've gone easy on you this time. Don't let me see you flirting like that again!'

Suzy was so dizzy, she staggered as she slid back down the wall onto her own feet again. He was a fright-

eningly strong man because he had held her suspended
all that time, but then she was a small and slender
woman. As Percy slammed noisily into the car he had
left parked across the street, she lifted her bag from
where it had fallen and headed back home, praying her
father would already be in bed. She massaged her aching head as she crept upstairs to her room. All of her
ached from being thrown against the wall and her face
was still stinging from that blow.

In the mirror she saw that she had had a nosebleed.
She was in shock, trembling and staring at her drained
and distraught face. She cleaned herself up in the bathroom, noting that her face was swollen while wondering
how much make-up it would take to hide what might
well be a bruise by morning. In her bra and pants she
inspected her body and recognised the purple bruising
already becoming visible on her arms and shoulders.
She hugged herself and shuddered.

Percy had been married before and nobody local was
aware of that fact. He was violent and territorial and had
seen flirtation where none existed. But she still had to
marry him, *didn't she*? She had to have that debt cleared
for her dad and, once that was achieved, if Percy laid
his hands on her again she would go to the police. On
that decision she went to bed.

In the morning she went by rote through her bridal
preparations. Her gown was all lace, ribbons and glittering crystals because Percy had instructed her to buy
'something fancy' and the ultra-feminine frills were the
sort of thing that Percy deemed fancy. Fortunately, the
long sleeves hid her bruises and cosmetics took care

of her bruised cheekbone. But as she finally looked at herself in the mirror it was as if she were only then emerging from a waking nightmare: suddenly she knew she *couldn't* go through with the wedding—not for her dad, not for any reason could she face marrying a man who clearly believed that it was his right to beat her up.

'Hey, love, I'm just off down to the off-licence for later... OK? I'll only be half an hour,' her father told her from outside the door. 'We've got plenty of time.'

She yanked open the door and gave him a hug. 'I love you,' she told him, but she didn't have the courage to tell him that she was about to leave Percy at the altar. She would write a note but there could be no explanation because her father would kill Percy if he knew what he had done to his daughter and she didn't want to cause a fight in which her much smaller father might get hurt.

She was going to run. She had no car, not even a bike and very little money, her brain reminded her. Where was she planning to go? What she was hoping to do? But just at that moment the practicalities honestly didn't matter to her. All that mattered to her was that she had finally made a decision and that there would be less dangerous fallout all round if she simply vanished. In haste she wrote a note to her father, telling him that she was sorry, but she simply couldn't go through with the wedding and that she'd phone him as soon as she was able. No note necessary for Percy. When she failed to show he would know that he had shown his true colours too clearly to her the night before. She kicked off her bridal heels and reached for her biker boots.

As she was bending over, tightening the multicoloured laces, her attention fell on the window and the view across to the church. She saw Percy climbing out of his car in a dark suit and then turning to stare across at the pub. *Why* was he arriving so early for the ceremony? Did he already suspect that she might not turn up?

Sheer dread grabbed Suzy as she wondered if he would try to see her, *check* on her. Her stomach heaved with nausea, her brow banged with stress. The bag she had been planning to pack, the clothing she had been meaning to change into…it all totally fled her mind and panic took over instead, washing away every other consideration, including common sense. Grabbing her bag, she pulled out her purse and extracted what cash she had within it. Thrusting the banknotes she had down the front of her dress into her bra, she simply ran down the stairs and out into the beer garden, which was surrounded by the dense woods that ringed the village. She had run wild in those woods as a child and, even in the cold air with actual snowflakes starting to fall, they had never looked more enticing to her than they did at that moment.

Hoisting her full skirts high round her legs, Suzy ran for the cover of the trees. Behind her she heard the echo of the doorbell seemingly thundering through the flat and she felt sick, grateful that she had run rather than taking the risk of hanging back to face Percy again. She didn't owe him that courtesy. If he had felt violent the night before he would feel even more violent when she told him she wasn't coming to the church. And no man was *ever* going to hit her again!

* * *

'Something's set off one of the motion sensors on the fence,' Ruy's security phoned to inform him. 'It's probably an animal but it would be safest if you stayed indoors, sir, and let us handle this.'

Reflecting on the state-of-the-art security he had originally set up to ensure his privacy rather than his personal security, Ruy almost rolled his eyes. He had not wanted security of any kind with him, but so successful had he become in his role at Valiente Capital that his insurers now wanted him protected everywhere he went. He had been forced to build the necessary accommodation for bodyguards even though in his opinion the chances of a kidnapping deep in the wilds of Norfolk, where he was entirely unknown, were extremely low.

'It's fine. I'll handle it myself,' he imparted before dealing with the polite attempt to argue that inevitably followed.

He slung on a thick coat and scarf because the temperature had dropped radically once it began snowing. Snow and it was almost May, he reflected in wonderment; what a barbarous climate that could go from spring one day back to winter the next! He had bought hundreds of acres of woodland with the house and had surrounded it with an impenetrable security fence. Reflecting on the peaceful beauty of his surroundings with satisfaction, he jumped into his four-wheel drive and drove down the track into the woods, parking a few minutes later to get out and stride through the trees to head for the west sector of the fence, which lay nearest the village.

Trapped in the dilapidated tree house, Suzy shivered

violently. She didn't know where her wits had been when she had run off into the trees. She could have done with the knowledge in advance that someone had mysteriously cut the woods in half with a giant metal fence, which meant that it was no longer possible to reach the main road on the other side of them. Getting over the fence had entailed climbing a tree and jumping and, in that mad panic that had gripped her where only adrenalin ruled, she had managed those actions fine even if the dress was the worse for wear as a result. The snow coming on had persuaded her to head for the old tree house to take shelter for a while.

And then everything else that could go wrong *had* gone wrong. The tree house she remembered from childhood had lost its roof long ago and offered no shelter whatsoever. She had only just managed to make it up onto the platform when the ladder, which had cracked under her weight, fell and smashed to pieces. Now she was stuck until she had gathered the energy to climb back down the tree, but she was horribly cold and she no longer trusted her arms and legs to keep her safe. Worse still, it hadn't even occurred to her to snatch up her phone when she ran and, dazed with physical misery and aches and pains, she was feeling very sorry for herself even while she wondered vaguely why she wasn't more actively concerned about her predicament.

Ruy walked along the fence and found the obstruction. It was a branch, he assumed until he reached it and saw that it was the remains of a very roughly put-together ladder. He tossed it away from the fence.

'It *would* have to be you,' a woman's voice pronounced in a tone of loathing. 'Just my luck.'

Startled when he had believed himself utterly alone, Ruy swung round and glanced up in sheer disbelief at the woman swinging her boot-clad legs on the edge of a tumbledown wooden structure that he had not even known existed in his woods. A tree house, he realised, or at least the remains of one, something he had craved as a child but had never been allowed to have.

'Is this the part where I say, "Rapunzel… Rapunzel…let down your hair"?'

'You're *not* my prince!' Suzy hurled at him accusingly, not in the mood for a fairy-tale allusion. 'But you can still get me down from this blasted tree!'

'*Sí*, Your Highness,' Ruy countered with appreciation at such rudeness and the novelty of it. 'The use of the word please might be sensible in the circumstances.'

'You've got smartass written all over you!' Suzy raged down at him incredulously.

'I'm stuck… I'm freezing and it's snowing. So, please, please, *please*!'

Ruy stared up at her, dark-as-pitch eyes narrowing in disbelief and flaring gold as he registered the veil fluttering into view behind her fall of copper spiral curls. 'Are you wearing a wedding dress?' he almost whispered.

'Are you going to help me get down from here? Or are you planning to keep on asking me stupid questions until I'm a frozen corpse?' Suzy snarled, her tongue stumbling round the words and slurring the syllables.

Involuntarily, Ruy grinned. 'You're not that far from the ground. Jump down and I'll catch you,' he told her.

'And you're *smiling* at seeing me in this condition!' Suzy framed, almost incandescent with fury at such stupidity while she wondered why she could no longer speak properly. 'Don't you recognise an emergency?'

All that passion fired her eyes to green-glass brilliance in her pale little face. His fingers itching for a stick of charcoal and a blank page, he studied her with the fierce enchantment of a born artist and walked beneath the tree house. 'Just push yourself over the edge and fall,' he instructed.

'I'm scared of heights, you dummy!' Suzy launched.

'So close your eyes and trust me,' Ruy advised without sympathy, 'while you're telling me how you got over my fence.'

'*Your* fence…should've guessed. I climbed a tree and jumped down.'

'I thought you were too scared of heights,' Ruy pointed out, since she had yet to move an inch.

'I was running on adrenalin just then,' she mumbled shakily, and he regretted mentioning the height because he had already noticed the shivering and the slurring of her speech and the pale colour of her lips and he suspected she was suffering from hypothermia.

'You've left him at the altar…haven't you?' Ruy gathered harshly, keen to distract her because she was shaking so badly without seeming to be aware of it that he was beginning to appreciate that she could also be deep in some kind of shock.

She nodded her head jerkily in silence.

'Not a very kind thing to do,' Ruy dared.

'How dare you?' Suzy shot as hotly at him as he had

hoped, and she slid off the edge of the platform and down into his arms.

Ruy staggered as he caught her because of the force of her fall but she was a slight weight, a small, curvy shape that smelled of oranges and sunshine. Weird, he thought, abstractedly drinking in the scent of her hair, liking it in some even weirder way. 'I just wanted you down from the tree as fast as possible,' he murmured soothingly as he tried to put her down again. 'Winding you up seems to work a treat.'

Her legs buckled and he told her to lean against him while he removed his coat and wrapped it round her before lifting her again.

'I don't know why you wind me up so much…well, actually I do,' Suzy muttered jaggedly, from the depths of his giant warmly lined jacket. 'If you hadn't been in the bar last night talking to me, it wouldn't have happened…but maybe I'm lucky it happened because I had no idea he would do what he did, so maybe I should be thanking you instead of thinking it was all your fault because *he* thought you were flirting with me.'

'How was it my fault? And what did happen?' Ruy pressed, strong arms closed firmly round her and making her feel oddly safe for the first time after long hours of agonising while she had lain sleepless throughout the night.

'Nothing…nothing happened,' she muttered, struggling to concentrate.

In the stark harshness of the spring light, Ruy looked down at her and registered the bruise on her cheekbone and the reddening and hint of swelling round her little nose. 'He *hit* you? That's why you left him standing?' he demanded rawly.

'Let's not talk about it. And then he arrived early at the church... I saw him from the window,' she admitted unevenly. 'He came over to the flat and Dad was out and I just panicked because I couldn't face him again. I knew he would pile on the pressure and make threats. He knew what he had done, and he wanted to make sure I would go through with the wedding. He'll be in a towering rage with me now and I didn't want to risk that confrontation.'

'Cabrón!' Ruy bit out the insult in Spanish, settling her carefully into the passenger seat of his vehicle and tugging out his phone to ring his sister for advice; as a GP, she was generally home at weekends. He spoke to her in French because Cecile's mother had been French, and he didn't want to take the chance that Suzy might understand what he was saying. Cecile was shocked and told him what to do best for Suzy while promising to call round to check her over.

'Shouldn't we be contacting the police to report the assault?' Ruy prompted as he turned the car.

'No...*no*!' From the depths of his coat, Suzy shot him a look of pure horror. 'It would only make Percy more vindictive and I can't afford to do that.'

'We'll see,' Ruy said lightly, although he had no intention of standing back while the abuser got off scot-free because he had literally terrorised his victim into such fear that she couldn't currently see the situation as it was. He wanted more information but knew it was unfair to press her when she was in a weakened state of confusion. He was also experiencing an extremely strong urge to protect her from further harm.

'He has a lot of power,' she mumbled thickly. 'You can't afford to antagonise people like that.'

Ruy was outraged by the depth of her fear of a small-time local businessman. It was the strangest feeling. He could not recall ever being so angry about anything that did not directly affect him. After all, he did not get involved in other people's problems. On the one occasion when he had abandoned that rule years earlier the situation had blown up in his face when, by trying to help, he had simply done more damage, or so it had seemed. But Suzy was different, he told himself soothingly, because he had no personal or sexual interest in her. She wasn't his type, absolutely *not* his type. Ruy was drawn to quietly spoken brunettes, not short, curvy redheads with sharp tongues.

'Gosh, I'm so sleepy,' she whispered through chattering teeth.

'You can't go to sleep, not yet anyway,' Ruy responded, ramming the vehicle to a halt in front of his property and racing round to the passenger side to lift her out at speed.

He strode up the stairs to the bathroom off the bedroom and laid her down with care on the floor. 'You need to get undressed. You have to get out of your wet clothes,' he told her as he rang his housekeeper to order a drink and a snack for her.

'So you can paint me?' Suzy asked with a giggle, entirely removed from the urgency of her condition.

'Not just yet,' Ruy countered, crouching down to

extract her from his coat and unpinning the wilted veil
with ease to toss it aside. 'How the hell do I get you out
of this dress?'

'H-hooks!' Suzy advised with another inappropri-
ate giggle.

Suppressing a groan, seeing by the state of her pale
bluish hands that there was no way she was capable of
undressing herself, Ruy gently bent her over and em-
barked on the many hooks. His wide sensual mouth
clamped down in a hard line as the bruises began to
appear. Against her naturally pale skin purple finger-
prints ornamented her slim shoulders and upper arms
while a long painful scrape and bruising marred her
slender spine. He knew he wanted to find the guy responsible and thump him hard where it hurt most. The
knowledge shook him because Ruy was very controlled
and disciplined and he virtually never gave way to emotional reactions. After all, he had spent his entire life
suppressing natural inclinations to concentrate on what
he saw as his duty.

He stalked into his bedroom to dig a tee shirt out
of a drawer. After his conversation with his sister, he
was wondering if Suzy had been sexually assaulted as
well and he felt murderous as he dropped the tee shirt
over her down-bent head and threaded her limp arms
through the holes before propping her up. Suzy was still
shivering violently, mumbling to herself, barely aware,
it seemed, of her surroundings or of him. That was a
novel experience for a man used to being treated like
a billionaire trophy to be acquired at any cost. Lifting
her up with ease, he carried her into his bedroom, laid

her down and rolled her into the soft blanket he had laid out, finally settling her back against the carved head-board like a cocoon.

'Now you eat and drink,' Ruy announced.

'Not hungry,' she muttered.

He wasn't listening because Cecile had given him his instructions and he would follow them to the letter.

'A hot bath would have warmed me up,' Suzy complained.

'Your body temperature has to be restored slowly,' Ruy contradicted. 'It's safer that way. It would have hurt like hell anyway if I'd plunged you into a hot bath.'

'It...*would*?' Her head fell back against the head-board. 'Where am I?'

'My house.'

'How did I get here?'

'It's not important. What's your fiancé's name?'

Suzy stiffened, drooping eyelids lifting high on her wide green eyes. 'Percy Brenton.'

Percy Brenton, you are toast, Ruy reflected with sat-isfaction at acquiring the name. 'Why were you mar-rying him?'

'Dad...' Her voice faltered and she blinked rapidly. 'That's private, I can't discuss that.'

'You can discuss it with me. It will remain confiden-tial. You have been harmed. I will not harm you in any way,' Ruy informed her levelly, his sheer confidence leap-ing out at her in his stance, his tone, his bright golden eyes that were no longer darker than pitch. Gorgeous eyes, she thought absently, totally gorgeous, exotic eyes.

A knock sounded on a door somewhere and her eyes

slid off him to bump up against unfamiliar views and the huge window overlooking the snowy woodland scene outside. It was raining now, and the unseasonal fall of light snow was already melting fast. She was disorientated because she had never been in such a big bedroom or seen such furniture or the kind of classic paintings ornamenting the rough stone walls. It looked incredibly opulent and that was quite outside her experience.

Ruy stalked back into view with a tray. He sank down on the edge of the bed and extended a glass in a metal holder to her.

'Not thirsty,' she admitted.

Ruy ignored her, raising the glass to her lips. 'Drink,' he urged.

'You're very bossy.' She sighed, sipping with difficulty and grimacing. 'What is it?'

'Milk and honey—'

'Brandy would have been nicer,' she told him, settling her dilated gaze on his and internally swooning, not from the sweetness of the drink, but from the sheer carnal impact of those lean bronzed features and the dark golden eyes so intent on hers. He packed a real punch in the charisma stakes, and he had the most amazing long black curling lashes fringing his eyes, the sort a woman would have killed to have.

'You're not allowed alcohol… Cecile's orders,' Ruy told her apologetically.

'Your sister's really nice,' she told him lamely.

'And I'm not?' Ruy grinned, having caught the unspoken comparison.

'You're just very…forceful,' Suzy framed.

'Don't you dare compare me to *him*!' Ruy warned in a husky undertone and something about that tone, something about that smouldering dark golden appraisal, set a fire alight in her pelvis and, without even thinking about it, Suzy leant forward and pressed her parted lips against his.

And for a split second he froze, and she thought, *I've got it wrong,* along with, *What the heck am I doing?* as astonishment at her aberrant invitation rippled through her. But that was before he responded, a lean hand coming up to cup her nape and tip her head up and he was kissing her back and it was *amazing*, literally the most electrifying kiss she had ever had. The firm seal of his sensual lips against hers, the delving exploration of his tongue, the very taste of him were overwhelming.

He jerked back from her with such abruptness that she was startled. 'I'm sorry,' he said flatly. 'That shouldn't have happened. You are not yourself right now.'

'I don't know what you're talking about,' she began, her face burning hot with mortification because she, unbelievable as it was to her at that moment, had made the first move.

Ruy rested the plate with the sandwich down on her lap. 'Eat…it'll help.'

At that point, Suzy wanted to sink through a hole in the mattress rather than try to eat. Her brain felt as if it were in a swamp. She remembered the attraction but not why or how she had succumbed to it. Her body was warming up now, indeed she was nearly too warm, and her hands came up from under the blanket to push it down and free her fingers. Like a drowning swimmer, she snatched at a sandwich as though it were a lifebelt.

Ruy was standing circumspectly now by the side of the bed. 'You're confused right now.'

Suzy nodded. Whether she liked it or not, it was sadly true because her brain cells still felt as though they had been plunged into sludge.

Striving to breathe less audibly, Ruy swung away to the window, fiercely aroused, not wanting her to notice the tight fit of his black jeans at the groin. He didn't know what had happened either. That conflagration of passion had come at him out of the blue and he didn't like that, he specifically didn't want *any* woman to have that much of an effect on him. It was too risky; it didn't fit into his life plan in which everything was to be in moderation. No wild passion, no fierce sympathy, no anything that made him feel vulnerable or out of control, because that path could lead to devastation and guilty regret and he was determined never to revisit such unnecessary and dangerous feelings again.

The urgent knock at the door sent his head twisting round, gratitude flaring at the awareness that his sister must have arrived, a welcome interruption indeed to the tense atmosphere that was forming.

'That will be Cecile. I'll bring her in, leave you to it,' Ruy intoned with a relief he couldn't conceal.

Mortified beyond bearing, Suzy lowered her head and cringed inside herself for the mistake she had made.

CHAPTER THREE

CECILE WAS BRISK and kind, the very best she could have been in such circumstances. She gently insisted on documenting and photographing Suzy's abrasions, informing her that it was a matter of legal procedure.

'But I don't want the police involved,' Suzy proclaimed.

'Have you really thought that through? Has it occurred to you that he has probably done this sort of stuff before and got away with it? Or that if you don't make a complaint, some other woman after you will suffer the same as you are now? It could have been much *worse* for you, Suzy…and he could come after you again.'

All those sensible points got through to Suzy and made her squirm and feel sick and ashamed and frightened, because Percy's attitude *had* given her the impression that she was not the first woman that he had attacked. 'I know it could have been worse…look, I'll think about it,' she muttered uneasily.

'Obviously what you do is up to you,' Cecile conceded gently. 'For now, I recommend that you have a nap, because you look exhausted.'

'I'd love a shower first... I don't suppose—' Her voice ran out as the other woman helpfully tugged open a door on the other side of the room.

Alone, Suzy crept barefoot into the fanciest bathroom she had ever seen outside a magazine. Natural stone with veins of quartz that glimmered like gold covered the floor and the walls and provided a massive shower, while the bath sat up a short flight of steps by the window and looked very much like the sort of backdrop a film star might have used. Eyes wide, Suzy peeled off her clothing, picking up the pitiful roll of banknotes she had thrust into her bra earlier that day. She glowered at her own reflection, seeing the shadows beneath her eyes and the ugly bruising on her body before turning away from the view and switching on the shower.

Downstairs, Cecile surveyed her younger brother. 'I know you must want your peace back. I suppose you want me to take her out of here for you,' she assumed. 'She doesn't want to go home yet because of the bruises.'

'No. I want her to stay.'

'*Stay?* But where are you planning to put her?' the vivacious brunette asked in surprise. 'You haven't got a spare room.'

Put on the spot while cursing his stubborn refusal to consider extending the house when he had bought it , Ruy shrugged a broad shoulder with something less than his usual cool. 'I'll sort something out. I have the studio. I'll buy a bed. I want her to stay because I want to paint her.'

'You want to…*paint* her?' Cecile shook her dark head in visible disbelief. 'Right now, she needs support and understanding, not some guy who just wants to use her in some other way!'

'I have no plans to use her in *any* way,' Ruy retorted drily.

'I'm sorry, but seeing her like that upset me. She's such a kind girl and usually so lively.' His sister sighed. 'I think that awful man, Brenton, must have some kind of nasty hold on her because I can't understand why she's reluctant to report him to the police. I bet it's something to do with money. Ever since we moved here I've heard rumours that the pub is going bust.'

Ruy tensed, his hard, expressive mouth compressing. 'May I ask if—?'

'No, you can't ask me anything confidential about a patient and you should know better!' Cecile told him firmly. 'Now, tell me, have you accepted the invitation to our brother's wedding yet?'

Ruy grimaced. 'Not yet. Had he extended the invite to you and Charles as well I would have accepted immediately.'

'Rodrigo isn't prepared to recognise me as a sibling yet. He's a complete snob,' Cecile commented with the dry amusement of indifference on that score. 'I'm just grateful he has a twin who isn't. I think you should give him a second chance, Ruy, and trust that there will be no unpleasantness this time.'

Ruy said nothing. The history of what Cecile called

unpleasantness between the brothers had begun when they were children and eight years earlier had significantly worsened to the extent that the brothers no longer spoke at all. He refused to think about the murky secret in their past, the reason behind that complete breakdown in communication. Yet that was why Ruy had been astonished by the wedding invite and he was as reluctant to refuse it and cause offence as he was to attend and risk an angry scene.

What he really needed, he reflected uneasily, was a female companion to act as a buffer between him and his brother and his bride, but any woman of his acquaintance whom he invited to accompany him to a family wedding would immediately assume that their relationship was more meaningful than it was. That was a hassle he didn't need but it made him think of Suzy again, Suzy who struck him as more a wild and free young woman than a conventional conservative one. Someone like her would make the perfect companion. She would be different enough to intrigue his relatives and his brother but too young and restless to harbour any serious expectations of him afterwards.

A couple of hours later, Suzy stirred and awakened, stretching with a wince because pushing her head into the pillow ensured she felt the tender swelling on the back of it. Cecile had tried to persuade her to go for a hospital scan, but Suzy was confident that it was simply a painful bump. She lay there picturing the guests who must have turned up for her wedding and their incredulity over her non-appearance and she flinched, wiping her mind free of the embarrassing images again. What was done was done, she told herself, and she could not regret backing out of her agreement with Percy.

She had returned to bed with her wet hair wrapped in a towel and it took inventiveness to make herself even vaguely presentable because her curls had gone crazy. She finger-sorted and flattened and dampened and gave up in the end, glancing in the mirror and frowning before putting on her biker boots again and leaving the room.

Emerging onto a landing she didn't even recall seeing before, she headed for the stairs since there didn't appear to be anywhere else to go.

Ruy looked up from his sketch pad and saw her on the stairs, long pale, shapely legs thrust into those ridiculous boots, his capacious tee shirt almost hanging off one slender white shoulder. Her hair was wild and untamed, a messy mass of curls surrounding her triangular face in a cloud of Titian glory, huge green eyes striking his. He was entranced and he knew it, *knew* it was the artist in him, not the man, because for the first time in her presence he hadn't got hard.

'Ruy,' she said, awkward in the buzzing silence, her attention falling to the slew of discarded sketches littering the coffee table and squinting at the nearest image, involuntarily impressed by the few slashing strokes on the page, which even she registered as recognisable. 'Have you been drawing me?'

Ruy tossed the pad down on the coffee table, the faintest colour defining his remarkable cheekbones, dark eyes flaring gold as ingots as he looked up at her.

'You look *so* guilty!' Suzy carolled in unexpected delight, a teasing grin forming on her lips as she settled down on a capacious sofa and curled up. 'You *know* you should have asked permission first.'

Unaccustomed to being read that accurately, Ruy suppressed a sardonic retort because she was smiling, and then the entirety of his attention was stolen by a glimpse of slender inner thigh that sent a pulse thrumming directly to his groin. It was that flawless skin of hers, so translucent and smooth that he could only wonder how it would feel beneath his fingertips. 'I should have done,' he agreed in a driven undertone, averting his gaze and willing his hormones to stop derailing him, disconcerted that she could make him react with so adolescent a lack of restraint. 'But occasionally the desire to draw pushes me beyond the limits of courtesy. I apologise.'

'You don't need to,' Suzy told him immediately, wondering why his admission that the pull of his art tempted him into forgetting his manners should strike her as so very, very sexy. She didn't think like that, at least, she never had before meeting him. It was downright unnerving, in the wake of that first kiss initiated by her, to appreciate that around him she *still* didn't seem capable of behaving normally. 'You helped me today and I won't forget that.'

'I could scarcely have abandoned you in the tree house,' Ruy pointed out. 'That would have been manslaughter at the very least.'

And there it was: that *other* side of his nature, Suzy labelled straight away, that very controlled, pretty ar-

rogant and almost chilling attitude of detachment that
had set her on edge at their first meeting. 'Never mind.
I owe you a few sketches,' she told him dismissively.

'What I would *really* like is some clarification on the
score of the wedding that misfired,' Ruy admitted as
he slid fluidly upright. 'We'll talk over dinner, which
should be ready in a few minutes...'

'Oh...' Suzy said uncertainly, his sheer confidence
that she would choose to confide in him leaving her
bemused. 'Can I help?'

'I have a housekeeper. She does the catering.' Ruy
thrust open a door into a dining room with a contemporary glass table that was already set with cloth nap-
kins, crystal glasses and gleaming cutlery.

Intimidated by that very formal setting, Suzy quickly
dropped down into the chair he had tugged out for her.
'Did you build this house? I didn't even know it existed and yet it can't be much more than a mile from
the village.'

'No, I bought it as is. The original owner of the property was something in showbusiness and this was to
be his retirement home, but he passed away before he
could move in,' Ruy explained.

'It's a beautiful house,' Suzy remarked, a little more
relaxed by the assumption that Ruy was not personally
responsible for the profound luxury of their surroundings. The property wasn't in a fashionable area and although the rooms were very spacious there didn't seem
to be that many of them. The house was a quirky one-
off, so possibly he had got it cheap, she reasoned. On
the other hand, equally possibly, he was a very success-

ful artist. How would she know? That she had not recognised his name meant nothing because she had no
knowledge of the art world.

'The woods sold it for me more than anything else,'
Ruy told her. 'Now, some things you said earlier today
have worried me and I can't pretend you didn't say
them. You said Brenton had too much power and that
he would pile on the pressure and threaten you. Aside
from the assault, why are you so frightened of the man?'

Suzy flushed from cheek to temple, the heat of mortification engulfing her in a tide, for she hadn't realised
just how much she had revealed while she was in the
grip of hypothermia. 'I'm sorry, I can't discuss that.'

Undaunted, Ruy stretched his big powerful body
back into his seat and lifted his dark head high, narrowed dark eyes of astonishing intensity locked to her.
'Does it relate to your father's ownership of the village
pub?' he enquired smoothly. 'I've already learned that
Brenton has a reputation for unscrupulous behaviour
and that his financial dealings may be questionable.'

Hugely disconcerted by that statement, Suzy was
grateful when the door opened and an older woman
bustled in with plates. The interruption was welcome
but at the same time Suzy was desperate to know how
Ruy had acquired such information, bearing in mind
that she had lived in the area all her life and had not
heard so much as a whisper of such rumours.

'Who told you that about Percy?' she pressed as soon
as they were alone again.

'When I make financial enquiries, I have good

sources.' Ruy shook out his napkin with infuriating cool. 'Let us enjoy our meal.'

Fizzing with frustration, Suzy settled her attention on her tomato and mozzarella first course and ate with an appetite that surprised her. Only when she thought about it did she recall that she had skipped her evening meal the night before and breakfast that morning and had only had the sandwich that Ruy had given her. Yet it felt to her as though weeks had passed since the previous day, because the future she had expected had suddenly vanished and she had no idea what would take the place of her acting as Percy's wife. She supposed that after they had lost the pub she and her father would move to the nearest town in search of employment.

The main course, another sophisticated dish, arrived and Ruy offered her wine with the quip that Cecile wasn't present to police her.

'I've still got a bit of a headache and I took painkillers, so no, thanks, for the moment.'

'Now,' Ruy breathed with blistering assurance. 'Enlighten me about your father's financial dealings with your ex.'

'How on earth do you even *know* that he has dealings?' Suzy exclaimed, dropping her knife and fork with a clatter to emphasise her annoyance.

'I refuse to believe that love had anything to do with your planned marriage to Brenton,' Ruy intoned drily. 'By nature, he's a thug and a bully.'

'You only met him for about ten seconds!' Suzy snatched at her glass of water to occupy her restless hands, unnerved by Ruy's steady stubborn persistence. 'How could you even know that?'

A grim light shadowed Ruy's gaze at that question. Being raised by a bully had made it very easy for him to recognise the warning signs. He had not had a pleasant childhood but, in many ways, his more sensitive twin brother, unable to handle their father's lacerating tongue, had suffered much more in failing to meet the standards that Armando Valiente demanded.

'Just tell me the truth, because you *have* to confide in someone.'

'No, I don't.' Suzy sucked in a ragged breath and picked up her cutlery again with determination.

'And you have to stop being scared for long enough to go to the police,' Ruy contended.

Colour flooded the pallor that had spread across her small stiff face. 'I want to go to the police...but I daren't do it,' she muttered shakily.

'Tell me why not,' Ruy prodded afresh.

And a tempestuous mixture of desperation and resentment assailed Suzy. Green eyes flashed with defensiveness and she lifted her chin as though daring him to judge her. 'Dad borrowed from the bank to update the bar but we didn't do enough business to keep up the loan. When Dad was threatened with repossession, Percy stepped in. The old loan was repaid and Percy extended a new one with lower payments.'

'How did you become involved in that arrangement?' Ruy enquired, resting back in his chair with his wine glass elegantly cradled in one lean brown hand, so stunningly handsome in that moment that she momentarily lost the thread of the dialogue. As she gazed almost blankly back at him, her mouth dry, her pelvis thrumming with the strangest pulse that made her thighs twitch and tense, he had to repeat the question.

'I wasn't involved until six months ago,' Suzy admitted in a rueful rush. 'Then Percy said he'd write the loan off if I married him and that if I *didn't* marry him he would take the pub off Dad. After a couple of discussions, I agreed but I... I told him I wouldn't have sex with him. I would be his wife in all other ways though and nobody else would know the truth of our relationship,' she completed with scarlet cheeks.

'*Dios mio*...and he *agreed* to that?' Ruy marvelled.

Suzy nodded miserably. 'But I'm not sure now that he planned to stick to the rules and that he didn't start hating me for them.'

'How much does your father know about Brenton's blackmail?'

At that question, Suzy frowned. 'He knows nothing about any of it! Dad would never have agreed to let me marry Percy for his benefit.'

'And the loan outstanding amounts to fifty thousand pounds or so?' Ruy queried, startling her with his accuracy and, when he met her troubled gaze, dealing her an eloquent smile. 'That *was* why you plucked that particular sum out of the air, wasn't it?'

'A ridiculous amount,' she mumbled in severe chagrin as she recalled that conversation in the bar when he had urged her to name her price for modelling for him. 'I wasn't serious, of course...you do know that, don't you? I'm truly not a greedy person. It's just, Percy was starting to scare me, and I'd pretty much do anything for my dad.'

'That's not a sin. It's proof of loyalty and of your love for a parent. You were willing to make a sacrifice to protect your father.'

'But I tumbled at the last fence and now I've just dug Dad into a deeper hole!' Suzy argued with a guilt-ridden shake of her head. 'Now, after being left at the altar, Percy will be out for blood.'

'He's already had as much blood as he's getting and he's not taking any more out of your particular hide,' Ruy asserted with scorching conviction. 'Surely you realise that Brenton will now want to approach you with some suggestion aimed at saving his own skin? If you choose to prosecute him for assault his reputation will be ruined. He may well offer to write off that loan in an effort to keep you quiet.'

Suzy's eyes widened. 'No way would he do that. Percy has the reputation for collecting on all his debts.'

'You have to report him to the police,' Ruy continued. 'And I can offer you a way to do that that will protect you *and* your father's business.'

'I'm not a kid, Ruy. There's no magic fix for this mess,' Suzy told him heavily as she pushed her plate away. 'And in many ways, it's a mess of my own making. I was stupidly trusting. I should never have agreed to marry Percy in the first place. That wretched money seemed to give him the impression that he was buying me body and soul and that that deprived me of any right to respect or decency. What I agreed to was wrong, though, and perhaps I deserve what happened.'

'*Valgame Dios!* Of course, you didn't *deserve* it!' Ruy argued in heated dissent.

'And now you're talking about making me an offer… presumably money,' Suzy gathered with a little moue of distaste and a look of reproach in his direction that made him seal his wide, sensual mouth shut again. 'Please… *don't*. I'll think over the idea of modelling for you, but I don't know how it could be organised now because Dad and I will probably be leaving the village soon. But please, please, do *not* try to buy me like Percy did… I've learned my lesson and I'm off the market now.'

Unusual frustration currented through Ruy, but he was adept at steering paths round obstacles and varying his approach. Being flexible, innovative and highly intelligent had made him a living legend in the financial world and he recognised that Suzy would naturally be highly resistant to any offer of cash assistance after the experience she'd had at Brenton's hands. The germ of an idea struck Ruy and at first he rejected it, deeming it not to be his place to interfere in a family matter or, indeed, in a family business. Even so, as he ran the concept swiftly through his brain he saw *how* he could extend his help without making Suzy feel that he had bribed, bought or blackmailed her. And how he too would benefit from the arrangement beyond her modelling for him. He would ask her to accompany him to his brother's wedding.

Even so, his most pressing concern should be protecting Suzy from her ex, shouldn't it? His thoughts froze on that startling point. Exactly when had he developed that strange notion? When had he last become this involved in problems that were not his to solve? He wanted to paint Suzy, which put her in an entirely different category, he assured himself. Having shaken off his unease over that uncharacteristic urge to protect, Ruy found that he could think with clarity again. To ensure Suzy's security from further threats, or indeed dodgy proposals, he would need to view first-hand the loan agreement her father had signed. Once that problem was settled, he would consider his own needs and wishes, proving that he was *not* the selfish bastard his sister had implied, he reasoned with satisfaction, his momentary tension evaporating.

'So, what sort of stuff do you paint?' Suzy asked.

'People, mainly portraits, usually women.'

'Nudes?' Suzy suddenly prompted in a slightly strangled voice.

'I have done, but generally my models remain clothed,' Ruy responded with a glint of amusement in his gaze, because she was shifting in her seat like an embarrassed child, her dismay at the prospect of posing nude for him clear as day. A prickle of interest in seeing those pale luscious curves unveiled shimmied through him like a sudden shot of some dangerously addictive drug. Taken aback by that loss of artistic objectivity, he struggled to suppress that leap of desire, all amusement buried by his own far too personal response.

Dessert was served as Suzy confessed, 'I know nothing about art.'

'Why would you when it's not an interest of yours?' Keen to stick strictly to business as he saw it, Ruy added, 'If you agreed to model for me, you would have to first sign a non-disclosure agreement, which would prevent you from mentioning my name or indeed any details about me. It's a standard safeguard I use with every model I employ.'

'Why would you do that?' Suzy surveyed him, eyes as green and fresh as spring leaves wide with curiosity and surprise. 'Don't artists need publicity to boost their careers and the prices their work commands?'

'Privacy is more important to me,' Ruy said quietly.

Suzy waved an expressive hand at the elegant table and her surroundings and laughed. '*And*, it doesn't look like you're hurting for a spare penny or two!' she teased.

It was that playful quality, which his sister had called liveliness, that appealed to him, Ruy decided, his attention locking to that full pink lower lip, recalling the taste of her, the taste of temptation. When she smiled she practically lit up the room. Yet when she had danced, even before he had seen her face, he had wanted to capture her in oils, to somehow magically meld her innate grace of movement into the painting. Obviously, there would have to be more than one canvas, he conceded, to capture her different moods.

'I would like you to consider granting me another favour,' he divulged.

On the brink of asking why she would consider doing him any favours, Suzy caught her tongue between her teeth, recalling how supportive he had been.

'I have to attend my brother's wedding in a couple of weeks and it would be easier if I had a woman with me, a woman willing to pretend that she was engaged to me.'

'Why on earth would you want that?' she exclaimed, too disconcerted to guard her tongue.

'I have a troubled relationship with my brother. My presence at his wedding would be smoother if he were to believe that I had found a woman of my own,' Ruy revealed reluctantly.

'Very strange…and not for me,' Suzy said ruefully. 'I was Percy's fake bride and it didn't work out well for me. I don't want to be faking anything for anyone now.'

'Consider it. I think it would suit you right now to escape the local gossip for a while. The wedding is in Spain.'

'Spain!' Suzy rolled her eyes as though he had suggested the moon as a destination, but the reference to local gossip made her grimace. It annoyed her that he was right once again. Leaving the village even for a few days was a welcome idea, particularly as it would put her out of reach of Percy, she acknowledged. 'But, I'll think about it.'

Smothering a yawn over coffee, Suzy began to droop, the events of the past few days catching up with her again. Ruy urged her to have an early night.

'I shouldn't still be here,' Suzy registered abruptly, absently amazed by the way she had simply taken Ruy Rivera's hospitality for granted. 'I should go home.'

'Where were you heading when you went into the woods?'

'I had a vague notion of hitching a lift to the railway station. Can you imagine it? Me in that wedding dress and probably not even having enough money to buy a train ticket…' She shook her head and sighed. 'I'm sorry I involved you in all this.'

'You're welcome to stay. At least here, you are out of Brenton's reach,' Ruy pointed out sneakily.

'And it's handy to keep me around if you want to paint me.' Suzy's bright gaze glimmered with humour. 'I've got your measure, Mr Rivera…you will never be slow to take advantage of a useful opportunity.'

Ruy's rare grin slashed his expressive mouth, his dark eyes flashing gold with appreciation at the intelligence sparkling in her appraisal. 'Exactly,' he agreed.

Suzy paused at the foot of the stairs and glanced back at him, her delicate profile and the scattering of freckles on the bridge of her nose as fascinating to him as the fragile white shoulder poking through her spiralling auburn curls. 'Thanks for helping me today. The wedding thing sounds challenging, I'm afraid, and I don't think I fancy trying it. I'll do the model thing for you, though, as long as I can keep my clothes on,' she announced with a gauche bluntness that almost made Ruy laugh out loud.

Involuntarily he was entranced by that kind of modesty. Was it an act? Understandably, he was suspicious. After all, the majority of women Ruy met couldn't wait to get their clothes *off* for his benefit, be it as a model in the studio or as a one-night stand. And then there were the unwelcome invitations like the maid who had sashayed into his bedroom with his breakfast one morning naked as a jaybird, or the PA who had just stripped off down to her fancy lingerie on the first and last day of her employment with him.

'I'll see you in the morning.'

'Ah…' Ruy shifted a fluid hand. 'Would it be possible for me to first remove some clothes from the bedroom?'

On the stairs, Suzy froze and whipped round. 'It's *your* bedroom? I'm putting you out of your own bed? Oh, that won't do at all! I'll sleep on one of the sofas.'

'That's not necessary,' Ruy declared, striding up to crowd her on the stairs and with his very height and breadth somehow persuading her to move on up to the landing.

'But—?'

'I'm sleeping in my studio,' Ruy countered firmly, having already procured a bed for his use. 'When I bought this place it was a ground-floor bedroom.'

Suzy hovered uncomfortably as Ruy removed items from drawers and a closet and returned to her side.

'I'm going out tonight. I wouldn't want to disturb you when I return,' Ruy murmured softly, scorching dark golden eyes welded to her.

Suzy was bright pink with self-consciousness, the sort of deep dire self-consciousness that she had suffered as a schoolgirl. 'It just doesn't seem right, me putting you out.'

Ruy rested a long brown forefinger gently across her parted lips. '*Silencio, por favor*…it is nothing.'

Her lips prickled even below that light touch and her pupils dilated. 'Ruy—'

'It is very sexy that you *didn't* suggest that I share the bed with you,' Ruy murmured softly, gazing down at her for all the world as though that omission on her part were an act of astonishing restraint.

Thoroughly taken aback, Suzy shot the vast bed a glance, acknowledging that it was large enough to absorb two couples, never mind one, but she was still struggling to get her head around the telling fact that he found her failure to ask him to join her in the bed sexier than an invitation would have been. And that concept lay so far beyond her grasp of the male outlook on sex that she could only gaze back at him in incredulity at the comment.

'Sleep well, *buenas noches*,' Ruy husked, striding out and leaving her standing there in a fog of confusion.

Did Ruy get women coming on to him so often that it had become the norm for him? He was extraordinarily good-looking, she conceded thoughtfully, picturing that lean, strong, sculpted face and those stunning eyes that could go from dark to smouldering gold. Very, very good-looking, she concluded as she made use of the new toothbrush laid out for her and prepared for bed. She had studied him throughout their meal, seeking a flaw, nonplussed to be unable to find one. Those gorgeous looks of his had briefly mesmerised her into stealing that kiss. She winced for herself afresh. Talk about making a production out of being attracted to a guy! She had practically shouted it in his face. But she was comforted by the conviction that most women probably found Ruy Rivera extremely appealing and he was clearly used to it and bored by it, so her foolish little kiss would soon be forgotten.

As she would soon forget him, once he was out of her radius, she told herself soothingly. She was a very down-to-earth and sensible woman, always had been, always would be. Accepting Percy's offer had been a mistake, a glitch caused by panic on her father's behalf. She felt quite nervous and sick at the thought of what her rearranged future might now hold for her and her father, but she was well used to making the best of what she got in life even if it often wasn't what she wanted or felt she needed. And she would handle whatever happened, she told herself squarely, slipping into the gloriously comfortable bed.

As Suzy drifted inexorably into the deep sleep of emotional exhaustion, Ruy was striding into the village pub to introduce himself to her father. No sooner had he intimated that he had news of Suzy than the bar maid was left in charge and he was ushered into a private room where he sat down to discuss business over a revered Scottish malt while thinking that Suzy might try to object but he was sticking strictly to the guidelines she had given him...

CHAPTER FOUR

SUZY SLEPT IN and scrambled out of bed in a rush to head into the bathroom, stumbling to a halt when she saw clothing lying across the chair by the wall, clothing that was familiar. She stared in frowning puzzlement at a pair of her own skinny jeans, her favourite green sweater with its asymmetric hem, and in the bag beneath the chair she discovered fresh undies, socks and both her make-up and toiletries bags.

How on earth had her possessions arrived at Ruy's house? Had Cecile told Suzy's father where she was and had her father packed a bag for her and brought it over while she slept? Sudden guilt that she had still not phoned her father washed over her. But in truth, she had yet to work out how much she could risk telling the older man about the breakdown of her relationship with Percy.

She washed and dressed very quickly and didn't bother with any make-up, sensitive now to what Ruy might assume if she appeared to be gilding the lily for his benefit. After all, a man who could thank a woman for *not* inviting him into bed had shameless confidence and a daunting, meteoric awareness of the strength of his own attractiveness. Suzy planned to do nothing and say nothing that might encourage such arrogance. Hadn't she already done enough with that stupid kiss? Hopefully he would put that down to her disorientation after she had almost been frozen into a Popsicle.

As she moved towards the door, a knock sounded on it and she tugged it open, startled to find Ruy standing there holding a tray. 'What's this?' she muttered.

'It was supposed to be breakfast in bed, but I can see I left it too late,' Ruy fielded with amusement.

'Ruy,' Suzy admonished with a raised auburn brow. 'I've never had breakfast in bed in my life. I'm more likely to be serving it to other people than enjoying it myself.'

'That may be but there is always a first time,' Ruy retorted, refusing to be sidetracked and settling the tray down on the circular table by the window. 'Sit down, eat...'

'Gosh, you must keep your housekeeper busy,' Suzy remarked in wonderment at the beautifully set tray with its ornamental cloth and fresh orange juice, pastries, fruit and tea, all proffered in the finest china along with a seasonal lilac blossom in a tiny vase. 'This is beautiful. Make sure you thank her for me. She went to a lot of trouble.'

'I will,' Ruy promised, impressed by her thoughtfulness because so many of the women he knew took excellent service entirely for granted.

'When did Dad drop my clothes off? You should

have wakened me,' Suzy scolded as she drank her orange juice, still pacing the room.

'He gave the bag to me last night. Mrs Liggett brought it up but found you asleep.'

Her smooth pale brow had furrowed. 'You saw my father last night? Oh, you went to the pub for a drink.'

'No, I went specifically to see him and we talked in private,' Ruy extended, lounging back against the bedroom door with folded arms and narrowed dark perceptive eyes locked to her restless movements. Sunlight burnishing her hair, she was full of energy but growing tension was threaded through that energy like iron bars strengthening concrete, he conceded, amused by that analogy but well aware of the questioning onslaught of her bright eyes and the volatile force of nature that powered her deceptively small and slender frame. He found it strange that her volatility, which had troubled him at the outset of their acquaintance, now only drew him in faster.

'Why would you go to see my father?' Suzy asked with a frown.

'To make life a little smoother for you,' Ruy countered lazily. 'When I see a problem, I tend to solve it. In fact, I excel at solving problems.'

Suzy tossed her head back in irritation. '*My* problems are not *your* problems!'

Unperturbed, Ruy spread the fingers of one lean hand and began marking off points. 'One... I detest abusers and I wanted you to feel free to report your ex to the police. Two... I knew that you wouldn't accept the money to pay off Brenton from me...you told me so. Three... I want to make it possible for you to act as my model without other concerns getting in the way. Four... I would also like you to accompany me to my brother's wedding. Five...if you think of this situation from a logical point of view, our mutual needs can dovetail perfectly.'

Suzy's chest heaved as she snatched in short breath after short breath in an effort to control her temper. She wanted to slap his point-scoring fingers off his hand. She wanted to deprive him utterly of the ability to stand there telling her without embarrassment that he had approached *her* father behind *her* back on her supposed behalf. 'I don't know what you've done... I'm not even sure I *want* to know!' she exclaimed. 'Did you tell Dad that Percy attacked me?'

'Yes, and while he was very angry he knows that you're not seriously hurt.'

'You have no right to interfere in my life!' Suzy hurled at him.

'The pub belongs to your father, *not* to you, and what arrangements he chooses to make with me are entirely his business,' Ruy spelt out, dropping her back down to earth again with a crash. 'As it happens, I've bought a share in the pub. I will be a silent partner, but it takes the pressure off your father. He will be able to repay Brenton without difficulty, although, as I told him, he could take him to court over the paperwork, which did not clearly specify the interest rate Brenton was charging. But your father prefers to let that go—he's not keen on the idea of calling in a solicitor.'

Suzy had gone white with mounting shock and dismay. 'You've bought a share in our pub?' she gasped in disbelief. 'But why the heck would you do that?'

'I live locally now, although I won't be resident here throughout the year. It's an investment. A pub is an asset in a village,' Ruy pronounced, as though he were not aware that the business was struggling. 'Now it will stay open and your father remains the landlord.'

'I just don't believe this!' Suzy confessed in seething frustration.

'I had to find some way around your reluctance to accept my financial help,' Ruy pointed out without shame.

'But don't you see that what you've done is *wrong*?' Suzy demanded angrily. 'That you've simply found another way of bribing me and getting me to do what you want? Evidently, you only bought into the pub to manipulate me!'

'Your father is happy, and you love your father. I don't see what the problem is or how it can be wrong when I have only good intentions,' Ruy declared, brilliant dark eyes challenging hers.

'I know you're not likely to beat me up, but you leave Percy standing in the ruthless stakes!' Suzy condemned.

'That is possible,' Ruy conceded without surprise or regret. 'I always play to win. When I want something, I do go all out to get it.'

'I'm a person, not a something!' Suzy hissed censoriously. 'I already agreed that I would try to model for you. At no cost! There was no need for you to go behind my back and invest in the pub!'

'Set aside my financial investment in your father's business,' Ruy advised. 'It is nothing to do with you, except insofar as it means that you can now stop worrying about your father's security.'

In a passion of confusion and incredulity, Suzy folded her arms and spun away from him. 'Nothing will convince me that you had a sincere interest in buying a share of the pub!' she shot at him.

Ruy shrugged a broad shoulder. 'I'm not trying to convince you. I don't have to justify what I've done, but I would make the point that your father is very happy with his side of the bargain and even more relieved to know that Percy is out of both your lives.'

Suzy's slender hands knotted into fists. 'Damn you!' she snapped at him, because every time she thought she had him on a weak spot he leapt away and put her there instead. 'You drive me insane!'

'And your passion lights me up,' Ruy confided in a raw undertone, needing to touch her almost as badly as he needed to paint her, flexing his long fingers and coiling them up again, rigid with the tension of unsated arousal.

Never before had he been with such an emotional woman. He had learned to repress his own emotions. He slept with women who had no drama to irritate him and he could not begin to explain or understand what it was about Suzy's volatility that made her so very desirable. That trait, that essential fire in her, *should* have been a turn-off and yet, it wasn't. She was not his type, categorically *not* his type, but when she went toe to toe with him, fists knotted, eyes shimmering in challenge like polished malachite, pink pouty lips parted to display little pearl-like teeth, it turned him on so hard and fast that the zip of his jeans bit a pattern into his throbbing flesh.

'Your control, your coldness, has the opposite effect on me,' Suzy confided tautly. 'It makes me want to shake you up.'

'Success...*major* success on that score,' Ruy purred with an emphasis that seemed to glide down her rigid spine like caressing fingers.

Suzy's knees wobbled a little. 'We really are oil and water,' she muttered uneasily.

'No, we're more like a conflagration,' Ruy husked, stalking closer, suddenly seeming to snatch all the oxygen out of the air she needed to breathe. 'And it's a fire I don't want to put out because, like any man, I *love* the burn, *querida*.'

'I'm shouting at you. You can't change the subject in the middle of an argument,' Suzy told him loftily.

'That's the look I want when you lift your chin... just like that.' Ruy angled up her chin with a fingertip, let it slide back down the cord of her neck to her clavicle, where it lingered. 'And you look at me like you're a queen and I'm a filthy peasant. No woman has ever looked at me like that.'

'You have the most wildly extravagant imagination,' Suzy remarked unevenly, stepping back a few inches, the skin of her neck tingling, tenderly aware of that light touch, so very different from Percy's harsh, careless grip on her arm, her elbow or her shoulder. Her shoulders met with the wall. She had honestly believed that Percy didn't know his own strength. How naïve had she been in believing that that occasional roughness was simply masculine, careless and unintentional?

Her gaze locked to Ruy's lean dark features and something sweet and yet almost painful clenched low in her pelvis and for the first time she recognised what was happening to her body. She regretted that she had got halfway through her twenty-second year before experiencing normal sexual attraction. The race of her pulse, the hammer of her heart, the sudden tightening of her nipples as well as the dryness of her mouth held her fast because she had never felt anything that powerful before and she was remembering *that* kiss, that brief but glorious adrenalin rush.

Dark golden eyes welded to hers, Ruy stalked slowly closer and her heart raced so fast it felt as though it were thumping at the foot of her throat. He reached for her and if he hadn't reached for her she reckoned that she would have shamelessly grabbed him.

'You want this?' Ruy breathed in a driven undertone, easing her closer, one hand braced on her hip, the other braced against the wall behind her.

'I want…you,' she heard herself say and she didn't know where the words came from, only that it was a truth so new to her that she *had* to say it, *had* to share it.

'*Gracias a Dios,*' Ruy groaned above her head, crushing her mouth under his with an urgency that shook her to her very depths. His mouth contrived to communicate everything she didn't have the words to express and the explosive effect of his hunger meeting hers set her on fire.

It took a while in that passionate exchange of kisses

for Suzy to notice that he was extracting her from her sweater and for a split second she stilled, checking with herself that that was all right. And because it was Ruy, because she was so worked up that she was wound up tighter than a spring, it was fine. She was a big girl now, she reminded herself abstractedly, not a teenager keeping a handsy first boyfriend within acceptable limits. Yes, she could take her clothes off now, of course she could.

'Of course, you would have to have *the* boots on.' Ruy sighed, lifting her up into his arms and bringing her down onto the side of the bed, crouching down lithely at her feet to remove her boots. 'I love these boots. You're going to wear them in the studio for me when you pose—'

'Am I?' Amusement softened Suzy's gaze as she stared down at him, spearing her fingers into his black luxuriant hair, smoothing it back from his brow, admiring the dark slashing brows and the ridiculously long ebony lashes framing his gorgeous eyes. Absently she wondered what she had thought about before she met him.

'In a wedding dress…but not the one you put on for *him*,' he asserted, tossing aside the boots and gently pushing her back to embark on the zip of her jeans.

'You have the most crazy imagination.' Suzy sighed.

'I'm not an imaginative man.'

'But you're an artist. You've got to be imaginative,' Suzy told him, sensing that for some reason he was in denial of that reality. 'I mean, imagining me posing in my boots and a wedding dress…how eccentric is th…

that?' She stammered to a halt as, with one hard yank, he succeeded in tugging the jeans down her long slender legs.

'But that's not imagination, that's the reality of how I saw you in the woods,' Ruy argued, lifting her dangling legs up onto the divan and coming down beside her. 'We're talking too much… I don't talk in bed—'

'Tough,' Suzy whispered, touching a fingertip to his slightly reddened lips. 'Two people here, two votes, not just one…you just revel in being bossy, Ruy.'

He hauled off his sweater and leant over her, shimmering dark golden eyes alight as flames against his bronzed complexion, the corner of his mouth hinting at a smile. 'Maybe a little.'

'I should've run like hell when you told me about buying into the pub,' Suzy remarked with sudden anxiety. 'Maybe you're one of those controlling guys, who tries to own a woman.'

'I've never tried to own a woman in my life. And you see this is why you don't talk in bed—it gets too serious and now you're freaking yourself out and stressing again,' Ruy censured, dropping a kiss down on her parted lips, trailing his own slowly down her neck to her shoulder, lighting up a tingling trail of arousal through her trembling body.

'I'm still furious with you!' she protested, struggling to ground herself again and yet at the same time inwardly rejoicing at the concept of her own freedom from constraint, the precious ability to do as she liked for once.

All her life, after all, she had been the good dutiful daughter, instinctively tailoring herself to the role her father needed her to fill. She hadn't had the liberty to choose a career once she had grasped that her father couldn't afford to pay anyone else for the work she did. In the same way she hadn't experimented with any young men because, working at the pub, she couldn't risk acquiring a free and easy reputation, which would only encourage the often married men who tried to chat her up.

'Why would you be?' Ruy reasoned in what appeared to be genuine surprise as he stared down at her with smouldering dark golden eyes. 'I'm solving problems for you.'

'But I don't *need* you to solve my problems.'

'There's no shame in accepting help when it's available.' Ruy kissed a rousing trail across one delicate shoulder, lingering on her collarbone, making her shiver convulsively, heat curling at the secret heart of her. 'I'll be disappointed if you decide not to model for me or accompany me to Spain but if those are the choices you make, I will respect them,' he swore.

With those words, that assurance that she was still free to do as she wished, he broke the last chain of constraint holding her back. Bribery and blackmail only worked with the addition of pressure and he was removing the threat of that pressure. 'You promise?' she pressed tightly.

'I promise, *querida*,' Ruy husked, lean fingers spreading across her curvy derriere to angle her into collision with his erection. 'I can take no for an answer when to do otherwise would make a woman feel intimidated.'

Her heart raced as she felt his readiness. 'Take off your clothes,' she urged helplessly, impatient and greedy now that he had soothed her fears.

Ruy vaulted off the bed and stripped at speed. Boots, sweater, jeans hit the floor in a messy heap, leaving him standing there before her for a split second, almost naked, and breathtaking in a way she had never known a man could be. He was very tall, very lean and all muscle from his sculpted torso and flat, corrugated stomach to his powerful arms and legs. Her attention lingered on the thrusting evidence of his arousal, clearly delineated by the boxers he sported, and her face burned, curiosity and anxiety melding as he strode into the bathroom and reappeared to toss a handful of condoms down beside the bed.

A handful? Surely he wasn't planning on them doing the deed more than once?

He released the catch on her bra, cupped a firm full mound and suckled a straining nipple and an arrow of damp heat raced through her and settled into a dulled throb between her thighs. Her spine arched as she surged up to him, alight as a crackling fire craving oxygen. His mouth crashed down on hers again and the heat inside her surged even higher. Her hands danced over every part of him she could reach, toying with his hair, caressing his wide smooth shoulders, skating down the long line of his flexing back, fingers curling as he addressed his attention to her other breast and tugged on the sensitive tip until she moaned low in her throat.

An impatience more powerful than anything she had ever felt assailed her. Hunger clawed at her, a wanting, a need she had never before experienced. He took her mouth again, urgently tasting her, and every delve of his tongue made her temperature rocket.

He lifted his dark head, struggling to catch his breath. 'Slow down,' he urged. 'We're not in a hurry.'

Her eyes closed tight against the compelling contours of his beautiful face, defiance racing through her trembling frame because she didn't like to be controlled and just then, as the giver of pleasure, he was controlling her. He might not be in a hurry, but she *was*. She ran a hand down over his flat stomach and stroked him, surprised by how smooth and yet hard, like steel wrapped in velvet, he was, delighted when he shuddered against her and groaned out loud, as responsive to her as she was to him and she liked that, really *liked* that feeling of power. She pressed him back against the pillows.

A glint lighting his dark golden gaze, Ruy used his hands to roll her over instead. 'This that two-vote equality thing you mentioned earlier?' he teased huskily, stretching a hand down to whisk off her panties before reaching for protection.

'Maybe…' Arms wrapping round him, Suzy pulled him down to her again, nibbling at his lower lip before passionately kissing him, unable to sate her longing for his mouth on hers again.

Ruy traced a finger over her swollen wet centre and a whimper of sound was torn from her as she lifted up to him by instinct, desperate to ease the drumbeat of need driving her, barely recognising herself when she was lost in that fierce craving. He slid between her trembling thighs and entered her in a powerful surge, and she jerked at the burn of his entrance into her untried body. It hurt and she gritted her teeth, shocked because she hadn't expected pain. She closed her eyes tight and endured until the burn lessened, faded, turned into something else, a something that soothed and aroused and entrapped her afresh.

A ripple of excitement built in her pelvis and the promise of pleasure was so strong it held her spellbound. He felt extraordinary. Waves of heat and sensation shimmered through her sensitised body, exquisite sensation tugging at her with every thrust of his lean, powerful length. He ground down on her and went deeper and her world just exploded round her in a white-hot electrifying shower of response that lit her up inside and out. She tumbled back against the pillows, shattered by that climax, fascinated by an experience that had been so much more powerful than she had ever dreamt it could be.

Ruy pulled back from her and immediately saw the blood on her thighs and on him and he remembered the way she had hidden her face, the incredible tightness of her, and suddenly he registered that he had been a complete idiot and he was furious. Nobody was less able to cope with the suspicion that he had slept with a virgin than Ruy. Indeed, he had gone through a phase after his nightmare with Liliana of checking beforehand that no woman he slept with was an innocent. As a rule, though, the risk wasn't great because Ruy rarely took younger women to bed.

'How old are you?' he suddenly demanded of Suzy.

Her smooth brow furrowing at the rawness of that enquiry, Suzy sat up. 'Twenty-one…why?'

Dark golden eyes as hard and unyielding as the stone in his bathroom, Ruy surveyed her grimly and sprang off the bed. 'You were a virgin. I had no idea and I wouldn't have touched you had you warned me.'

'*Warned* you?' she repeated in shaken objection to his attitude. 'Why would I have warned you?'

'Because I didn't sign up for this scenario,' Ruy lanced back chillingly. 'I don't sleep with virgins… *ever*! I don't want you attaching expectations to what just happened between us because sex means virtually nothing to me. I'm not about to fall madly in love with you and suggest that we have a serious relationship either… I don't work that way. I'm sorry.'

A shuddering wave of humiliation engulfed Suzy as she stared back at him in shock. Unapologetic eyes challenged hers before he swung away to stride into the bathroom and the door slammed shut.

CHAPTER FIVE

Suzy STAYED STILL for only a few moments and then she leapt off the bed and ran around scooping up her clothes, clambering back into them as fast as she could. At the same time, a phone started buzzing somewhere, a phone she suspected to be in Ruy's discarded jeans. Ignoring it, she sped downstairs, not even sure where she was going. She felt hurt, humiliated, utterly and cruelly exposed after his cutting words in the aftermath of their intimacy. She had got into bed with the wrong guy, totally the wrong guy.

In the spacious lounge area, she looked around in search of the studio he had mentioned or at least the possibility of another bathroom facility because she knew she had to wash the memory of him off her skin. She peered into an empty kitchen, a cloakroom and then a big airy room with full-height windows that overlooked the dense woods. It contained both an easel, a stack of canvases and a bed. One of the doors off it led into a bathroom and with a sigh of relief she began to undress again.

She had gone to bed with a man she barely knew,

and she cursed her impulsive nature for that blunder. She had leapt in where angels feared to tread. All the worst mistakes she had ever made could be laid at the door of that flaw in her character. Well, lesson learned, she told herself urgently, frantically striving to fill the deep well of pain inside her with more positive feelings. Her body ached, reminding her of what she wanted to most forget.

How on earth had she put herself in a position where Ruy Rivera could reject her as if she had chased after him begging for his attention? Was he so arrogant, so vain that he assumed every woman would try to entrap him if she got the chance? What else was she to think after that speech he had made? Plenty more fish in the sea, one of her friends at school used to quip when some boy let her down, but just then Suzy didn't believe she would ever dare to look at a man again with covetous eyes.

On the floor above, Ruy almost punched the wall of his shower, drawing his clenched fist back with a curse at the last possible moment. What the hell had come over him when he verbally attacked Suzy like that? But he *knew*, didn't he? He knew all too well where that attack of paranoia had come from. His brain had succumbed to a flashback of Liliana and the catastrophic trail of events that she had initiated in his life. Cold revulsion and disquiet had drenched Ruy like an acid bath and he had lashed out accordingly at an innocent. He gritted his teeth. Ruy had never liked being in the wrong and even less did he like the prospect of apologising.

A virgin though, he hadn't been prepared for that

possibility at all. Why not though? She was still very young, *too* young for him, he censured himself. He had given in to lust like a sex-starved teenager with no thought of the consequences. As a result, he had destroyed any trust Suzy might have had in him and any hope of her being willing to do anything for him. He towelled himself off grimly and stooped to snatch up his phone when he heard it buzzing.

Damp and breathless from her haste, Suzy emerged back into the lounge, having decided what she would do next. She would nip back upstairs, collect her stuff and then go home to her father. She would have to walk back by the road, which would take ages, but she didn't feel as though she had a choice. She reckoned she would sooner walk over hot coals than spend another hour under Ruy Rivera's roof.

Someone thumped loudly on the front door knocker. Suzy frowned, knowing the housekeeper wasn't around and that Ruy was probably still in the shower. After a moment of hesitation, she opened the front door and took a dumbfounded step back as Percy confronted her with knotted fists and an enraged red face.

'You slut!' he launched at her accusingly. 'So, the rumours were true!'

'Leave me alone!' Suzy exclaimed as he extended his thick arms to grab at her and she snaked backwards into the safety of the house.

As Percy lurched past the door she attempted to slam shut in his face, two things happened. She saw several men racing across the driveway towards them and heard someone coming down the stairs to her rear.

With an explosive Spanish curse, Ruy thrust Suzy to safety behind him and as Percy ploughed forward Ruy punched him hard. Percy went down like rock and, venting a hissed imprecation, Ruy grabbed him by the scruff of the neck and dragged him out of the house. Suzy was frozen to the spot, shocked by the speed of Ruy's reactions. She watched as four men rushed up the steps, frantically apologising to Ruy in Spanish while grabbing hold of Percy to haul him away.

'Who the heck are they?' Suzy whispered shakily.

'Staff,' Ruy breathed curtly. 'Did he hurt you?'

'No…you got here just in time.'

'My staff let him onto the grounds because they knew you were staying here and they assumed that he was your father,' Ruy explained with a shake of his head, damp black hair tousled above dark deep-set eyes that shone gold with strong emotion. 'Well, they won't make that mistake again and we will ensure that Brenton stays away.'

'Don't know how we're going to do that… Percy likes to have his say,' Suzy muttered as Ruy paced away from her, punching a number on his phone and speaking rapidly.

'Legal counsel will meet us at the police station…'

Suzy dealt him a dazed look, still reeling from Percy's sudden appearance and the shockingly efficient violence of Ruy's response. She watched as the men Ruy had labelled staff levered Percy back into his car and stood back waiting for him to drive away. 'Why would we need legal counsel?'

And *why*, in concert with Ruy, was she suddenly employing that royal 'we' as if Ruy were as ensnared in the ongoing problem of Percy as she was?

'You have to apply for a non-molestation order to keep Brenton at a distance but first you must report the original assault to the police,' Ruy told her firmly. 'You really can't afford to wait to do that now.'

'No,' Suzy conceded with a shudder, her ex's second attempt to assault her having shaken her up badly and made her appreciate that she did need the law to protect her.

'It'll take an hour for the solicitor I've instructed to arrive.'

'I don't know why you would be instructing a solicitor to help me,' Suzy told him flatly, shooting him a bemused glance. 'You know your moods change like the wind, Ruy. One minute you're Mr Nice guy, the *next*—'

Watching her warily, Ruy expelled his breath in a hiss. 'Will you allow me to apologise and explain?'

Suzy stiffened and flushed; her expressive eyes carefully veiled. 'You don't need to explain anything to me.'

'I apologise for what I said upstairs,' Ruy murmured in a driven undertone, thoroughly surprising her with that candid opening.

'Unfortunately,' he continued flatly, 'after an experience I had with a woman eight years ago, I'm a little paranoid about having sex with a virgin.'

'A *little*?' Suzy stressed. 'Anyone could have been forgiven for thinking I was ready to set a wedding date!'

But his frankness and the speed of his apology had already struck a reassuring note with Suzy. Clearly, Ruy had faults and baggage just as she did, a little voice piped up inside her head, and he was strong enough to admit those facts. He had helped her, had dealt with Percy and was still fully committed to ensuring that she stayed safe. Yes, Ruy had also said stuff he shouldn't have said and made assumptions that he was not entitled to make, but if he was willing to explain she decided she would listen even if it was only out of curiosity. Stiff with nervous tension, she dropped down on the edge of a sofa and studied him with caution.

Ruy was currently engaged in buttoning the shirt he had put on with his jeans. He had been bare-chested when he repelled Percy, the shirt fluttering loose. He was now covering that broad slice of bronzed muscular torso. As a little spark of heat awakened low in her belly, she turned pink and swiftly averted her attention from him. 'Eight years ago, you must have been quite young,' she remarked uncomfortably.

'I was twenty-two,' Ruy admitted flatly. 'I took a woman home from a club one evening. She was a virgin and afterwards she spooked me by announcing that she had always known that we would make a wonderful couple. I had never met her before and, at that age, I was more into one-night stands than anything else. Regrettably, she decided that that one night constituted a relationship and she turned into a stalker, who caused me a lot of trouble and unhappiness.'

'Oh, my goodness,' Suzy groaned in surprise and sympathy at his explanation.

'So perhaps you can now understand why I forgot my manners for a moment with you and dived straight into mistrust. What happened with that woman did a

lot of damage to my life. Since then I have generally
been much more careful about the women I take as lovers and they have, until now, always been more mature
and experienced.'

'I think the lady's problems had very little to do with
her lack of sexual experience.'

'You're right, but that lack was the only thing that
made her different from her predecessors. I'm afraid
discovering your innocence unleashed my worst memories.'

'I can understand that…now that I know about your
past,' Suzy extended, wanting to ask him more about
his stalking experience, but, sensing that he had shared
as much as he felt comfortable sharing with her, she reluctantly suppressed her curiosity.

'Now go upstairs and put your boots on. We're going
to the police station,' Ruy informed her.

'Right now?' she gasped.

'No better time.'

Apprehensive at the prospect of reporting Percy to
the police, Suzy got to her feet, ruefully amused that
she had left her boots upstairs and had been running
around in her socks without realising it. Putting on her
boots, she came down again clutching her bag and tossing it into the car that Ruy stood beside.

'You'll feel relieved when it's done,' he assured her
confidently.

Some time later Suzy emerged from the police station, answering the urbane solicitor, Ellis Johnson's
query about the nearest good hotel. The imaginary
weight she had felt on her chest had lifted and, for the

first time in several days, she felt a little more like herself again. Ruy planted a light hand to her slender spine to urge her back into his vehicle while Ellis headed for his own car. She knew that she had to go back home with Ruy to fill out the paperwork for the non-molestation order with Ellis. The recollection of Percy forcing his way into Ruy's house still had the power to make her blood run cold. She registered that it would take time for her to stop feeling jumpy and feel safe again.

'Will you consider signing a non-disclosure agreement with Ellis at the same time?' Ruy enquired without warning. 'With a view to modelling for me? I know you're probably not in the right mood to contemplate anything extra and understandably you may feel that you can't trust me now.'

Without even thinking about it, Suzy lifted her hand to rest it soothingly down on a long powerful thigh in disagreement. 'No. I don't feel that way. You were very honest with me and I appreciate that but, after all the strife and hassle I've brought into your life, I can't believe that you *still* want to paint me.'

'That hasn't changed.'

'OK, then,' Suzy breathed. 'But I'm not sure about going to Spain yet…although the thought of the locals piling into the pub just to stare at me and speculate about what happened with Percy makes me cringe.'

'Someone somewhere will talk. They won't have to speculate for long,' Ruy forecast. 'As to Spain, I haven't been very professional in my approach, but I can assure you that I'm not about to put pressure on you to continue our liaison.'

'Not sure I can make the same promise,' Suzy confided without thinking through what she was admitting,
because she was thinking that that word, 'liaison', had
a certain sensual buzz on his lips and lent their brief
encounter a distinct sophistication.

Ruy flashed her a startled glance from glittering dark
golden eyes and then threw back his handsome head
and laughed out loud with appreciation. 'Suzy…where
have you been all my life?'

'I shouldn't have said that,' Suzy muttered, her face
burning, only then lifting her hand off his thigh where
it had lingered. Somewhere deep down inside her she
felt extraordinarily comfortable and relaxed with Ruy
and she was mortified, particularly after he had declared
that sex meant nothing to him.

And she completely understood that attitude if he'd
had the amount of practice she suspected. Sex was neither new nor particularly tempting for him. It was an activity he had taken for granted and freely enjoyed, most
probably with women who were a great deal more beautiful and sensually talented than she was. For her their
encounter had been a major event but it was highly unlikely that it had been equally exciting for him. Why else
would he be telling her that he would be putting no further pressure on her to repeat the experience? And why
had she said what she had? She had been joking, trying to
lighten her embarrassment at the topic being discussed,
but that particular joke had backfired on her. Surely, he
wouldn't think that she had meant that seriously?

Back at the house Ellis Johnson explained the non-
disclosure agreement to her in fine detail. Signing the

document would prevent her from ever speaking or writing about anything relating to Ruy, or indeed posting photos of him or his work, but it didn't strike her as an onerous promise to make because she had never been much given to gossip or social media. In any case she was fairly certain that, once Ruy had painted her, he would have no further interest in her and, by the sound of it, he spent most of his time in Spain. He would melt back out of her life as quickly as he had entered it, she reasoned ruefully, wondering why that should be a deflating thought. Perhaps prior to meeting Ruy, and even prior to Percy, she had allowed her life to become too boring and predictable.

'If I could just get my bag out of your car I can go home now,' she told Ruy as Ellis stood up to leave.

'You have to stay for lunch. You still haven't eaten… and your father was planning to call in here to see you this afternoon,' Ruy imparted while Ellis stared at her and then at Ruy as though he was fascinated by the exchange.

'Dad's coming *here*?' Suzy said in surprise.

'When you go through a traumatic event you have to sit down and catch your breath after it,' Ruy informed her. 'Now it's time to rest and *relax…*'

Her green eyes widened. 'Is it professional for you to still be telling me what to do?' she enquired.

Ruy shrugged, impervious to insult. 'I have more common sense than you do, *querida.*'

'Says the man who thinks he knows everything. Why am I not surprised?' Suzy tossed back, flushing when she noticed Ellis still staring as he departed.

'If you do decide to come to Spain to accompany me to my brother's wedding, I will need to know everything about you,' Ruy admitted over lunch. 'Your birthday, likes and dislikes, everything a fiancé would be expected to know.'

'If I decide to go, I'll draw up a cheat sheet for you and you would need to do the same for me,' she pointed out. 'I'm good at memorising stuff.'

'Why did you choose to stay in the village at the pub instead of moving somewhere that would have offered you more options?'

'Dad needed me. Sometimes you have to do things you don't want to do. My life's always been like that. I've learned to deal.'

'Your father adores you,' Ruy incised. 'He would hate to know how you really feel.'

'It's always been Dad and I against the world...it's all I know. He has often suggested that I go off travelling or try working somewhere else, but I persuaded him that I was a home bird. I don't want him to feel guilty about it. How much did you tell him about Percy?'

'That's your department. I glossed over the nastier elements, played ignorant. I don't think your father needs to know that Brenton was blackmailing you right under his nose, but I do think he suspects that you were only marrying the man to help him.'

Suzy gave him a grateful look. 'Thanks. That was tactful.'

Her father wrapped her into a tight hug as soon as he arrived and studied her with tears shining in his searohing gaze. Ruy went into his studio to leave them in peace to talk.

'I can come home now,' Suzy told the older man.

Roger Madderton frowned. 'I thought you were staying on here, because people are asking a lot of nosy questions and—'

'Don't you need help at the pub?'

'I'm managing fine.' He reminded her that he had hired Flora to cover for her. 'If you'd married Percy, you'd have been gone for good and as it is now, with that loan off my back, I can afford to pay for any help I need.'

Her father was also keen to share exciting news for the future with her. A stately home a few miles away was opening up to the public for the first time and he reckoned that the pub would gain custom from tourists. 'Ruy knew about it, of course. He's very much on the ball when it comes to business,' he opined with a slow admiring shake of his head. 'Taking yourself off to Spain with him for a week is a brilliant idea. You deserve a break after what Percy has put you through.'

'Ruy told you about Spain?' Suzy gasped in surprise.

'Getting away is exactly what you need and if he wants to paint you sitting under an orange tree or some such weird arty thing, let him do it...no skin off your nose!' The older man chuckled, his amusement at such an ambition unconcealed.

Registering that her father had no knowledge of the pretend fiancée role that Ruy wanted her to accept, Suzy smiled without committing herself. It hurt a little that her father wasn't gasping to bring her home, but then that was partly because he knew how much she would cringe at receiving pitying looks and awkward questions from their customers. What astonished her, however, was his faith in Ruy.

'You like him...why?' she asked baldly as the older man was leaving.

'He stepped up for you when you needed it—it wasn't his problem but that didn't matter to him. He did what was right. I respect that in a man,' Roger Madderton replied, and then turned to go back to his car.

Suzy knocked on the studio door, opening it when Ruy called out.

'How did you make my father your biggest fan?' she asked softly.

Tossing aside his sketchbook, Ruy lifted a broad shoulder in a fluid shrug of dismissal. He knew that the truth would be tasteless. Her father had been worn down with worry about the pub and losing that fear had given him a new lease of life. 'Although he's furious that you were hurt, he's very relieved that you're not marrying Brenton.'

'He's not the only one of us relieved,' Suzy conceded, spiralling curls of copper falling across her pale cheek, her green eyes reflective, her skin translucent in the stark daylight, her lips a plump and rosy contrast.

Tensing, Ruy glanced away, suppressing his response to her because it was destroying his concentration. No model had ever had that effect on him before. But then, until Suzy, his relationship with his models had been strictly business and devoid of any sexual element. Why was it different with her? Why couldn't he retain his detachment with her? He had assumed that sex would remove much of her mysterious allure, although that was not why he had ended up in bed with her.

No, he had ended up in bed with her because hunger had overpowered restraint and passion had silenced every logical reservation. That had never happened to Ruy before and such a weakness, such an inability to withstand temptation, disturbed the legendary even temperament that he cherished. It was even more daunting that in spite of acknowledging the folly of a sexual connection with his model he still only had to look at Suzy to want her afresh. And *this* was the woman he was choosing to take home with him? The very first woman who would learn that Ruy Valiente was also V, the famous portrait painter, who scrupulously conserved his anonymity? He crushed the thought in favour of focussing on what was most important to him.

'Will you come to Spain with me?' Ruy pressed softly.

Suzy wondered if Ruy had always had that innate ESP that told him the optimum moment to pose a thorny question. She studied him, her gaze lingering on the black spiky lashes framing his stunning eyes, the angle of a hard cheekbone in sunlight, the sensual curve of his moulded lips. He was beautiful but it was the sheer driving force of will behind that façade that worried her the most. He hadn't been joking when he said that when he wanted something he went all out to get it. He never, it seemed, forgot his objective for an instant. It was a decidedly unnerving trait, but her father's opinion of

him had eased her misgivings and even made her feel
a little foolish for backing nervously away from Ruy
and his proposition.

'Yes, I'll accompany you,' she stated. 'I'll start my
list of cheat-sheet questions today.'

'You'll also be trying on wedding gowns for me this
afternoon.'

'I beg your pardon?' Suzy believed that she had mis-
heard him.

'I want to paint you in a wedding dress but *not* the
same one I found you in. I've ordered a selection to be
brought here this afternoon and I'll choose the most
suitable. Then you can go for a walk in the woods or
something and dirty it up…add a strategic rip or two…'
Ruy shifted a careless hand that implied such behaviour
was so normal as not to require further explanation.

'You'll have to cut the dress if you want rips,' Suzy
told him, striving not to sound as though she considered
the concept to be strange. 'I tore my dress climbing the
tree and jumping out of it and I'm not doing that again.'

'You can pose for the rough drawings here, but I
plan to set the background in Spain. There's an orange
grove at my home there.'

'You live on a fruit farm?' she asked with interest.

'There are orange orchards nearby,' Ruy parried,
knowing he ought to tell her the truth, but holding out
for as long as he could because he enjoyed her resolutely
unimpressed attitude to him and he was afraid that un-
veiling the reality of his astronomic wealth would fa-
tally change that.

And he preferred her as she was: an ordinary girl

from an ordinary working background. Her breezy irreverence stemmed from that solid base. She had strong values. She respected hard work and was entirely free of snobbery. He had observed her in the pub and interacting with his nieces, learning that she was considerate towards the elderly and that she loved children, who loved her back because she was one of those adults who had never quite buried their inner child. Right now, she was relaxed with him, which was exactly how he needed her to be before he could paint her. How much would her outlook shift once she knew the truth about him?

'The stylist who is bringing the gowns will also be taking your measurements for the clothes you'll need to have for Spain,' Ruy volunteered casually.

'I don't need any new clothes for Spain. I have all the stuff I got for the honeymoon I was supposed to be having in Barbados,' Suzy pointed out.

'I doubt if there will be an outfit suitable for a high-society wedding. It won't be similar to a beach holiday where you throw on anything that's comfortable,' Ruy murmured drily.

'You can dress me however you like for painting… that's what artists do, isn't it?' Suzy asked uncertainly and then her triangular face tightened, her chin lifting, her bright eyes glinting back at him. 'But you don't get to tell me what to wear any other time or in any other place.'

'The clothes are merely props for the role you'll be carrying out for my benefit and I wouldn't be engaged to a woman who was poorly dressed.'

'My goodness, what a superficial person you are!'

Suzy scoffed in exasperation. 'I said no, Ruy. Accept a refusal with grace.'

'Be realistic, Suzy,' Ruy breathed coolly. 'If this is about me buying you clothes, dump them when we part, but don't make this venture of ours more difficult than it needs to be!'

Suzy spun away from him, feeling rather as if she were trying to face down an invasion force. Given the smallest chance, Ruy would encroach a little way over the line, but if his initial incursion was successful, he would then flood in and take over at ridiculous speed and it infuriated her. She knew very well that nothing in her wardrobe would pass muster at an upmarket wedding. Ruy had been correct when he surmised that most of the stuff she had could be categorised as casual, rather than elegant or expensive. But he set her back up every time he came over all macho and bossy. Six months of having to dance to Percy's tune had made her touchy on that score.

Even so, Ruy had done her a huge favour when he'd helped her deal with Percy, she reminded herself, and now it was payback time. She whirled back to him, eyes defiant. 'You're making me feel like I'm the unreasonable one!' she condemned.

'It's a week of dressing up and acting attached to me...no big deal!' Ruy shot back at her.

Suzy settled her keen gaze on him. 'Ruy? Learn to quit when you're ahead. This is not the time to lay down the law and score points. I don't work for you. I'm not going to salute you and say, thank you, sir, what would you like me to do next?'

Ruy levered fluidly upright, long lean limbs effortlessly graceful, the power in his smouldering dark golden gaze illuminating his lean, devastatingly handsome features. 'No, you definitely don't want to ask me *that* question because you might not like my answer,' he breathed thickly.

Sixth sense prompted Suzy to back away until her shoulder blades met the window behind her. Sometimes when Ruy looked at her a certain way it felt like straying perilously close to a roaring blaze.

'On the other hand, you might like it too much,' Ruy completed huskily, gazing down at her with extraordinarily compelling golden eyes. 'And so might I.'

He traced her full lower lip with his fingertip and her stomach turned over and her head swam and her knees felt weak, because he was close enough for her to smell the rawly familiar cologne-tinged scent of him. She teetered forward a few inches, *closer*. It was dangerous and she knew it was, knew that they were both attempting to respect boundaries and that, maddeningly, it was the most terrible struggle to do so.

'Kiss me,' he husked, his breath fanning her cheek, making her shiver with awareness.

And she stretched up and he stretched down and their lips collided, hers brushing back and forth with a tantalising lightness of touch, his hotter, harder, claiming her mouth with a fierce, impatient hunger that sent a shower of sparks licking up through her entire body. She had never wanted anything so much as she wanted that kiss to continue, but she also remembered the sensible limits she had promised herself that she would respect. She twisted her head away and sidestepped him, snatching in oxygen as though she had been drowning, denying the sensations rippling through her body in a seductive tide of response. The pulsing ache between her thighs hurt.

'I choose any clothes and I leave them behind when I'm done,' Suzy specified tightly, mentally washing away what had just happened between them, ignoring it as best she could.

Ruy clenched his teeth hard, rejection not being a reaction he had much experience with. It galled him that she had backed away first and that it had been the rational thing to do. Sex would muddy the waters of what was essentially a business arrangement, although it wasn't business when he wasn't paying her a fee, was it? And business didn't make him as hard as a rock with frustration either, he reasoned grimly.

'*And* we try to keep our connection friendly and… er…distant,' Suzy suggested shakily.

'Choose your battles with care, *querida*,' Ruy murmured sibilantly. 'I suspect we're both bad losers.'

CHAPTER SIX

'*SERIOUSLY?*' SUZY WHISPERED helplessly in Ruy's ear when he picked the wedding gown with the feathers. 'I'll roast alive wearing that in Spain.'

He spoke to the stylist about alterations with all the panache of one who knew what he was talking about, but his belief that the internal structure of the dress could essentially be ripped out to make it lighter simply exposed his ignorance. Suzy suppressed a chuckle, marvelling at his obstinacy and amazed by the dress he had picked while he continued to discuss options, expense clearly no drawback as it was agreed that the dress would literally be remade for the occasion. She had been expecting him to choose something severe and elegant, not extravagant and frothy and trailing white feathers like the ghost of Christmas past.

'Mr Rivera knows what he likes,' the stylist remarked when Ruy had left them alone and Suzy was able to get down to describing her requirements, which consisted of a single smart gown and accessories that would hopefully pass muster at his brother's wedding. But her taste in fashion was more quirky than conventional and it took time to identify a suitable dress for the wedding and the perfect shoes to wear with it.

The next morning she had to attend a court hearing in town for the non-molestation order Ellis had lodged on her behalf. Percy wasn't in attendance and the magistrate granted it. Ruy had accompanied her and she felt enormously grateful for his support and relieved when it was over. Afterwards, Ruy asked her to pose for him in the studio, wearing her jeans and sweater. She would have preferred to put some make-up on first, but he insisted that he didn't want her 'all painted up', as he called it. Sadly, that was only the start of their differences that afternoon. Ruy sketched while telling her how to pose in innumerable different positions. Every time she moved an inch or so out of a pose to ease a tight muscle, he growled in complaint and she shot comments back at him, telling him he needed to be more adaptable, more tolerant if he expected her to relax. Ruy liked his models quiet and biddable but as Suzy performed a handstand and then segued down into the splits with the easy flexibility of a dancer, he was too entertained by her joie de vivre to be exasperated.

Over dinner, she asked when they would be going to Spain.

'The day after tomorrow,' Ruy imparted.

'But the clothes won't have arrived by then.'

'They will. I made it clear that a longer wait wasn't an option,' Ruy extended calmly.

Suzy studied him in dismay. 'Ruy…someone could be up all night stitching that feather dress to meet a deadline like that!'

'I would expect that they will be handsomely remunerated if they are. I pay over the odds for good service,' he parried.

'Employees don't get those kinds of choices and I would assume that the boss usually keeps the profits.'

'That's the world we live in. Not my personal responsibility,' Ruy returned, impervious to the hint that he should be ashamed of his willingness to use money to ensure that he received exactly what he wanted when he wanted it, no matter how inconvenient and unreasonable his requests were. 'A jeweller will be calling here this evening for you to choose a ring for our supposed engagement, and at some stage you will have to go home to pick up whatever else you require for Spain.'

'You organise everything right down to the last tiny detail.' Suzy sighed. 'It doesn't leave much room for manoeuvre or going with the flow.'

'I wasn't raised to go with the flow,' Ruy murmured drily. 'I was brought up to respect rules and meet every demand that was made on me. It turned me into a high achiever. It's true that I don't turn handstands in the middle of a work session, but I value the discipline I learned.'

In receipt of that crack, Suzy felt the hot colour of embarrassment flood her cheeks. 'Sorry about that.'

'No, it was refreshing. One minute you were in place and the next you were upside down on the other side of the room,' Ruy pointed out with amusement. 'I won't get bored with you in the studio.'

Dinner was followed by the arrival of the jeweller complete with a security guard. Trays of rings were set out on the coffee table and Ruy closed a hand over hers and tugged her down beside him. 'Choose,' he urged calmly.

All Suzy could see was a crazy bank of glittering jewels. 'No, you choose.'

'Suzy,' Ruy murmured with the faintest emphasis.

The heat of a long thigh was against hers, warming her entire body and tugging at that insistent ache that stirred in her pelvis whenever she got too close to Ruy. It made her want to melt into him, over him, any way she could, but she resisted the urge to leap away, reminding herself that this was supposed to be a joyful occasion for a couple and that in a sense she was on stage and expected to act her part. She reached for a solitaire ring in the very centre.

'A most discerning choice,' the jeweller told her, practically purring at that selection, which implied to her that it was a very, *very* costly ring. 'The rarest of diamonds, a beautiful blue.'

'Perfect,' Ruy said, reaching for her trembling hand to thread it onto her finger, where it proved to be a little loose.

'Are you sure you like it?' Suzy prompted with anxious eyes.

'It's yours.'

Her finger was measured. The ring, she was assured, would be with them the next day. The jeweller and his guard departed.

'The ring will be yours to keep,' Ruy informed her.

Suzy froze in astonishment in receipt of that assurance, angry resentment flaring inside her. 'No, you are doing it again—stop trying to buy me, bribe me, whatever you want to call it! I don't want that! I don't want you believing that you're paying me for any of this, but you don't listen, do you? Look, I have to collect my cases at home. I'll call Dad to pick me up and I'll go now, spend the night there,' she completed doggedly.

Ruy stilled in front of her, so tall, so dark, so devastatingly handsome, her senses hummed that close to him. *'Stay...'*

And it disturbed her that she *knew* he didn't want her to leave and that on some very basic level she was equally reluctant to move any great distance from him. Feeling that way was foolish and would hurt her, she told herself firmly. Was she planning to turn into some sort of clingy woman? That wasn't her, would *never* be her. She was sailing too close to the wind, risking her emotions for a guy who had no serious intentions whatsoever towards her. She was forgettable, *disposable* as far as Ruy was concerned. He had not once referred to their fleeting encounter beyond quickly assuring her that he did not expect her to continue that intimacy. How often did a guy turn his back on the chance of sex?

A guy that wasn't that keen, her brain told her bluntly, but then why was he so reluctant to let her leave his house? It was simple: Ruy wanted her to be on the spot and immediately available when the desire to sketch assailed him. Convenience meant everything to Ruy, who seemed to have a terminal objection to having to wait for anything.

'I'll run you back home,' Ruy volunteered when she said nothing.

Suzy breathed in deep and slow to ease her constricted lungs, knowing that she needed a little space to figure out why she felt so tied to Ruy. Because he had been around to save her when she was terrified? Because he had advised and supported her and made her feel safe? Was her brain, were her very emotions, really that basic? Or was she catching feelings for a man who would never catch them back?

She sat up late with her father and then went through her cases, discarding anything that seemed superfluous. Her father took her back to Ruy's the next morning and by then the wedding dress and her outfits had arrived and she went straight upstairs to try everything on. She walked downstairs in the feathered dress and Ruy sprang off the sofa where he was using a laptop and stared at her. In the gown, her fiery curls tumbling round her shoulders, she was a vision, a distinctly beautiful vision, not at all what he had originally planned.

'Do you still want me to dirty it up a bit?' Suzy enquired doubtfully.

'No, that idea won't work with that gown,' Ruy conceded. 'You could end up looking like a bedraggled bird after a rainstorm.'

Suzy giggled. 'That's what I thought.'

'I'll come up with something else.'

'From that non-existent fertile imagination of yours,' Suzy teased absently.

Ruy merely quirked a brow. He would still paint her in the gown, but he would also paint her in her own clothes, immortalising those lovely delicate features of hers, the glow of her translucent skin and the grace of her. 'Let's do some work now,' he suggested with renewed enthusiasm.

The following day, Suzy rose early. She put on capri pants and a silky tee teamed with a short boxy jacket, aimed at giving her a more finished look. Her very high-heeled red sandals necessitated a slow descent of the stairs. She was surprised to see Ruy already downstairs, sheathed in a dark business suit that just screamed personal tailoring and expense. It fit him like a glove, accentuating his broad shoulders, narrow waist and long powerful legs.

'You're very formal,' she remarked, sitting down for breakfast.

'I like the pompoms on the shoes,' Ruy replied, evading that comment as he passed her a ring box. 'Very different.'

Suzy opened the box, removed the ring and slid it onto her finger without ceremony before eating with appetite. She had only been abroad once and that had been a trip to Greece with a school friend's family the summer that she was sixteen. She was excited about visiting Spain, her late mother's birth place, but striving to act mature and hide the fact. When her cases had been carted away and she walked out of the house to see a limousine awaiting them, she was startled.

'Is this what you call travelling in style?'

'Something like that.'

'Which airport are we heading for?'

'I use a private airfield nearby. It's not far and it'll speed up our journey.'

A private airfield? How did that work? Reluctant to betray her ignorance, Suzy said nothing while wondering if he knew someone who had offered them flights on his plane.

They drew up at the office at the airfield. Ruy requested her passport and it was handed out of the limo to the man who emerged from the office. Suzy idly appraised the sleek white jet parked on the runway nearby. It bore a V logo and the Spanish flag on its tail.

'Time for us to board,' Ruy advised as the passenger door was opened by the driver.

The pilot and two stewardesses greeted them at the foot of the steps. There was a lot of what Suzy regarded as bowing and scraping and the ladies were very flirty with Ruy. Suzy frowned as she mounted the steps and moved into what struck her as the very last word in opulent cabin interiors. There were reclining seats, coffee tables, polished wood, pale leather surfaces, and through the arch at the foot she could see an actual conference table surrounded by chairs. She stepped back as the four men she had seen at Ruy's secluded home passed by them and headed towards the back of the plane, where they disappeared from view.

'Make yourself comfortable,' Ruy advised.

'A private jet?' Suzy queried, settling stiffly down into a reclining seat but keeping it upright, quite unable to relax in so sumptuous a setting.

Ruy vented a rueful laugh, raw charisma in the lazy

half-smile he angled in her direction. 'I suppose it's time to come clean.'

'I think it is,' Suzy agreed with a dangerous glint in her clear green eyes. 'You have access to a private jet or is some friend allowing you to use it?'

'Strictly speaking the jet belongs to Valiente Capital, the Spanish investment firm. I am the CEO of Valiente Capital. That I also paint is a secret, a diversion from my normal life as a hedge-fund manager and I use the pseudonym V for my portraits to conserve that privacy,' Ruy explained with cool precision.

Investment, hedge funds? Suzy's brain swam. She would probably have been less taken aback had he announced that he was a bullfighter. But some sort of financial wizard? That was so far removed from what she had so far seen of Ruy that she was wildly disconcerted, and then her thoughts took a step back and she recalled that cool, arrogant side to his nature. 'Why weren't you honest with me about who you were from the start?' she demanded tightly.

'My two identities are kept very much separate and few people know the truth. Cecile is one of the few. I'm not sure our investors would be happy to learn that I'm an artist as well. I bought the house in England as a bolt-hole where I could paint when I take time off and I see no reason to tell anyone that I'm also involved in the financial markets.'

'How rich *are* you?' Suzy shot at him thinly, an unpleasant thought suddenly occurring to her. 'Rich enough to have paid me that fifty thousand pounds I mentioned that night in the pub and think nothing of it?'

Steady dark eyes with only a gleam of gold in their depths rested on her as Ruy compressed his lips and jerked his chin in confirmation.

'And I laughed and asked if you thought you were Mr Rockefeller or something!' Suzy recalled with a shudder of humiliation, her cheeks burning. 'You've had a lot of fun at my expense!'

'What's that supposed to mean?' Ruy countered, taken aback by the charge.

'I may not have the right to know your secrets, but I *did* have the right to know the identity and status of the man I slept with. I was entitled to be told who you really were *before* that happened,' Suzy condemned. 'Because I can tell you right now that if I'd known you were some flash hedge-fund whizz-kid, I wouldn't have gone to bed with you in the first place!'

'Why the hell not? What possible difference could it have made?' Ruy slammed back at her, angry for the first time in her presence, thoroughly nettled by that word, 'flash', which seemed to suggest that he was some sort of untrustworthy braggart.

'I don't even know your real name!' Suzy yelled back at him above the roar of the engines as the jet rolled down the runway.

'Ruy Santiago Valiente,' Ruy supplied with icy precision. 'Rivera was Cecile's mother's surname and I borrow it when I don't wish to be identified.'

'How convenient to have an alternative name!' Suzy snapped between clenched teeth of scorn.

Ruy exhaled slowly, cocked an ebony brow and murmured, 'I really don't see what the problem is. I've told you now.'

Suzy gripped her right hand with her left because she wanted to hit him. 'You deceived me. You betrayed my trust.'

'Those are serious accusations,' Ruy bit out, his temper stirring even more.

'And they're *true*. You didn't give me a choice. I feel like an idiot for not seeing that, the way you behaved, you couldn't possibly have been the forthright artist you were pretending to be!'

Ruy gritted his teeth. 'Most women would be ecstatic to find out that I'm a wealthy man.'

Suzy's hands both flew up in the air to emphasise her furious frustration with him and his refusal to look at the situation from her point of view. 'If they're greedy, if they want you to spend your money on them, but I don't! Now I can see that you've used your wealth like a weapon against me from the moment we met!' she framed with bitter resentment.

The jet was finally in the air and Ruy released his seat belt and vaulted upright to his full intimidating height. He stared down at her with scorching dark golden eyes. '*Valgame Dios!* How do you make that out?'

Suzy released her belt and got up as well, moving away several feet before spinning back round to face him. 'You tried to bribe me.'

'And it would have worked a treat had you known who I was at the time because you were desperate to save your father and his livelihood,' Ruy reminded her drily.

Suzy stamped a pompommed toe. 'That is not the point!'

'That is exactly the point. Everything has turned out very well for you and your father...*why*?' Ruy prompted expectantly, as if he were a teacher giving a young, not very bright child a lesson in life. 'Because I have money, and I was able to use that money you deride to protect you and your father from further interference and intimidation from Brenton. Don't you dare snipe at me for telling you the truth you don't want to hear or accept!'

As Suzy angrily parted her lips the cabin door opened and a stewardess appeared. Deeply flushed, Suzy backed down into her seat again and sat there frozen in place while refreshments and snacks were served. She was so angry she was trembling with the force of her feelings. On one level she knew that Ruy was right. He *had* saved the pub from her ex's machinations. He *had* made her father's life a lot easier by releasing him from years of worry about money. But, ultimately, she was convinced that Ruy had bought into the pub to ensure that Suzy agreed to model for him and accompanied him out to Spain to pose as his fiancée.

'Yes, what you did may have delivered a happy result for my father, but it doesn't change the unscrupulous way you operate. You bought into the pub to put pressure on me.'

'I bought into the pub to take pressure *off* you,' Ruy stressed curtly.

'I had the right to know your true identity before I slept with you,' Suzy sliced back at him sharply.

'It was casual sex, Suzy...not a life-changing choice!' Ruy raked back at her cuttingly.

Her face flamed at the wounding reminder. What had meant a great deal to her had meant considerably less to him and that hurt, yes, it did, no matter how hard she resented that reality. Ruy had lied to her and that scared her and made her very wary, particularly after she had innocently chosen to trust Percy. She had already suffered the knowledge that she was not that perfect a judge of character and she knew she needed to be more careful.

'Yes, it worked out so well for you when you ended up bedding a stalker!' Suzy reminded him helplessly, needled by the statement that their encounter had been casual on his terms when it had been anything but casual for her when he had become her first lover.

A muscle pulled taut at the corner of Ruy's unsmiling mouth. 'You slept with me because you wanted me. It would have been wrong had I been married or concealing some other relevant fact that you needed to know, but I *wasn't*.'

'I wouldn't have chosen to become intimate with a guy so far removed from my own world!' Suzy retorted fiercely.

'That's inverse snobbery,' Ruy countered, marvelling at the stubborn manner in which she held onto her ire, refusing to be soothed or to accept that he had done nothing wrong.

'No, it's not. You're rich and I should've worked that out for myself because you don't really hide it that well. You're very arrogant. You think you can buy whatever you want and that your wishes and needs are more important than other people's. You rearranged my life and my father's purely to suit yourself.'

'It suited you as well,' Ruy incised coolly, all logic and calm, which only increased the frustrated rage she was suppressing.

'Oh, shut up!' Suzy finally launched at him in exasperation, ramming down the hurt feelings tugging at her that he was *not* the man she had naively assumed he was. Once again, she had made the wrong judgement call and that scared her. 'I've heard enough of your smooth, specious arguments. You could probably talk your way out of murder but I'm not listening any more!'

And with that ultimate strike, Suzy rose from her seat, swiped up the magazines the stewardess had brought her and stalked to the end of that section of cabin to sit out of his view. Ruy brooded on his rage, even white teeth gritted. He was very wealthy, he had always been wealthy, and he supposed a certain level of arrogance and selfishness afflicted most men in his position. He was accustomed to getting his own way. He was used to paying more to get it too, it being his experience that those he dealt with *expected* him to pay more because he could afford it. How was that wrong?

What difference did his status in life make to her? Would she honestly have rejected him had she known that he was rich? And why was she the very first woman in his life to fight with him over the reality that he was as rich as Midas? The first woman to criticise him... aside of Cecile. And his sister adored him and only offered occasional nuggets of unwelcome truth in an effort to improve his character.

'I have a business call to make,' Ruy informed her as he came to a halt in the archway next to her seat. 'But before I leave, allow me to have the final word.'

Suzy lifted her head, green eyes glittering like emeralds, soft pink mouth flattening with tension.

'You had sex with me for the same reason I had sex with you, *querida*,' he imparted softly.

'Which was…?' Suzy dared, enraged by the heat she could feel hotly flooding her cheeks.

'*Hombre!* Reason had nothing to do with it. We were so hot for each other we couldn't control ourselves. At least I'm honest about it,' Ruy told her mockingly.

CHAPTER SEVEN

As the limousine that collected Ruy and Suzy from the airport pulled away from the kerb, the silence within the vehicle was frigid. Suzy played with her phone and did everything she could to avoid looking in Ruy's direction while he passed his time with business calls, switching with enviable ease between several different languages. Having no idea exactly where they were heading and still too angry with Ruy to ask, Suzy was exasperated with both him and herself by the time the limo turned off a rural road to move up a long straight driveway. The lane was bounded by tall dark cypress trees that cast spear-shaped shadows across the pale sunlit gravel.

A gargantuan building came into view at the top of the drive. The substantial house in the centre was extended on either side by wings. It was a mansion, composed of several storeys and countless windows.

'Welcome to Palacio Valiente,' Ruy murmured as the limousine drove below an archway and came to a halt in a cobbled interior courtyard, adorned with a marble fountain.

An arched veranda with polished floor tiles ringed

the entire space. Elegant urns of colourful flowers tumbled from every corner. Suzy climbed slowly out of the car. A hand lightly cupping her elbow, Ruy moved forward to greet the small middle-aged man awaiting them. They moved indoors down a short corridor into a vast echoing marble entrance hall in which life-sized classical statues stood in niches.

'Manuel is scolding me for bringing you into the house for the first time by the rear entrance,' Ruy told her with amusement. 'He manages the staff and the household—'

Suzy was still in shock at the size and style of Ruy's home while telling herself that she should have guessed by his attitude that he would live in a literal palace. How he had accommodated his pedigreed expectations to that relatively small, if spacious, house in Norfolk she had no idea because by his standards he had been roughing it. Ruy had not only grown up with the proverbial silver spoon, he had grown up with an entire silver canteen. The entrance hall was cool, splendid and thoroughly intimidating, designed, she felt, to remind less high-flown mortals of their lowlier place in life.

A sweeping staircase that split in two higher up to curve in opposite directions sat before her. Suzy thought in sudden horror, *Oh, my goodness, my clothes just aren't going to cut it here!* He had said a high-society wedding, but she had seriously underestimated the level of glitz and expense that would be expected. And once again that was all *his* fault for not being more honest. He had worn an elegant business suit to travel home, she had put on cropped trousers and a tee and that contrast said it all.

Ruy thrust open the door of a room off the landing and stood back. Her delicate profile tight, she moved ahead of him into a breathtakingly magnificent bedroom. A superb canopied and draped ornate bed sat at the far end of the room. 'This looks like somewhere royalty would sleep,' she whispered uneasily, feeling as if she should be standing behind a rope reading a guidebook on some official tour.

'No, this is where we sleep,' Ruy countered.

'*We?*' Suzy almost gasped.

'It may be an old house but expectations here are as contemporary as anywhere else. Engaged couples share a bed,' Ruy informed her smoothly.

'Even when they're barely speaking?'

'Particularly in that case. Never let the sun go down on anger,' Ruy quipped.

'Any more clichés to offer?' Suzy was playing for time because back in England she had become accustomed to having a bed to herself. Ruy had stayed in his studio, she had stayed upstairs. After their fleeting bout of intimacy, that division, that privacy, had provided a welcome escape from the turmoil of emotions Ruy's presence incited inside her. But whether she liked it or not, he was correct in his assertion that people would expect an engaged couple to share a room.

Ruy crossed the room to tug open a door onto a balcony. 'I want you to put on the feather dress and your boots and I'll meet you down…there.' He indicated the wrought-iron staircase that ran down to the charming inner courtyard below them.

'It's an orange grove,' she whispered in recognition, gazing down on the plump fruit bright against the rich evergreen leaves of the trees.

'Yes... I'll get changed. I don't usually paint here but for you I will make an exception. After all, there is no one alive now who cares what I do,' Ruy breathed abstractedly, dark shadowed eyes lightening as he glanced up at the azure-blue sky above. 'I should celebrate that freedom whenever I can.'

Her luggage and his arrived while Suzy was still mulling over his words and trying to fathom why he had sounded both regretful and energised. A maid appeared to tackle her cases and Suzy quickly lifted the feather dress in its garment bag and her boots and vanished into the bathroom to dress in private. As she descended the outside steps into the courtyard the intoxicating sultry scent of the oranges rose in the midday heat.

A few minutes later Ruy strode down the stairs, his attention welded to the slender silhouette of Suzy standing in the white dress beneath the trees. In that instant, reality and fantasy smoothly merged into a perfect whole for him. He directed her down onto the worn stone bench below one of the trees and arranged her in a sideways pose, one booted foot braced on the bench, the other on the ground, her face turned towards him, her riot of vibrant copper curls spiralling round her slight shoulders, slender legs edged with a jagged white feather hem. With her luminous skin warmed to a hint of a soft pink glow by the heat, she looked utterly amazing.

Suzy studied Ruy as he sank down opposite her. She had no other choice when she was not permitted to move her head. In his suit he had looked sleek and sophisticated and distant. In well-worn jeans and a shirt, he looked overwhelmingly masculine and somehow rougher and sexier round the edges with dark stubble outlining his hard jawline and accentuating his wide, sensual mouth. Her body clenched as she remembered the taste of him, the pounding urgency of his lean, hard body on hers. A very slight shudder slivered through her, her nipples pinching taut, her skin prickling with that unstoppable tide of awareness and tightening her flesh round her bones.

A phone was buzzing. It had to be his because he ignored it, ebony brows flaring in annoyance. A door opened nearby. Manuel appeared, wringing his hands apologetically and imparting the message that someone just wouldn't take no for an answer. Ruy swore under his breath and tossed aside the sketch pad. He dug out his phone, stabbed buttons, paced away before swinging back to her to take a photo of her and that particular pose. 'We'll have to call it a day. I have to go into the office. Feel free to explore.'

'I will.' Suzy rose slowly and straightened her stiff muscles. She was hungry and thirsty and tired but determined to make the most of her freedom. She climbed the stairs and unzipped the dress, removing it to drape it over a chair arm. She kicked off the boots and pressed her warm feet against the relief of the cold tiled floor before going for a shower. Her clothes had been neatly put away for her in the cabinets and wardrobes in the same room that Ruy had used. She pulled out shorts and a vest top, more suitable for the heat. Manuel was waiting for her when she came downstairs to usher her into a wonderfully air-conditioned room and serve her with a beautiful salad while offering to show her round the *palacio* after her meal.

Ruy couldn't settle at work. He dealt with the minor crisis that had erupted but his laser-sharp concentration swiftly evaporated. He looked several times at the photo of Suzy on his phone and wondered what she was doing, grimly amused by his wandering thoughts. Of course, he was always driven and obsessed in the first fine flush with a new model, a new painting, he reminded himself. His fascination would ebb once he had finally contrived to pin down and capture Suzy's effervescent spirit on canvas.

His sexual fascination? That, he sensed, might be another story because that was without precedent. He paced his office, wondering why that hunger refused to quit. One and done was his pattern. He took a woman for one night and treated her like a queen for that night but there were no repeats, no extended interludes. He didn't get involved in relationships. He had tried a couple of times, but within the space of a handful of dates the women concerned would get on his nerves and begin assuming that they were more important to him than they were and then he had to let them down gently. In truth, he didn't like hurting people, women in particular, and some individuals, like Liliana, were dangerously fragile. It was easier simply to stick to one-night stands. Nobody misunderstood what was on offer then and nobody got hurt.

But, unfortunately, one experience of Suzy hadn't been enough to satisfy him. He hadn't even got a whole night with her. And worst of all, every moment of that impulsive, hasty encounter was etched on his mind like a scar. From her point of view, it must have been a pretty poor introduction to sex and that dented his ego and shamed him, but he hadn't known, couldn't have guessed that she would be that innocent. Even so, he didn't believe that let him off the hook. And now he would never have the chance to show her how different it could be. After her experience with her ex and then his own callous words in the aftermath, the last thing Suzy needed now was another man trying to put pressure on her. He had promised that he wouldn't do that. He had to keep that promise.

Ruy arrived home in time for dinner and found Suzy in the long portrait gallery with Manuel. Manuel was carefully naming pieces of antique furniture in Spanish and correcting Suzy's pronunciation while giving her a potted history of the characters in the portraits. As most of them had led lives of stultifying boredom, Ruy was surprised to hear her laughter ring out. He was already trying not to let his gaze linger too long on her long shapely legs in denim shorts and the perky tilt of her unbound breasts or even the glorious messy tumble of her curls. That silvery peal of laughter only energised the throb at his groin.

'Ruy!' she exclaimed when she noticed him, tall and

dark and devastatingly handsome in his silvery grey designer suit.

Manuel smiled and left them alone.

'Poor Manuel,' Suzy sighed. 'He thinks you're going to marry me and so he's trying to get my Spanish up to speed and educate me about your home and your ancestors.'

'My family were bankers to royalty for centuries. That's just about all you need to know. What made you laugh?'

'The one who had a whole string of wives,' Suzy confided, an irrepressible twinkle in her bright eyes. 'Your family's version of Henry the Eighth.'

'Except Diego's five unfortunate wives died in childbirth,' Ruy explained.

'I suppose back then that was very common,' Suzy remarked thoughtfully. 'Thank goodness it isn't now.'

'My mother died in childbirth and my baby sister with her,' Ruy heard himself admit in argument, startled to hear himself proffering that confidence, but there was something in the freedom with which she spoke and behaved with him that smashed his usual reserve and brought his own barriers crashing down. Somehow she made him *want* to tell her stuff and he couldn't explain that to his own satisfaction. 'It's less common, but it still happens.'

'What age were you?'

'Rigo and I were five. Our world fell apart without her. She was very loving. My father, on the other hand, was more of a "spare the rod and spoil the child" parent.'

'I'm so sorry. At least I was too young to be aware of my loss and Dad was very caring.'

'You were fortunate. Our father didn't have a kind bone in his body. He punished my brother and I for the smallest infraction. I excelled at school, but I still got punished for not doing well enough to please. Rigo, regrettably, was not academic. As you can imagine, he suffered more,' Ruy told her grimly. 'My father made Rigo compete with me and never let him forget that I was the elder, the heir, the *important* son. It destroyed our relationship.'

'So, you were never close to your twin?'

'No. He grew up resenting me and that never went away…in our twenties, something occurred that destroyed any hope of a closer relationship.'

'And what was that?' Suzy prompted, hungry for more detail, conscious that Ruy rarely spoke so freely with her.

'Rigo was addicted to drugs for a while. I don't wish to share his history,' Ruy admitted very stiffly. 'That is his business.'

Suzy reddened, aware that she had asked one question too many and mortified as she took a determined step back from that angle. 'What was it like for Cecile?' she asked.

'Cecile's mother was my father's mistress. She didn't grow up with us and he never officially acknowledged her as his daughter. Rigo wants nothing to do with her because according to him accepting Cecile into the family is dissing my father's memory. Even though our father was cruel to him, he still regards him as the ultimate standard of what he should aspire to.'

'Life's too short for an outlook like that.' Suzy sighed ruefully, passing by him into the bedroom, relieved to have finished that conversation and backed away from it. 'Do I need to change for dinner or anything?'

'Not for my benefit, particularly when you look as incredible as you do in those shorts,' Ruy told her with a slow smile.

Her face went pink as she watched him remove his jacket and tug his tie loose. The little intimacies of a shared room tugged uneasily at her and she walked restlessly over to the window. 'Is that orange grove in the courtyard the one you were referring to?'

'Yes, but there's another wilder, larger version of it at the far end of the gardens beside the estate orchards. I remember playing hide and seek there as a child,' Ruy imparted, his voice closer than she expected.

Suzy whirled round and there he was, a couple of feet away, clad only in boxers, almost every inch of his magnificent body bare for her perusal. Involuntarily her eyes roamed over the expanse of his bronzed torso, lingering on the corrugated slab of his abs and flat stomach. Her mouth ran dry, her tongue glued to the roof of her mouth.

'Don't look at me like that. I'm not good at self-denial,' Ruy warned her.

'Neither am I,' Suzy croaked, noticing, well, she really couldn't help noticing that he was aroused. Those boxers didn't hide much. 'How was I looking at you?'

'Like you want me…like I look at you,' Ruy framed hoarsely. '*Dios mio!* Even my grammar's going to hell!'

Warmth mushroomed inside Suzy at the confirmation that he still wanted her but that, just like her, he was in conflict over it. Still being tempted by him had seemed weak until he made that same admission. 'I was so angry with you this morning…still am, because you aren't the guy I thought you were and that threw me… and now I don't have the right clothes.'

'I'll get you more clothes,' Ruy swore impatiently. 'Little problems of that sort aren't important.'

'You're not allowed to buy me anything more,' Suzy reminded him. 'You keep your money to yourself.'

Ruy reached out and closed his big hands round her smaller ones to tug her closer. 'Anything you want. I need you to be happy.'

'It doesn't take money to make me happy,' Suzy mumbled. 'Well, except when it came to saving Dad from Percy.'

'There's an exception to every rule,' Ruy conceded generously while stilling in the act of edging her even closer. 'We're not supposed to be doing this.'

'That's your rule,' Suzy pointed out helplessly.

And he kissed her, and a long breathless sigh of relief escaped her. The tension holding her fast snapped and propelled her into the muscular heat of him, her hands sliding up to his shoulders and stretching round his neck, her entire body melting and pliant. 'I want you,' she whispered daringly. 'But not if you're liable to freak out afterwards.'

'Absolutely no freaking out,' Ruy swore raggedly

half under his breath. 'Are you sure about this? I'm still the same guy who doesn't want a relationship.'

'Do we have to put a label on it? I don't want a relationship right now either, not after escaping Percy. Do you think you could go with the flow just for once?' Suzy murmured softly as she backed him towards the bed.

An unholy grin lit Ruy's lean dark features as he realised what she was doing. 'Just for once,' he agreed, angling his lean hips against her, further acquainting her with his arousal.

A kernel of pure exhilaration, unlike anything Suzy had ever felt before, sparked and glowed at the heart of her, igniting an impatient pulse of need. He tugged her down on the bed and kissed her until she was pushing up against him, eager for more. She was with him every step of the way. He extracted her from her top, teased the pouting tips of her breasts and buried his mouth there to take advantage of her passionate response before beginning to remove her shorts. Her body felt as though it was already racing ahead of her, taut and trembling with seething anticipation.

'You'd run away if you knew the things I want to do to you,' Ruy growled against the slender column of her white throat, his mouth nipping along the tender slope of her neck, making her squirm and gasp while he delicately stroked and traced the damp triangle of cloth stretched between her thighs.

Her heart was racing at an insane level. It was a crazy challenge simply to catch her breath. Sheer physical excitement had gripped her in an unbreakable hold.

He peeled her out of her last garment. The burn at her core was relentless, tiny ripples of tension already ringing her pelvis and building in demand. He spread her trembling legs, lowered his head and used his tongue on her tender flesh while he eased a finger into her. Irresistible sensation engulfed Suzy in a heady wave and a rosy flush warmed her entire skin surface as she rocked her slender hips. Erotic bliss, a whole world of sensual extremes, captured her and wrung powerful responses from her sensitised body. Flung up to an ecstatic height that made her cry out, she felt fireworks flare through her entire being and light her up until she fell back against the pillows to marvel at the tiny convulsions of pure pleasure still currenting through her.

Her shimmering green eyes locked to him. She lifted a feathery copper brow. 'You're allowed to shock and awe me in bed,' she conceded with deadly seriousness and no small amount of complacency.

After a disconcerted pause, Ruy flung himself back on the bed and laughed with raw appreciation. No other woman had ever given him such a sense of freedom. He reared back up again to crush her parted lips under his and let his tongue delve deep, that carnal kiss reawakening the sensual hum deep inside her. '*Dios*... I'm burning up for you,' he told her hoarsely.

He reached for protection, carefully rearranged her supple body and plunged into her hard and fast. Her back arched, her hips rose, a formless sound of need quivering from her lips. His fierce rhythm sent compelling surges of delight through her and the excitement climbed, little paroxysms of convulsive sensual heat tying her into a tight knot of anticipation until the pleasure rose to an uncontrollable height, loosened the knot of need and blew her away again.

'See…no freak out,' Ruy breathed huskily in the aftermath, gazing down with smouldering dark golden eyes at her hectically flushed face.

'The earth definitely moved,' Suzy told him with dancing eyes of admiration as she smoothed a possessive hand down over his heaving ribcage. 'Do you think you can keep that standard up for a whole week?'

'A week…why only a week?' An immediate frown tensed Ruy's lean dark features.

'Because I'm only here for a week,' Suzy reminded him cheerfully.

Ruy unclenched his taut jawline and thought about it. A week was a very long time for him with a woman. In fact, he had never spent that much time or that many nights with one particular woman. The sex was spectacular but that could possibly be a mere side effect of his artistic obsession with her. By the time he completed his sketches and started to paint her, he would probably be far too preoccupied by his art to care too much about her departure.

Ruy closed an arm round her. 'I intend to make the most of this week.'

And so did Suzy, lying there dreamily compliant in her sensual daze. She would make the most of Ruy and her trip to Spain and then return to her normal life. A life in which she would make changes, she planned reflectively with a little leap of anticipation that for once had nothing to do with Ruy. If her father no longer needed her to work at the pub, she would be free to decide her own future and there were a dizzying number of options available. Although perhaps there weren't quite so many options open to someone like her without higher-level education, she acknowledged ruefully. Perhaps the first move she would have to make would be signing up to study towards better qualifications.

'What are you thinking about?' Ruy pressed, sensing her abstraction and irritated by it.

'Going home,' she told him truthfully.

His brilliant dark eyes glittered like polished jet. At that moment he didn't want her thinking about anything but him, and the very strangeness of that thought disconcerted him.

It was because that desire of hers to return home put pressure on him to complete the painting, he reasoned uneasily. And possibly just a little because he wanted her full attention to be on him—and that was normal, wasn't it? Particularly for a guy who had never had to fight for a woman's attention before...

OK, Ruy thought with sudden ferocity, *challenge accepted.*

CHAPTER EIGHT

'DON'T MOVE YOUR HAND,' Ruy instructed. 'And, no, don't twist your face up like that. You're a creature of perpetual motion, *querida*. You must learn how to sit still.'

'Were you like this as a kid?' Suzy queried impatiently. 'Did you make your friends sit like statues while you drew them?'

'My friends didn't know about my artistic propensities.'

Suzy studied him intently, taking in the gleaming black hair, the proud high cheekbones, the dark deepset eyes that flashed gold in sunlight or emotion. He was gorgeous, particularly when dressed down to paint in worn jeans and a tee that showcased every inch of his lean, beautifully muscular body. The sensuality of that thought brought colour to her cheeks but six days of pretty much constant intimacy with Ruy had wrecked her ability to step back and maintain her cool. Now she looked at him and her own body clenched and throbbed in reaction even though she ached from their mutual enthusiasm.

'And why was that?'

'My father punished me for drawing or for showing any interest in art.'

'But *why*?' she exclaimed in disbelief.

'My father's younger brother, Lorenzo, was an artist. He was also defiantly gay. My father was a bigot and he cut his brother out of his life, but he grew up associating any kind of artistic leanings in a man with homosexuality. My desire to draw horrified him and he tried to beat it out of me.'

'That's appalling!' Suzy gasped in shock at his calm manner of talking about such inhumane treatment.

'I learned to hide my interest at an early age,' Ruy admitted, his sensual mouth quirking. 'But, perhaps, Armando *was* rather unlucky with his sons. Rodrigo, after all, has a similar creative streak. He's become a successful art dealer and is the owner of a fashionable art gallery in Seville. This *palacio* is, after all, the home of one of the most valuable private art collections in Spain, consisting of paintings assembled over many hundreds of years by my ancestors. Art and collecting is in our blood.'

Her smooth brow furrowed. 'Your father sounds like a monster. Is that why you keep your artistic side a big secret?'

Ruy's strong jawline clenched. 'It was the start of it, certainly. I wasn't strong enough to fight my father off and stop those punishments of his until I was a teenager and by then a lot of damage had been done and the secrecy had become a habit.'

'Your brother must know about your art,' Suzy assumed.

'No, he doesn't, and I must ask you to remember not

to mention it to anyone at the wedding tomorrow,' Ruy warned her grimly.

'You know I won't if you don't want me to,' Suzy told him soothingly. 'But why is it *still* a secret? Why do you feel the need to hide such an important part of yourself from the rest of the world?'

Ruy had never asked himself that question, which struck him as an odd glaring omission. 'Custom, privacy,' he responded. 'For many years, it felt like the only thing in my life that was truly mine and I guarded my secret zealously.'

'Would you give up Valiente Capital to paint full-time?' Suzy asked.

'No,' Ruy answered without hesitation. 'Once I believed that, given the choice, I would do that, but since then I've come to appreciate that I also very much enjoy the cut and thrust of the financial world. I think that's in my genes as much as the need to paint.' He set down his palette. 'That will do us for today. Manuel is providing a picnic lunch for us. I did promise to show you the estate.'

'I thought you'd forgotten... I want to see the orange grove where you used to hide.'

Ruy closed a hand over hers as she rose and tottered slightly on her stiff limbs. His other hand winding into her curls, he drew her slight frame up against him. The heat of his skin and the aroma of clean, fresh male engulfed her and the pulse at the heart of her quickened. The strength of the hunger Ruy ignited in her unnerved her because she had never thought of herself as a particularly sexual being and now she was learning that she hadn't known herself as well as she thought she did.

Her nipples prickled and peaked and her body dampened, her pupils dilating.

'Sometimes I want to eat you alive,' Ruy groaned hungrily against her ripe mouth. 'I thought this would fade...*why* isn't it fading?'

'Feed a cold, starve a fever,' she framed shakily. 'Maybe you were right and we shouldn't be doing this.'

'*Que pasa?* What's the matter with you?' Ruy growled, ravishing her parted lips passionately with his own in punishment for that suggestion, his tongue delving deep enough to make her shudder against him as if she were in the teeth of a gale. 'This is us. *This* is how it is.'

But she felt consumed by him, by the passion she couldn't deny, by the boundaries she couldn't make herself respect. He walked her indoors to the air-conditioned cool but still she felt as though her skin had shrunk too tight over her bones and her heartbeat was pounding as if she had run a mile. Ruy wanted to lift her up into his arms and stride upstairs with her, but instead he forced himself to stay in control with her simply to prove that he could do it...*this once.*

Manuel was beaming at them from a discreet corner. They were definitely putting on an authentic show of being lovers, Ruy acknowledged without the satisfaction he had expected to feel. She would be leaving in a day and a half, straight after the wedding. He already knew that he would miss her. Not just the passion, but the new life she brought to the *palacio.*

A huge bunch of sunflowers gathered from the edge of a field by Suzy sat in a giant vase on a table, transforming the splendid marble hall into a much warmer space. Suzy cast a kind of spell over the old house, changing practices that had been in vogue for decades. A cardigan she had abandoned over a carved chair provided another splash of colour. She could be rather untidy, Ruy conceded, because he had tripped over the boots she'd left lying on the bedroom floor the night before. Not that on the way into a bed containing Suzy he had felt remotely tempted to complain.

They now ate their meals in the airy orangery, not in the formal dining room, where she had confessed to feeling oppressed by the heavy tapestries on the wall and the giant table. She had taken a notion for fish and chips one afternoon and had casually suggested it to Manuel and, lo and behold, Ruy's *cordon bleu* chef had served fish and chips for the first time ever and had then emerged from the kitchens he ruled like a tyrant to enquire as to whether she had any other special requests. Informed that Suzy loved to be surprised, the chef had grinned and Ruy had appreciated that his regimented menu of meals—for *he* did *not* like to be surprised by what was on his plate—would be changed for ever. Suzy smiled and said thank you and the staff couldn't do enough for her.

On the landing he succumbed to the allure of her soft pink mouth and crushed her to him to extract a hungry kiss. They walked into his bedroom and Suzy stopped dead. Ruy frowned at the display of rails holding a wide selection of women's clothes.

'What's all this?'

'You said you weren't sure that your clothes were what you needed for your stay here or for the wedding.

I ordered a selection of designer garments in your sizes. I'm sorry I forgot to mention it,' he completed truthfully as he closed a hand over hers. 'You can look at them later.'

'Ruy,' she muttered in frustration. 'For goodness' sake, I'm leaving soon!'

'I thought you could donate them to a charity afterwards,' Ruy suggested, feeling quite pleased with that community-minded advice. 'Or even auction them off for a good cause.'

Suzy gritted her teeth at the prospect of garments so expensive that it would be worth auctioning them and groaned. 'I tell you not to be sneaky and you just get *sneakier*!' she complained. 'And what's in that giant chest sitting on the dressing table?'

Ruy shrugged. 'Some jewellery I had Manuel take out of the vault. It belongs to my family and it's overdue an airing. If you don't want new clothes, I can guarantee that festooning yourself in diamonds that haven't been seen in a couple of generations will work as an alternative. Nobody will look beyond the Valiente jewels.'

Suzy sucked in much-needed oxygen. Ruy caught her fingers in his again.

'Stop trying to distract me,' she warned him. 'And unzip this dress.'

Ruy watched her peel off the dress, her slender but delicately curved body emerging from the feathered folds. She kicked off the boots. He automatically toed them out of the way beneath a chair. Wearing only bra and panties, Suzy vanished into the dressing room and appeared mere minutes later in a casual yellow sundress, standing on one foot in the doorway and then on the other as she donned canvas sneakers.

Suzy watched him watching her, tensing as her mouth ran dry and her heart thumped with the excitement she couldn't suppress. Ruy might often infuriate her but she knew that she was falling in love with him in a very big way. Nobody had ever made her feel as he did and very probably nobody would ever make her feel that way again. The hours she spent with Ruy raced by at supersonic speed because he fascinated her. His sheer passionate intensity enthralled her and had given her back the confidence that Percy had stolen from her, because it was impossible to feel like a lesser being with a guy like Ruy, who could not hide his desire and appreciation from her. He wasn't just lethally attractive and insanely sexy, he was clever and entertaining and complex. The more she got to know him, the more she wanted to know. But she also knew that their time together was fast running out and that she wouldn't figure in his future except as a girl he had once painted.

Suzy wasn't fanciful and she didn't believe in miracles. She knew that Ruy viewed her as an enjoyable fling and nothing more. He had warned her that he didn't have relationships as such with women and she had listened, but her heart and her body had overruled her common sense. She had given in to temptation. She had honestly believed that she could stop her emotions getting too deeply involved but that had proved to be a naïve hope. Now she knew that heartbreak loomed on her horizon. She had been too trusting, too confident in her assumption that she could protect herself and too ignorant of how intimacy could change and strengthen everything between a man and a woman.

Even so, she wasn't one to cry over spilt milk and she didn't think that she had any true regrets. She couldn't say that she wished that she had never met Ruy because she had revelled in every high and low of being with him. She was almost twenty-two years old and he was the first man in her life—she didn't count Percy. At her age, it was normal to succumb to physical attraction and hope that it would develop into something deeper. It was equally normal to fall in love and get hurt. She would learn to live with the disappointment, she told herself fiercely.

Ruy answered his phone and began to talk in Spanish. It was his sister, Cecile, and Suzy saw him frown and start to pace as the conversation heated up. After several strained responses when she could clearly see that he was hanging onto his temper by a thread, the call ended.

'I'm afraid I'll have to ask you to remain one full day longer after the wedding.'

Her brow furrowed. 'Why?'

'Cecile was phoning to warn me that my family are throwing an engagement party here for us the day after Rigo's wedding,' he explained. 'Manuel refused to make any arrangements without the go-ahead from me, which is why Cecile has shared their plans in advance.'

'No, I can't stay any longer,' Suzy interrupted worriedly, keen to stick to the timetable initially agreed between them.

'Would you really leave me to face an engagement party without a fiancée?' Ruy demanded in astonishment.

Suzy reddened. 'What's the point? I'll be leaving and disappearing from your life soon anyway.'

'*One* day,' Ruy emphasised, dark golden eyes brilliant. 'We're talking about one day. Why are you in such a hurry to get home?'

'Because I've got plans,' Suzy responded with determined cheer. 'Dad doesn't need me working at the pub any more. I'd like to work with children in the future and I'm going to look into studying towards that goal. I'll need to get applications in now if I want to get onto a course.'

'One more day, *querida*,' Ruy murmured drily. 'Don't make it a big deal. I didn't ask for this party either.'

Suzy sucked in a sustaining breath, wanting to be fair and yet resenting him for putting pressure on her. 'I'll agree because it would be unreasonable to say no in the circumstances, but no is really what you deserve...' She waved a meaningful hand at the racks of clothing and the antique box of jewellery. 'You constantly chip away at what I want to try and turn it into what *you* want instead. I don't like that.'

The faintest colour edged Ruy's sculpted cheekbones. 'I enjoy smoothing out problems for you, solving them,' he argued as he moved forward. 'You're letting me paint you. You're faking being my betrothed for my benefit. I owe you and I like to pay my debts.'

'Some things in life are free, Ruy,' Suzy declared,

her pulses pounding at the smouldering glitter in his gaze. 'You don't owe me anything and I don't owe you anything either. Let's keep this simple.'

'You want me to return the clothes?' he prompted tautly.

'Not until I've picked out something suitable for a fancy engagement party,' Suzy responded with a rueful roll of her bright eyes. 'And now Cecile knows about our pretend engagement as well.'

'Cecile knows the truth…that you're doing me a favour,' Ruy contradicted.

'Like I'm about to complain about a week in a palace abroad where I'm being waited on hand and foot!' Suzy quipped, flashing him a look of amusement, needing to come across as light-hearted and fully aware that nothing between them was real or lasting. 'And the sex isn't bad either.'

'Cheeky,' Ruy remarked with a sizzling smile, reaching for her and discovering that at the very last minute she wasn't there any more.

'Lunch,' she reminded him from the bedroom door. 'I'm starving!'

She would keep it light and chirpy right up until the moment she departed. She wasn't the clingy, needy type and, worse, he would be repelled by any hint of clinginess after suffering the attentions of a stalker in the past. No, there would be no behaviour of that nature on her part. She would laugh and she would smile, and she would stay normal and buoyant right to the bitter end.

CHAPTER NINE

'YOU LOOK FANTASTIC,' Ruy murmured as Suzy emerged from the dressing room, a flirty net fascinator anchored in her vibrant curls. She was an amazingly sexy vision. No man in the world would wonder why he was with such a beauty. That emerald-green shade accentuated her translucent skin and vibrant curls.

Her elegant gown, with its strategic panelled splits, revealed an occasional discreet flash of long shapely calf and tiny feet shod in high-heeled shoes that were a curious mix of bondage boot and sandal, with narrow straps that bared her toes while accentuating the delicacy of her ankles. 'I notice that you're not wearing any jewellery.'

'I'm wearing the engagement ring, but I decided it was best not to borrow anything from that chest,' Suzy told him gently. 'I'm not a member of the family and it would be tasteless of me to be seen flaunting any of it *before* we were married. Your brother's bride would have more excuse than I would have.'

'The collection was offered to her and refused,' Ruy sliced in coolly. 'Of course, Rigo is marrying an heiress and the bride probably has her own inherited gems to flaunt.'

Suzy flushed a little. 'I wasn't being rude. I just don't think it would be appropriate for me to be showing it off in my current role. You've told me nothing about the woman your brother is marrying. Tell me more,' she urged, keen to leave the topic of the jewellery she had rejected behind.

'Her name is Mercedes Hernandez Ortega. She's the only child of a prominent industrialist and well known for her charity work. I've never met her because she's more in your age group than mine. As my father would have said, however, in a worldly sense, Rigo has done very well for himself *this* time.'

'*This* time?' she questioned as they walked downstairs.

'This is Rigo's second marriage,' Ruy admitted rather stiffly.

'He's divorced?'

'Widowed,' Ruy corrected. 'His first marriage wasn't a happy one, though.'

'Well, then, it's lovely that he's met someone else and that he wasn't soured by his first experience,' Suzy declared in that upbeat way of hers, so very different from his own more pessimistic outlook on relations between the sexes.

Ruy was almost tempted to say that his twin had been very much soured by his first marital venture and that he had put *all* the blame and responsibility for that failure squarely on his brother's shoulders. But he didn't want to talk about the past or dig up its ugly secrets, particularly not on a day when he was hoping his sibling, Rigo, had finally chosen to move on from that divisive past into a new era. That Ruy had even been invited to share his brother's big day signalled a very positive change in attitude. Even so, he would have felt a lot less comfortable attending without a woman of his own by his side.

The wedding ceremony was taking place in a huge church in Seville. It was late afternoon as they walked in the sunshine into the big building and the instant she crossed the threshold Suzy felt as if every eye in the place swivelled in her direction. A moment later she caught the whispers about *'la pelirroja'*—the redhead—and faint self-conscious colour mantled her cheeks as she sank into her seat. Ruy was a wealthy, important man in Spanish society, she reminded herself. Naturally the sudden appearance of an English fiancée, whom no one had ever met, would rouse considerable curiosity.

She studied the bridegroom waiting at the altar. Rodrigo's features were similar enough to Ruy's for Suzy to have guessed his identity, but he was less ruggedly masculine than Ruy, his build finer and he was more edgy in the fashion stakes, with his trendy-cut narrow suit and his long hair in a ponytail worn with a jewelled clasp. His bride came down the aisle in a flowing off-the-shoulder dress, her pretty face wreathed in smiles. She was a small curvy brunette with big brown eyes.

Afterwards, when Ruy greeted his brother in the crush that formed outside on the steps, Suzy immediately recognised the tension between the two men. It was there in the tightening of Rigo's mouth, the rather forced smile, and in the taut flex of Ruy's braced fingers against her spine. Ruy introduced her and she did feel as though her presence and the many questions asked of her got them all through what might have been an awkward moment. Mercedes recognised the tension as well and she was beaming and very talkative, chattering freely about her last trip to London. Suzy didn't dare tell the bride that she had only visited London twice in her entire life and that one of those occasions had been to attend a funeral. She had no knowledge whatsoever of the luxury hotel where Mercedes had stayed or of the designer shops she had enjoyed.

'How long is it since you last spoke to your brother?' Suzy asked in the limo that collected them outside the church.

'Several years,' he said stiffly.

'And how do you feel now?'

'Relieved that that first awkward meeting is over,' Ruy revealed flatly. 'I suspect I have his bride to thank for my invitation. I could see that she was very keen to stress the family connection.'

'Like me she has no siblings and she is probably struggling to understand the situation between you and Rigo.'

'I'm sure Mercedes is as well acquainted with the gossip as everyone else,' Ruy commented in a decidedly raw undertone.

Suzy stilled. 'What gossip?'

'It's nothing that you need to concern yourself with,'

Ruy parried, exasperating her by putting up an immediate stone wall.

'If other people know whatever it is, shouldn't I know too?'

'If we were genuinely engaged to be married, *yes*,' Ruy agreed, cutting her to the quick with that blunt distinction. 'But as we're not, my past is not your concern.'

Painful colour flooded Suzy's face and she twisted her head away to look out of the windows at the busy streets of Seville as evening fell. Slowly the colour ebbed from her cheeks again, but she still felt quite sick at being slapped down so hard for her curiosity. Well, that was putting her in her place and no mistake, wasn't it?

Without warning, Ruy closed a hand over hers. 'I'm sorry. I'm in a filthy mood,' he breathed in a savage undertone. 'I shouldn't be taking it out on you. You deserve better from me. I simply don't want to revisit the past because what's in the past can't be changed and that frustrates me.'

Suzy snaked her fingers back from his with the instinctive recoil of hurt pride and mortification. 'That's all right. I understand,' she told him.

Ruy settled gleaming dark eyes on her in reproach. '*Please* forgive me,' he urged.

'I have.'

'No, you haven't,' Ruy contradicted. 'I know you too well to be fooled.'

But his wounding words had only reminded her that soon she would be travelling home and that Ruy and Spain and everything that had happened between them would then only be memories of a few stolen days in a world that was not her own. It hurt that he could shut her out so easily. It hurt that he wasn't willing to confide in her, even though it seemed that other people already knew that same information. It hurt to appreciate that he wasn't falling in love with her, that he would watch her walk away with the same recollections but neither the pain nor the regret that she would experience. *Well, that's the way the cookie crumbles,* she told herself sharply, *toughen up!*

'Suzy...' Ruy pressed.

'It's fine.'

'Prove it...' he breathed, releasing her seat belt and lifting her into his arms to settle her across his lap.

Suzy shivered, suddenly gathered into the heat of him, cornered when she was striving to keep her distance, and yet she couldn't have said that she wanted him to set her free because on some level she couldn't bear to be at odds with Ruy either. 'You'll mess up my make-up.'

He pressed a button and told his driver to take the long route to Mercedes' home where the reception was being held. He ran his mouth lightly down the cord of her slender neck and inhaled deeply as her head tipped back. 'You know even the smell of your skin turns me on hard and fast. You smell delicious, like oranges in sunshine.'

'Fruity hair shampoo,' Suzy mumbled weakly, because he could make even that sound so much more romantic than reality. Ruy, she conceded, was a mass of contradictions. He said he wasn't romantic or imaginative and then he said stuff like that and made her pose in a floaty, feathery, very romantic dress in an orange grove in which only her boots cast the discordant note he seemed to like in his paintings.

He skated a teasing fingertip up the length of her thigh beneath her dress. 'I knew those slits would come in useful,' he husked.

'Ruy...*no*,' Suzy said firmly.

The fingertip flirted with the lace edge of her knickers and she snatched in a ragged breath, the promise of sensation tugging at her greedy senses while she could feel the hard thrust of his arousal beneath her. A wave of heat travelled through her entire body, leaving her weak.

One hand meshed in her curls, he ravished her parted lips with his own and every nerve ending in her body went wild with anticipation. 'Do I have a "maybe"?' he prompted thickly.

'I hope you're capable of finishing what you started,' Suzy told him starkly, her fingers meshing helplessly into his luxuriant black hair to bring his carnal mouth back to hers.

'*Hombre!* Only *you* do this to me!' Ruy growled.

'What do I do?'

'You make me desperate,' he complained, skating skilled fingers over the tender folds at her core, discovering the damp welcome there, delicately penetrating her silken sheath, listening to her gasp and feeling her arch before retreating to a more sensitive spot that was even more responsive to his attentions.

Suzy reached a climax shatteringly fast and it left her limp, gasping against the heat and urgency of his marauding mouth, her whole body quivering with the aftershocks of pleasure. He held her close in the aftermath and breathed in slow and deep. 'I wrecked your lipstick.' He sighed. 'I'm sorry. I don't know what came over me.'

Ruy settled her down beside him again, reached for her seat belt and did it up before lifting her clutch bag from the floor and helpfully placing it on her lap. Disconcerted, Suzy glanced back at him. 'But you...er...'

'Not in the car. I draw the line at that. I'll have to wait until later,' Ruy breathed, laughing as she leant forward with a tissue to wipe his face free of her peach lipstick. 'I deserve to suffer a little.'

That quick charismatic and entirely uninhibited smile made her want to kiss him again. Inside herself, she rebelled from that thought. Tomorrow evening, after the engagement party, she was flying home: it was arranged. It was time she forged a little distance between them and stopped throwing caution to the four winds with every kiss and every smile he gave her. Their little fling as such was almost over and he had only just finished reminding her that they *did* have boundaries, closing her out when he could have let her in...had he wanted to. Only he didn't want to and that told her all she needed to know. She was on the outside with Ruy and always would be.

The limousine dropped them off at an enormous mansion milling with beautifully dressed guests. From the moment she entered she was conscious of female eyes clinging to her. Mercedes made a special point of greeting her again while from every corner Ruy was hailed as though he were a very important guest indeed. Before very long he was the centre of a crush of men, gamely answering every question aimed at him.

'Ruy seems very popular,' she remarked to Mercedes.

'He always has been. That level of success impresses most people. He was also every girl's pin-up when I was at school and he hasn't lost his appeal to the ladies,' Mercedes responded.

'I noticed that he attracted a fair amount of attention at the church,' Suzy admitted uncomfortably.

'It's vulgar, but all the women who made a play for him and got nowhere are madly curious to know what you had that they didn't and why you have that ring on your finger.' Mercedes wrinkled her nose with distaste. 'I'm afraid that Ruy acquired the reputation of being a commitment-phobe.'

'I can't think why.' Suzy laughed although she could taste bitterness behind her fake amusement because Ruy was exactly what everyone had thought he was: a commitment-phobe. She had never been in the running for anything deeper with Ruy. From the outset he had made it clear that he didn't want a relationship and he had stuck to his rules.

Ruy retrieved her and they took their seats and a long elaborate meal began, accompanied by many speeches. It was a relief to get up and stretch her legs on the dance floor afterwards. 'If I ever get married,' Suzy told Ruy, 'there will be no pomp and ceremony to it.'

'Weddings are very much family affairs. The bride and groom don't always have a choice. I have very stuffy relatives. This type of ritual and tradition is exactly what they appreciate and respect. Some of them have come to speak to you today but most of them are too busy observing you and gossiping and they won't officially meet you until tomorrow.'

'You're scaring the life out of me!' Suzy censured, slender hips moving in time to the pulsing beat of the music as she moved back from him.

Another man hovered, requesting permission with a look at Ruy to step in to partner Suzy. Ruy wanted to say no but he was mindful of the occasion and reluctant to act possessive, even knowing that he was hellishly possessive when it came to Suzy. He backed to the edge of the floor, taking the chance to watch her dance, appreciating the fluid grace of every movement, her perfect synchronisation with the music. His replacement moved in with a great deal more panache than Ruy had in the dance department and a wry smile curved his sardonic mouth.

'Who is he?' he asked his brother as he drew level with him.

'Don't you recognise him?' Rigo said in surprise. 'Jorge's a professional...stars in that dance show Mercedes adores on Channel—'

'I don't watch dance shows. Do you think she needs rescuing?' Ruy interrupted, his entire attention glued to Suzy's animated face.

'I don't and maybe you need to let her have some space,' Rigo murmured thoughtfully, turning to study his twin. 'Never thought I'd see you being clingy with a woman.'

'I'm not.'

'Never thought I'd get married again either though,' his twin continued as if Ruy hadn't spoken, a relaxed note to that admission that impressed Ruy. 'But I don't need pills or booze to get through the day with Mercedes around. She lights up my world.'

'Congratulations. I'm very happy for you both.' Ruy breathed in deep and slow, suddenly appreciating how important such an exchange was with his long-lost twin, opening the possibility of a closer, more normal relationship. It heartened him, made him realise how much Suzy's presence had lightened the atmosphere between him and his brother.

At the same time, Rigo's words had made Ruy reluctantly recall his world pre-Suzy. It had been very well organised, and every moment had been scheduled to maximise efficient productivity. He had fallen off that relentless train, however. He didn't think that way any more because Suzy had driven a coach and horses through his schedule. Only now was it dawning on him that in less than twenty-four hours Suzy was leaving and he would be returning to that rigorous cult of maximum efficiency. The prospect was not enticing, not the way he had dimly assumed it would be. She had changed him...somehow she had contrived to change him in a fundamental way...and Ruy was no fan of change or innovation. He was much more likely to fight it off than embrace it.

'Maybe we could meet up for dinner some evening once we get back from our wedding trip,' Rigo said hesitantly. 'Mercedes was very taken with Suzy. '

Ruy was still struggling to deal with the awareness that Suzy would no longer be around the following evening. 'That…that would be good, *great*,' he stressed, endeavouring to express his gratitude for that invite with greater warmth.

Rigo swung away to greet an older man who had grabbed his arm to get his attention. Ruy strode onto the dance floor to reclaim Suzy. She and her partner had gathered an audience with their display and he judged it time to intervene, not because he objected to her dancing or attracting attention, but because he intended to make the most of every moment he had left with her.

'Gosh, that guy was very *intense*,' Suzy hissed, breathing heavily from her dance moves but visibly grateful to leave her partner. 'He wanted me to audition for some television competition show and he was so pushy. I'm not good enough for that sort of thing.'

'I'm no expert but I think you probably are good enough,' Ruy overruled.

'But it's not me. I'm not a performer. I never was. I like teaching kids. I like dance as an exercise but I'm never comfortable with people watching me when I do it,' she whispered. 'It drove my teacher mad when I was a teenager when I wouldn't apply for stuff but that's the way I am.'

'Nothing wrong with that…' Ruy looked askance at her as she pulled away from him.

'I'm hot. I need to freshen up. I won't be long,' she told him, walking off into the crush.

The overpowering plush opulence of the large cloakroom made her roll her eyes. Emerging from a stall to wash her hands at the vanity counter, she jerked in surprise when she saw an older blonde woman seated in a chair in the corner and staring at her. 'Sorry, I didn't see you,' she muttered in taut Spanish.

'I wanted a closer look at the woman Ruy Valiente is planning to marry,' the blonde informed her, rising from her seat. She was so thin she was almost emaciated, the bones of her chest visible through the glittering diamond necklace she wore.

'Why?' Suzy asked baldly as she dried her hands, rather creeped out by the suspicion that she was being ambushed on purpose.

'Only a very confident woman could attend this wedding with Ruy and still hold her head high.'

'And why's that?' Suzy enquired, removing a lipstick from her clutch.

'A decent woman would have been too embarrassed to show her face so boldly. After all, Ruy slept with Rodrigo's first wife and she killed herself when he dumped her. It took his brother a very long time to get over that betrayal.'

Suzy was so shocked she was frozen in suspended animation with her lipstick tightly caught between her fingers. The blonde departed with a malicious smile. In a haze of disbelief, Suzy renewed her lipstick and stared into space, blank with shrinking horror at what she had been told. Was it true? It *couldn't* be true! That could not be the reason that Ruy had a troubled relationship with his brother! Ruy could not be guilty of such an indefensible act, she reasoned in consternation.

And yet...*and yet* he had been unwilling to admit

the story behind the gossip she had mentioned. Surely only a man ashamed of his past behaviour would behave that way? Rigo's wife had killed herself? After having an affair with Ruy and being ditched? Suzy was appalled at that claim. But she also knew that gossip, even cruel gossip, was often based more on entertainment than fact. She was leaving the cloakroom when Mercedes approached her.

'I saw Elisa Torres coming out looking smug,' she said anxiously. 'Did she speak to you?'

'The skinny blonde with the diamonds?' Suzy checked and nodded. 'She didn't seem friendly.'

'No, she wouldn't be. Elisa's daughter, Fernanda, made a big play for Ruy last year, probably with her mother's encouragement.' Mercedes grimaced. 'There is no man in Spain more likely to be more turned off by a woman chasing him than Ruy and he froze her out. Seeing him engaged to another woman will have enraged Elisa. Did she say anything to you?'

'She said something in Spanish, but she spoke too fast and I didn't catch it. The look on her face was sufficient warning,' Suzy fibbed for the sake of peace, because she knew she could have asked Mercedes for the truth but she had sufficient consideration for the bride's feelings on her special day to swallow her nosy questions. The brunette would not wish to be drawn down that path and it would make her uncomfortable, not only because it was intensely private stuff but also because she had only just met Suzy. In such circumstances, silence was golden.

'That's good, because Elisa is usually critical rather

than pleasant,' Mercedes confided, accompanying Suzy back to the main reception room.

For the remainder of their time at the reception, Suzy kept on smiling and trying to behave normally. But the whole time she was stealing stricken glances at Ruy and wondering. Did he? *Could* he have? Could she have fallen in love with a man that immoral, disloyal and seedy?

And the moral of that story was that she had once agreed to marry Percy Brenton, crediting that he was, at heart, a decent enough older man worthy, at least, of her respect and trust. How could she ever have been that gullible about a man who had literally blackmailed her to the altar? Events had proven her to be badly wrong in her naïve assumptions when it came to Percy, she reminded herself painfully.

How much did she really know about Ruy? And did it even matter if he was guilty as charged when their brief affair was virtually over? Why would she confront him now with such explosive accusations? Their relationship as such was already almost over, bar her final departure. Was there any point in stirring up such sordid unpleasantness? Particularly when, with Ruy's stake in her father's pub, she might well be forced to see him again in the future. No, she would keep her lips firmly sealed and endure her curiosity. What else could she do when Ruy had already refused to discuss the gossip she had questioned? Obviously, he didn't want to talk about such sleazy stuff, not now when it was all over. And why would he even want to discuss it with Suzy when he had already made it clear that his past was none of her business?

'You did really well today,' Ruy told her on the drive back to the *palacio* after midnight. 'Thank you.'

A tense smile curved Suzy's mouth. 'Well, that appearance was what I was here for,' she reminded him quietly.

'You were very convincing,' Ruy continued.

'I must be a better actress than I ever appreciated,' Suzy demurred, relieved that she had less than twenty-four hours left to spend in Spain. Stepping back from Ruy and the level of intimacy they had indulged in was a challenge and to behave normally while accomplishing that feat was an even bigger one.

Her feet were killing her. She wondered if it was a rule that new shoes always had to pinch, but even if she had been warned she would have picked them because they had been the perfect match for her dress. In the marble hall, she kicked them off and lifted them to pad barefoot upstairs.

'I could carry you,' Ruy proposed with amusement.

'Not required.'

She got ready for bed quickly. From below lowered lashes she covertly watched Ruy undress, marvelling at how familiar his every move had become to her. He was so organised, so methodical. Everything had a place, and nothing got lost because it always went back in the same spot. She was the exact opposite but sharing a room with Ruy had made her tidier, not only because that was his preference, but also because she was now mortifyingly aware that in the *palacio*, if she left something on the floor, someone else had to pick it up.

The mattress gave a little with Ruy's weight. The lights went out. He reached for her and she tried not to freeze.

'Er…we *can't*,' she muttered, cheeks burning as she brought out the excuse she needed. 'It's that time of the month.'

The heat of his lean, powerful body spread slowly through the chill that gripped her.

'Not a problem,' Ruy murmured, still holding her close.

Suzy had expected him to let go of her and retreat, but he did neither.

'Are you feeling all right?' he asked, a shade awkwardly.

'I'm not great,' she fibbed.

And he let go of her immediately, switched on the lights, emerged from the dressing room in jeans and left the room. Suzy sat up, wondering where he was going. She lay down again, planning to fake sleep, but a few minutes later Ruy reappeared with tablets and a glass of water, sitting on her side of the bed and feeding them to her. That he would be that considerate hadn't occurred to her and she was embarrassed, forced to swallow pills she didn't need.

'Try to go to sleep,' he urged as he doused the lights again.

He didn't put his arms round her again and, absurdly, she wished he would because it would have been the very last time they were that close. She squeezed her

eyes tight shut and ordered her brain to shut down but
there was no closing out the revelation that Elisa Torres had made.

Had Ruy fallen in love with his brother's wife? He
must've done, she assumed. Surely he would not have
betrayed his brother's trust for anything less than an
all-encompassing love? And yet it did not excuse him
because love didn't turn a sordid affair into a case of
Romeo and Juliet. Ultimately, Ruy had ended the relationship but Rigo must still have been devastated.
And then his wife had died, and he could hardly have
got any sort of closure from that tragic conclusion. She
marvelled that Ruy's twin had invited him to his second
wedding and could only admire Rigo for his ability to
accept the past and forgive.

The next day, she had to work hard at keeping her
spirits up. She was determined not to reveal the truth
that she was dreading returning home when in reality it
was what any sane woman would want after discovering
such bad news about the man she cared about. Before
lunch, which they would be sharing with Ruy's closest
relatives, she laid out the dress she had selected from
the rails. It was a dark blue dress that barely showed
any skin, extremely conservative. She had picked it after
meeting a couple of Ruy's very starchy aunts and uncles
at the wedding the previous day. It helped to remember
that she was merely fulfilling a pretend role and that
in a few hours she would be taking off the truly beautiful ring for ever. None of it was real, she reminded
herself doggedly. It was her own foolish fault that she

had dived too deep into her first affair even after being warned that it wouldn't be a relationship.

And she had no real grounds for complaint, had she? He had told her with candour that they had no future and he had treated her well and with respect. He hadn't shared his deepest secrets but then who did in a casual fling? If she were discovering that in reality she couldn't do casual comfortably with a man, that was her problem, not his.

Ruy studied her in surprise as she came downstairs. 'You don't look like you in that outfit,' he remarked.

Suzy wrinkled her nose. 'I might as well serve up what your relations like and expect from your future wife. Why ruffle feathers when it's not real?'

'I don't care what they think,' Ruy intoned almost harshly.

'Ruy…you agreed to a fake engagement celebration for their benefit. Of course, you care. You were raised to care, weren't you? You can't help that,' she reasoned.

'I try not to follow my father's rules,' he countered.

'I suppose that family is simply family and your father's rules don't come into it,' Suzy murmured, connecting briefly with his stunning dark golden eyes and feeling her heart pound and her mouth run dry before swiftly evading that direct connection.

He wasn't the man she had believed he was, she reminded herself fiercely, heartbroken at the idea that he could have behaved so badly. He was neither loyal nor trustworthy. He was a cheater, and a man who would cheat with his brother's wife would probably be unfaithful in future relationships as well. Of course, there was a chance that that vindictive woman had been lying, but Ruy's own refusal to discuss the gossip he had acknowledged had convinced Suzy that there had to be a nasty secret in his past, one that, quite understandably, he didn't wish to discuss.

But what sort of judge was she of any man? Particularly after her foolish trust in Percy? That had been a big fail on her part, and she couldn't forget how naïve she had been.

Why was she so angry with Ruy, though? It wasn't as though she had been in the running for something more serious with him. But she was disappointed in him, disappointed in herself, convinced that she should have sensed that moral vacuum inside him or at least suspected that Ruy didn't share her basic moral values. That discovery made him a lot less desirable, she told herself firmly. Or at least it should've done, she registered, gripped with anguish when he closed his hand over hers to walk her out onto the formal loggia where drinks and coffee awaited them following the leisurely lunch, which under Manuel's watch was conducted with many courses and great ceremony.

Time was running out for her and Ruy like sand running through an egg timer, leading to the inevitable separation. But if she had any real pride, she would be eager to leave him, she told herself urgently. It didn't help that she was simply devastated to credit that he could have slept with his brother's wife.

'I wish Cecile hadn't had to work. She always lightens the atmosphere on her visits,' Ruy breathed with a frown, but his tolerance also showed her that he was very generous towards his demanding relatives. 'You seem very…stressed, tense—'

'I haven't much experience of being on show like this,' Suzy pointed out in a taut whisper, drawing her head back from his proximity as the achingly familiar scent of his cologne and his skin enveloped her. 'And why *would* Cecile have made the effort to attend? She knows that this event is only an unlucky consequence of you having persuaded me to act a part at your brother's wedding. She knows we're a fake.'

'Not quite as fake as you're suggesting when I don't want you to go home,' Ruy disconcerted her by declaring with the utmost calm. 'I want you to stay.'

Utterly taken aback by that astonishing statement, Suzy momentarily froze. 'You're not done painting me yet?' she hazarded with a stilted laugh.

'Probably not but that's not the only reason,' Ruy breathed, shooting her a narrow-eyed appraisal that questioned her attitude. 'What's the matter with you?'

'I suppose I'm homesick. I can't wait to see Dad,' Suzy exclaimed in desperation, ranging away a few feet from his tall, still frame, determined not to let him pierce her defences, weak as they were.

'You won't consider remaining here with me?' Ruy prompted on a dangerous note, his dark deep accented drawl dropping in pitch, purring down her spine like a caress.

Suzy lifted her chin. 'It's not possible. I think we've run our course, don't you?'

And with that she lifted the coffee poured for her and strolled away. It wasn't hard to sidestep Ruy in a family gathering. As soon as she stepped away, his relations closed in and clumped around him like a wall, full of deference and desperate for his attention. They told him about business upsets, family problems and financial challenges. Over lunch he had promised to check out the fiancé one of the daughters was planning to marry, had agreed to look over a cousin's business plan and had promised to contact a friend to help a son find a suitable job. It was ironic that she had begun to see exactly how Ruy had developed his arrogant belief that he could solve every problem in her path. His family had convinced him that he was all-seeing, all-knowing, the ultimate oracle.

Even so, his tolerance of those same demands impressed her with his generosity although she did see why he guarded his privacy because his relatives recognised few boundaries.

Yet how had those same prim and prudish aunts and uncles overlooked his behaviour with Rodrigo's first wife? Had they simply closed their eyes? Did their reverence for his social position, his wealth and his spectacular success excuse every flaw he had in their estimation?

The younger generation of his many cousins chatted casually to her and she talked freely to them, admitting that she hadn't had the chance to further her education but that she was still hoping to rectify that oversight. But at the back of her mind, she couldn't really think of anything but Ruy and the suggestion he had made that she stay on in Spain in his home.

What on earth was he proposing? And why had he

waited until the eleventh hour to mention it? Of course, the wedding had taken up the whole of the previous day and evening and there had not been an opportunity for them to talk about anything serious. But then, Ruy didn't *do* serious, so what was he talking about? She had a life to live and it wasn't in Spain. Most probably he found their liaison convenient. The sex was off-the-charts amazing and wasn't that, according to popular report, what the average guy reputedly valued the most? In addition, she made no demands on him. High colour mantled her cheeks at the humiliation of such thoughts in which she was reduced to rating her precise value like some product and she lifted her bright head high as she smiled at the last departing guests.

'Now perhaps you'll tell me what's wrong with you,' Ruy breathed in the marble hall.

'I have to pack,' Suzy told him with urgency.

Impervious to the hint that she intended to be very busy, Ruy followed her upstairs. He strode into the bedroom. 'I ask you to stay on and you don't even want to discuss it?' he pressed incredulously.

'It's not possible,' Suzy told him, hauling her case out in the dressing room, wishing he weren't able to see that it was almost fully packed already. 'Thank you for the offer but I'm saying no, we're done.'

'Why?' Ruy demanded rawly, swiping the heavy case from her and planting it noisily down on the luggage rack in the bedroom. 'Why wouldn't it be possible?'

Suzy felt trapped. She hadn't wanted such a confrontation, had seen no advantage to it, indeed had only foreseen future repercussions. 'It just wouldn't be,' she muttered evasively.

She yanked comfy clothes out of her case and carried them into the bathroom, closing and locking the door for privacy.

'I want... I *need* an answer,' Ruy growled outside the door.

Suzy stripped off the dress and pulled on yoga pants and a loose sleeveless sweatshirt. She was all shaky. She didn't want to leave the bathroom, but she was no coward. Breathing in deep, she padded out again barefoot, to head back to her case to dig out canvas shoes.

'I don't want to talk about this with you,' she warned him stiffly.

'I'm afraid you have no choice but to talk about it. That jet won't take off until I get an answer,' Ruy spelt out flatly.

That hard assurance warned her that there was no way she would be getting home without satisfying his curiosity, but she was still very reluctant to tackle so controversial a topic with a male she knew to be fiercely private and determined not to confide in her.

'Suzy...' Ruy breathed.

As she looked at him involuntarily, it was as if a cruel hand squeezed her heart inside her tight chest. Black hair slightly tousled, a dark shadow of stubble accentuating his jaw and sensual mouth, his dark eyes smouldering gold, he was rawly masculine and very much the man she had fallen madly in love with. She had become accustomed to the man in the sharply tailored business suits that he wore with such panache. At first that sophisticated image had intimidated her, and then he had simply become *her* Ruy and what he wore and where he lived and how much money he had hadn't mattered to her any longer. When he had rescued her and her father from Percy, when he had supported her through that frightening experience, she had begun to believe that Ruy Valiente was everything she had ever wanted in a man. Discovering that he was not that man had shattered her faith in her own judgement.

She straightened her shoulders, lifted her head, green eyes veiled. 'Is it true that you slept with your brother's first wife and that she...er...died when you ditched her?'

As she'd spoken, Ruy had become as still as a statue, his lean dark features wiped clean of all expression, but his healthy colour had evaporated and his shock stabbed her to the heart because she took that reaction as confirmation. He compressed his lips and it took a few seconds for him to master his surprise at that question and respond. 'In essence the facts can be interpreted in that light. People who know me are aware of the true facts and if you knew me better—'

'I don't *want* to know you any better!' Suzy let loose at him because her tension had climbed and climbed unbearably while she awaited his answer and the ferocious disillusionment she suffered at his lack of argument did not make her feel generous. 'What I was told convinced me that I want nothing more to do with you!'

Suzy was devastated when he failed to contradict her. She had hoped against hope that he would have an explanation, a miraculous excuse, but then that weak hope only reminded her of how poor her own judgement was and of how she could not trust her own feelings. She might love him but that did not automatically mean that he was a decent person. Hadn't she once believed that Percy was decent too? That unfortunate acknowledgement tore her down even further in her estimation.

'That is, of course, your choice even if I'm surprised that you would be so judgemental when you can be in possession of few facts,' Ruy retorted icily.

A kind of rage more powerful than anything Ruy had ever felt before was roaring through him. Liliana had forced him to live through a nightmare and she had cost him and his unfortunate brother so much. He refused to believe that her spectre could cost him Suzy as well. 'You believed whatever seedy gossip you were told, then.'

'I didn't want to, but, yes, I believed it because you wouldn't discuss anything private with me, which implied that there *was* something shameful in your past.'

'Everyone's got something shameful in their past, Suzy,' Ruy incised with gritty cynicism at such innocence, and his rage was now roaring inside him like a forest blaze. 'But logic should tell you that things aren't always what they seem.'

'I don't want to hear some devious explanation that paints *you* white and *her* scarlet! That such a thing ever happened is unpardonable. It should be enough for me to say that I can't be with a guy capable of behaving that way,' Suzy framed in a pained rush.

Ruy was outraged, deeply offended and hurt by her complete lack of trust in him. His deep anger and his ferocious pride drove him, preventing him from making any further attempt to explain himself or reason with her. 'Then I too have nothing more to say,' he bit out with savage brevity.

The silence stretched thick as a blanket and it felt claustrophobic. Pain burning inside her, Suzy gazed silently back at him, willing him to pull a miracle out of his pocket and fix everything but somehow knowing now that that wasn't going to happen. She felt sick and she simply nodded on the least said, soonest mended rule because his past was still not really her business. And any prospect of it being her business had died when that horrible woman had made her sordid allegations and Ruy had then confirmed the facts.

'I'll finish packing, then,' she said jerkily.

He walked out of the door. If he had slammed it, she would have felt a little better, but he didn't. She removed the diamond ring on her finger and set it on the dresser. She left the green dress and the blue one she had worn that afternoon over a chair because she wanted no reminders. Didn't need them, she conceded wretchedly. She suspected that it would be a very long time before she forgot Ruy Valiente and the happiness he had given her before she'd discovered that it was all as much of an illusion as their fake engagement.

CHAPTER TEN

'You can sit in the car while I nip into the off-licence,' her father wheedled. 'Save me parking across the road.'

'You usually go on your own... I'm kind of busy here,' Suzy argued, barely lifting her head from the academic website she was studying.

Roger Madderton frowned down at his daughter. 'I'll be blunt, then. *I'm* tired of you moping about the place like a wet weekend. Two weeks of that is enough. You need to get out of the flat, even come down and help behind the bar—'

'Flora's managing fine,' Suzy reminded her parent stiffly, because it had been something of a shock to discover on her return that her place had been filled more than adequately by the older woman, who was also cooking up a storm of popular meals to sell to their weekend customers. That had stung when Suzy had only contrived to serve up pizzas and paninis, her catering skills being rather more basic.

And then there had been the mortification of all the tales about Percy Brenton that had come her way whenever she was seen. The locals seemed to think it was their bounden duty to tell her anything that related to her ex. Percy had been charged and arrested. As soon as he had got out on bail, he had put his house on the market and he had not been seen since. There was a rumour that his assault on Suzy had not been his first offence and that he had a bitter ex-wife now living in York. It didn't seem to occur to anyone that Suzy couldn't have cared less and that she was merely grateful not to have to see the man again.

'Come on,' her father urged, and with great reluctance Suzy rose from her seat at the desk in the lounge of the flat and followed him downstairs to his car.

She *wasn't* moping, she thought resentfully. She had done her best to be cheerful and helpful since she came home. But most of her attention had been reserved for the different educational courses available to anyone planning to work with children. The variety of options had made it hard to choose because she wasn't sure how high to set her sights or whether or not to settle on a short course or a lengthier one. In short, she had done everything possible to avoid moping and stay busy and if she was miserable she had done her best to hide the fact.

A broken heart was a broken heart, and she couldn't eat or sleep without thinking about Ruy and feeling a great gush of pain and hollowness engulf her until she felt as if she were drowning.

In truth she had left her heart behind in Spain and she remained furious in her bitterness with Ruy. He hadn't wanted her enough to fight for her! He hadn't wanted her enough to defend himself! It was even more galling that she had shut him down before he was forced to define exactly what he had meant by asking her to stay in Spain with him. After all, if you didn't have a relationship to begin with how did one move on from that point, particularly with the complication of a fake engagement in play? Yes, Suzy would very much have enjoyed hearing Ruy explain what he was asking her to consider. Not, of course, that she *could* have overlooked what she had discovered about him, but she was only human, she would still have liked to *know*.

Her father was unusually quiet on his way to the off-licence and when he emerged she was surprised that he was only carrying a little crate of beer.

'That was a small order,' she remarked as he reversed the car and drove off again.

On the drive home, she said, 'Have I really been that hard to live with?'

Roger Madderton groaned. 'You're inconsolable. How am I expected to feel as your dad? I want to fix it for you.'

'You can't fix it. He wasn't the guy I thought he was,' Suzy sighed, patting his knee soothingly. 'I'll get over this. Don't worry about me.'

'I can help you fix it,' her father asserted, disconcerting her. 'You're very stubborn. He's very stubborn as well but he's also a few years older and a little less short-sighted than you can be.'

'Why are you talking about Ruy like this?' Suzy twisted in her seat as her father turned off the road down a familiar lane. 'Why are we driving down here?'

Her father stopped at the electric gates that secured

Ruy's house in the woods. The gates whirred open and Suzy stared in disbelief at her parent while he marvelled out loud at the camera-recognition technology that had given them automatic entry.

'Dad!' she gasped in frustration. 'What are we doing here?'

'You had a row with him, and you didn't talk it out. This is your last chance to get it sorted,' her father told her squarely.

At the realisation that Ruy was back in England, Suzy froze in consternation. 'I'm not going in there!'

'If he's made the effort to fly over here, you can make the effort to at least listen to what he has to say. You don't have to forgive him for whatever he's done,' her father pointed out levelly.

'I can't believe you're doing this to me!' Suzy protested, shooting him a shaken glance.

'I hope you don't still feel that way in ten minutes—'

'Ten minutes?'

'I'll wait here for ten minutes. If you aren't back out again by then I'll go home.' Her father switched off the engine with a flourish.

'Did Ruy somehow force you into doing this for him?'

'No, he was planning to come to the pub, but I didn't want to find myself in the middle of your drama and it's not very private there. This is the better option,' Roger Madderton opined and leant across her to swing open the passenger door in invitation.

Suzy snatched in a sustaining breath and leapt out. 'I'll be out in less than ten minutes!'

'Famous last words, my love,' her father said equably as she slammed the door shut again.

Furious with Ruy for using her dad to do his bidding and mysteriously contriving to shift the older man's loyalty away from his daughter, Suzy stomped up the steps. Ruy opened the door himself and her heart skipped a beat straight away. His black hair was still damp from the shower, his jawline freshly shaven. Sheathed in jeans and a shirt, he should have seemed familiar but he was definitely changed with his lean, strong face rather fined down, his spectacular dark eyes under-shadowed. Her first thought was that he had been ill, and alarm clutched at her and only with the greatest difficulty did she resist the urge to demand proof of his health.

'Ruy…' It was all she could do to squeeze those syllables from her dry throat.

'Don't blame your father for this. I phoned him last night and persuaded him that this meeting was for the best.'

'But it's not,' Suzy whispered, sidling past him, careful not to brush against him.

'Hear me out and *then* say that,' Ruy framed harshly.

What Suzy wasn't about to say to him was that seeing him again and refreshing her memories only made their separation more painful for her. 'OK,' she agreed. 'I'll listen.'

Ruy strode into the spacious reception area. 'I told you about my stalking ordeal eight years ago.'

'Well, you didn't tell me how you settled it,' Suzy remarked in a brittle voice.

'I didn't settle it, but eventually I involved the police and she was charged. I had to do something. The longer it went on, the worse it became. She assaulted a woman I took out to dinner. When the police arrested her and searched her apartment they discovered that she had gathered a huge amount of information about me long before I met her. She had deliberately targeted me in the club the night we met.'

Suzy was frowning. 'That's creepy. What happened to the poor woman she assaulted?'

'She was shaken up, but she managed to get away from her. Although I was convinced it was my stalker who had attacked her, we weren't able to prove it. The assault made me bring in the police,' Ruy admitted. 'After she was arrested, her parents approached me and begged me to drop the charges. They said the prosecution would ruin her life. They promised to get her psychiatric treatment and swore that I would never see her again. I dropped the charges and to this day, I don't know whether that was the right or wrong thing to do.'

'I don't understand what all this has to do with your brother's wife—'

'Bear with me,' Ruy cut in. 'Would you like a drink?'

'A white wine.'

Ruy filled a glass for her, his lean brown hands deft, and she watched him, studying his sculpted profile, his black hair gleaming as it dried in the sunlight arrowing through the tall windows. 'I was sympathetic towards my stalker's parents because my brother also had mental-health issues,' Ruy explained. 'Rigo had a nervous breakdown in his teens. He got hooked on prescription drugs and eventually he had to go into rehab to get clean. Six months after that he phoned me to tell me that he had got engaged and that he wanted me to meet his future wife, whom he had met in the same clinic. He was besotted with her. She *was* a beautiful woman. Her name was Liliana, my former stalker.'

'Good grief!' Suzy croaked, finally grasping the connection. 'What did you do when you realised?'

'I was honest with him. I told him that I had had a one-night stand with her, which quite naturally angered and upset him. No man wants the woman he loves to have already slept with his brother. I also gave Rigo chapter and verse on her stalking activities and I went to see her parents and asked them to be honest with him as well. They flat out refused. They believed Liliana was in love with my brother and that he was the best chance she had of a normal life. At the same time Liliana gave Rigo some nonsensical story about how I had led her down the garden path and broken her heart, which of course made him sympathetic towards her. I, on the other hand, was convinced she had chosen him *because* he was my brother…and in the end I was proven right on that score.'

Suzy gulped down a mouthful of wine. 'She really did put you through the mill. What happened?'

'He married her, and she began to stalk me again. She was very manipulative. My brother accused me of trying to lure her away from him when I would have done anything to be rid of her attentions!' Ruy admitted in a driven undertone. 'But, no, I certainly never wished her dead. She interrupted a business lunch I was having one day…my brother's wife, my sister-in-law, walking in and draping herself over me as though we were lovers. Her behaviour caused a great deal of talk and I warned Rigo that he had to rein her in or that I would take steps to keep her away from me.'

'My word, Ruy…she made your life hell.' Suzy sighed, understanding all at once why Ruy was so set on not getting into relationships. Liliana had scared him off and had probably made him wary and distrustful of every woman he met after her. 'And your brother's too.'

'The last time I saw her I tried very hard to persuade her to see a psychiatrist and I told her that there was no chance of her ever having a relationship with me, but she became hysterical and I had to drop the subject. That afternoon she bribed a cleaner to gain access to my apartment and took an overdose there,' Ruy related grimly. 'She knew my schedule and usually I would have been home that evening but a crisis had arisen and I flew to Brussels instead.'

Guessing the ending of his story, Suzy winced. 'Oh, Ruy,' she muttered, pained on his behalf and his brother's.

Dark eyes grim, he compressed his lips. 'I don't believe that she meant to kill herself. I think it was another cry for attention and a desire to punish me. She expected me to find her and get her to a doctor in time. Unfortunately, she wasn't discovered until the next day by which time it was too late. Rigo blamed me for her death.'

'I don't see how he could,' Suzy breathed, troubled at that unjust bestowal of blame in such tragic circumstances.

'He had to blame someone…why not me? As he saw

it, I had stolen his wife's affections, treated her with cruel indifference and destroyed her mental health. I tried to reason with him, but he was too bitter back then.'

'It wasn't your fault.'

'Wasn't it? Perhaps had I been a little more discerning the night I met her, I would have spent more time talking to her and then I might have realised that we were not suited in any way.'

'I don't think that would have mattered when she had already fixated on you. I'm sorry I misjudged you,' Suzy said truthfully. 'I shouldn't have listened to gossip.'

'None of us should but we all do it,' Ruy murmured wryly.

'I didn't trust my own faith in you because of what Percy did to me,' Suzy admitted in a shamed rush. 'You see, I trusted him once too and then I realised how foolish I had been and, after that, I didn't see how I could trust you…particularly when you seemed too good to be true.'

'I like the sound of being too good to be true,' Ruy confided.

Suzy went pink. 'We were talking about Liliana and your brother,' she reminded him. 'I think she married Rigo simply to get closer to you. She used him.'

'Although it's taken him years of therapy to get over her, he's stronger now and Mercedes is, thankfully, a very different woman. Now I want to show you something…' Ruy paused at the foot of the stairs and regarded her expectantly, a catch in his usually level dark drawl, almost a slight hint of nervousness. 'Your portrait.'

'You finished it?' Suzy prompted eagerly, springing up to approach him.

'It's upstairs.'

He cast open the bedroom door and there it was, resting on an easel by the window in the far corner. Suzy slowly crossed the room to stand in front of the vivid image and study it with wondering eyes. Her hair and her skin seemed luminescent. She looked as though she were about to leap off the bench and walk right out of the painting. It was an extraordinary likeness. 'You've made me look as though I'm beautiful, though,' she whispered self-consciously. 'And I'm not.'

Ruy smiled. '*Sí, querida*...you are. And you destroyed my artistic objectivity. You modelled for my very first romantic portrait.'

'You don't do romantic,' she reminded him.

'I do for you. I do a lot of things differently with you,' Ruy murmured, reaching for her left hand and showing her the diamond ring he was holding as he dropped down very deliberately on one knee. 'Will you do me the very great honour of becoming my wife?'

Thoroughly taken aback by that proposal of marriage, Suzy stared down into anxious dark golden eyes and she dropped down onto her knees as well, covering his lean, strong face with kisses and grabbing the ring in the midst of it. In fact it was a bit of a free-for-all between him trying to get the ring back on her finger at the same time as he claimed her mouth in a fierce ravaging kiss designed to prove to her that she was being claimed for all time as his.

'Oh, my goodness, Ruy... I love you so much and

I wasn't expecting that…but we've only known each other a few weeks,' she exclaimed in reluctant protest.

'If I had known what love felt like I'd have proposed the first day but I hadn't ever been in love before so I didn't recognise what I was feeling,' Ruy explained, appraising her dazed face with adoring intensity. 'At first I assumed it was an overwhelming desire to paint you. But I needed to keep you close as well and prevent anyone and anything from ever hurting you. I wanted to kill Brenton…slowly. I wanted to wake up with you in the morning and go to sleep with you beside me every night. I didn't just fall in love with you a little. I fell obsessively in love with you.'

'That's good…that's good. Stop saying it as if it's peculiar when it's not. I thought I would break in two leaving you behind in Spain because it hurt so much.' Suzy framed his lean dark face with unsteady hands. 'And you didn't try to *stop* me leaving!'

'I was so angry that you could believe me capable of such sleazy behaviour, angry…and, *si*—' he sighed '—also hurt. I expected you to have more faith in me.'

Suzy flinched at that quiet admission. 'I didn't trust my own judgement enough after Percy,' she confided heavily as she closed both arms round him with so much determination that she almost toppled him. 'But I swear I'm getting over that now…and look at you, I can see that you haven't been sleeping, you haven't been looking after yourself properly…*and* you've lost weight!' she condemned with ringing disapproval.

'Our chef is grieving your absence. I've eaten Thai, Malaysian, Vietnamese, Indonesian, Indian and Mexican dishes every day you've been gone and not one British or Spanish meal. I need you at home with me so that I can eat again and regulate the menu. I need you round the clock.'

'But marriage—'

'And soon,' Ruy urged as he lifted her up off the floor and brought her down on the welcome softness of the bed. 'Like really, *really* soon, like possibly this week, and a casual, relaxed wedding that you would like here with your father and Cecile and her family attending. And then possibly a more traditional do for Spain and the rest of my family. You get to pick your own wedding dress too and it doesn't have to have feathers.'

'You *are* insane,' Suzy told him lovingly as he came down over her. She speared her fingers happily into his tousled black hair. 'I'm going to drive you nuts sometimes...you do know that? I'm untidy and impulsive and—'

'You are the woman I love, and I can't do without you in my life another day,' Ruy swore vehemently.

'I've got so used to you too. I thought I disliked so much about you, but you made me feel safe, protected, *cared* for even though I fought with you about your bossiness,' Suzy told him, hauling him down to kiss her again, revelling in the weight of his body on hers. 'I couldn't believe how much I missed you. I fell like a ton of bricks for you and now you're going to be stuck with me and my irritating habits for ever.'

'You wouldn't believe how good for ever sounds,' Ruy admitted with a brilliant smile.

'But you didn't do serious relationships! How has this happened?'

'Liliana scared me off. I saw how devastated Rigo was by her betrayal. And her death. I thought it was safer to keep my distance from deeper relationships with women and that then I could control things. But you broke through my defences, you made me want stuff I had never wanted before…and I wanted you more than anything I had ever wanted in my life and all of a sudden nothing else mattered. Not my pride and not all the anger and bitterness I had suppressed over Liliana. I suppose, a little like my brother, I was ready to make a fresh start and there you were in your tatty wedding dress, swinging those ridiculous boots over the edge of that tree-house platform and being very cheeky.'

Suzy grinned and traced a fingertip along his full lower lip. 'And you *like* cheeky.'

'I didn't know that until you fell into my arms in the woods.'

'That's not how it happened!' Suzy argued, her pride stung by that claim.

'Technically it is and you smelled so good and felt so amazing in my arms, *mi corazón*,' Ruy husked, running the very tip of his tongue along the finger she still had resting against his lips. 'I started to fall for you that same moment, but when you did that handstand in the middle of a modelling session I knew I was definitely in trouble.'

'How?'

Ruy dealt her a look of wicked amusement. 'I would have strangled any other model who pulled a stunt like that but when you did it, I thought it was cute,' he confessed with a chuckle. '*Cute!* Should've realised that I was in love with you then.'

'You're my first love too,' Suzy admitted, her hands sliding below his shirt to find the silky skin of his long smooth back, making him flex against her and grind his hips into hers.

That was the sole invitation that Ruy required to ravish her parted lips with his and before very long the breathless kisses they exchanged were interspersed by impatient attempts to rid themselves of their clothes without separating their bodies. And when that was finally accomplished, and they lay skin to skin, there was no more conversation. They made love with frantic passionate energy and lay in each other's arms afterwards, sated and blessed with a quiet sense of having finally come home.

'So you want to get married this week,' Suzy remarked when she had her breath back enough to talk. 'You realise that there are formalities that have to be met?'

'Special licence…already have it in the pipeline.' Ruy dealt her a victorious look. 'I never suggest anything I can't do.'

'I'll wear the feather dress… I loved it and you painting me in it made it kind of special,' Suzy told him dreamily. 'And I may just be persuaded to borrow the small diamond tiara in that family jewel chest you let me rake through—it was very pretty.'

'Do you want children?'

'Oh, at least a dozen!' she replied.

'A dozen?' Ruy exclaimed in disbelief.

'Well, more than one, less than ten. I always kind of saw myself with a little team of kids. You should have asked that question *before* you proposed,' Suzy pointed out with a grin. 'You look so horrified. We can negotiate. Don't worry about it.'

As a slender hand ran down appreciatively over his abdomen, Ruy discovered that he didn't have it in him to worry about anything at all. *'Te amo, tesora mia.'*

Suzy sat up in sudden dismay. 'Oh, my goodness, I left Dad sitting outside in his car and forgot about him!'

Ruy tugged her lazily down to him again. 'He had driven off before I even brought you up here. I told him I was proposing.'

'Oh…' Suzy flopped back. 'It's going to be a constant game of one-upmanship with you, isn't it?'

Ruy kissed her again and she forgot to talk.

EPILOGUE

Four years later

'I'M AMAZED RUY let that painting out of the *palacio* from its place of honour at the top of the stairs,' Mercedes teased as she glanced at the huge portrait of Suzy at the centre of the exhibition, the one of her in her feather dress in the orange grove. 'Rigo had to really work on him to get him to loan it out for this and he's gnashing his teeth now because he could have sold it ten times over! And, of course, Ruy will not sell a picture of you to anyone.'

'Or of Mateo,' Suzy added, thinking warmly of her two-year-old son and of the pair of little girls she was currently carrying.

It was only a few weeks since the gender scan and only a couple of weeks more since she had learned that she had conceived twins. Her pregnancy with Mateo had been easy but the twin one was proving a little tougher in terms of nausea and tiredness and she would be glad when her due date arrived. Although she was wildly excited at the prospect of two little girls to dress, she adored her son. He was a black-haired dark-eyed little replica of his father, full of energy and personality. She was already wondering what the girls she was carrying would be like and was considering the names Rosa, after her own mother, and Ramona, after Ruy's late mother. She liked names with a family connection.

'We wouldn't ever sell the one Ruy did of Javier either.' Mercedes laughed, mentioning her little boy, who was barely six months older than Mateo. 'I don't know how he got either of the boys to sit still long enough for him—'

'He made me amuse them. I tried balloons and that was a disaster, so were the bubbles because the boys got up to chase them, but turning handstands worked and plain bribery worked. Your son is particularly fond of ice cream with multicoloured sprinkles. Mateo's more into crisps.'

'It meant so much to Rodrigo that Ruy came out as V at his gallery with that first exhibition he allowed him to put on for him. That's when the frost really started to melt between them,' the curvy brunette opined.

'Or it could have been the fact that we simply ignored the frost and kept on forcing them together by making dinner dates!' Suzy commented with dancing eyes, loving above all things that, along with Ruy, she had married into a happy family. Rigo had also finally met Cecile and a cautious friendship was beginning to grow between him and the half-sister whom he had once refused to acknowledge.

Mercedes had become Suzy's best friend, always ready to offer advice in the early days of Suzy's marriage when she had been less sure of herself dealing with Ruy's relatives and entertaining. That they were almost the same age, married to brothers and both had young children had undoubtedly helped as well. Suzy's Spanish had come on by leaps and bounds once she was living in Spain.

Ruy had retained the house in Norfolk but he had had to extend it to accommodate their family. Their last wedding anniversary had been spent in England and Suzy had been stunned when Ruy took her through the woods to show her the tree house he had had built. It was a monster of a construction with proper stairs and loads of safety features and Mateo was going to love it when he was old enough to use it. It had provided Suzy with yet another glimpse of her husband's essentially romantic and passionate soul. He had been determined to commemorate that meeting of theirs in the woods when she had been so rude to him.

When they were in England, Suzy spent time with her father and Cecile's family. Roger Madderton was now in a relationship with Flora's daughter, Maddie, a divorcee, who had recently moved to the village. Suzy liked the effervescent blonde and reckoned that it was past time her father found someone of his own.

After the court case in which Percy had been fined for assault, Suzy had heard no more of the older man. He had sold up his businesses locally and moved. Ruy had bought up those same businesses and they were thriving since the opening of the stately home to tourists. He had also financed the rebuilding of the community hall after the place was vandalised and set on fire.

'What's wrong?' Mercedes whispered and then followed the direction of Suzy's eyes.

'*Dios mio*...leaving Ruy alone is like setting down a roast chicken in front of sharks!' the brunette exclaimed.

At least four very beautiful women were circling Suzy's husband and striking poses.

'Every one of them wants to become his next model because featuring in a V painting gives you a definite cachet.'

'And here I am, obviously pregnant and not at my sleekest and they think this is a good time to pounce and try and tempt him,' Suzy completed darkly. 'Excuse me...'

Ruy was talking to an art critic, quite impervious to the predators hovering nearby. Suzy slid a possessive arm through his and he smiled down at her before continuing his conversation. Moments later he pulled away from the other man and leant down to Suzy to say, 'Are you feeling all right? You're a little flushed.'

'I'm pulling the possessive-wife intervention because other women are hovering hoping to steal your attention.'

'You are the only woman who gets my attention, today and every day,' Ruy countered with amusement. 'And well you know it, *mi vida*.'

Suzy stared up at him with a glow of appreciation in her eyes, thinking of how much he had changed from the man she had first met. For a start, he was infinitely more relaxed and less driven. A wife and a child had given Ruy another focus and had taught him that neither art nor finance were the be-all and end-all of life.

As for Suzy, she had never known that she could be so happy or so contented.

Later that evening, she studied Mateo as he slept at an angle across his junior bed, the covers heaped on the floor. He was a very restless sleeper. He looked angelic with his ruffled hair and fan-shaped lashes resting on his flushed cheeks, something he never looked awake because he was full of mischief.

Ruy paused in the doorway of the nursery and then crossed the room to scoop her off her feet. 'You're tired,' he told her. 'You were standing too long.'

'If you've got legs, you can't escape standing,' Suzy scoffed as he settled her down on the sofa at the foot of their bed. 'I'm not an invalid.'

Ruy knelt at her feet, sliding a very high shoe off one slender foot and gently flexing her crushed toes. 'I don't know why you bother with shoes like these.'

Suzy knew but she didn't tell him. He loved her legs, he particularly loved them when shod in glitzy heels. As the other foot received the same gentle treatment, she wriggled the zip down on her dress with its cowl neckline. A silk and lace apricot and grey bra came into view, a bra she filled to capacity when she was pregnant. The dress slid to her waist. Eyes burnished with heat, Ruy vaulted upright. Suzy stood, shimmied her hips so that the dress fell away and revealed matching panties. He breathed in deep.

'You are so beautiful, *mi corazón*,' her husband husked with pride and satisfaction.

He believed it too, she thought fondly, and even she had come to believe that, in his eyes, she *was* beautiful. He lifted her up in his arms and crushed her mouth hungrily under his, his tongue stabbing deep, sending a flare of white-hot excitement shafting through her There was no more talk now of her tiredness. Sometimes Ruy's protectiveness got in the way of her need to be a desirable woman but triggering his hot-blooded nature always overcame that obstacle.

'*Dios, me encantas*...you enchant me, *mi preciosa,*' he husked. 'I love you.'

'To the moon and back,' she slotted in. 'For ever and ever.'

Ruy brought her down gently on the bed and dealt her an appreciative smile. 'You always have to get in that final word...'

But Suzy had always known that she could safely leave that final word to him.

* * * * *

CINDERELLA'S NIGHT IN VENICE

CLARE CONNELLY

To the indomitable spirit of the people of Italy,
and for the city of Venice.

CHAPTER ONE

'OH, MY GOD.' Bea stared at the fast-spreading blob of coffee with a look of sheer mortification on her dainty features. 'I'm so sorry. I didn't see you.'

The man—at least, he *looked* part-man, yet he was also part-warrior, all broad shoulders, lean muscle and hard edged face—stared at her with surprise first, and then displeasure. 'Evidently.'

'Please, let me—' She cast an eye around for something—anything—she could use to mop up the man's shirt, which now bore the marks of her early evening energy boost. 'I just made it. It must be hot. Does it hurt?'

'I'll live.'

She grimaced, looking around the office, but it was past six and almost everyone had left. 'Let me just grab—' She plucked a tissue from a box on a nearby desk, lifting it to his shirt and wiping furiously, all the colour draining from her face when she realised she was only making it worse. Little white caterpillars of tissue detritus were sticking to the coffee stain, damaging the obviously expensive shirt even more.

His fingers curled around her wrist, arresting her progress, and warmth enveloped her out of nowhere, shocking her into looking up into his face properly for the first time. At five foot ten she generally found she was almost at eye level with most men but not this guy. He stood a good few inches above her, at least six foot two, she guessed.

There was something familiar about him, though she was sure they'd never met. She'd definitely have remembered him. His face was angular and strong, like his body, a square jaw covered in dark facial hair—not a look that was cultivated or painstakingly trendy so much as a fast-growing five o'clock shadow. His lips were curved and bracketed on either side by a deep groove, like parentheses in his face, his cheekbones were prominent and his brows were thick and dark, framing his grey eyes in a way that turned the already spectacular specimens into works of art.

Her breath caught in her throat and she pulled at her hand on autopilot, a familiar instinct to deny anything approaching closeness marking her actions, her lips twisting in a silent gesture of rejection and simultaneous apology. 'Naturally the London Connection will cover the dry-cleaning fees,' she offered, her cheeks growing hot under his continued inspection.

He held up a hand in a gesture of silence.

Bea swallowed, taking a step back. 'I didn't see you.' *Quit talking, Captain Obvious*, she derided. It was a tendency she'd worked hard to curb—speaking when nervous was a girlhood habit she'd kicked long ago. Or *thought* she had.

'Where is Clare?'

'Clare?' Bea parroted with a frown, flicking a glance at her wristwatch to be sure she had the time right. Was her friend and founder of the London Connection—a woman who was as well-regarded for her business nous as she was for being notoriously disinterested in romance and relationships—dating this guy? She hadn't mentioned anything, but something *had* been different with Clare recently. Perhaps this explained it?

'Clare Roberts—about this tall, dark brown hair? Given that you work here, I imagine you've heard of her?'

Bea's eyes narrowed at his tone, which was innately condescending. It was on the tip of her tongue to tell the man that not only had she heard of Clare, but they'd gone through almost every major event in their lives, along with Amy Miller, side by side together. The three amigos, from way back.

'We had a meeting and I do not appreciate having my time wasted.'

'Oh.' She grimaced; the oversight was unprofessional and unexpected. 'She's not here.'

'She must be.' His nostrils flared as he exhaled a deep breath. 'Please go and find her.'

'Find her?' Bea felt like a parrot, but her senses were in overdrive.

'You know, walk through the office until you discover where exactly she is?' He spoke slowly, as though Bea was having difficulty comprehending what he was saying, when his English was perfect, albeit tinged with a spicy, exotic accent that was doing funny things to her pulse points.

Old feelings of inadequacy were stealing through her, making her stomach swirl with a very familiar sense of unease. She tried to banish it, forcing a tight smile to her face. 'Clare was called away on urgent business,' Bea explained, a pinprick of worry at her friend's inexplicable and urgent departure pulling at her. 'Is there anything I can help you with, Mr...?' She let her question hover in the air, allowing him time to offer a name.

His brows knitted together, and every cell in his body exuded impatience. 'You must be mistaken. This meeting has been scheduled for weeks. I flew in this afternoon for this specific purpose.'

Bea's eyes opened wide. If that was true, then they'd

bungled something—badly—and that ran contrary to every instinct she possessed. 'Oh.'

'Yes,' he clipped, crossing his arms over his chest and glaring—there was really no other way to describe his expression—at her across the space. The air between them seemed to grow thick with a tension that made Bea feel as though she was continually cresting over the high point of a roller coaster. She dug the fingernails of one hand into her palm, forcing her expression to remain neutral with effort.

'As I said, something urgent came up, otherwise I know Clare wouldn't have left you in the lurch.' She waved a hand in the direction of Clare's office, the lights off, door closed. 'If you give me a moment, I can try to get in contact with her, or log into her calendar and see if—'

He scowled fiercely. 'This is completely unacceptable.'

Bea hesitated, unprepared for this man's obvious frustration. When he was cross, like this, his accent grew thicker, more mysterious and honeyed.

'I do not have time to be messed around, nor to accept excuses from some secretary or cleaner or whatever the hell you are. I've worked with Clare a long time, but this is—'

Bea felt as though she were drowning. She'd only been with the London Connection for a few months but she knew what this company meant to her friends. Not to mention what it meant to her! This PR firm was important to all of them and, whoever this man was, she didn't want to have a disgruntled client on her hands.

'Yes, very disappointing,' Bea inserted, belatedly remembering that while she was relatively new to the firm she was also the head of the legal department, having been recruited across from her senior partner role in a top tier City firm. She wasn't accustomed to being spoken to as if she were the dirt on someone's shoe. Modulating her voice to project an air of calm authority, she met his eyes straight on, her spine jolting at the clarity of their steel-grey pigment. They were like pewter; she wasn't sure she'd ever seen anything like it before. 'Unfortunately, standing here firing scorn and derision at me isn't going to achieve very much, is it?'

His shock was unmistakable. His eyes widened, flashing with an emotion she couldn't register, and then his jaw moved as though he was grinding his teeth together.

'I am not—'

She expelled a soft breath as she cut in. 'Yes, you were, but that's okay. I understand you're disappointed. And I am truly sorry that you've flown to London from—'

He said nothing.

She waved a hand through the air. 'Wherever, only to find Clare not here.' She turned, moving towards her friend's office. 'You mentioned that you've worked with Clare for a long time, so obviously you're aware how unusual this is. I hope you're able to overlook this rare mistake.'

'I am not generally in the habit of forgiving mistakes, rare or not.'

A shiver ran down her spine at the steel in his words. She didn't doubt for a second that he meant what he said. There was an air of implacability about the man that she'd felt from the minute he'd arrived.

Bea had, at first, thought his accent was Italian, but as he spoke more, her appraisal changed. She was almost certain he was from Greece—one of her favourite places in the world. She'd spent a summer there during her degree, and had fallen in love with the sun, the water, the history and, most of all, the anonymity. When she travelled abroad, no one knew Bea as Beatrice Jones, daughter of Rock Legend Ronnie Jones and Supermodel Alice Jones.

'Then I hope you'll make an exception just this once,' she implored as she flicked Clare's screen to life, typing in her friend's password quickly. 'Please, have a seat.'

He glowered at her without speaking.

A dislike for this rude, arrogant man was forming in her gut. She knew she couldn't treat any client of the firm's with disrespect but the way he was acting was truly unforgivable! So Clare had made an unusual mistake. It obviously wasn't ideal, but nor was it the end of the world.

'Now, let's see if Clare's left any notes here,' Bea murmured, reaching for a pen and tapping it on the edge of the desk.

'Should you be doing this?'

She frowned, looking up at him.

'I cannot imagine Clare would want just anyone accessing her files. There'll be sensitive information in there, including financial documents.' Suspicion crept into his voice. 'What exactly is your role within the company?'

She double-clicked into Clare's calendar as she prepared to answer him but, before she could speak, all the breath whooshed out of her lungs. His name hovered on the screen before Bea, in black and white pixels.

Ares Lykaios.

AKA the firm's most important, gazillionaire, global tycoon client. This man had a finger in just about every corporate pie imaginable. From transport and logistics to airlines to textiles and telecommunications, as well as casinos and hotels, Ares Lykaios had been given the nickname 'Gold Fingers' at some point because, as the press liked to say, everything he touched had a habit of turning to gold.

He was also a man both Clare and Amy had pulled Bea aside to warn her about.

'He's intelligent, demanding, ruthless and loaded. Deep down he's a good enough guy, probably, but he expects top level service—and doesn't suffer fools gladly.'

'Should your path ever cross his, which it likely won't because he only deals with Clare, do whatever you can to keep him happy—we can't afford to lose his business.'

Bea gulped, her eyes straying to the man's stained shirt with renewed panic.

'Mr Lykaios.' Her voice was strangled in her throat, unwanted nerves robbing her of any confidence. She shook her head, forcing herself to project professional authority. She stood, wiping her palms surreptitiously down the sides of her pencil skirt. 'I'm Beatrice Jones, head of legal here at the London Connection. Allow me to apologise once more—'

'No more apologies.' His eyes, grey like the strongest steel, seemed to lance her. 'I am not in the mood.'

'Then why don't you allow me to organise you a drink—perhaps something to eat?—while I familiarise myself with your file. I don't have Clare's or Amy's experience, of course, but I'm sure I'll be able to—'

'I have absolutely no desire to be palmed off with someone who, by her own admission, doesn't have the skill set required to manage my interests.'

Bea's jaw dropped. 'Mr Lykaios—' her voice shook a little with indignation '—please don't misunderstand the situation. While Clare isn't physically here right now, she's as involved in the business as always. As is Amy. You're in very good hands, I assure you.'

'Really? Because it certainly doesn't feel that way.' He pushed his fingers through his hair, which was thick and dark, cropped to the nape of his neck. The action conveyed obvious irritation. Bea's eyes, though, were drawn to his torso; she couldn't help noticing the way his expensive business shirt pulled across his obviously taut abdomen, the spilled coffee highlighting the definition of his pectoral muscles.

For as long as she'd known them, Amy and Clare had pushed Bea, telling her she needed to be more assertive. To tell her parents how she felt. To speak up about the hurt rendered in her childhood, and to stand up to the part-

ners who'd pushed their workload onto Bea's desk, all the
while claiming the hours for themselves. Her best friends
had pushed her to speak up about *anything*, and Bea always smiled and nodded, knowing their words were kindly
meant—and definitely not something she would ever act on.
Yet anger rushed through her suddenly, and for one ghastly
moment she was terrified of unleashing it all on this man.

With no Clare and no Amy in the office—and Bea new
enough to still be grappling with clients and staff—she'd
had a demanding enough day already. Straightening her
spine, she gestured once more to the seat across from her.
'Please, take a seat. Tell me what you need.'

'What I need is for my usual PR manager to discuss the
launch of a seven-billion-dollar operation in Mexico and
Brazil. Do you feel you can discuss the nuances of that,
Miss…?'

'Jones,' Beatrice supplied and, despite the tension humming between them, she was glad he hadn't heard of her.
Glad for some of that Greek anonymity to be here in this
room.

'Well, Miss Jones—'

'Please, call me Bea,' she suggested, aware that she
needed to break down his barriers—and quickly—if she
was going to have any hope of defusing this situation.

Bea. The name was short and brief, jarring and unpleasant.
He dismissed it, wondering why she had chosen to use this
moniker instead of her actual name. In the back of his mind,
Ares knew he was being a first-rate bastard. He could see
the pretty young woman was close to snapping point and
it was an excellent indication of the kind of day—scratch
that, *month*—he'd been having that he didn't care.

But 'Bea' had raised an excellent point. He'd come to
Clare Roberts about three months after she'd opened the
firm a couple of years ago, and he'd never once wavered

in his choice to support her fledgling PR company. He'd witnessed her go from strength to strength and had always admired the work she'd done for him. Surely she'd earned a little leeway from him?

Yes, she had, undoubtedly, but at the moment all of Ares's leeway was in use.

His phone began to buzz in his top pocket.

'Now, just give me a moment, and I'll see if Clare's made any—'

He held up a hand to silence her, reaching for his phone and swiping it to answer. He understood the look of displeasure that crossed Bea's face at his obviously rude gesture.

Another tick in the 'bastard' column for him.

'Lykaios,' he barked into the receiver.

'It's Cassandra.'

He closed his eyes, his stomach immediately sinking. The fact that the nanny he'd hired for his infant niece was calling yet again was definitely *not* a good sign. The last time it had been to beg off the assignment, telling him she wasn't equipped to 'cope' with the child. Danica was only five months old! How hard could it be?

'Go ahead.'

'I gave it another shot, I did, but honestly, she's impossible.'

He tossed his head back, staring up at the ceiling as he rubbed his fingers across his neck. 'Isn't that what you're supposed to be trained to deal with?'

'I'm a nanny, not a magician.'

He could have laughed if he wasn't already at breaking point. 'Your résumé and references are excellent,' he reminded Cassandra.

'Yes, I know. But I don't generally work with infants, and definitely not infants like Danica. She needs—'

'Whatever she needs, she can have. But right now, I need you.' He compressed his lips, the sense of flailing out of control horrifying him, so he stood taller, straighter, staring directly ahead at the wall across the room. 'Double the agreed salary, Cassandra. Just do your damned job.' He hung up before she could answer, confident the exorbitant pay he was offering would be too tempting to turn down.

It wasn't Bea's fault, but when he turned back to her, his mood had dipped into oblivion.

'You are telling me Clare thinks so little of my business she has disappeared into thin air and left only *you* to help?'

The insult hit its mark. He almost regretted the words. It was beneath him to treat anyone like this. But the look of fire that stoked in the depths of her eyes was fascinating and somehow compelling. He moved closer, bracing his palms on the back of the leather chair she kept trying to wave him into.

'I'm not sure what your implication is,' she murmured, her cultured English accent irking him far more than it should.

'Aren't you?' he drawled, a mocking smile curving his lips. He wasn't amused though. He was frustrated and angry, just as he'd been since his younger brother had checked himself into rehab—thank God—after too many benders to ignore, stranding the infant Danica with Ares, a man completely unsuited to being responsible for anyone, let alone a baby. All his life he'd been taking care of others, and failing them at the same time. His mother. His brother. And now his niece. Why wouldn't they see that Ares was a loner—not meant to be depended on by anyone?

He dug his fingers into the back of the chair until the flesh beneath his nails turned white.

'Look, Mr Lykaios, I appreciate how you must be feeling. This is so unlike the London Connection. You mentioned you'd flown into London for the meeting. Will you still be here tomorrow?'

'I wasn't planning to be.'

Her delicate jaw moved as she bit back whatever it was she'd been about to say. Goading her was giving him the most pleasure he'd felt in weeks. Irrational and stupid, he knew he shouldn't bother, yet sparking off this woman offered a kind of tension release.

'If you could perhaps see your way to changing your plans, I can spend tonight familiarising myself with the campaign proposal and meet with you again in the morning.'

'And can you promise you'll offer me exactly the same level of service and expertise Clare ordinarily would?'

'Well, given that I'm head of the legal department and I'm more comfortable wading through hundreds of pages of technical contracts than analysing public relations, I can't promise *exactly* the same level of expertise, but I think you'll find me sufficiently well-informed.'

They stared at each other across the desk; it was impossible to say who was more surprised. Ares for having succeeded in stirring her into the outburst, or Bea for having given in to the sarcastic flood of words.

She clamped a hand to her lips, shaking her head. 'I'm sorry; that was rude.'

'Yes, it was,' he agreed, brushing aside her words and still taking a perverse pleasure in making her sweat. 'I have already told you though: I'm not interested in apologies.'

Her eyes swept shut, her dark lashes forming two perfect crescent fan shapes against her creamy cheeks.

'As for your offer—' he loaded the word with as much condemnation as he could, in no mood to be messed around after everything else he'd been through '—I'll take it into consideration.'

She frowned. 'What exactly does that mean?'

'That I'll see how I feel in the morning. Do your homework, Miss Johns. If I'm here, I'll expect you to be prepared.'

* * *

She hadn't even corrected him on her surname! 'It's Jones,' she'd intended to snap, but the words had died on the tip of her tongue, as they often did when confronted with people who treated her as he had just done. Instead, she'd watched him stalk away through the offices, his pace long and feral, anger emanating off him in waves.

She sank into her chair with a worried expression, staring at Clare's computer with wariness. She was *not* a public relations expert and she wasn't interested in becoming one, but she would protect this business with every fibre of her being. And that meant fixing this monumental mess-up, or risk losing their biggest client.

Not on her watch. It would be a long night, but that was nothing new to Bea. For the sake of the company, she'd do whatever it took. Even suffer through another meeting with that arrogant bastard of a man.

CHAPTER TWO

ADDICTION WAS A beast of a thing. While Ares's younger brother had struggled with it most of his life, following in the footsteps of their drug-addicted mother, Ares had never found that this demon resided within him. It was one reason he could pour himself a measure of Scotch some time before midnight, aware that one measure would bring him the sense of mental tranquillity he craved—but that one small measure would be sufficient. Unlike Matthaios, Ares had never drunk to excess, nor had he indulged in a penchant for drugs. Being in control was essential for him, and he sought that feeling whenever and however he could.

Drinking to excess or taking mind-altering substances was anathema to him. Perhaps that explained why he'd let his brother down so badly. If he'd shared the same proclivities as Matthaios, maybe Ares would have been better placed to help him. He might have seen the path ahead sooner, foreshadowing Matthaios's unravelling after Ingrid's untimely death. The loss of Matthaios's beloved wife in childbirth, coupled with the burden of a screaming newborn, had obviously been too much for a man who'd struggled with addictive impulses all his life.

Ares's grip tightened around the Scotch glass, his eyes chasing the lights of London's renowned skyline. It was a view he drew little comfort from—he far preferred the outlook from his home on Porto Heli. Yet tonight he stared across the ancient city with a feeling that this was the only place he wanted to be in the world.

Or was it that his home was the *last* place he wanted to be? With the screaming, unsettled, demanding infant in residence, and a nanny looking to break the contract he'd had her sign before undertaking the assignment, Porto Heli had temporarily lost its charms. Every time he looked into little Danica's eyes he felt a suffocating sense of failure.

The baby deserved better than him. Just as Matthaios had deserved better than to be raised by Ares, just as he should have been able to save their mother and hadn't. It was history repeating itself over and over and Ares had no doubt he was out of his depth. Which was why he'd hired the best nanny he could find, a woman who came highly recommended by several sources. It was something he would never have dreamed of affording as a teenager. He and Matt had been on their own: poor, starving, alone, and Ares had had to do the best he could—and live with the fact that it had never been quite enough. But for Danica it was different. He could provide her with a nanny for as long as necessary, making sure she would always have what she needed.

Except that Cassandra, the nanny, had been threatening to quit for over a week.

If he wasn't in Greece, perhaps human decency would force her hand. Perhaps she'd decide the right thing to do was stay. Perhaps she'd bond with the baby and decide she couldn't leave her. And perhaps a drift of pigs would fly past his window right now.

He threw back the rest of the Scotch, cradling the empty glass in the palm of his hand.

The meeting this evening had been the last straw. Clare Roberts from the London Connection was someone he saw a few times a year and corresponded with marginally more frequently. She was incredibly organised, professional and detail-oriented and he'd been needing someone like that today. He'd wanted to walk in there and know that everything was in order in at least one aspect of his life.

Instead he'd got *Bea*. Her name bothered him less now than it had earlier. In fact, when he heard it in his mind, he saw her cupid's bow lips framing the word and almost felt the soft rush of her breath across his cheek.

Something like shame gripped him as he recalled their interaction, everything he'd said to her slamming into him now, so he felt as though he'd taken out the hell his life had turned into on the first person he'd found he could blame for something. Yes, he'd used her to unleash his tension simply because he'd reached his limits, and that had been inexcusable.

Right before he fell asleep, Ares resolved to fix that— he'd been unreasonable, but he could undo whatever damage his tirade had caused. Tomorrow was a new day; perhaps things would look better in the morning.

'Mr Lykaios, please, take a seat.' Any hopes Bea had held that the arrogant billionaire might have become less good-looking overnight evaporated into thin air when he strode into the office a little after midday. Wearing a dark grey suit with a crisp white shirt flicked open at the neck to reveal the strong column of his neck, he was preposterously hot. Seriously, was it necessary for him to have *that* face, and *that* body? Wouldn't one or the other have sufficed? Strong features, chiselled jaw, eyes you could drown in, and a body that looked as though he could run marathons before breakfast. Bea's physical reaction was inevitable. Her mouth went dry and her stomach swooped, but she told herself the latter was owing to nerves.

After the disastrous 'meeting' the evening before, she'd spent most of the night reading every single thing she could on the man and his business, as well as swotting up on the current public relations undertakings the firm was making on his behalf. And that was no mean feat. He was a dynamo in the corporate world, with interests all over the globe. The London Connection was currently overseeing ten specific campaigns, as well as doing ad hoc PR work as the need arose. There were four staff members dedicated to him full-time, with Clare managing their work diligently, as—according to the file on Ares Lykaios, he preferred to have only one contact rather than needing to get to know 'new people'.

Strike one, she was out.

As with the evening before, he ignored the chair, striding towards Bea instead, his pewter-grey eyes latched onto hers in a way that made her tummy flip and flop.

'Miss Jones.' He nodded in greeting and her tummy stopped flipping and started feeling as though it were under assault from a kaleidoscope of over-excited butterflies. He held out a hand and she slid hers into it on autopilot, but the second his fingers curled around hers Bea's eyes flew wide, locking on Ares's in shock. Sparks of electricity seemed to be exploding through her, heat travelling from the pads of his fingers to the centre of her being. Her breath was burning in her lungs and heat stole across her cheeks. She dragged her eyes away; it did little to alleviate her physical awareness of the man. Great, that was all she needed: to be *attracted* to this mega-client.

Bea had a minuscule degree of experience with men, and had always been glad she was far too plain and dull to attract anyone's attention. That wasn't strictly true— she'd been asked out on dates before, but the very idea of a relationship had made Bea feel as if her skin was being scrubbed with acid and she'd always backed off. Meaning she'd never had first-date tingles or a blush of attraction when a man she liked looked into her eyes as though he might find the meaning of life in their depths.

Whoa. Hold on. She didn't *like* Ares Lykaios. He was a client first and foremost, and her ingrained professionalism and diligence prohibited her from thinking about him on any other level. But even if she were inclined to fantasise— which she definitely, truly wasn't—how was she forgetting the way he'd treated her the night before? She'd grown up with enough spoiled, entitled, arrogant people in her orbit to know that these were her least favourite qualities.

Their hands were still joined. She pulled away jerkily, wiping her palm on the side of her trousers. That did nothing at all to stop the tingling in her fingertips.

'I had some refreshments ordered in,' she offered politely, pleased when her voice emerged cool and crisp. She sounded far more in control than she felt. 'Pastries, fruit, sandwiches. Please, help yourself.'

His dark head dipped in silent acknowledgement, but he didn't reach for any food. Instead, she watched as he lifted the sterling silver coffee pot and poured a measure into a mug. His focus was on what he was doing, which meant she could watch him—unguarded for a moment. As he poured the coffee, his sleeve shifted a fraction higher, revealing the flicking tail of a tattoo—cursive script, perhaps?—running up his wrist. Curiosity sparked in her belly; she tamped down on it post-haste. This wasn't the time to be wondering about his tattoo, or his body.

Except...she found it almost impossible to stop.

He was tanned, as though he spent a lot of time outdoors. Given that it was only April, it suggested he lived in a warmer climate than London, which was just starting to see some clear blue sky and warmth thaw the ground. Bea had always hated the cold. It reminded her of long nights at boarding school when the blankets had never felt quite warm enough. Or perhaps it was more the ice in her heart, an ice that repeated rejections—first by her biological parents and then her adoptive ones—had locked in place.

His lashes were long and thick, the kind supermodels would kill for. As Bea knew first-hand—she'd witnessed her mother's attempts at enhancement for long enough to understand what went into procuring such thick and radiant eye furnishings.

Unexpectedly, he jerked his gaze to her face and heat spread through her. Guilt too, at having been caught staring. She looked down at the tabletop in a knee-jerk response.

'Coffee for you?'

She nodded quickly, taking up the seat at the head of the table. 'Thanks. I've already had three cups this morning but if it weren't for coffee I have no idea how I'd get by. I should have credited my law degree to the stuff.' *Stop. Talking. For the love of God.*

He was the opposite to her. Silent and brooding, pouring the coffee with his long fingers holding the mug midair, replacing the pot then striding to her side of the table. Close enough for Bea to inhale his intoxicatingly masculine fragrance. Her gut kicked. What the hell was happening? She'd made an art form out of ignoring the opposite sex. Why was she suddenly obsessed with details like his tantalising cologne and curly eyelashes?

To her chagrin, Ares Lykaios, all six feet plus of him, folded himself into the seat directly to her right, so close that if she hadn't moved quickly their legs would have become entangled beneath the table. Her pulse was in frantic overdrive at the very idea! She wrapped her hands around her coffee cup and stared at the swirling steam rather than look at him again.

'Try not to spill it on me this time.' The words were serious but she felt an undercurrent of amusement in their throaty depths. It unsettled her completely.

'Shall we begin?' She didn't sound remotely cool now. Her words were still crisp, but closer to being whispered, as though she were afraid of him.

Get a bloody grip, Bea!

She conjured an image of Clare on one side of her and Amy the other, their smiling, encouraging faces providing much-needed strength. But there was also the spectre of fear—what would happen if she bungled this and lost the firm's most important client? Clare had ploughed all her inheritance money into this place, and it had finally given her a sense of purpose and safety. Bea could never let anything happen to the London Connection on her watch.

'Soon.' The word dropped between them, shaking Bea out of her thoughts. She frowned, looking at him.

He was studying her now with the same intense curiosity she'd focused on him earlier. Bea *hated* to be looked at and actively did everything she could to discourage that kind of attention, but what could she do now? Tell him to stop? Tell him she didn't like it? When the truth was, a strange kind of warmth was bubbling through her blood and her lips were parted on a husky breath of surrender.

Why was he looking at her, though? Bea was under no false illusions regarding her looks. Her adoptive mother was a supermodel and her younger twin sisters had inherited their mother's looks, all slender and fine-boned, blonde and blue-eyed, with skin as translucent as milk and honey. She'd known from a very young age she didn't compare and, even if she hadn't understood that, the articles the press had run through her teenage years—when pimples and puppy fat had attached to Bea with gusto—had left her in little doubt as to her physical merits, or lack thereof. After suffering comparisons to her mother at the same age, and then the twins, Bea had eventually developed a thick skin, yet only after years of painful arrows had already hit their mark.

But who cared about that stuff anyway? she reminded herself staunchly. She'd never wanted to be known for her looks—how vapid and dull! That was just genetic lottery. Far better to build a reputation based on hard work and effort. Tilting her chin, it was on the tip of her tongue to say something to bring their meeting back on track, except he was staring at her mouth now, and logical thoughts were suddenly impossible. Self-conscious, she bit down on the edge of her lip, wiggling it from side to side. She stopped when she saw the way his forehead creased, his thick brows drawn together speculatively.

'I—' She spoke because the silence was like the beating of a drum, resonating in the air around them and deep within her, demanding action—inciting a physical response which was new to her. Her pulse was hammering in the same way, rhythmic and urgent, low and slow, echoing throughout her whole body.

But her attempt at starting a sentence seemed to rouse him. He shifted, reaching for his coffee cup, taking a sip before returning his eyes to hers. Sparks flew through her.

'I came to apologise.'

It was the very last thing she'd expected him to say.

'What?' She shook her head from side to side, a bemused expression on her features. 'I mean, I'm sorry?'

His lips twisted. 'You stole my line.'

Her smile was instinctive. 'But—what for?'

'You don't think my behaviour last night warrants an apology?'

She looked down at the gleaming conference table, unsure how to answer. She wasn't going to tell Mr Millions-of-Pounds-in-Revenue that he'd been incredibly rude. Besides, he evidently knew that already.

'It's fine, honestly.'

'It is *not* fine. The fact Clare missed our meeting was not your fault. I shouldn't have taken my displeasure out on you.'

Her pulse began to race for another reason now. His apology was limited specifically to her. The company wasn't out of the woods yet. Bea still had work to do.

'I'm a senior team member of the London Connection,' she said firmly. 'I should have known you were expecting to meet with Clare, and I should have been prepared. It was an oversight none of us has ever made before. It's I who should apologise.'

His eyes remained glued to hers as he took another mouthful of coffee, so a shiver ran down her spine. Not a cold shiver, though. More like that delightful sensation one experienced when sinking into a warm, fragranced bath on a cool night. Pleasure radiated through her. She jerked her eyes away, forcibly angling her head a little so there was no risk of meeting his eyes again.

'Then we were both at fault,' he agreed. 'But to different degrees.'

Something like amusement snaked through her at his determination to take the blame for their catastrophic meeting the evening before. 'You don't strike me as a man who apologises often, and yet you do it well.'

'I may have an ulterior motive to earning your forgiveness.'

'Oh?'

'There's an event tonight, and I need a date to accompany me.'

Bea's pulse ramped up. She quickly looked down at the iPad on the tabletop, trying to remember every detail from the files she'd read overnight. 'I—can't remember seeing that,' she admitted belatedly, curving her hands around her own coffee cup to stop them from shaking visibly. 'Is that something we usually arrange for you, Mr Lykaios?'

His eyes widened and then he tipped his head back on a laugh that reverberated around the room, rich in timbre and heavy in amusement. She sipped her coffee, simply for the comfort its familiar taste would bring.

'I am asking *you* on a date, Bea, not to act as an escort service.'

Now it was Bea's turn to be surprised. 'Just to be your escort then?'

The humour was gone. Something far more troubling flared in the depths of his eyes. Despite zero practical experience with men she'd still watched enough movies to recognise sensual appraisal. Her knees felt as though they'd been pumped full of water and she was grateful she was sitting or she might have fallen down.

'The event is high-profile and will be covered extensively in the press. I'd prefer not to arrive alone. Think of it as a PR service.'

Every fibre in her body screamed at her to say no. All the buzz words she'd learned to fear and hate were in that sentence. Press. PR. Event. High-profile. She stared at her coffee, sure her face must look whiter than a sheet of paper. 'Mr Lykaios, I'm afraid that's not possible.'

'You're involved with someone?'

Her heart thumped against her ribcage. 'No,' she said before she could think better of it, denying herself a simple explanation for her demurral. 'Not exactly.'

'What does "not exactly" mean?'

'I'm not seeing anyone,' she grumbled, biting down on her lip once more.

'Even if you were, it wouldn't matter,' he said after a pause. 'This isn't a romantic invitation, Bea. It's just work. A small way you can make up for the inconvenience of last night.'

His words were a form of torture. On the one hand reassuring, because she didn't *want* to go on an actual date with someone like him—or anyone. But the fact that he was taking such great pains to tell her this wasn't romantic speared her with unmistakable disappointment.

'Or,' she murmured thoughtfully, 'I can go through the information I ascertained about your PR concerns, and you can go through your no doubt extensive Rolodex of past dates and choose someone else to accompany you.'

Oh, my God. She lifted a hand to her lips again, her eyes drowning in his as the whip of her words cracked through the room. 'I'm sorry. Again,' she mumbled, shaking her head.

'I meant what I said last night. I do not have any interest in apologies.'

The hypocrisy of that stung. '*You* came here to apologise.'

'I was in the wrong.'

'I thought we just agreed I was too.'

He dipped his head. 'I'm asking you to show me you're sorry. That's far more valuable to me than empty words.'

'By going to some event with you?'

'Precisely.'

'But why?'

'I've already answered that.'

'Because you don't want to arrive alone?'

His eyes narrowed. 'In part, yes.'

'Then, as I said, perhaps you could consider—'

'Inviting someone else?' He brushed that suggestion aside. 'I'm asking you.'

'I don't understand why.'

'Because it's tonight, and you're here.'

'I'm here?'

'Yes. Available and in my debt.'

Her lips parted. 'I wouldn't exactly say that.'

His teeth were bared in an approximation of a grin. 'Wouldn't you?'

Damn him. He knew what he was worth to this business, and he knew she'd do just about anything to keep him happy.

And he was right. She sensed the jeopardy they were in, and no way would she do anything to worsen it. If going to some event with this man was the price she had to pay to keep him happy then she'd do it. She'd do it for Clare and she'd do it for Amy, even though it was the last thing she personally wanted!

'I'd have conditions,' she mused.

'I'm all ears.'

He definitely wasn't all ears. He was all hot, handsome face and Greek god body. That was a huge part of her problem. She'd never found a man it was harder to ignore.

'This isn't romantic in any way. Under no circumstances will there be any touching, kissing or flirting.'

'Agreed.' Why then did his droll smile feel exactly like flirtation? Inwardly, she groaned.

'It's only for one night. After which you'll drop me home and that's the end of it.'

'Isn't that covered by rule number one?'

'I'm a lawyer; what can I say? Specificity is my stock in trade.'

'Fine,' he agreed, his voice warm with amusement. 'I won't look to seduce you on a technicality then.'

Fire burst through her. She could no longer sit at the table, so close to him. Instead, she stood, pacing to the windows that overlooked the bustling streets of London. She wore a slightly oversized trouser suit but the sunlight streaming in through the window highlighted her slender silhouette. She was unaware of the way Ares's eyes lingered on her body, appreciating her shape—her breasts, the curve of her hips—or she would have sprinted from the natural light as though a tiger was on her tail.

'And you'll forget about yesterday completely,' she added.

She wasn't looking at him, and Ares didn't speak for a while. 'I can't do that.'

She gaped, turning to face him. 'It was a mistake, Ares,' she pleaded, forgetting momentarily to address him more formally, then wishing she hadn't when that same look of sensual appraisal appeared in his eyes. She was drowning, and there was no lifeline within reach.

'Not your mistake, though.'

'Yes, my mistake,' she rushed to correct him. 'I was here, and I should have—'

He stood abruptly, a warning in his gaze now as he strode towards her, fast and intent. 'I will not forget yesterday but I will forgive it, so long as you agree to accompany me this evening. Do we have a deal?'

Her heart shifted in her chest. He stood right in front of her, so close that if a gust of wind blew her forward by a matter of an inch or so they'd be touching. She took a stilted step back, an awkward gesture that didn't escape his notice, if his slightly mocking look was anything to go by.

'Not quite.'

'More details?'

Her lips twisted in wry agreement. 'Always. I don't need you to forgive me or forget yesterday, but I do need you to promise to give the London Connection another chance. Allow me to have this meeting with you now, seeing as I spent all night preparing for it. Or to call in one of my colleagues, who actually does most of the grunt work on your case and would be far better versed and able to answer your—'

He pressed a finger to her mouth and every cell in her body began to tremble. Her lips were like lava, her face bursting with heat.

'No.'

Her stomach dropped but Bea was unable to feel as much disappointment as she should have. Instead, her body was intent on making her aware of just how nice it was to be touched by him.

'I can wait until Clare returns.'

'I don't know how long she's away for, but I'm sure she can do a virtual meeting at the earliest convenience.'

'I will arrange this.'

Bea's heart thundered.

'I have some conditions of my own.'

His finger lingered on her lips. She was glad; already she feared its removal, her own rules be damned.

'Yes?'

'This is a ball. You will need to dress appropriately.'

More heat stole through Bea. A ball was so far down on her list of favourite ways to spend time, she practically classified it as a torture technique. She gritted her teeth. For the good of the company and all that. 'Fine.'

His finger drifted slowly across her lips, moving sideways, travelling down to her chin and lifting it slightly.

'I have drawn a line in the sand under yesterday. We do not need to discuss it again. Come tonight, be a charming date on my arm and I can promise you there will be no ramifications for the unprofessional mishap.'

She went hot and cold all at once. Bea had no doubt he knew exactly what he was doing—incentivising her cooperation with the most lightly delivered threat. But why would he care so much about having her accompany him?

His fingers stayed on her chin, the touch light, so she wanted more, and that very idea had her lips parting. 'You're already breaking rule one.'

Was it her imagination, or did Ares move closer? 'You think this is flirting?' he asked huskily.

Her heart skipped a beat. She nodded, dislodging his finger and telling herself she was glad.

He frowned. 'You're wrong. This is business, and it's best you don't forget it.'

CHAPTER THREE

As HIS CAR pulled up outside the London Connection offices, Ares wondered for the tenth time that day why he'd insisted on doing this. He'd initially gone to Bea's office intending to apologise and draw a line in the sand, leaving the matter behind him. Overnight, his temper had simmered down and he could clearly understand why he'd overreacted. Since his brother's spectacular breakdown and admission to rehab, and Danica's entry into his life, Ares had felt as though he were lurching from one disaster to another.

Clare forgetting their meeting had been the last straw and he'd taken that out on her hapless business partner.

An apology had been called for, but once he'd made it that should have been the end of it.

But the way she'd looked at him had stirred something inside him, a curiosity he couldn't quell, and Ares was determined to get the answers he craved.

He stepped out of the car, then was striding towards her office with a confident gait, pushing the door inwards and hailing the lift. The doors opened immediately; he stepped inside, watching as the buttons indicating each level glowed as he passed. When the doors pinged open to the London Connection, he acknowledged he was actually looking forward to tonight.

It was unexpected but, given it was the first time in a month he'd felt anything other than a slight sense of panic, he wasn't going to question the emotion. Ares Lykaios had used to feel like this before. Before Matt. Before Danica. He liked women, he liked spending time with them, and for the first time in a long time he felt a rush of pleasure at the prospect of a night spent with a woman who was intelligent and interesting. There was nothing more complex than that behind this evening. He was scratching an itch, giving himself a reprieve, distracting himself from the dumpster fire of his life for a few hours.

It was just after five and the office was still a hive of activity. He announced himself at Reception and was directed to Bea's office. He strode towards it, pausing to read her name on the door: Beatrice Jones. Beatrice suited her better. He knocked twice then pushed in without waiting.

And froze.

She was looking out of the window, her expression— even in profile—taut, but he spared her face only the briefest of glances. Instead, his eyes roamed her body, cataloguing the effort she'd gone to—and the effect it had on him. Her hair, a soft brown, had been styled into loose, tumbling waves that fell over her shoulders and down her back. The dress was subdued and yet that didn't matter. Somehow even the fact it was minimalistic—a simple black with a halter neck and a full skirt that fell all the way to the floor—made her look elegant and regal. When she turned to face him her expression was troubled, but she smiled as he strode towards her and any doubts about why he'd committed to this course of action fled.

'You're stunning.'

Her lips quirked. 'That sounds a lot like something someone flirting with their date might say.'

'Only a fool would deny the truth.'

'Flattery will get you nowhere, Mr Lykaios.'

He shook his head. 'No. Tonight you will call me Ares, as you did earlier.'

Her lips parted and the regret was back. Not regret that he was spending time with Bea, but that it was to be at a ball, surrounded by other people. This was a woman he would have enjoyed spending time with—alone. Now *that* would have been an actual distraction...

'And I will flatter you whenever I see fit.'

Her eyes darted to his and then looked away again, as though she were actually panicked by the very idea. More questions.

She paused at the reception desk and Ares was aware of the eyes that were trained on them—curious staff members unused to seeing a senior member of the team dressed like this. Her cheeks grew pink at the obvious attention. 'I'll have my phone for anything urgent. Please call if you need me.'

The receptionist grinned, gesturing to the lift. 'We'll be fine, Bea. Have fun.'

'So what is this event, exactly?'

'It's to mark the opening of a children's hospital. My foundation was involved in the funding.'

'Ah.' She nodded, mollified by that, as it made it all the more obvious that this was, in fact, a work commitment. 'I read about your foundation last night. You do a lot of work with children's charities.'

'Yes.'

'I didn't realise you were involved in any in the UK though.'

'Our foundation has many partners. Often our work is indirect.'

'Silent philanthropy?'

'Attention isn't exactly the point. I do not support charitable acts because I'm looking for praise.'

'Don't you?'

The grey of his eyes turned stormy like the ocean. 'That's a rather cynical viewpoint to have.'

She laughed, unexpectedly caught off guard by that. 'You're right, it is.' How could she feel otherwise, though, given the way her adopted status had been brandished by her adoptive mother only when it suited her purposes? If she ever needed the world to see her as a Mother Teresa figure, out would come Bea, some photoshoot or other arranged to convince the world of the Jones family's altruism.

She looked towards the car window, her mood slightly dampened by the bitter reflection. 'You didn't say where we're going tonight.'

'No,' he agreed laconically. 'You're new to the London Connection?'

His change of subject was swift and she frowned, but reminded herself that he was the client and she couldn't afford to offend him again. It had nothing to do with what *she* wanted—if she had her way she'd be home bingeing Netflix, definitely not on the way to some swanky affair with this Greek god brought to life.

Before she could respond to his question, he reached for the skirt that covered her knees, lifting it a little.

Surprise had her dropping her eyes, and then, as she followed his gaze, wincing. He'd noticed her shoes. Red high-tops with their trademark white star on the sides, a little scuffed at the toe. Coupled with the sheer black stockings she wore, she was well aware they looked ridiculous.

'In case you need to run away from me?' he pondered, his smile the last word in sexy.

It was the kind of smile designed to melt ice, but Bea's frozen heart was unlike anything Ares had ever known. She offered a cool smile in return. 'Oh, absolutely. A girl never knows when she might have to break a world record.'

'Usain Bolt, eat your heart out?'

'You better believe it.'

'Seriously, though. Did you leave your shoes at home? We can stop and get them if you would like?'

Bea didn't want to admit that she'd chosen to wear these shoes out of habit—that at five foot ten she always wore flats to avoid looking like a giraffe.

'Nobody will see them beneath the dress. I'll be fine.' She just managed to avoid adding 'Won't I?'

But when she looked at him he was scrutinising her thoughtfully. She uncrossed her legs and rearranged her skirt so the hem covered her shoes.

'You were telling me about your job at the London Connection.'

'No, you were asking,' she reminded him, relieved the conversation had returned to something less personal than her choice of footwear.

He waited, watchful in that unnerving way of his.

'It was a few months ago,' she relented. 'Though Clare's been asking me to join for years.'

'You've known her a long time?'

Bea's expression assumed a nostalgic air as she thought back to her teenage years. 'The three of us went to school together. They're my best friends.'

'You're very different to Clare and Amy.'

She was, but his perceptiveness surprised her. 'In what way?'

'Many ways,' he said, the answer frustrating for its lack of clarity. The car turned towards the river. She couldn't think of any hotels here, but it had been a while since she'd ventured this way. Perhaps they were going to a converted warehouse?

'Is being similar to friends a prerequisite to friendship?'

He put his arm up along the back of her seat, his fingers dangling tantalisingly close to her shoulder. 'I couldn't say. It apparently works for you.'

That drew her interest. 'You don't have friends?'

He frowned. 'I didn't say that.'

'You kind of did.'

It was his turn to laugh. 'You're reading between the lines.'

'Do you mind?'

As the car slowed to go over a speed hump, his fingers briefly fell to her shoulder. An accident of transit, nothing intentional about it. The reason didn't matter though; the spark of electricity was the same regardless. She gasped and quickly turned her face away, looking beyond the window.

It was then that she realised they had driven through the gates of City Airport.

She turned back to face him, a question in her eyes. 'There's a ball at the airport?'

'No.'

'Then why…?' Comprehension was a blinding light. 'We're flying somewhere.'

'To the ball.'

'But…you didn't say…'

'I thought you were good at reading between the lines?'

She pouted her lips. 'Yes, you're right.' She clicked her fingers in the air. 'I should have miraculously intuited that when you invited me to a ball you meant for us to fly there. Where, exactly?'

'Venice.'

'Venice?' She stared at him, aghast. 'I don't have a passport.'

'I had your assistant arrange it.'

'You—what? When?'

'When I left this morning.'

'My assistant just handed over my passport?'

'You have a problem with that?'

'Well, gee, let me think about that a moment,' she said, tapping a finger to the side of her lip. 'You're a man I'd never clapped eyes on until yesterday and now you have in your possession a document that's of reasonably significant personal importance. You *could* say I find that a little invasive, yes.'

He dropped his hand from the back of the seat, inadvertently brushing her arm as he moved, lifting a familiar burgundy document from his pocket. 'Now you have it in *your* possession. It was no conspiracy to kidnap you, Beatrice, simply a means to an end.'

Clutching the passport in her hand, she stared down at it. No longer bothered by the fact he'd managed to convince her assistant to commandeer a document of such personal importance from her top drawer, she was knocked off-kilter by his use of her full name. Nobody called her Beatrice any more. She'd been Bea for as long as she could remember. As girls, they'd formed a club: ABC—Amy, Bea, Clare, and the 'Bea' had stuck. But her full name on his lips momentarily shoved the air from her lungs.

'Why didn't you just tell me?'

He lifted his shoulders. 'I thought you might say no.'

It was an important clue as to how he operated. This was a man who would do what he needed to achieve whatever he wanted. He'd chosen to invite her to this event, and so he'd done what he deemed necessary to have her there.

'Your business is too important to our company, remember?' She was grateful for the opportunity to remind them both of the reason she'd agreed to this. It had nothing to do with the fact she found him attractive, and everything to do with how much she loved her friends and wanted the company to continue to succeed.

'And that's the only reason you agreed to this,' he said in a deep voice, perfectly calling her bluff. Was she that obvious? Undoubtedly. Her lack of experience with men meant she had no idea how to conceal her feelings.

Fortunately, the car drew to a stop at that point and a

moment later a man appeared, dressed in a smart navy-blue suit, opening the door.

He spoke in Greek, and Ares responded in English. 'Miss Jones will be joining me. Please have champagne brought to us after take-off.'

Bea stepped out of the car, her jaw dropping at the sight of a gleaming white aeroplane emblazoned boldly with the word 'Lykaios' down the side in bright red letters.

'Of *course* you have a private jet,' she said with a be-mused shake of her head.

'It's a practical necessity. I travel a lot.'

She refused to be impressed. 'You know how bad they are for the environment, don't you?'

He gestured to the steps. 'I offset my footprint in other ways. The reality is, my schedule cannot be made to fit in with commercial airlines.'

A flight attendant stood at the top of the steps, wearing a navy-blue trouser suit with a crisp white shirt.

'Miss Jones,' she greeted, word apparently having reached her of the unexpected guest. 'Good evening, Mr Lykaios,' she added.

'*Yassou*, Andrea.' He put a hand in the small of Bea's back, the touch light and impersonal, yet nonetheless doing very personal things to her insides. Large leather seats were on either side of the aisle, then there was a bank of four fac-ing each other. He indicated she should take one, which she did, spreading her skirt over her knees to conceal her shoes.

He sat opposite, one ankle crossed over his knees in a pose that was sexy and nonchalant and drew attention to his powerful legs. She'd realised he was wearing a tuxedo, of course, but, seeing him sitting directly across from her, the full impact of his appeal hit her like a freight train.

'You're quite ridiculously handsome, you know.'

He burst out laughing. 'Thank you, I think?'

'It's not really a compliment,' she hastened to assure

him. 'Just an observation. I mean, you'd be crazy not to realise that.'

'I always thought looks were subjective?'

'Sometimes, but some people are just objectively attractive. It's a bone structure thing.'

'Is it?' he prompted, teasing her with his eyes and his tone.

'Absolutely. But don't worry, I've never really thought good looks were anything to write home about, so I'm not going to break our cardinal rule.'

'I'm glad to hear it.'

For the briefest moment, despite her best intentions, Bea's eyes dropped to Ares's broad chest. Her temperature spiked; her tummy flipped.

Andrea arrived, proffering two glasses of champagne, but Ares waved his away. 'Coffee, *efcharistó*.'

Bea took hers gratefully. She needed something to soothe her frazzled nerves. 'Your first language is Greek?'

He dipped his head in acknowledgement.

'Yet you speak English flawlessly. Did you study here in the UK?'

'No.'

'How did you learn to speak it so well?'

His lips twisted in a smile that hid emotions Bea couldn't interpret. 'Speaking many languages was somewhat of a survival skill. I got good, fast.'

She quirked her brows. 'I don't understand.'

'No,' he agreed calmly, watching as she sipped her champagne.

She let out an exasperated laugh as the engines began to roar beneath them, the plane starting to move down the runway. 'So what does it mean?'

He stood suddenly, filling the void between their seats with his large frame and masculine aura. He reached down, his eyes holding hers as he buckled her seatbelt into place, fastening it so it sat low on her hips.

She was breathless, completely unable to look away. 'I could have done that.'

He took his own seat again, fastening the seatbelt just before the plane took off, a rush of adrenalin flooding Bea as it often did when she flew.

Once they levelled off Andrea returned, brandishing a tray. The aroma of coffee hit Bea squarely between the eyes. There was a small plate on the side, with crescent-shaped biscuits topped with flaked almonds.

'After my grandfather died, my brother and I spent some time on the streets. We made our way to Athens, where tourists were plentiful. At first we begged—' he said the word with disdain and her stomach clenched for him, the pain he felt at admitting just that palpable '—but once I had a decent command of English and Japanese I began to do odd jobs for the hotels. I earned a pittance—less than begging, most days—but I liked it far more.'

Bea found it hard to catch her breath. 'I had no idea. I presumed you were—'

'Go on,' he prompted.

She couldn't look at him. Shame at her preconception—her *mis*conception—made her mouth grow dry. 'I just presumed you'd had an easier journey to success.'

'You thought I'd been born into a wealthy family?'

'Honestly, yes.'

He laughed. 'Why?'

'Because you are *so* wealthy,' she said, gesturing around the plane by way of example. 'Amassing this kind of fortune, the empire you command, having come from what you've just described... How did you do that?'

'I was extremely well-motivated.' He lifted the plate, offering her the biscuits. 'Have one.'

She took a biscuit automatically. 'I love *kourabiedes*.'

'These are my pilot's grandmother's recipe,' he said with a smile that might have disarmed a less well protected heart.

She took a bite, moaning as the flavour infused her mouth. Almond essence, but not so much as to be overpowering, ran through her, sweet and addictive. The insides were a soft, melt-in-the-mouth consistency, while the top was crunchy, so the texture was a contradiction she longed to enjoy more of. The dusting of icing sugar on top was the *pièce de resistance*.

Closing her eyes to savour the flavour more fully, when Bea opened them it was to find Ares staring at her in a way that drove every thought from her head. The full force of his dynamic attention was focused on her lips, his own mouth held in a tight line, his pupils large in his stormy grey eyes, his body tense, as though holding himself absolutely still against his will.

She lowered the biscuit to her lap, her heart hammering against her ribs.

'You eat that biscuit as though you are making love to it.'

The husky words sent her nerve endings into overdrive. If he had any idea she'd never made love to anyone—man or biscuit—what would he say then? Panic flooded her body, awkwardness at her inexperience overpowering her. She dropped her eyes, staring at the floor.

'It's very good.'

'As all lovers should be,' he responded.

Bea wished the plane would somehow expel her onto a nice fluffy cloud she could hide out in and pretend that Ares Lykaios wasn't talking to her about lovers and sex.

'I'm sorry your childhood was so difficult.'

She risked a glance at him to find a speculative look in his eyes, as though she were a puzzle he wanted to make sense of.

'Another apology?' he murmured, but though it was in the tone of a joke, it wasn't. At least, humour wasn't flooding the air between them. Instead, there was a raw, sensual heat that pulsed with throbbing need.

'A turn of phrase, I suppose.' Her voice sounded strangled. She cleared her throat. 'What other languages do you speak?'

He sipped his coffee, his eyes holding hers. His hands were so powerful-looking, and the cup so delicate, she had to fight an urge to tell him to be careful he didn't break it. She imagined a man like Ares might drink from a goblet cast from stone, rather than pretty white porcelain with a fine gold rim. He replaced it on the tray, the action accompanied by a musical sound.

'Italian, French, Spanish. Some conversational Cantonese.'

She blinked at him, lifting her fingers and counting. 'Plus Greek, English and Japanese… That's six and a half languages.'

He crossed his legs, his foot brushing hers, sending arrows of desire through her body.

'Yes.'

'And you speak them fluently?'

'I couldn't write a novel in all of them, but I can hold a conversation like this.'

'You make me feel quite inadequate. I speak passable enough French to order my favourite meal in a restaurant, and that's about it.'

His smile sent butterflies into her belly. 'Which is?'

'Duck à l'orange.'

Something like approval glimmered in his eyes.

'I first had it when I was about twelve. I remember the trip so clearly.' She didn't go into the details—Paris Fashion Week, her mother's doting on the twins and their matching couture, Bea just growing into her hormonal body, feeling too big and too awkward, the photos the media had picked up of her bored, slouching, reading a book in the light cast by the stage. She pushed those sharp recollections away. 'We went to a restaurant and the waiter recommended it to my dad. He ordered one and so I thought I would too.'

Inwardly she grimaced, remembering her mother's displeasure. *'Darling, duck is incredibly fattening. And as for the sauce—'*

'It was so good. I made a point of ordering it from then on, whenever we ate out.' And not just to spite her mother, though that didn't hurt.

'If only we were going to Paris instead of Venice. I know the best restaurant, on a small cobbled street in Montmartre. It isn't famous, and has no Michelin stars or other plaudits, but the chef cooks traditional food as her father taught her to: each dish is perfection.'

'I'll have to get the name from you,' Bea said, more captivated than she cared to acknowledge by the image he was evoking.

'The restaurant is tiny. If you wish to try it, let me know and I'll arrange things. Ordinarily you have to book in months ahead.'

Bea hid a smile behind her glass of champagne. 'But, let me guess…for you, the chef makes an exception?'

He grinned that charming smile of his, pushing back in his chair and regarding her with all of his focus. 'Always. And therefore for you too, if I ask it of her.'

Bea had been to Venice a handful of times, always with her family, and when she was much younger. She'd been too caught up in the push and pull of their dynamic to enjoy the place fully, and certainly to appreciate its beauty. As the plane began to circle the curious, ancient water city with its glistening canals and baroque homes, she craned closer to the window, pressing her brow to the glass so she could see it better.

The sun was low in the sky, not yet disappeared but

obliging with an incredible palette of golden lights. Rays of orange burst towards them, and she sighed, something like calm settling over her.

As the plane touched down, she avoided looking in Ares's direction for fear the sight of him might diminish even the beauty of the spectacular sunset.

CHAPTER FOUR

'PUT THIS ON.' He held out a fine silk scarf towards Bea, pale pink and turquoise, unmistakably designer.

Bea frowned, looking down at her outfit with a frown. 'Why?'

He focused on her hair then lifted the scarf, wrapping it over her head, letting the ends drape behind her. His hands fussed to ensure it was tightly tucked and then he nodded, stepping back to admire his work. 'So you don't get windswept.'

Bea turned to follow his gaze towards a low black speedboat.

Of course it made sense, yet, years earlier, her family had taken a taxi to the airport, not travelled by water despite being in Venice.

With a sensation of fluttering nerves, she put her hand in Ares's so he could hand her down onto the boat. A man stood, wearing jeans and a dark shirt, a lightweight cardigan over the top and a beret on his head.

'Enrico,' Ares greeted, following Bea into the boat with a lithe motion. The engine purred beneath them and the sun cast spots of gold across the water as it dipped nearer to the horizon.

It was a warm enough evening but, as the boat began to move, Ares shrugged out of his tuxedo jacket, holding it towards Bea. She shook her head instinctively, afraid to be engulfed in something that was still warm from his body, terrified of being wrapped in his masculine aroma. Ares, though, wouldn't take no for an answer. Perceiving the fine goosebumps on her arms, he slipped the jacket over her shoulders, his hands lingering there a second longer than might have been, strictly speaking, necessary.

Bea concentrated on remembering that he was the most important client the firm had, and he was annoyed at having been let down. *That* was the only reason she'd accepted this proposition.

'Would arriving alone to the ball really have been so bad?' she prompted, having to shout above the roaring wind.

His eyes probed hers, his smile a sensual lift of one side of his lips. 'I prefer having company.'

'You're the opposite to me,' Bea said with a small smile, turning away from him. She presumed the boat would swallow her words, but if she'd stayed looking at him she would have seen a speculative glint ignite in Ares's eyes.

Murano was recognisable first, the low-set red and brown buildings familiar to Bea from a long-ago trip to a glass factory there. A few minutes later and the boat tacked south, then swept into a wide canal surrounded on both sides by Gothic-style buildings, the Moorish influence apparent in the curved windows and ornate decorative screens. She held her breath as they passed beneath a bridge, tourists above it waving and smiling. She waved back then looked to Ares instinctively to find his eyes trained on her. He hadn't waved at them.

She felt gauche and silly, focusing instead on the view ahead. Enrico, the driver, reached the Grand Canal, pausing to allow a water taxi to pass, then several gondolas, before he pushed across, moving in a northerly direction. She didn't need to ask where the ball was being held. A few hundred metres away stood a grand old palace, peach in colour with white detailing and a red tiled roof. Several balconies were adorned with candelabras and musicians playing string instruments, so the sound of an orchestra filled the canal. A crowd had formed out the front, including a group of paparazzi.

Instincts honed long ago fired to life. She straightened her spine and squared her shoulders, but it did little to quell the flipping in her belly. How she hated the press!

Ares's hand in the small of her back didn't help. Enrico slowed down the boat, pulling in behind another speedboat which was disposing of its elegant guests, a similarly attired driver helping them onto the platform. Ares moved to stand in front of Bea, his fingers working at the scarf until it was freed, but he didn't move away. He stood in front of her, staring at her, reading her, watching her, so her lungs refused to work properly and all she could do was watch him right back.

'Am I—?' She frowned, painfully aware of how often she'd let her mother down at events like this, and not wanting to do the same to Ares tonight. 'Do I look okay?'

His face bore a mask of confusion. 'Okay? Have I not already told you that you are beautiful?'

She shook her head, brushing aside his praise. 'I'm serious, Ares. I haven't been to anything like this in years.'

'Why not?'

Heat infused her cheeks. How to answer that? 'There hasn't been the need.' Her voice held a warning note.

'You look almost perfect.' He dropped the scarf onto a nearby seat, then put his hands on her lapels.

'Oh.' Belatedly she remembered that he'd provided his tux jacket for her to stay warm. 'Yes, of course.' She shrugged out of it as he slid it from her, standing where he was as he replaced it on his body. His scent still lingered though, and he stood close enough that his warmth did too. Enrico lurched the boat forward as space became available and Bea almost fell—she would have done so, had it not been for Ares's lightning-fast instincts. He shot out a hand, catching her behind the back, his legs like two powerful trunks securing them both to the centre of the boat, his body rigid as he drew her to him. It was the work of an instant, a quick movement to steady her, then he stepped away again, giving Enrico space to throw some ropes to staff atop the platform. The action drew the boat closer, and then Ares was holding out a hand to help Bea off.

She felt strangely shy as she put hers in his, glad when she reached relatively dry land and could relinquish his hand. The pins and needles stayed. Ares practically leaped from the boat, his natural athleticism easy to appreciate.

The sight of him was distracting enough that for a moment Bea didn't realise the photographers' lenses were trained on them—or rather, him—but when they began to call his name she instinctively shrank away, seeking to put distance between them.

Except Ares was too quick for that. His arm curved around her waist, drawing her to his side, fitting her perfectly against the muscular strength of his body, so that, despite the horrible feeling of being photographed, she was reassured by his proximity. Her mother's voice crashed into Bea's mind.

'Smile, darling. But don't show your teeth—your jawline is very horse-like. Straighten those shoulders—never hunch!'

It was over blessedly fast. Another boat pulled up, carrying a bona fide Hollywood celebrity, so Bea and Ares were allowed to walk in peace towards the double doors at the entrance to the famous palazzo. Hewn from ancient timber, thick enough to withstand any number of attacks, they were held open and guarded on either side by staff dressed in white tuxedo tops and slim-fitting black trousers. As they crossed the threshold, Bea used the move inside as an excuse to put some space between herself and Ares. After all, this wasn't a date.

The look he threw her was laced with mockery.

'This way.' He gestured across the tiled entranceway to a room that had Bea gasping at its splendid beauty. Paintings adorned the walls, either late Renaissance or Baroque, swirling scenes with clouds and angels, rippling torsos and long white-bearded men brandishing golden spears to offset the panel framing, which was a lustrous golden colour. Candelabras adorned the walls and ceilings, the floor was a polished parquetry. The room was filled with guests dressed in the most incredible ballgowns and tuxedos, so Bea was glad she'd dusted off the dress she'd bought for one of her parents' Christmas parties in the hope of fitting in.

'This is a lot of people,' she remarked grimly.

'Yes.' His eyes skimmed hers speculatively; trembles ran the length of her spine.

'I've never seen anything so beautiful,' she murmured as they moved through the crowd. He dipped his head closer to hers so that he could hear her better. People were staring at them. She felt a familiar prickling sensation on the back of her neck, aware that, as they cut through the elegantly dressed guests, heads were turning, scanning Ares first and then Bea, appraising her in a way that filled her veins with ice. She moved a little to the side, putting even more distance between them.

She didn't belong with him. She wasn't good enough for him.

It was just like being with her picture-perfect adoptive family. Bea was an outsider.

A waiter passed with a tray of drinks and Bea swiped a glass of champagne from it, her large hazel eyes almost the colour of burned caramel in the atmospheric lighting.

'Why did you bring me here tonight?'

His expression was quizzical. 'We covered this. I didn't want to arrive alone.'

She waved a hand through the air. 'Fine. But surely there are dozens of women who would have jumped at the chance to be your date?'

His lips flattened into a line that spoke of disapproval at her questions.

'So why not ask one of them?' she insisted.

'Because I do not want any complications.'

She frowned. 'What does that mean?'

He lifted his shoulders in a laconic shrug. 'It means that I didn't particularly want a date on my arm, just a companion. No expectations, no promises. No...romance.'

She nodded thoughtfully. 'And any woman you asked would have expected more from you?'

He grimaced. 'There is always that risk.'

'So you don't date?'

He nodded once. 'I date. But not in the way you might expect.'

She laughed unexpectedly. 'How many ways are there?'

His look was droll. 'There is dating because you believe in the fairy tale, and there is dating because you enjoy companionship and sex.'

Heat burst through her. She found it impossible to breathe.

'And I only do the latter.'

Bea opened her mouth to say something but a man approached them at that exact moment, and she was immensely glad. It was clear that the gentleman—Ares referred to him as Harry—was intent on having an in-depth discussion with Ares about an investment in Argentina. Bea shifted sideways, more than happy to leave Ares be—and to get her head together.

Ever since he'd arrived to collect her, things had been spiralling wildly out of control and yet his assertion just now that he didn't welcome the complications of romance only served to reinforce the parameters of tonight. After all, they weren't dating in the hope of the fairy tale and she certainly wasn't going to have sex with him. Which meant this was business, pure and simple. She should have felt relieved by that, shouldn't she?

Ares had learned, with difficulty, to control his emotions. As a child he'd frequently felt lost, angry, hurt, damaged and broken, and as a teenager he'd been terrified but he'd known he couldn't reveal that to Matthaios, who'd depended on him for everything. He'd also realised that the more emotionally he behaved, the worse things got for them. He'd always been big for his age and the sight of a glowering, thundercloud-faced seventeen-year-old had hardly endeared them to the tourists they were depending on for small change. He could control his emotions with a vice-like skill, except recently.

Since Danica had come into his life he'd felt that control slipping, and tonight it was basically non-existent. He watched Bea walk away, catching the tiniest glimpse of her shoes as her skirts swished with her, and wishing more than anything that she'd stayed by his side. He'd liked the way she'd felt there, tucked against him, her softness the perfect antidote to his muscular strength. Instead, though, she weaved through the crowd; an irritating number of other women were wearing black so that, despite her height and natural grace, she disappeared from view far too quickly.

Between scanning the walls for the world class art and making sure she looked busy and distracted so as to avoid entreaties for conversation, Bea was also aware of a young girl with blonde ringlets and a pretty pale blue dress. She stood to the side of a gaily laughing group. From time to time she'd make a foray into the group, tugging on the skirt of one of the women, only to be rebuffed with a shake of the head and a pointed finger back to the wall.

'I didn't know there was going to be a real-life princess here!' Beatrice remarked as she drew closer.

The little girl—Bea would have guessed her age to be six or seven—had eyes that shone when they lifted to Bea's face. 'A real princess? Is there really?'

Bea feigned bemusement. 'Aren't I looking at one?'

'Where?' the little girl asked, craning her neck to see behind her.

'Here.' Bea gestured to the girl.

She looked surprised then shook her head. 'I'm not a princess.'

'Aren't you? You could have fooled me.'

Pink spots appeared on the girl's cheeks and then she was giggling. 'I'm American. We don't have princesses.'

'Hmm. Technically, I suppose you're right. Yet I could have sworn you were. Are you having fun, Your Highness?'

The little girl's smile brightened and then dipped away completely. 'Um…honestly?'

'Of course.'

'Not really.' She ran the toe of her shoe across the lines in the parquetry. 'I hate stupid balls. They're so boring.'

'They can be,' Bea agreed. 'Do you attend many?'

'Way too many,' the girl groaned. 'Dad's job means we always have to come and I hate them. There's never any other kids here and nothing for me to do but stand quietly and wait.'

Bea nodded sympathetically. 'I used to feel exactly the same way.'

'Really? My mom says I'm ungrateful. She says she would have loved to come to fancy parties at my age.'

Bea wrinkled her nose. 'Everyone's different, but I always found this sort of thing incredibly tedious.'

'Did you have to come when you were little?'

'Oh, yes, all the time.' Bea shuddered at the memories. 'To parties and shows and I would get bored and then so tired that sometimes I'd fall asleep on a chair in the corner!' she half joked.

'What happened?'

'They stopped bringing me,' she murmured, not mentioning that once the twins had been born she'd been shipped off to boarding school and only seen her adoptive parents a few weeks a year.

'I wish mine would stop bringing me,' the girl said a little too loudly, so her mother turned in preparation to scold her, pausing only when she saw Bea in conversation with the child.

'You know, I used to keep myself busy by playing maths games. Want me to show you what I mean?'

The girl nodded eagerly.

'Well, first of all, I'd count all the women wearing pink.' She frowned as she surveyed the crowd. 'There aren't very many tonight, so that won't take you long. Once you've done that, look for men wearing black shoes. Then women wearing tiaras, then men with ties versus bow ties. You'd be amazed at how it helps to pass the time.'

Having spent almost thirty minutes locked in conversation with Harry, expecting Beatrice to reappear at his side at any minute, he'd moved beyond frustration and onto irritation when she seemed to have simply disappeared into thin air.

He'd circumnavigated the room for another twenty minutes, being interrupted too many times to count to make short conversation with acquaintances and business contacts. As he'd scanned the room, his eyes had landed on something that made very little sense, and he'd drawn his gaze back.

A woman sitting on the ground at a ball was a strange sight indeed, so he knew somehow instinctively that it could only be Bea. Sure enough, as he moved closer, assiduously avoiding several more attempts to draw him into conversation, he saw that she wasn't, in fact, sitting so much as crouching beside a little girl, who was cross-legged beside her. They were staring into the crowd, a matching expression of concentration on their faces. Bea pointed at something and the little girl frowned as she followed the gesture, then she burst out laughing.

Something grabbed at his chest at the unexpected sight and his impatience changed gear. No longer irritated by her disappearance, he was now irritated by the fact that there were so many people surrounding them when he wanted to be all alone with her.

It was a warning bell he heeded. He hadn't brought Bea to be distracted by her. He'd been honest with her earlier when he'd explained that he didn't want any complications. Perhaps ending this night prematurely was the wisest course of action.

'Ares—' she smiled to cover the rapid beating of her heart as she stood up '—there you are.'

'You sound as though you've been looking for me, but I suspect this is not the case.'

A guilty heat stole along her cheeks. 'You were busy,' she explained, fidgeting her hands in front of her.

'Yes. Harry is a partner in a project—'

'In Argentina, I gathered.'

'Indeed.'

'Who's this?'

Bea turned to the little girl. 'Emily, this is a friend of mine. Ares Lykaios, this is Her Royal Highness Princess Emily of Connecticut.'

'Hello, Your Highness,' he volleyed back without missing a beat. 'I'm pleased to meet you. Thank you for keeping Bea entertained while I was talking to someone else.'

'You're welcome.' Emily grinned. She pointed to his shoes. 'Thirty-nine!'

Bea nodded. 'You're right! Well done.'

'Are you enjoying yourself?' Ares asked.

Bea smiled at Emily. 'We're having a good time, aren't we?'

Emily nodded. 'Much better.'

Ares compressed his lips. Children made him uneasy; they always had done. Bea, on the other hand, seemed completely at ease with this little person. 'We can leave any time. If you're ready?'

Bea's eyes lit up. 'Really? You don't have to stay?'

'No. I've made an appearance; that's all that was expected of me.'

She looked down at Emily apologetically.

'It's okay.' The little girl pressed her hand to Bea's. 'I'll be fine. I'm looking for wigs next.' Emily wiggled her pale eyebrows so Bea laughed softly.

'That's a delicate one. Make sure you don't point or count too loudly.'

Emily tapped the side of her nose. 'Promise.'

Ares's hand was firmly insistent as he guided Bea away from Emily. 'A friend of yours?'

'A new friend.' Bea sighed. 'A lovely little girl rather too young to be dragged to events like this.'

'It's not exactly a child-focused evening.'

'She reminds me of how much I used to hate this kind of thing,' Bea said with a shiver.

'Used to?' he prompted, and again she was struck by how insightful he was.

'You caught me. I still do, generally speaking. In fact, you'd normally have to drag me kicking and screaming to something like this, so you should take it as an indication of how important your business is to the London Connection that I'm here with you tonight.'

She wondered why the words felt slightly disingenuous. As if to prove that he knew she was lying, he lifted a hand, catching a thick wave of brown hair and tucking it behind her ear. A *frisson* of awareness shimmied down her spine.

She gulped, trying to remember what she was saying, desperately hoping her voice emerged with a semblance of control.

'As a child, I was made to attend so many functions with my parents. Parties like this, with fancy clothes and beautiful music, and I came to hate them. Everything about them. The food, the forced laughter, the social interactions.' She lifted her shoulders. 'Give me a good book and a quiet living room and I'm all set.'

'And do you wish you were in your living room now, instead of here?'

The challenge lay between them. She feared they both knew the answer to that...

'I...am having a better time than I anticipated,' she said unevenly.

It was like stepping off the edge of a cliff and into an abyss. She was in freefall, losing herself in the depths of his silver-grey eyes, with nothing to hold onto. He stared at her long and hard and turned away from her, but not before he uttered under his breath, 'As am I.'

CHAPTER FIVE

THE GONDOLA HAD been a mistake. He should have refused. But her eyes had been so hopeful as she'd looked out on the canal, watching the little boats bobbing past, and before he'd been able to stop himself Ares had heard himself say, 'Would you like to take a ride?'

Of course, he'd simply been being polite. She'd smiled awkwardly and for a moment he'd held his breath, thinking she'd say no, but then she'd nodded, a simple shift of her head.

It was tighter than he'd imagined in the boat, the seat designed for lovers, so they had no choice but to sit hip to hip, her body lightly pressed to his side, her warmth permeating him. 'You're good with children.' The words were cool, and he was glad. This wasn't a date—she wasn't a woman he was looking to bed.

'Thank you.'

Silence stretched between them, long and taut. He should continue it, ignore her, get this evening over. But again, almost against his volition, he asked, 'Do you have siblings?'

Her smile seemed to communicate something he couldn't understand. Uncertainty? Pain? 'My adoptive parents had twin girls when I was seven. Annelise and Amarie.'

'So you must have been given plenty of opportunities to babysit?' The moon overhead was almost completely full, only a fingernail snippet missing from one side. It cast the canals of Venice in a glorious silver light, the water lapping gently at the edges of the wooden boat.

'I went to boarding school shortly after the girls were born. I really only saw them during the holidays—a few weeks a year at most.' Her words were robotic, as though she'd practised the line many times.

'How old were you when you were adopted?'

Her fingers fidgeted in her lap; she stared down at them, the matte black nail polish the perfect complement to her dress. 'Three.'

He waited for her to continue and was eventually rewarded with a shaky explanation.

'Ronnie and Alice tried to fall pregnant for a long time. Years and years of IVF and fertility treatments, all with no luck. Adoption was their last resort—definitely not the kind of parenthood Alice had envisaged, but better than nothing.'

Ares was very still, the rejection she was describing making him pity the little girl she'd been.

'The twins were a miracle. She was in her forties when she conceived, and without fertility assistance, after years of being told it would never happen. You can imagine how doted on the girls were.'

'And you felt pushed aside?'

Bea's smile was iced with years of pain. 'I felt that way because I was.' She fixed him with a gaze that was like steel, and yet it didn't deter him. He could see through it easily. 'Anyway, I don't really like to talk about my family.'

But he wouldn't let her turn away. His finger caught her chin, guiding her face back to his, and now he was so close to her, grey eyes morphing to silver in the moonlight reading her as he had been all evening. What the hell was he doing? She was pushing him away with her words, and he should let her do exactly that. Not caress her face and draw her towards him. 'Families can be complicated.' His voice was throaty.

'Yes.' Just a whisper, the word caught on the air, brushing across his cheek towards his ear. She was a beautiful woman, but he hadn't brought her to Venice with this in mind. Yet sitting in the gondola, his body so close to hers, he felt a drugging desire to throw sense to the wind and act as though she was any other woman. What harm could come from that?

'Amy and Clare are my family.' It was a strange thing to say. Was she simply explaining that she didn't need her adoptive parents and siblings? Or was she looking to remind him—and herself—of her best friends and business partners?

The gondola moved to the side to let another boat past, and some waves formed in its wake that caused the craft to rock from side to side, lurching Bea towards Ares. She made no attempt to resist the gravitational movement and he was glad.

Her hands lifted to his shirt; her face stayed tilted to his. He stared at her, torn between doing the right thing and getting the hell back to Enrico and sending her back to London, or doing what he desperately wanted and closing the distance between them completely. His eyes dropped to her lips, staring at their pouting form, aching for her. She lifted one finger to her mouth, tracing the line his eyes were taking, her fingertip trembling at the intimate gesture. It was an invitation and an entreaty; what she wanted was blatantly obvious.

And so? Why fight this? He'd explained to her that he didn't believe in romantic relationships. He'd been explicit in telling her that all he looked for when he dated a woman was sex. If she was interested in him, and what he was offering, then he'd be a fool to resist. Right?

'Tell me, Bea, did you have a rule about kissing?'

Her breath hitched in her throat at his low-voiced question. She tried to think straight but it was almost impossible. 'We agreed no kissing.'

'I think you said no touching too,' he suggested, dropping the hand that held her chin to her knee, where he cupped her flesh there, sending sharp arrows of pleasure through her skin. She leaned infinitesimally closer to him, her skin lifting in a veil of goosebumps.

'And definitely no flirting.'

'Tell me, Counsellor, how does one go about revising the rules?' he asked.

Her mouth was dryer than dust. She was on the precipice again, nudging closer to the edge even when she knew she should turn and walk away.

'You're a client,' she reminded herself and him, saying the words aloud in a desperate attempt to bring sanity back to her mind.

'Not tonight.' His head dropped closer to hers, so close that if she pushed up she could take his lips for her own. Blood formed a pounding cacophony in her ears, an orchestra of need like a tidal wave she was cresting over.

'No? What are you then?'

She sucked in a gulp of breath but the stars in her eyes didn't go away.

'They are your rules,' he responded without answering directly. 'To break or ask me to abide by. I'm in your hands.'

The imagery conjured was too much. How could she explain to someone like Ares Lykaios that she was nothing like his usual companions? How could she explain to him that she didn't simply go on dates with handsome strangers and kiss them beneath the bright Venetian moonlight? How could she explain to him that she was, of all things, a twenty-nine-year-old virgin?

'I don't think this is a good idea,' she whispered. Because surely whatever happened next would be wildly disappointing for him—and possibly earth-shattering for her.

The imbalance in their experience was terrifying. 'I'm really, really not your type.'

Despite the tension thickening between them, his smile reached inside and calmed Bea's nerves. Her body was, if anything, moving closer to his.

'If you want to retain our original agreement, then I'll respect that. But make the choice based on *your* feelings, not what you believe mine to be. I know exactly what I want right now.'

Her heart lurched completely off-balance. 'And that is?'

He moved so close that their lips brushed and whatever willpower she had left to resist him disappeared completely. 'I want to spend the night with you.' His finger ran along her cheek, and she was trembling against his body, the desire he was invoking too much to resist. 'Just one night, nothing more.'

It sounded so simple! So easy! Sex, plain and simple — except nothing with Ares Lykaios would ever be plain.

'But I'm—' The words trailed into nothing.

Then, to hell with the rules, he was kissing Bea and she was kissing him back, their lips enmeshed in a way that blew all Bea's preconceptions of such a thing well out of the water. Unlike the passionless encounters she'd had in the past, every movement of his mouth stirred flame in her blood, so that she couldn't sit still. If she did, the fire would engulf her; she had to move.

The boat rocked from side to side as she pushed up into his lap, needing to be closer to him, so much closer than their clothes and public location allowed. His hands moved inside his jacket that she wore, wrapping around her slender waist, holding her there as he drove his tongue into her mouth, the rhythm fast and urgent, leaving her in no doubt as to just how badly he did, in fact, want her. One hand on her hip moved lower, cupping her bottom, and she groaned, flinching a little at the completely foreign contact but welcoming it too, needing it—and him—in a way that shook her to the core of her being.

She often felt too tall, too ungainly, but in Ares's hands she was dainty and petite, his size engulfing her, his strength dominating her completely as he shifted and by degrees moved her with him, so she was straddling him, the voluminous skirts of her dress forming a circle around them, her fingers pushing through his hair and joining behind his neck, her breasts crushed to his chest as his mouth continued to torment hers, his expertise and experience meaning that the kiss alone had the power to make her stomach swoop all the way to her toes.

But then he rolled his hips, lifting a little on the seat of the gondola, so she felt something unfamiliar and unmistakable between her legs, his hard arousal striking panic into her heart even as ancient feminine instincts came to the fore, reassuring her that she'd know what to do when the time came. Her hand dropped to his shoulder, then lower still to his shirt, her fingers curling into the fabric and squeezing, holding on tight.

He tore his mouth away but held her head steady where it was, calling Italian words over his shoulder.

He was kissing her again before she could ask him what he'd said, but the gondolier took a side canal, so she could only presume Ares had given a change of course. And, with any luck, to a hotel!

Why was it that he, of all people, could affect her like this? She'd spent her entire adult life believing she was immune to the opposite sex and yet here he was, stirring her to a fever pitch on a boat in the middle of Venice.

'To hell with the rules,' he growled.

His hand pushed under the fabric of her dress, resting on her thigh. He kept it there, not pushing higher, as though he sensed it was a limit for her, that she needed time to process that sensation first, to reconcile herself to the intimacy before he took another. And God, she hoped he would take another and another and another. Sparks of anticipation flew through Bea's blood as she realised what was about to happen: Finally, she was going to have sex. She was going to lose her virginity, so she could have some understanding of what all the fuss was about. And with Ares Lykaios she knew it would be a night to remember!

A low, throbbing noise was sounding in her ears, running through her body, vibrating in her chest. She attributed it to her heart until her brain kicked into gear. Pulling back from him and staring dazed—into his hooded grey eyes, she pressed a hand to his torso. 'You're ringing.'

He looked as swept up by passion as she felt. He stared at her for a beat before the words resulted in action. He lifted his shoulders, pulling her closer. 'I don't care.'

She moaned softly as he parted her lips with his, sliding his tongue in more slowly this time, the enquiry gentle, but no less urgent. She rolled her hips, a primal wisdom beating in her heart, showing her how to answer her needs, how to act.

The throbbing began once more, vibrating through Bea's chest, so she pushed away, her breath laboured, her eyes sparkling. 'Answer it, then switch the damned thing off.'

His brows flexed and with a forceful exhalation he reached into his pocket. A frown crossed his face as he glanced at the screen, and then he swiped it to answer, his other hand still on her thigh, his thumb stroking gently over the skin there, as though he knew he could keep her in his sensual thrall with that slight contact alone.

'Yes?' Frustration emerged in the clipped tone, taking Bea back to their first meeting, when he'd spoken to her like that. She was glad not to be on the receiving end of his impatience any more, and pitied whoever had called.

They were in close proximity and she could hear the string of high-pitched words without being able to understand any of them, owing to the language in which they were being spoken. His thumb stopped moving; the weight of his hand on her thigh grew lighter.

He barked something into the phone in Greek, his eyes on Bea's face without, she suspected, seeing her. Ares was gentle yet insistent as he dislodged her from his lap, shifting her back to the seat at his side, his features looking as carved from granite as ever but harsher now so they were jagged and sharp. For no reason she could think of, a shiver ran down Bea's spine.

He said something short and then disconnected the phone. It was the only movement he made; the rest of him was completely still. Shocked? She couldn't tell. It only lasted a small beat of time and then he was speaking to the gondolier once more.

'Ares? What is it?' Her voice was still husky, the passion flooding her veins slow to recede.

When he looked at her it was almost as though he'd forgotten she was there. 'Beatrice,' he muttered. Her heart lurched. She'd been treated as an inconvenience often enough to immediately understand his meaning.

'I have to return home, immediately. It cannot be delayed.'

Concern eclipsed her own feelings of rejection. 'Has something happened?'

A grimace was his only response. Mentally she derided herself for asking such a stupid question. *Obviously* something had happened. But what?

Everything felt different now. The buildings of Venice still sat on either side of the canal but now it was as though they were looming watchfully, bathed in too-bright yellow rather than a gentle gold, and even the lapping of the water seemed to inflame Bea's uncertainties and anxieties.

They had not travelled far and, using a series of shortcuts, the gondolier had them back at the speedboat a short time later. He pulled up to the pontoon, moving to help Bea disembark, but Ares was there first, his strong hand guiding her out of the boat even as his face bore an unrecognisable mask of stony intent. Another shiver spread through her as she shrugged out of his jacket and looked around behind her.

'You go.' She nodded towards the sleek black speedboat. 'I'll catch a water taxi to a hotel.'

His frown was just the slightest shift of his lips, then his hand was on her back, drawing her with him. 'I doubt any will have space available. Between the ball and the opera, Venice is packed.'

'Surely somewhere—'

'Nowhere reputable.'

She nodded, relying on his better knowledge of Venice at that point, stepping into the speedboat with him. At the airport, she could arrange a flight to London. Disappointment was a visceral ache rapidly spreading through her. She refused to think about where the night had been heading only moments earlier; she refused to think about the heat still pooling in her abdomen, demanding fulfilment. She refused to imagine Ares naked on top of her, and what the weight of his body would feel like over hers; she refused to go down that path even when it was dragging at her every second of the torturous, silent boat ride to the airport.

Relief flooded Bea's veins when they arrived; she wanted Ares more than she could say, but at the same time she desperately needed to get away from him so she could process what had just happened.

He walked quickly away from the speedboat and she had to take long strides to keep up. He was taking the same path they'd trodden earlier—a partly concealed sign declared *'Aerei Privati'*. Private Aircraft.

She stopped walking and, despite the fact he was marginally ahead of her, some sixth sense must have alerted him to the change because he halted and turned to her. 'Come. I must be quick.'

His accent was more noticeable, his words rushed with something like panic.

'You go on. I'll make my way to the terminal and see about getting a ticket to London.'

His brow furrowed, as though he hadn't expected that. 'There won't be any commercial flights at this time.'

Beatrice glanced at her wristwatch, groaning because of course that was true! It was almost midnight. She looked around with a growing sense of unease. 'Then an airport hotel—' She gestured to a low building in the distance bearing a familiar logo, associated with three-star hotels the world over.

'No.'

She startled at the word. 'I beg your pardon?'

He compressed his lips, turning to her in a manner that made Bea feel as if she were a recalcitrant child. She stood her ground.

'I do not have any time to spare, Beatrice. I cannot take you to that hotel, and I will not leave you to make your own way there. So you need to come with me.'

'Where to?'

'My home.'

'I don't even know where that is.'

'Does it matter?'

She glared at him with hauteur.

He sighed. 'In Greece. It is an emergency; I do not have time to argue with you.'

'Then don't argue with me,' she said quietly, practically on the brink of tears at how the night had turned out. 'You do your thing and I'll do mine. I'm a big girl, more than capable of getting myself to that hotel and checking in for the night.'

He shook his head. 'I won't have it on my conscience if something goes wrong, and I do not have the time to see you there safely myself.'

'We're going around in circles here, Ares, because I've already said I'll be fine, and you're saying you don't know that for sure. But I can see no reason to come with you, especially when something's obviously happened that requires your attention, so, short of kidnapping me, you're going to have to accept my decision.'

He stared at her, his bright eyes bitter; she could feel her skin burning under their assault. And then he moved, taking one step towards her and lifting her easily, as though she weighed nothing, hoisting her over his shoulder. She was too shocked to make a noise; he had already resumed his earlier path and taken several steps before she squawked in indignation, 'What the hell are you doing?'

'Kidnapping you.' The words obviously came from between gritted teeth. 'Just as you suggested.'

CHAPTER SIX

HE HAD TO give his flight crew credit. They acted as though seeing him arrive hauling a very cross woman over one shoulder was a totally everyday occurrence, running through all the normal pre-flight checks without batting an eyelid. For his part, Ares was grateful for their professionalism, and only slightly shocked by his own behaviour towards Bea.

It hadn't been about wanting to kidnap her and drag her to his home, even though such thoughts had been tormenting him all evening, so that he'd imagined her against the sheets of his bed, her languorous hazel eyes staring up at him, begging him to make love to her.

This had been a question of practicality alone.

The call from his housekeeper, Xanthia, had pushed all other considerations aside. Cassandra, the nanny, had walked out after hours of the baby's screaming. Xanthia, herself a grandmother, had sounded beside herself. What choice did Ares have but to go straight home and assess the situation?

His eyes drifted to Bea, who was sitting opposite him, a belligerent expression on her face that—at any other time—he would have been very tempted to erase from her pretty features using far from respectable methods. As if to torment him even further, his fingers tingled with the memory of her silky-smooth thigh beneath his palm, the way she'd juddered at the contact, her body begging him for more.

He'd held back, telling himself they had all night, that the pleasure was better savoured than rushed, but now he wished he'd ignored that impulse and let his hand drift higher, finding her sweet femininity and brushing her there, feeling her heat and watching as she exploded in his arms.

'I wish you'd tell me what's happened,' she said quietly. 'It seems like the least you could do.'

It was the first time she'd spoken all flight, and they were almost in Athens. He stared at her, the words locked deep inside. But he had to say *something*. She was about to walk into a scene that would make it perfectly obvious he'd been left—literally—holding the baby.

'Five months ago, my brother's wife died.' He spoke clin ically, no sign of the ensuing trauma in his words. 'It was a complete shock—something went wrong during child-birth. Ingrid was delivered of their baby, a little girl, but then wouldn't stop bleeding, and the doctors could do noth-ing to save her.'

Bea gasped in that way she had, lifting her fine-boned hand to cover her lips.

'Now my brother is…not well…' he glossed over the nature of Matthaios's illness out of instinct to protect him '…and has left me with the care of his child while he seeks treatment.'

The sympathy in her eyes was unmistakable. Ares hated it. As a teenager he'd seen that look on countless faces and he'd sworn he'd show them. He was not an object of pity. Strengthening his spine, he infused ice into his bones. 'Naturally, I hired an exceptional nanny. My workload is hardly conducive to the care of a child, and young children particularly need a lot of care. Unfortunately, the woman I hired has been almost as much work as my niece since day one. My housekeeper just called to inform me that the nanny had walked out.'

'Cassandra,' Bea prompted thoughtfully.

'How did you—?'

'She called while you were in Clare's office.' Pink bloomed in Bea's cheeks. He looked away, controlling his body's response to the betraying gesture with difficulty.

'Yes, Cassandra.' He spat the name with derision, almost missing the way Bea's lips lifted a little at the corners. She was smiling at him? Trying not to laugh at him? It didn't make sense and Ares liked things to make sense.

'I have to get back there, to see what's going on,' he snapped.

Her eyes, clear pools of burnt butter, appraised him for several seconds and then she nodded slowly. 'If you'd explained this sooner I wouldn't have fought you at the airport.'

His lips tugged downwards. 'It didn't occur to me. I was too preoccupied.'

Again, sympathy crossed her face. It took Ares a moment to realise it wasn't sympathy for him so much as for the unknown baby, and the entire situation.

'Naturally, I'll arrange for you to fly back to London tomorrow.'

She barely reacted, yet in the depths of her eyes he was sure he saw something unexpected—something akin to disappointment? Or maybe that was wishful thinking: ego?

'Don't worry about me,' she insisted quietly. 'I can take care of myself.'

Bea's adoptive parents owned a grand old country home in the English countryside, the kind of place with rolling green lawns, a stream filled with trout, stables that had been empty for many years until the twins asserted a desire to learn to ride, and horses were therefore acquired from top breeders. The desire had lasted three weeks, the horses longer—they were now given free rein of the western paddocks and, from time to time, found their way into the orchard and ate their body weight in fruit, much to Alice Jones's displeasure. As an organic-only fruitarian, the orchard represented almost her sole source of food, so the horses' act had been seen as a declaration of war.

The house itself dated to the early Tudor period, though much modernisation had occurred in recent years, and now boasted ten bedrooms, each with its own bathroom, three swimming pools—one for diving, courtesy of Amarie's insistence that she was going to be an Olympic diver. The pool had been completed about a week too late—she'd moved onto playing the drums by then and, despite the fact that Ronnie had a full studio in the basement of the house, a separate drums studio was built for Amarie, perhaps to save Ronnie from the torture of listening to her murder the tempo of any more classic rock music.

So it wasn't as though Beatrice hadn't been surrounded by wealth. But ever since arriving at the airport in London and being ushered into Ares's private jet she'd felt as though she'd been exposed to a whole other level of extravagance. Upon touching down in Athens they were ushered to a limousine which drove them a very short distance to a gleaming black helicopter with darkly tinted windows. The upholstery was brown leather and the details oak. Her companion was as silent as a tree himself and his manner became colder, more intimidating with every minute that passed.

Bea distracted herself by staring out of the window, trying not to compare him to the way he'd been on the gondola. Then, she'd almost felt as though she could say anything to him, tell him anything, but now he was so distant it was impossible to think of him as anything except an incredibly successful self-made businessman who was also a very important client—a man whose business the London Connection needed to retain.

And, for some reason, all she could think about was the time she'd been sent home from school with suspected chickenpox and somehow the message had never reached her parents. The doors to the house had been locked—Bea never had a key of her own—and so she'd walked around to the drawing room, peering in through the windows. The sight of her parents and sisters having dinner together had made her heart ache in an unforgettable way. It had been easy to lie to herself until that night, to make excuses for why she was treated one way and her sisters another, but seeing them enveloped in the warmth of their home, the focus of such obvious parental love, had made the literal point to Bea that she was an outsider.

It had made her see that she had never had that. Not from her biological parents, and not from the parents who'd adopted her. No one had ever wrapped her into their warm embrace and made her feel as though she was special and irreplaceable.

She'd never looked to her family for affection again, nor did she seek it from anyone else. Being on her own was better, easier and infinitely safer.

The helicopter circled lower to the ground. The full moon shone on the coastline, showing the ocean as a shimmering expanse of black with a silver trail through its centre and, along the shore, set several miles apart, a handful of houses. The helicopter headed towards one that was boxy and modern, elegant lighting illuminating the sides in a warm glow that was somehow at odds with the stark white walls. A swimming pool was lit with turquoise lights, lending it the impression of a five-star resort. The helicopter came lower, confirming the fact that this was Ares's house, landing squarely on the rooftop.

The helicopter had barely touched down before he had

unbuckled his seatbelt and was standing, moving to the door at the side. Bea couldn't take her eyes from him. He was completely absorbed, focused only on reaching home and finding out what had happened. She unbuckled her own seatbelt, the fierce throb of disappointment in her body not worthy of her in that moment. There were far greater things to worry about.

'What happened?' he demanded as he moved from the stairs and into the living room. He had to speak loudly to be heard above the infant's screaming. Every two seconds the little baby paused to suck in a gulp of air, then made a bubbling sound as she pushed it out, wailing into the night. If he allowed himself to feel fear he knew it would overtake him, so he refused to admit the possibility that something could be physically wrong with Danica. Not on his watch.

'She will not stop crying,' Xanthia said in Greek.

Despite the fact he'd barely spoken to her since leaving Venice, Ares was ever conscious of Bea just behind him, and switched effortlessly to English. 'What caused this?'

'Nothing.' Xanthia did the same, herself fluent in many languages, a prerequisite to the job as he required his housekeeper to oversee the management of his properties in various countries. 'She had a bath and then refused her evening meal. When Cassandra attempted to put her to bed she began to wail, and nothing could calm her.'

'Why?' he asked with obvious disbelief. 'Shouldn't she be tired?'

Xanthia pursed her lips and looked at him as though he were an idiot and, to be fair, in that moment he felt like one. But shouldn't this be easy? Weren't babies supposed to just need food and sleep?

He ground his teeth together, the sense of inadequacy overwhelming. 'For God's sake, has she been like this the whole time?'

'Yes,' Xanthia confirmed, rocking the baby from side to side, which only caused Danica to scream more loudly.

'You said she didn't eat—' the voice came from behind him '—could she be hungry?'

Xanthia's green eyes turned to Bea, appraising her quickly. 'She is only little. Dinner consists of some spoons of cereal and a bottle of milk.'

'Nonetheless,' Bea continued, moving towards the baby. Despite the screams, the gentle rustle of her skirts reached his ears, reminding him of the way they'd felt bunched in his hands. He formed a fist at his side, an act of determination, a refusal to be distracted by his body's base impulses. Bea lifted a hand to the baby's head, checking for a temperature.

'She's warm,' Bea said gently. 'But that's probably because she's so agitated.' She held her hands out. 'May I?'

Xanthia's jaw dropped. 'Oh, please. I have been holding her for hours. Please, yes, take her.'

'Would you go and prepare her bottle?' Bea prompted, taking the baby and barely flinching at the noise. Without lifting her attention from Danica's face, she addressed him. 'Ares, I think a cool facecloth might help to calm her. Would you get one?'

He stared at her, totally unprepared for this turn of events. He'd expected Bea to fade into the background at best, or, at worst, be something of an inconvenience if she'd continued to fight with him about coming to his home, but her cool manner and air of control knocked him sideways.

Even Danica seemed mildly less hysterical in Bea's arms.

'Yes, of course,' he said belatedly, turning on his heel to fetch what she'd asked for. He noticed as he waited for the cloth to dampen sufficiently that he wasn't wearing his tuxedo jacket. It was still wrapped around Bea's shoulders. The thought tightened his body, making him far more aware of her as a woman than was appropriate, given the circumstances.

He entered the lounge at the same moment Xanthia did, and both stopped walking and simply stared at each other.

Danica was silent. Not quite, he amended. She was making lots of little breathy noises, rapid and urgent, as she calmed down from so much screaming. Her cheeks were mottled pink and tear-stained, her hair damp from crying, her nose sticky with snot, but she was no longer wailing.

As he approached, he heard Bea's voice, soft and gentle, singing words in a language he didn't know, like English but different. Almost elvish, reminding him of Middle-Earth.

'Oh, my ears,' Xanthia whispered, smiling broadly, her dark grey hair piled high on her head in a loose bun, frazzled after hours of trying to console a screaming child.

He held out the facecloth to Bea but she shook her head. 'She's cooler now that she's stopped crying. Perhaps a tissue though?'

He nodded without moving, simply standing, awestruck at the sight of someone so completely *comfortable* with the child. Not since Danica had arrived at his house had he seen her actually seem halfway to peaceful.

Xanthia held the bottle out to Bea. She took it, returning to singing as she looked around. Her eyes momentarily met Ares's and something passed between them, something fierce and intractable, a magnetic force that demanded acknowledgement. He ground his teeth together, jabbing one hand into his pocket.

'The tissue,' she reminded him with a pointed look and the hint of a smile, jolting him into action.

'Right, the tissue,' he repeated, still reluctant to leave the scene. He bypassed Xanthia, pausing beside her. 'You should go to bed. Thank you for holding the fort tonight. I'm in your debt.'

'Of course, Ares,' she said with a shake of her head, switching back to Greek. 'The poor little dove simply couldn't be settled. Not until you showed up with the baby whisperer. This nanny shows much more promise than the other.'

He was about to correct her but, instead, Xanthia's words settled inside his chest, landing there with a soft thud. *This nanny.* He cast a glance over his shoulder.

It was easy to see why Xanthia would have made that mistake. Despite her formal dress, Beatrice was unmistakably at home holding the baby...

'Where's her nursery?' she whispered, stroking the darling little infant's shoulder with the pad of her thumb.

Ares had been standing, watching for the twenty minutes it had taken to feed Danica and rock her slowly to sleep. 'I'll show you.'

Bea stood slowly—it had been years since she'd held a baby, though it was surprising to realise how easily it all came flooding back. Memories of helping her friend Priti with late-night feeds and colicky tantrums filled her with confidence. This, though, was different.

Holding Danica, feeding her, lulling her to sleep, had caused something to flicker to life inside Bea that had caught her completely off-guard. A stirring of maternal instincts she absolutely didn't expect and definitely didn't want. She'd decided a long time ago that she was *never* having children.

She walked beside him and, without the ticking time bomb of a furiously upset infant, was able to take in the details of his palatial home. It was a temple to modernity, all crisp white walls, polished cement floors with Danish-style furniture. The only concession to colour came in the form of abstract paintings which hung in niches along the walls, lit with art-gallery-style spotlights. The stairs were highly polished wood. As Ares walked ahead of her Bea had a perfect view of his powerful legs and firm bottom and the sight of both made her mouth go dry.

She looked away, concentrating only on her steps, one after the other, holding Danica close to her chest so that she would stay comforted and warm.

Ares paused on the landing, pointing to an open door a little down the hall. Bea walked towards it, trying not to speculate on which of these doors might lead to his room. The nursery was a guest bedroom with a cot in the corner and a rocking chair by the window. Bea stood above the cot for a moment, singing 'Calon Lân' to Danica, gently lowering her over the sheet. She startled a little, so Bea placed her on the mattress quickly then held her hand on Danica's tummy, reassuring her she was still there, lifting her fingers lightly, gradually, until it was clear that Danica had settled. She turned to Ares and smiled, overcome with shyness now, uncertain what to say.

Nothing within the baby's earshot, that was for sure! What the poor little thing needed more than anything was a good night's sleep.

As she stepped through the door, Ares pressed his hand to her back, guiding her towards the stairs. The lightest touch made her nerves go haywire. She moved a little ahead of him on the steps, her own hand seeking the reassuring firmness of the railing.

In the lounge, he strode across the room, throwing open the glass doors and quirking a brow by way of silent invitation. Bea hesitated a moment, then moved in his direction, keeping her face averted as she brushed past him.

It was cool outside; she was grateful to still have his jacket on. Salt filled the air; the sound of rolling waves made a gentle background rhythm.

'You're good with kids.'

She turned to face him, a tight smile on her face. 'She

was just overwrought. Babies don't always know how to calm themselves down; they need us to do it for them.'

He shook his head dismissively. 'The nanny I hired came highly recommended but she couldn't manage Danica. No one could.'

'I find that impossible to believe.'

'I'm not making it up.'

She tilted her head. 'I'm not saying that. It's just—she's just a baby, Ares. She's—did you say five months old?'

He nodded once.

'That's so little! And she's had a lot of change in her life so far. Babies are more perceptive than people realise.'

'And you are the only one who can calm her,' he said quietly.

'That's not true.'

'How did you know what to do?'

Her smile was tinged with the best kinds of memories— sweet ones, those that were solely good. 'When I was at university, my flatmate Priti fell pregnant. It was a one-night stand, completely unexpected. The dad wasn't in the picture. She really wanted to be able to keep studying and, seeing as we were doing the same course, we came up with a schedule for school work and baby-minding. It was a crazy time.' Bea laughed softly, recalling the madness of it. 'I'd go to lectures and record them for her, we'd cram over buckets of soaking laundry—nappies and bibs—and study while Nikki slept. She wasn't an easy baby. In fact, I'd say she was downright difficult. Some nights it would take hours to get her to sleep. *Hours*, no exaggeration. Some babies are just like that,' she said with a shrug.

When he didn't respond, she rushed to fill the silence. 'If it's any consolation, I can assure you that that difficult baby is now a confident, intelligent pre-teen who rarely has a temper tantrum and absolutely sleeps through the night, so it does get easier.'

Ares seemed to stiffen. 'Hopefully she won't be my problem for much longer.'

Bea's lips parted on a soft sound of outrage, her expression full of chastisement. 'That's no way to talk about your niece.'

He winced at the reprimand. 'Ever since she arrived she has been like this. Screaming. Red-faced. Angry.'

In spite of his words, Bea smiled. 'She wasn't angry. Misunderstood is a better way to describe her.'

'I paid a nanny to understand her.'

'It doesn't sound like that worked out very well.'

'Cassandra clearly wasn't the right choice.'

'Apparently not.'

The silence between them throbbed and every second that passed did something to Bea. She felt herself being pulled towards him, as though a ribbon was wrapped around her, dragging her closer. She resisted it, but the effort it took was monumental.

'My brother is likely to be in hospital for another few weeks.'

Bea frowned at the swift conversation-change.

'I need someone to help with Danica while she's with me.'

'Perhaps you can find a nanny who has more experience with unsettled babies? It's quite a specific skillset, but if you let the agency know—'

He shook his head, moving towards her with urgency. 'I'm not going to contact the agency again.'

Bea looked confused. 'Then how will you find someone?'

Ares pressed a finger to her lips, silencing her as he'd done in the office earlier that day. Had it really only been a day? 'I've already found her.'

Bea stared up at him, unable to think straight when he was so close.

'Danica is a difficult child, you're right. But you were able to calm her easily.'

'That's just experience.'

'It's experience I need.'

She stared up at him, her expression wary. He couldn't possibly be suggesting…? 'You do realise I have a job?'

His eyes glittered with ruthless determination. 'Unfortunately, *agápi mou*, you showed your hand too early.'

Bea was silent.

'We both know what my business means to the London Connection.'

Her heart stammered, her jaw dropping in surprise.

'And we both know you'll do almost anything to keep me happy.'

'Ares,' she whispered, a plea in her voice, 'I was happy to help you tonight, but I can't just walk out of my job—my real job—to play babysitter. No matter how cute the baby is.' Or how sexy the uncle, she added mentally.

'Unfortunately, I'm desperate. Otherwise I'd never think of blackmailing you into staying here for the month.'

'A *month*?' she repeated on a wave of something that was terrifyingly like excitement.

'My brother's treatment will take a few weeks, at least. Let's say a month, to be safe.'

'We can't "say" anything, Ares. I'm not agreeing to this.'

'Of course you are,' he dismissed easily. 'You have no choice.'

She shook her head.

He made a frustrated sound. 'I would prefer not to bully you into this, Beatrice. Stay because we—I—need your help. Because I must do whatever it takes to help Danica. Stay because it's the right thing to do, just like it was the right thing to help Priti finish her degree. Stay because I am desperate.' He moved closer, his body finishing the intoxicating job his words had started. 'Stay because you want to finish what we started on the boat tonight, and a month gives us ample time to do that.'

Her stomach squeezed on an exhilarating wave of hope and need, but her brain was reluctantly firing to life. Disbelief hit her. On the gondola he'd been offering one night, not a whole month of them… Alarm bells sounded at the intimacy of that. It was all impossible. 'It's not that simple. I can't just click my fingers and walk out of my life.'

His nostrils flared; it was obvious Ares Lykaios was not used to hearing the word no. She'd expected him to kiss her in an attempt to persuade her, or to throw money at her, or maybe even to remind her of the blackmail angle. Instead, he addressed the realities of making this work.

'I do a lot of work from here. I have office space to spare, with all the latest facilities and technology, excellent Wi-Fi, and if you're worried about how you'll manage Danica and whatever work you cannot pass off to someone else then we can work around that.' He paused a moment, lost in thought. 'Xanthia told me of a girl in the village who babysits. She can come and help during the days—so long as you agree to step in if there's a problem—so that you have time to yourself. Deal?'

She wanted to say no, just to thwart him, because he was moving the pieces of her life so effortlessly, showing such control and intuition.

But that ribbon around her chest was being tugged again, drawing her to him, showing her a glimpse of a more impulsive life. Weren't Amy and Clare always telling her to follow her instincts more? To listen to her gut? Well, both her instincts and gut were telling her to jump first, look later. They'd been telling her the same thing all night. And now Ares was making it easy for her to do just that.

'What is the expression about having cake and eating it as well?'

She lifted a hand to his chest, tempted beyond words. 'To have one's cake and eat it too,' she supplied, distracted.

'Exactly. Isn't this a way to do that?'

She sighed. 'It's...complicated.' The kiss they'd shared on the gondola felt like a lifetime ago—as though it had happened to a wholly different person. She couldn't believe how free she'd felt then!

'Why?'

Embarrassment rolled through her. She dropped her gaze, unable to look directly at him. 'I'm not someone who just casually...gets involved in relationships.'

He was quiet and, despite the fact they'd only known each other a short time, she knew exactly how he'd be looking at her, appraising her, trying to understand what she wasn't saying. Nerves flew like butterflies inside her belly.

'I mean, I never have before.'

She risked a glance at him; he was frowning.

'Been in a relationship?' he prompted. 'Let me reassure you, Beatrice, I'm not offering anything serious. This would be a strictly short-term arrangement.'

Her lips twisted in a half-smile. 'I don't mean that. I mean... I've never...' But she couldn't finish the sentence. She was twenty-nine and had never had sex. That didn't usually bother Bea, but now she found it mortifying to confess.

'What is it?' he pressed. 'Are you trying to tell me you're a virgin or something?'

Her stomach swooped but she knew there was no sugar-coating it. Tilting her chin defiantly, she forced her eyes to meet his. 'Yes. That's exactly what I'm telling you. I'm a twenty-nine-year-old virgin. Are you sure you still want to make sex a part of what you're offering?'

CHAPTER SEVEN

ALL THE AIR evacuated his lungs at once. He felt as though her words were rattling through his ears like a freight train on a looped track. It didn't make sense.

'You said you're twenty-nine.'

She fidgeted her hands at her sides, not meeting his eyes.

'And prior to taking up your role at the London Connection you were a senior partner in a law firm?'

'A top tier firm,' she confirmed, in that habit she had of babbling a little when she was nervous.

He nodded anyway, taking the titbit of information and filing it away.

'You are an intelligent, beautiful and kind woman. Twenty-nine years old. And yet you've never slept with a man?'

Her cheeks were bright pink and it was an unfortunate consequence of the situation that he found that mesmerising. His desire increased rather than doing what he wanted—and abating completely at her pronouncement.

But the way they'd kissed on the boat, the way her body had moved over his, her hips pushing down on his masculine strength, showing with her body how much she needed him... 'So you've never had sex with a man,' he said with narrowed eyes. 'But you've obviously had some experience with other elements of lovemaking.'

Her throat moved in a delicate knot as she swallowed. 'You want my dating résumé now?'

'I think I'm entitled to some explanation.' It wasn't exactly the truth—he didn't feel entitled to anything, but he *wanted* an explanation and he hoped she'd give one.

Her eyes lifted to his, her mouth parting on a small sigh before she bit down on her lower lip. 'It's not a big deal.'

'I beg to differ.'

Hurt washed over her features; he regretted the words instantly. Hell, he was out of his comfort zone by about a thousand feet.

'I didn't intentionally mislead you. I didn't go to Venice expecting anything to happen between us. It was just work for me, nothing more. The gondola ride...' Her eyes assumed a faraway look as she tried to draw in breath. His gut rolled with a desire to kiss her. He stood his ground, his body like stone. He couldn't—wouldn't—give in to his instincts now. Not until he understood exactly what he was dealing with. A reformed nun? A runaway cult member? The idea of a twenty-nine-year-old virgin in this day and age beggared belief.

'The gondola ride was a total surprise. Put it down to the magic of the moonlight or something.' She laughed uneasily, awkwardly. 'And, as you know, coming back here wasn't on my agenda. You kidnapped me, remember?'

He remembered every detail of the evening they'd shared, and he knew this part would be forged in his memory banks in particularly vivid detail. 'Was your intention to save yourself for marriage?'

Her face scrunched up in a visceral reaction to that statement, a reaction he would have found amusing under any other circumstances. 'Don't be absurd. I'm never getting married.'

'That makes two of us. So what then?'

She closed her eyes, tilting her head towards the ceiling at the same time. 'Do we have to talk about this?'

'Help me understand and then I'll let it go.'

He had no real right to make demands of her, and yet Ares knew himself well enough to know he wouldn't rest until he understood. He liked things to make sense and this, quite simply, didn't.

'Is it really that big a deal? I just never met anyone I wanted to have sex with, that's all.'

'You didn't go through puberty?' he asked sceptically. 'It's my experience that at a certain point in everyone's lives hormones take control.'

She spun away from him and his fingers tensed with the desire to reach out and grab her, to turn her back to him, to pull her against his chest and listen to the rest of her explanation with her breasts crushed to him, her breath warming his throat. He ignored those instincts, aware that they were part of what had got them here in the first place.

'I was studying my backside off at an all girls school,' she said stiffly, sounding ever so prim. 'I didn't have time for boys.'

Despite himself, he smiled. He could imagine her saying exactly that to any friends who'd tried to lead her astray at the time. 'At university then?'

'Same deal, Ares. I studied. All the time. Some people seemed to be there to socialise, but not me. I worked hard and in any spare time I did have, I was helping Priti with the baby. I graduated with a first, and was offered a graduate role to start that summer.'

'And you didn't date that whole time?'

Her eyes sparked with something when they met his. 'I wasn't *interested* in dating. I wasn't interested in men. I wasn't interested in being lied to, told I was the love of someone's life just so they could get me into bed. I've seen it happen enough times to my friends to know that's the drill. I saw the way heartbreak torpedoed their lives and chose to avoid that for myself. Men, frankly, suck.'

Her words whirled around him. It was a speech laced with bravado, but he heard the hurt that underscored it. 'Heartbreak and sex don't have to go hand in hand. I'm sorry you've missed out on something so wonderful for so many years, simply because you were afraid.'

'I'm not afraid,' she rejected, so quickly it was obvious she hadn't given it a moment's thought.

For Ares, it was all he needed to push home his advantage. He hadn't realised he'd been laying the pieces of a trap—he'd played to win without even intending to—and now it was set.

'If that is true, you'll consider my proposition more seriously.'

Her eyes widened; he could feel her temptation.

'I will not break your heart, Bea, because I don't want it. I will not make you promises, I will not lie to you. I'm offering only sex.' His lips twisted with a hint of mockery. 'Nothing more complicated than that.'

He could feel her wavering, her certainties eroding, but it was too soon to celebrate. Too soon to rejoice in the fact that he would make her his. A heady rush of adrenaline at the prospect of being her first lover flooded his veins, but it wasn't time to act on it yet. She was staring at him appraisingly, a battle clearly being waged inside her mind.

'I think it would be foolish to stay here,' she said stiffly, so whatever jubilation he'd been feeling a moment earlier evaporated. But Ares Lykaios intended to win and there were two objectives for him that evening.

'Oh, make no mistake about it, you're staying here, Beatrice. At least you are if you value my business at the London Connection.'

He knew it was beneath him, but desperation to find someone who could help with Danica forced his hand there.

'I don't believe you,' she whispered. 'One minute you're asking me to make love to you and the next you're black-mailing me?'

'Not to sleep with me. Only to look after Danica,' he clarified, as though that made it any better. Since when had he become someone who stooped to this level? The answer was simple. On the streets of Athens, broke and starving, he'd done things as a teenager he knew to be reprehensible. Things that were against his strict moral code, all to ensure Matthaios's survival. He'd stolen food from grocery stores—not a lot, just enough to survive, but it had offended every cell in his body to do it. He'd hated that their impoverished state had required it of him. On one occasion he'd even stolen money from a tourist. A ten-euro note had been sticking out of her pocket, so close to falling. He'd walked behind her, waiting for it to drop and, when it hadn't, he'd brushed past her and taken it, aware that the money could make all the difference to Matt. He'd done what he'd needed to protect his brother, and now he was doing what he needed to protect Danica.

He didn't have to like himself for it though.

'Just to be stranded in this luxurious fortress for a whole month?'

He ground his teeth together. 'Think of it as an assign-ment.'

'I'm a lawyer. I don't get "assignments".'

'You're also a senior member of the London Connec-tion, aren't you?'

'Stop banging me over the head with that,' she demanded haughtily. 'You don't need to keep reminding me of your importance to the company, and I'm well aware of the com-pany's importance to me.' Her gaze clashed with his, cold anger stirring in their depths. 'But if you knew me, Ares, if you'd listened to anything I've said tonight, you would have known how unnecessary it was to go to such crude, bullying means to achieve your ends.'

He felt as though a boulder was pressing down on his chest, but didn't visibly react to her condemnation.

'I told you how I put my whole life on hold to help Priti with her baby. Tonight, at the ball, I spent an hour with a little girl I didn't know just because I felt sorry for her. You could have pleaded with me on Danica's behalf and won me over. You didn't need to show yourself to be such a callous bastard.'

She sniffed, a sound of anger not sadness.

Provoked into responding with total honesty, he spoke unapologetically. 'I had to be sure of your cooperation. I could have played on your sympathy, certainly, but then you might have said no. In my experience, people are always motivated by money.'

She laughed dismissively. 'It's not *money* that's motivating me, you idiot. It's basic human decency, and love. Love for Clare and Amy and the business they've built up. Love for the clients they take care of with every breath in their bodies.' She pushed her hands onto her hips, looking at him as though he were scum. 'Even *you*,' she said witheringly. 'To think, Clare works her butt off for you and this is how you behave!'

Strange that earlier that very same day she'd gasped any time she said anything approaching an insult, apologising profusely. There was no sign of apology in her face now, just scathing condemnation.

It stirred an ache in his gut he'd never felt before.

'I take it that means you'll stay?'

Her eyes swept shut, her features taut and skin pale. 'Obviously.' The word was seething with disgust. He felt every measure of it in the core of his being.

'But as for sleeping with you,' she said coldly, moving

towards him, pressing a finger to his chest. 'That's something I no longer have any interest in doing.'

It was a split-second decision. No, there was no decision-making about it. He acted purely on instinct, the same instinct that had seen him steal out of desperation as a starving teenager—he wasn't proud of it; it showed his darker side—roared to life now. He took hold of her finger, moving her hand to their sides, his eyes flashing with intention before he acted, his mouth claiming hers. Not like on the gondola—this wasn't a kiss of gentle, moonlit exploration, with waves splashing at their side. This was a kiss of desperate anger, a kiss of dominance, a kiss designed to entreat submission. Other than his hand holding her finger, he didn't touch her anywhere else. His mouth ravaged hers and she moaned, her body swaying forward, her abdomen pressing to his arousal. She made a low, keening noise as he grew harder against her, a whimper, and then a plea in his mouth.

How easy it would have been to take it further, to undress her and show her the full extent of her dishonesty. But Ares knew his limits, and he'd already stretched them well beyond an acceptable level. He broke his mouth free, staring down at her with darkly glittering eyes.

'You can lie to yourself all you want, Beatrice. Tell yourself you do not want to sleep with me, if you like. But don't lie to me, or I will take great pleasure in showing you the truth.' He stalked across the room, picking up the airphone and speaking a few words into it. He had his back to her—time he desperately needed to cool his temper and put a halt to the raging blood in his body. When he turned to face her, shame washed over him. She was shaking like a leaf, so pale and fragile-looking. Regret chewed through him, but he refused to show any form of weakness. 'A member of staff is on their way to show you to your room. Goodnight, Beatrice.'

* * *

She wanted to strangle him. She wanted to put her hands around his throat and strangle him for what he'd done, but at the same time her anger was really all directed at herself. Her stupidity in kissing him back, in immediately begging him to make love to her. The way she'd pleaded with him, over and over, his name moving from her mouth to his, begging him for so much more than a kiss, wanting satisfaction and fulfilment as she never had before.

He'd been right about hormones. That was all this was. Some kind of pre-programmed biological response. Her oestrogen responding to his testosterone, causing a hurricane of desire she'd been unable to ignore.

All night she lay in the luxurious bed, staring at the ceiling, trying to work out if he'd carry out his threat if she were to leave. He was hugely important to the London Connection but it wasn't a one-way street. They were important to him too. He wasn't a man to suffer fools so, without knowing the details of previous PR campaigns and the ongoing management they did for his various business interests, she had to believe Clare was doing an excellent job for him. Surely he wouldn't rip his business away simply because she'd said no to helping him with a baby—a job for which, despite what he might think, she was manifestly unsuited.

Except, at the same time, Bea had to acknowledge there was a risk. Although the London Connection was fast gaining recognition for its client management, there were other firms out there that had been established for much longer, that had more resources, bigger teams, larger reach. How many of the London Connection's clients had come across to them simply because they had someone like Ares Lykaios on their books?

It wasn't just about losing Ares's business then, but about losing the prestige that came from his association with them. Beatrice couldn't be responsible for that, and yet she was sorely tempted to roll the dice and see what happened. Despite his words, there was a part of her that suspected he was bluffing. She couldn't say why, but she had an undeniable faith in his inherent goodness and fairness—it was incompatible with his threat, and yet she felt almost certain that if she were to tell him she was leaving his home—come what may—he'd let her go, and continue working with Clare regardless.

But being almost certain wasn't good enough.

She prevaricated all night, veering from one opinion to the other. She tossed and turned and, somewhere in the early hours of the morning, before the sun had started its ascent into the night sky over Greece's Argolic Gulf, she gave up on trying to sleep and pushed out of bed. Her ballgown was where she'd left it—hardly suitable attire, but for lack of other options…

She had a quick shower and as she reached for a towel she saw that some clothes had been left folded on the cupboard beside the linen. The trousers were a size too big; she had to knot them at the waist to keep them from falling down, but the shirt—long-sleeved and a pale yellow in colour—was a perfect fit. She finger-combed her hair and rubbed a scented moisturiser over her face, regretting that sleep deprivation had left two brown smudges beneath her eyes, then defiantly reminding herself she didn't care.

She moved through the house, intending to hunt down a coffee, but a noise stopped her. Crying.

Baby crying.

Her feet moved towards the sound quickly and silently, piecing together the route to Danica's room. It wasn't easy. The house was huge and she'd been turned around by everything that had happened after she'd put Danica to bed. The crying grew louder though, leading her there, and she pushed the door inwards without hesitation, without a pause for what she might find on the other side.

It certainly wasn't this.

Ares stood dressed in only a low-slung towel, his chest bare, his hair damp, the crying infant in his arms. A lamp had been turned on near the bed, casting them both in a warm glow.

Bea's heart thumped painfully at the sight. He turned to look at her, his dark eyes defensive and then utterly bleak.

The baby howled. Bea held her ground, unable to move.

'Beatrice…' His voice was thick, groggy. 'Please…stay. We need your help.'

CHAPTER EIGHT

BY LUNCHTIME HER HEAD was swimming.

Leave a baby to cry it out. Never leave a baby crying longer than a minute. Leave them to cry but stay in the room so they can see you at all times. Put toys above the bed to distract them and comfort them. Never over-stimulate a baby at bedtime: remove all toys from their line of sight.

So much contradictory advice, all from reputable-seeming parenting authorities, none of them particularly good at agreeing about how to soothe an unsettled baby.

'And you've definitely ruled out medical factors?' she asked, tapping her pen against the thick pile of pages she'd printed off the internet. Going back to her law school roots, she'd spent Danica's fitful daytime naps with a highlighter and notepad, intending to distil what she'd presumed would be a sort of parenting manual onto paper—a guide for both of them to ease Danica into a better routine.

'Cassandra had her checked over by several paediatricians,' he said darkly. 'None could find anything wrong with her.'

'Well, that's good,' Bea said, returning her attention to the pages because it was preferable to looking at Ares. She was still angry with him, she reminded herself, even when the image of him shirtless and comforting Danica was now imprinted on her eyeballs. 'With Nikki, it was just about routine,' Bea murmured thoughtfully. 'If we missed her naptime by even ten minutes, she'd be a nightmare for days. It was hard because Priti and I were both trying to study, but we ran the house like clockwork. It meant we could have a semblance of a normal life,' Bea concluded. 'I wonder if Danica is the same?'

Ares's only response was to lift—by a degree of millimetres—his shoulders.

Bea compressed her lips. 'Did Danica's nanny keep to a tight schedule?' she prompted.

Something flickered in Ares's face. 'I don't know.'

'Well, were her daytime naps all at roughly the same time? What about bedtime?'

'I am not someone who sticks to a strict routine,' he said eventually. 'The reason I hired a nanny who was so highly regarded was because I'm often away from home. Xanthia would be better placed to answer any questions about that.'

Bea shouldn't have been surprised. She tried to keep the judgement from her expression but unfortunately his remark hit way too close to home. How familiar that was to her! The notion of an adoptive parent outsourcing the parenting and consoling themselves with the fact that they'd hired 'the best'. Ares wasn't Danica's adoptive father but he was her uncle, and he was—for the moment—her closest family.

Ice chilled her heart as her own experience of familial rejection spiked through her, paining her all over again.

'I'll speak to Xanthia then.' She scraped her chair back, walking towards the door with a spine that was ramrod-straight. Unusually for Bea, she had the strangest sense she might cry.

'Wait.' His voice was commanding and insistent. Oh, how she'd have loved to ignore it! But that would be petulant and childish, and she refused to indulge either emotion.

She half turned to face him, her neck swan-like, her brown hair piled onto her head in a loose bun.

'What time will you put her to bed tonight?'

Bea had drawn up a schedule which seemed to contain a lot of overlap from the various parenting sites and books. 'Six-thirty. Why?'

'Once she is asleep, we'll go to Athens.'

She gave up on the half-turn and spun back to face him completely. 'What for?'

'You're here for a month. You'll need more to wear than a ballgown and Xanthia's husband's clothes.'

Bea looked down at the misshapen outfit with a raised brow. 'Really? I had wondered...'

'Meet me on the roof at seven.'

Bea pursed her lips, jolted back to the present. 'I can't do that.'

A scowl darkened his face.

'I don't know if she'll go to sleep straight away, and if she doesn't I'm not going to leave her to have another exhausting and traumatic screaming episode. It's not fair to Xanthia either.'

Tension arced between them, an argument in their eyes, and then finally he relented—after all, he could afford to lose the battle. He'd already won the war. 'I'll be waiting. Come up when you are ready.'

Bea should have been relieved that Danica went to sleep so easily. Surely that was a good sign that something about the routine she'd implemented was working? In the end, she'd followed her instincts. An early dinner, a warm, lightly fragranced bath, a calm book-reading in an almost dark room, followed by a bottle with Bea singing softly as Danica fed, a quiet cuddle and burp and then into bed. Bea kept her hand on Danica's chest lightly, as she'd done the night before, watching as the baby's beautiful blue eyes grew heavy and finally dropped closed, her breathing rhythmic as sleep swallowed her.

Xanthia was hovering on the other side of the door, her face lined with worry.

'She's asleep,' Bea whispered.

Xanthia's look of shock brought a smile to Bea's face. 'Already? But…how? It isn't possible!'

'She was tired, I think,' Bea said with a shrug. 'I've switched the monitor on. You'll keep an eye on her?'

'Of course, of course.' Xanthia was glowing. She looked as though she wanted to hug Bea. Instead, she clapped her hands together. 'Peace, at last! I have been so sad for the little girl—so much heartbreak and no one—' Xanthia cut herself off abruptly. 'I'm glad she has you.'

Strangely, so was Bea. Despite the fact it had only been one day, so much had happened that her London life already felt strangely distant. Almost as though she was looking at it through a sort of screen.

'Ares asked me to remind you he's waiting,' Xanthia added belatedly, as though just remembering the reason for being stationed outside Danica's door.

'Like I could forget,' Bea muttered. 'Please call if anything happens with the baby. I don't want her to be upset like she was last night.'

Xanthia nodded. 'Tomorrow morning, Ellen will come. A girl I know from the village. She has two younger brothers and three younger sisters, all of whom she helped raise. You'll like her.'

It had only been hours since she'd last seen him, but Bea still felt a jolt of something like awe at the sight of Ares Lykaios when she pushed open the door to the rooftop helipad some ten minutes later. He wore a suit that must have been made for his body, the darkest navy blue with a crisp white shirt open at the throat. He was designer, delicious and dangerous. Far too handsome for any one man.

Butterflies burst through Bea's belly and her legs were unsteady as she walked towards the gleaming black helicopter. As she approached, he lifted the aviator-style sunglasses from his eyes, hooking them in the top of his shirt and pinning her with a gaze that hollowed out what was left of her tummy.

'She's asleep?'

Bea nodded. She wanted to stay cross with him, to remember that he was palming off the care of his infant niece to a virtual stranger, and that he'd blackmailed her into being here, but at the same time images of him in just a towel, comforting Danica in the small hours of the morning, showed that to be a lie. He did love the baby, and he was doing what he could to care for her. He simply felt bewildered by the enormity of being thrust into the role of parenthood out of nowhere. Relenting, she offered him a cool half-smile. 'She seemed tired. Hopefully she'll sleep well.'

His relief was obvious. 'Thank you.'

And because she'd heard the helplessness in his voice that morning, when it had been just the two of them in Danica's nursery, she understood the depths of his gratitude.

'You're welcome.'

The air between them seemed to spark with awareness, or perhaps that was all coming from Bea. Close to Ares, alone on the rooftop, she wanted more than anything to feel the strength of his body close to hers once more, to lift her face to his and have him kiss her as though that were the most normal and natural thing in the world. And maybe it was—for other people. But not for Bea. She'd never wanted a relationship with a man, and even the kind of relationship he had suggested seemed fraught with danger.

Dragging her eyes away from his with determination, she realised they weren't in fact alone. A man in dark trousers and a pale shirt opened the door to the helicopter, smiling at Bea in an invitation for her to step inside. She took the same seat she'd occupied the night before, presuming Ares would do the same, but before he sat down he hovered over her, reaching for the straps of her seatbelt and fastening it into place, just as he'd done on the plane. Her breath held, her gaze was drawn to his face as if by magnetic force. She couldn't look away.

He pulled the seatbelt tight, his fingers lingering at her hip as he lifted his attention to her face and she had to bite back a moan. Awareness crashed through her like a tidal wave, a desire she'd never known before pressing bright sparks of light into her eyes.

His gaze roamed lower, landing on her lips, so she remembered every single sensation of having him kiss her the night before, the way he'd plundered her mouth with his, proving a point. And he had proved that point—she wanted to sleep with him, no matter what she'd thrown at him in the anger of their fight.

Desire stormed through her blood; she was helpless to fight it.

She surrendered a part of herself in that moment, acknowledging how much she wanted him. She was taken back to the way she'd felt on the gondola, when she'd been tempted to throw all caution to the wind and experience, for the first time in her life, what sex was all about.

'Ares—'

His name on her lips was a plea, drawn from deep within her.

And he understood. She saw it on his face that he knew how she felt, and what she wanted. So it made absolutely no sense when he stepped back, taking the seat across from her, his expression neutral as he buckled his own belt in place.

Her cheeks felt as though they'd caught fire. She stared

at him in disbelief, then blinked, turning her attention to the window. Uncertainty and need were looping through her. She felt completely out of her depth, an experience Bea had always hated.

Before she could contemplate pulling the pin on the whole idea of a shopping trip in Athens, the helicopter's blades began to whirl, the engine noise cutting out any possibility of conversation as the craft lifted up into the sky.

For a moment the view distracted her. The night before it had been pitch-black, and she'd spent the entire day enveloped in baby-related research. For the first time, as the helicopter took the trajectory of an eagle over the coastline, Bea realised how stunningly beautiful it was. The sun had not yet set but was on its way, painting the sky a dramatic palette of fiery oranges and pinks; the ocean below them was a deep turquoise, enhanced by the dusk light. She could see how sparsely populated the coastline was too, each house spaced several miles apart, each luxurious and modern, though Ares's most of all.

'Champagne?' The throaty-voiced offer had her turning to face him. A recognisable label on a piccolo bottle was being held towards her. She stared at it a moment before nodding, watching as he curled his palm around the cork and lifted it, the sound muted by his hand's tight grip. He placed a straw in the top, handing it across to Bea, and she took it gratefully.

'How long have you lived here?' she asked, simply to fill the silence—a silence that was throbbing with a drugging awareness.

'I bought the house ten years ago.' His lips twisted in a way that suggested to Bea he was concealing something.

'For any particular reason?' she asked.

'I liked it.'

She nodded thoughtfully. 'You look as though there's more to it than that.'

Surprise briefly flashed in his features and he was quiet for a moment, thinking, before he shifted his head once. 'When I was a boy I used to live just over there.' He pointed across the glittering bay to a small town on the water's edge. Unlike the sparsely populated coastal region where Ares's mansion stood, this village looked full to the brim, tightly packed houses jostling for space. 'My grandfather was a fisherman, and I'd go out with him sometimes. There were barely any houses here then. Two or three enormous sprawling homes that—to my eyes—looked like palaces.'

Bea sipped her champagne, listening intently.

'When I made my first billion American dollars I bought one of these homes.'

Bea gaped. 'Your first billion?' She shook her head a little ruefully. 'Exactly how many billions do you have?' She grimaced, regretting the forthright question immediately. 'Don't answer that. I shouldn't have asked.'

He flexed a brow. 'It's a matter of public record. I have no issue with you knowing.'

'Oh.'

'Current estimates put my wealth around the hundred-billion-dollar mark. It fluctuates a little, depending on international markets and world events.'

Bea blinked. 'I can't even imagine what that's like.'

A muscle jerked in his jaw. 'The thing about money is that once you have enough to feed yourself and your family, buy a secure home, a warm bed, it doesn't really change that much. There's not a huge difference between ten thousand dollars and ten billion, to my mind.'

Having lived through homelessness and poverty, Bea supposed he was uniquely placed to comment on that.

'You must have felt pretty damned good walking in that door for the first time though,' she said, nodding back towards his home, now a distant speck far beneath them.

'I felt better when I bought our first home, actually,' he said quietly.

'Our?'

'My brother, Matthaios, and mine. He was still at school. Back then I'd amassed what I thought was a fortune—spare change now, really, but to me, at the time, it was a king's ransom. Being able to buy an apartment outright, to know that, whatever happened, Matthaios would have somewhere safe to live—that was the best feeling I've ever known. This was enjoyable, but nothing will ever compare to that.'

'He's your younger brother?'

He nodded but his demeanour shifted, so that he seemed closed off and distant. 'He's two years younger.'

'You're close?'

A terse nod.

'You said he's sick?'

Ares's eyes flashed to hers, dark emotions tumbling through their depths. 'Yes.'

'I'm sorry. Is it serious?'

'It's a…lifelong condition.'

She frowned, sympathy tugging at her heart-strings.

He sighed heavily. 'My mother was a drug addict. My brother inherited her…tendencies. I should have realised sooner what was happening.' Self-directed anger thickened his voice. 'As teenagers, we had no money—he couldn't drink or do drugs; it simply wasn't an option. But, once things improved for us financially, he found it easy to procure whatever the hell he wanted.'

Bea's heart tightened.

'I worked a lot. I didn't see what was right in front of me, despite having witnessed my mother's addiction play out for years. I should have known he was losing himself to drugs, alcohol—whatever he could get his hands on.'

She shook her head to dispel the blame Ares was laying

at his own feet. 'You were working so you could support him,' she reminded Ares gently.

'That's no excuse. I should have realised.'

The helicopter changed direction, so that the ocean gave way to verdant land far below.

'By the time I saw what was happening, he was so far gone. It took years to convince him to go to rehab, and in the end I had to let him hit rock-bottom before he finally got there. You cannot imagine what that was like, Beatrice. Watching him self-destruct, knowing there was only so much I could do.'

Her throat shifted as she swallowed. Strangely, he didn't mind the sympathy on her face now.

'I could only keep him safe,' Ares admitted gruffly. 'I hired security to guard his house—and him—so that at least he was watched.' He shook his head angrily. 'They called me one morning when he wouldn't wake up. He'd come this close to an overdose.' He pinched his finger and thumb together.

'That's horrible,' she whispered.

He nodded. 'He spent two nights in hospital and then he chose to go to rehab. He begged me for help. I've never been gladder than I was in that moment.' He grimaced, because that happiness hadn't lasted long. As so often in life, a downfall had already begun to approach. 'He got sober, and turned his life around. He started an investment firm which did incredibly well, then met Ingrid and fell in love.' Ares's expression had assumed a faraway look and Bea knew that, though he was speaking aloud, he was really recounting the facts to himself, going over them as if he could make better sense of them somehow. 'Their wedding day was one of the happiest of my life. To know how far he'd come, to see the hope on his face, the love in his eyes… I felt…such immense relief, as though finally everything was going to be okay.'

'And then Ingrid died,' Bea said softly.

He lifted his eyes to her face, torment in his features. 'Yes. Ingrid died and my brother was left with a black hole of grief and a tiny, dependent child. I should have done more. I should have—'

Bea made a frustrated sound and leaned as far forward as she could, putting a hand on his thigh to draw his attention fully. 'You can't blame yourself for this.'

'Can't I?' he asked quietly, his voice still ringing with self-condemnation. 'I'd seen what he'd been through before. I'd seen my mother grapple with her demons for years. I knew how desperately he needed to blot out the pain. I should have done more to help him.'

'What more could you have done?' she asked logically.

Ares stared at her.

'He's a grown man. Your job isn't to live Matthaios's life for him, Ares. It sounds to me like you've done the best you can for your brother all your life, and you're still doing that now.'

'You don't understand. I should have seen what was coming. I should have predicted he'd turn back to drugs. I should have—'

'Kidnapped him to your mansion for all eternity?' she couldn't help teasing, despite the serious tenor of their conversation.

His eyes flared, showing surprise at her quip.

'You couldn't chain him up until his grief passed. And you couldn't watch him twenty-four hours a day. Did you support him, Ares? Did you call to check on him? Ask how he was, how the baby was?'

His face paled. 'I spent a month with him, after her death. Then I had dinner with him several times a week. I hired security, as before, to keep them both safe. I hired nannies—he fired them. But still I thought he was doing well, given the circumstances. He seemed heartbroken but well, at the same time. I looked for signs of addiction. I checked his house when he was occupied with Danica, and I called at unusual times, wondering if I would detect something in his voice that spoke of drug use or alcohol abuse. I detected *nothing*. I missed the signs.'

'Or maybe he was holding it together and then something happened and he had a bad few nights. Or maybe he was just that good at hiding his behaviour from you...' She paused, frustrated that he couldn't see how much help and support he'd offered. 'But look at what you've done for him now. He's getting treatment and help, and you've stepped in to care for Danica, so that when he comes out his beautiful baby will be waiting for him. If you hadn't done that she would have ended up in foster care, Ares. Do you have any idea what that would have meant? It would have been far from guaranteed that Matthaios would be able to take Danica back when he was ready. You've given him a second chance to be a father—that's something to be proud of.'

His gaze shifted to her hand, still on his thigh, and he looked at it for so long that her fingers began to tingle and warm. She was about to retract it when his own hand came down on hers, keeping it right where it was.

'You were adopted.'

The statement shattered something inside her. A shame Bea worked hard to rationalise away burst through her at the unexpectedness of his words, a shame that came from knowing how unwanted she was: by her birth parents first, by her adoptive parents ultimately. A sour taste flooded her mouth and she went to pull her hand away again, but he held on tightly, his eyes loaded with warning when they met hers. Under his intense scrutiny her pulse began to go haywire.

'So?' Her voice shook with defiance, dredged from deep within her soul. She didn't need anyone to love her; what did it matter that she'd been rejected by all the people who were meant to love her most? She'd worked herself into the ground to build her career, and she had Amy and Clare.

'I just wondered if you're speaking from experience.'

Her breath evacuated her lungs on one huge whoosh. 'No.'

She pulled away then and he let her. Bea tried to ignore the coldness spreading inside, and the fear that he was seeing more of her than she wanted him to—more than she'd ever let anyone see. To the world, Bea was an in-control lawyer, intelligent, bright and driven. No one needed to know the gaping wounds that existed in her heart, the feeling that there must be something inherently wrong with her to have been rejected so consistently. Her secret fear—that no one would ever love her or want her enough—was just beneath the surface, though

She wouldn't let Ares know how broken she was inside. For some reason he was the last person she wanted to see beyond her façade.

CHAPTER NINE

SHE WASN'T LIKE any woman he'd ever known. She'd shunned the high-end boutiques his chauffeur had brought them to, wrinkling her nose up at the clothes the assistants had suggested, repeatedly walking out empty-handed, despite his insistence that he wanted to furnish her with a wardrobe to get her through the month they'd agreed on.

Had they agreed? He couldn't precisely remember. The night before had gone as far from his expectations as possible, and yet somehow he had taken the fact that she was still here as tacit consent that she'd remain.

He'd wondered if she was just being contrary to spite him, but as they'd passed a department store she'd stopped walking and pressed a hand to his chest. 'Perfect. Wait here.'

He'd ignored her suggestion, following behind as Bea whipped through the chainstore's women's fashion offerings. She scooped up clothes as she went. A pair of jeans, a denim skirt, some shorts, several T-shirts in the same style and different colours, before turning around and pushing the selection into his arms.

'Hold these.' Her eyes challenged him. 'Do not follow me into the lingerie section, Ares. I mean it.'

Oh, how sorely tempted he was to do exactly that! But her innocence put him in an unusual position—torn be-

tween his desire for her and a need to tread gently, reminding himself that she wasn't like his usual lovers.

Oh, she was beautiful and smart, sophisticated and intelligent, but she was also a virgin, and for a man like Ares
who'd only ever offered one part of him to the women
he slept with—his body—surely that innocence made her
off-limits? All the more so because he couldn't offer her
more than a physical relationship. Sex. His temperature
skyrocketed and in the middle of the department store his
body grew hard, his arousal tight against the seam of his
trousers so he lowered the bundle of clothes a little. What
the hell was wrong with him? The fact she was a virgin
should have been a huge red flag. He shouldn't be interested in being her first, but hell, he wanted her regardless.

He hovered on the edge of the section, determined not to
look in her direction. Instead, he wandered, finding himself
amongst Lycra swimsuits and picking several out simply to
keep busy. The deep red bikini would complement Bea's
complexion, but so too the cream with gold straps. He ignored the black one-piece even when he knew, somehow,
that the bland, unflattering style was the one she would
have gone for. He returned to the clothing section then,
picking up a floral dress with a cinched-in waist and buttons down the front, adding it to the clothes she'd chosen,
before Bea approached him, already carrying a plastic bag
with the store's logo emblazoned on the front.

'Let's go pay for those,' she said, unable to meet his eyes.

His stomach clenched at her coyness. She'd bought the
underwear already, rather than risk him seeing them? It was
yet another reminder of how different she was to the kind
of women he usually dated—women who would happily
swan around semi-naked in silken lingerie.

He knew he shouldn't tease her, but he couldn't resist.
'Did you find what you were looking for?'

She nodded, reaching out for the clothes without looking, but he shook his head. 'I'll take care of it.'

'Then I'll go wait outside,' she said breathily, apparently desperate to escape.

He watched her make a beeline for the exit and then turned on his heel, heading back into the lingerie section. He had no doubt she'd chosen boring cotton panties and bras. That was fine. But Ares wanted to add something else to her wardrobe, something that she might wear and imagine him removing...

There was a meagre selection of sensual nightgowns in this family-friendly store, but he managed to find a slinky black negligee with lace detailing, and a matching pair of French lace panties. He whistled as he made his way to the checkout, unable to think of anything except Bea in sexy lingerie, against the sheets of his bed.

'We really should get back,' she said quietly, as much to herself as Ares. The truth was, she didn't want to return to his home just yet. Being in Athens with Ares, it was almost possible to forget what had happened the night before, the way he'd bullied her into staying with him, to help take care of Danica.

No, it wasn't that she'd forgotten. It was simply that the more time she spent with him, the more she understood him. She saw how motivated he was by his love for his brother, his desperate need to care for his family—and that included Danica. He'd move mountains to be sure the little girl was cared for, and last night Bea had represented the best chance for him to do that.

'We should eat,' he contradicted firmly, taking the bags from her hands and passing them to the waiting chauffeur. 'There is a nice French restaurant near here. Shall we see if they have duck à l'orange?'

His recollection of the small detail sparked something in her blood, something she found very difficult to suppress.

She wasn't used to anyone paying that much attention to her. Amy and Clare aside, and Priti when they were at university, Bea had never been important enough to anyone for them to care about the small things she said. It had been a throwaway comment, for goodness' sake!

But she wasn't important to Ares. That wasn't what this meant. He was just a control freak with an eye for detail. How else could he have achieved what he had in the business world?

'Danica...' she reminded him weakly.

'Xanthia would have called if there was a problem. I'm sure she's fast asleep.'

Bea bit down on her lip, tempted.

'A quick dinner, and then home,' he insisted, putting a hand in the small of her back, taking advantage of her prevarication.

'I suppose so.' And, despite the fact it was a suggestion of practicality, a burst of anticipation spread through her limbs, so she felt a smile crossing her face as they walked. It was dark now, the sky an inky black. The hand at the curve of her spine moved sideways, catching her hip and drawing her closer as though it were the most natural thing in the world. He held her close to his side, moulding her body to his, and she indulged a need for that closeness, lingering beside him, feeling the power of his steps as they moved through the cobbled streets of Athens.

'This is where you lived when you were a teenager?' she asked, partly to fill the silence and partly because she wanted to piece together everything there was to know about Ares.

She felt him tense and wondered if he wasn't going to answer. 'Yes. After my grandfather died we had nowhere to go.'

'Your mother?'

'She'd left us with him many years earlier. She disappeared; we didn't know how to contact her.'

'I'm sorry.'

He slowed down so she looked up at him, and their eyes clashed with a fierce strength of emotion that almost toppled Bea. She sucked in a gulp of air and turned her face forward once more, her skin prickling with goosebumps.

'We came here, thinking it would be easier to find work. It wasn't. Hostels were often full, so more nights than not we were on the streets.'

Her heart was heavy, imagining the teenager he'd been then. 'You must have been terrified.'

'I was many things,' he said cryptically.

She tilted her face to his once more.

'The hardest part was the hunger. I'd never known anything like it. My grandfather didn't have much money but fish were plentiful, and he grew vegetables in pots. We ate well enough. When we came to Athens it was so hard. I will never forget trying to sleep through that dull, throbbing ache in my gut, knowing my little brother was feeling it ten times worse.'

Emotions throbbed in Bea's chest, sympathy chief amongst them.

'Having enough money to buy food became my primary concern. I used to watch people walk past in their expensive clothes and shoes, looking so happy and carefree. I promised myself, and Matthaios, that one day that would be us.'

His lips twisted in a dark grimace. 'Being carefree isn't something any amount of money can buy though.'

She jerked her head in agreement. 'There's no correlation between wealth and happiness,' she said softly.

'You have experience of this?' he prompted, leading them down a smaller alleyway. Buildings were tightly packed here, with bright flowerpots bursting with lavender and geraniums, some with small citrus trees, making the already narrow lane a tight squeeze, so he had to hold her even closer to his side.

'My adoptive parents had money,' she said quietly. 'But I don't know if I'd ever describe them as happy. My mother is...hard to please. In my experience, that's kind of the enemy to happiness.'

He nodded slowly, bringing them to a stop outside a brightly painted turquoise door. It had a glass panel and a moment later it was pulled inwards, so that any response Ares might have been poised to make was swallowed by the greeting of the waiter. He spoke in Greek, addressing Ares as an old friend, pulling the door open wider.

'You come here often?' Bea prompted, feeling self-conscious now in Xanthia's husband's clothes and wishing she'd taken the time to change into some of the items she'd chosen at the department store.

'From time to time,' he replied, gesturing to a table by a window. A candle was set in a round wine bottle, with long tendrils of wax showing that various others had melted in the same bottle top well before this one.

He held the chair out for her, and as she took her seat his hands brushed across her shoulders, sending little flames scurrying through her veins.

'Was she hard on you, when you were growing up?'

It took Bea a moment to realise he was talking about her mother again. She never liked talking about her childhood, but she especially resented its intrusion now. She pushed a bland smile to her lips, reaching for a menu instead of answering.

'What do you usually order here?'

His long, confident fingers reached over and removed the menu, replacing it on the tabletop. 'I always let the chef choose. Answer my question.'

She blinked at him. She shouldn't have been surprised

by his demand. After all, this was the man who'd point-blank insisted she remain at his home even when she'd told him she wouldn't. Ares got what he wanted, and right now he wanted to know something about her.

She swallowed past the bundle of nerves in her throat, relieved when another waiter approached their table, asking if they'd like a drink.

She remembered enough Greek from that long-ago summer spent in the islands to respond in his native tongue, asking for a soft drink. Ares opted for a glass of red wine.

'You speak some Greek?'

'Just a little,' she said. 'I travelled around the islands for a few months, back when I was in school. I picked up a bit.'

'I didn't realise you'd been here before. Where did you go?'

She listed the islands, smiling as memories of that time swept through her. 'I could be completely myself here; I loved it. The people were so welcoming—no one knew anything about my parents or me. There were no god-awful British paparazzi following me, looking for an unflattering photo, trying to turn me into some kind of B-grade tabloid fodder.' She winced, too distracted to care that she'd revealed so much of herself.

He immediately pounced. 'Why would paparazzi chase you?'

She waved a hand through the air dismissively. 'My mum was a supermodel, my dad a rock star. Despite the fact he hasn't been on tour since I was a young girl, in Britain he's still idolised, and Mum loves to "stay current", as she says. She has all the glossy mags do interviews with them every year; some come to the house for in-depth features. You know the kind of thing—"what life's like in the Jones family".' She rolled her eyes, wondering if the few sips of champagne she'd had in the helicopter had loosened her tongue so much, even when she suspected it was far more likely to be the effect of the man sitting opposite.

'Let me just say this…' She paused as the waiter appeared with their drinks, and so Ares could advise the waiter that they'd eat what the chef recommended.

'Do you have any allergies?' he asked Bea.

She shook her head.

Once they were alone again he reached across the table, putting his hand on hers. 'Go on.'

That simple gesture, as well as his prompting her to continue, warmed something that had been frozen in her chest for a very long time.

'Oh, just that what life looks like in the pages of those magazines is often a far cry from the truth.' A sense of disloyalty had her dropping her gaze. 'Or perhaps that's just being mean-spirited. I shouldn't have said it.'

'Is it true?'

Sparkling hazel eyes lifted to his. After a moment's hesitation, she nodded silently.

'Then you can say it.'

Nonetheless, perhaps sensing her reluctance to share further personal details, he moved the conversation to safer ground, asking about her studies instead, and her time as a senior partner, her career ambitions, and then her friendship with Amy and Clare, so, before Bea knew it, the dessert plates were being cleared and her stomach was full of the most delicious food she'd ever eaten.

'Oh, my goodness.' She stared at her watch with a look of panic. 'That wasn't a "quick meal"! We've been hours!'

'Yes,' he agreed, leaning back in his chair, completely confident and content. 'And while you were in the restroom earlier I checked in with Xanthia. Danica is still sleeping soundly. See? You are a magician.'

Relief and pride spread through Bea. 'I'm so glad. I hated seeing her as she was last night.'

'She has been like that most nights since she came to live with me.'

Bea tilted her head to the side a little. 'Babies are very intuitive,' she said thoughtfully. 'It's often believed that because they look helpless they are, when really they're capable of understanding so much more than we give them credit for.'

He waited for her to elaborate.

She chose her words with care. 'It sounds like Danica's life has already known no shortage of trauma and grief. The loss of her mother, her father's grief, and now his absence... It doesn't really surprise me that she's been struggling to settle.'

'So why were you able to calm her last night?'

Bea had her own theories on that, but she wasn't about to spout them to Ares. He hardly needed to know that Bea wondered if her own latent childhood traumas and grief had somehow spoken to Danica on some level, bonding them in a unique, unusual way, reassuring the little girl that she was in the company of someone who understood her pain.

'I don't know.' She shrugged. 'But I'm glad it worked.'

His laugh was unexpected. It spread like warm butter over her body. 'As am I.'

He ran his finger around the rim of his glass, his eyes probing hers in a way that sent shivers down her spine.

'I find it impossible to believe you've never dated before.'

The observation was completely unexpected and it roused her out of the heavenly state of relaxation she'd allowed herself to fall into. Sitting up straighter, she looked around.

'You must have been asked out?'

Bea bristled. 'I can't see how that matters.'

His smile was lightly mocking. 'Can't you?'

She looked down at her own drink, then his, mesmerised by the way his finger was moving.

She pursed her lips, searching for words. 'I'm twenty-nine. Of course I've been asked out.'

'So you've never said yes?'

She bit down on her lip, nodding warily.

'That makes no sense.'

'Apparently it takes a kidnap scenario to get me to go on a date,' she responded, only half joking.

Undeterred, he leaned forward, his legs brushing hers beneath the table. Her eyes widened. 'Haven't you ever wondered what it's like?'

'Dating?'

He shook his head slowly from side to side, not touching her, and yet heat spread through Bea's body as though his hands were on hers. 'No, *agápi mou*. Being made love to, slowly, gently, until you can barely breathe for how turned on you are.'

She gasped at the fever his words had incited.

'Or being made love to hard and fast because your lover cannot wait to make you theirs.'

Her lungs worked on overdrive.

'Have you never touched yourself, imagining your hands were those of a man you wanted? Touched yourself and wished it was your lover's mouth, worshipping you in your most sacred place?'

'Ares...' Again, his name was a plea on her lips. 'Please...' She didn't know if she was asking him to stop or begging him not to.

'I would like to show you what you're capable of feeling, *poulaki mou*,' he murmured. 'If only this were not so complicated.'

Oh, she wanted that too. She wanted it so badly she was terrified to admit her feelings. 'Why is it complicated?' she asked instead. 'I should have thought it's the most basic biological act.'

His smile was cynical. 'And yet you're a virgin.'

Her eyes dropped to the table.

'I do not sleep with virgins.'

She gasped. 'Is that a rule or something?'

'It might as well be.'

Disappointment speared her belly. She wanted to shake him, to tell him he was being silly. But then what?

Confusion, heat, need—all these feelings rushed through her like a live wire of electricity.

'Then…what…?'

When she risked a glance at him, he was appraising her silently.

She gathered her courage, forcing herself to speak her mind. 'Why are you flirting with me?'

His eyes were mocking, but was it directed at himself or her?

She waited, breath held, for his response, and yet she wasn't prepared for what was coming.

'Because I want you. Even though I know it's wrong, and that I can't offer you what you deserve, I look at you and feel as though I am fighting a losing battle.' Now his expression held a challenge, as though he were laying down a gauntlet. 'You've never had sex before and, despite what I just said, I find myself obsessing over being your first lover. I want to be the one who awakens you to the physical pleasures of intimacy. I have no doubt that's selfish of me, and yet here we are.'

Her breath wouldn't come easily. She stared at him in disbelief, her pulse racing, her mind blank. 'Ares…' But what could she say in response to that? He was offering her exactly what she wanted. She finally managed to suck in a deep breath, doing her best to think straight.

'I don't want more than sex.' She blurted the words out

loudly and blushed to the roots of her hair, looking around to make sure that she hadn't been heard. 'Perhaps that's part of what's held me back from dating. The idea of a relationship is anathema to me. You don't need to worry I'll want more from you. Just…sex…is fine.' She cleared her throat. 'More than fine, in fact.'

What the hell was she doing? The water was up to her neck; she was about to drown. Or was she swimming? She couldn't tell. She knew only that it felt good and right to speak like this—two adults outlining a new set of rules, an agreement that would protect them both. There was comfort in the sanity of that when every other part of her felt disconnected from reality.

'It would change nothing between us.' There was wariness in his voice, but also the hard edge of control, as though he was on the brink of losing it.

'Fine by me.' A breathless agreement.

Their eyes met and it was like the signing of a contract. Without words, Ares stood, holding his hand out. Bea stared at it long and hard and then slid hers into his palm, fire zapping through her veins.

He didn't speak as they left the restaurant, but she answered him—and herself—nonetheless. 'I'm ready.'

CHAPTER TEN

HE'D TAKEN THE helicopter ride from Athens to Porto Heli thousands of times, but never quite like this. The tension in the helicopter could have been cut with a knife. She sat opposite him without talking, her hands fidgeting in her lap so her anxiety became all he could focus on. Not her anxiety so much as how he could alleviate it, show her that her body knew what it wanted and could be trusted to guide her. He knew that once they were home he could take charge, pleasuring her until all doubts fell from her mind.

There were no familiar landmarks beneath—it was too dark to see anything properly, but he knew—to the minute—the time it should take to arrive. He checked his watch, relief spreading through him when they reached single digits and then, finally, his home came into view. Her eyes were on him, watching, appraising, and anticipation spread through him. He ached to touch her, to feel her warm softness beneath his palm, her silky hair in his fingers, entangled in his grip, her beautiful body beneath his, welcoming him, losing herself to the heady rush of sensual euphoria.

The fact that he would be her first tightened his arousal to the point of pain. Now that he knew there was no risk of emotional entanglement, he could simply enjoy the pleasure of Beatrice Jones. The helicopter had barely touched down before he was moving, unclipping his own belt before attending to hers. Bea's fingers were shaking when he took her hand in his, but when she looked at him he didn't see what he'd expected to. There was no hesitation in her face, only the same blinding urgency that was exploding in his chest.

The night was cool and he held her close as they moved to the door, partly to keep her warm and partly because he was selfish and simply wanted to touch her, to feel her. Her body was slender but curved; he hungered to feel her in his hands. At the stairs, he dropped his arm, taking her hand in his as he led the way, pausing only briefly at the bottom, waiting for her to take the last step before he strode down the corridor, towards his bedroom.

Bea was right there with him. Until he opened the door and drew her through it, shutting them in his room, he didn't realise he'd been half terrified she'd change her mind. He turned to face her in the dimly lit space, just a lamp near the window casting the room in a gentle glow, and every rush of need that had been tormenting him since they'd left the restaurant burst through him now. His chest rocked with the torturous act of breathing, his body tense. He stared down at her and she looked up at him, and then he moved.

He'd kissed her twice before and this was like the second time, full of urgency, a kiss that overtook him with need, that seemed to happen almost without his control—something Ares would ordinarily despise. But anything that could bring his body to hers like this and have her dissolving against him in a soft, whimpering form of surrender had his approval. He took a step forward, pressing her against the back of the door, his tongue duelling with hers, demanding her supplication. Over and over she said his name, moaning it into his mouth as best she could, her hands pulling his shirt from his trousers, pushing at the buttons until her fingertips could touch bare flesh.

Her need to explore and touch was as real as his own.

Despite her inexperience, she was guided by instincts and they were strong, so that if she hadn't told him she'd never been with a man he wouldn't have guessed it. Bea made a growling sound as she yanked at his shirt, separating it finally, removing it from his body as though she couldn't live another second without seeing him naked. He understood.

His hands completed the same task, removing the unsophisticated clothes she wore, stripping her down to her underwear and then dispensing with them so she was naked against him, her body warm and soft, just as he'd fantasised. Her hair was still up in a topknot; he pulled it loose as he kissed her, spilling her hair over her shoulders and down her back, before stepping back to admire her. The sound of their harsh breathing filled the bedroom, loud and demanding. He needed a moment though to commit her to his memory banks just as she was. Her cheeks pink, her chest too from his stubble, her pert breasts with peach nipples tautened by desire, her flat stomach and gently curved thighs.

He swore under his breath, holding out a hand. She put hers in it and he drew her to the bed, knowing he had to curb all his own selfish impulses—the desire to simply drive himself into her sweet sex and lose himself there, to take her hard and fast until they were both incandescent with pleasure. There'd be time for that—a month, in fact. A month to enjoy her sweetness and to teach her how great sex could be.

Tonight was about being gentle. Gradually introducing her to lovemaking without overwhelming her and, hell, without hurting her.

He scooped her up without warning, laying her down in the middle of the bed, kissing her as he moved his body over hers, still kissing as he extended an arm and lifted a condom from the bedside table. He discarded it near them on the bed—for later. First, he wanted to taste.

* * *

The sensation of his mouth on her breasts sent sharp arrows of pleasure-pain spiralling through Bea so she lifted her hips in a sudden, jerky movement. It was almost too much. Too intimate—too personal. He took one nipple between his teeth, rolling it there a moment before flicking it with his tongue, while his hand moved between her legs, brushing her femininity lightly at first, so she didn't know what to focus on, nor which feeling was more overwhelming. She knew only that she was coming apart at the seams in some vital, unmistakable way.

His hand between her legs was heaven-sent, but also not enough. She bucked her hips again, silently begging him for something she couldn't explain. He understood though; she felt him smile against her breast as he kissed his way downwards, his tongue swirling invisible circles around her belly button, over the plane of her stomach and low, teasing her hipbone before moving between her legs.

She groaned as his tongue touched her there, lightly at first and then with more intensity, more speed, more everything, delivering her towards a destination she'd never heard of, never even known about. She dug her nails into the bed first, then his shoulders, as her moans grew louder and louder and eventually she was tipping off the edge of the earth, pleasure swallowing her whole, changing her for ever.

But before she could recover she was dimly aware of the sound of foil and then his knee was parting her legs, his body over hers, his mouth kissing her softly as he pushed the tip of his arousal against her sex.

Despite the heavenly pleasure he'd already delivered, tension filled her. She whimpered, fear widening her eyes so she stared up at him for reassurance. His response was to speak in Greek, his words gentle and soft, words she didn't understand but which succeeded in reassuring her.

He wasn't gentle now. At least, not *so* gentle. He pushed into her, watching her the whole time as his arousal stretched parts of her previously untouched, his body possessing hers for the first time, breaking through an invisible barrier so that briefly she felt a sting of pain, a sharp, visceral response to his presence. It abated almost immediately, and she nodded, a silent encouragement to a question he hadn't asked.

It was then that he began to move. Then that Bea realised whatever pleasure she'd felt a moment ago, it was nothing to the overwhelming, all-consuming delight of this. His body mastering hers, his weight on top of her, the roughness of his chest hairs against her breasts, his hard erection deep inside her, being squeezed by muscles that were trembling in pleasure. Stars danced against the lids of her eyes; she was falling from heaven, or perhaps flying through it? She tilted her head back, capitulating to this madness completely, utterly lost and completely found all at once.

'How do you feel?'

It was a question with no answer. How could she describe how she felt in words? She turned her head to face him, her hooded eyes roaming his features with renewed speculation and interest. She felt a primal claim to him— as though he were hers in some vital, unchangeable way, and always would be.

Oh, it was a stupid way to feel. She recognised that almost immediately. No one person could belong to another and, even if they could, sex wasn't a gateway to possession. For someone like Ares, this had probably been a perfectly run-of-the-mill bout of sex. Just because the very parameters of Bea's world had been significantly redefined didn't mean it had meant anything to Ares.

He frowned, his finger lifting to trace her lips. She

sucked in a breath, the small act somehow seeming intimate despite what they'd just shared.

'Fine.' She cleared her throat. The word was banal and inaccurate. She felt so much better than fine. She felt shiny and new. She felt desirable and sensual. She felt wanted.

The realisation had her smile dropping, just by a fraction.

Careful, Bea.

She knew the inherent risks of that feeling. Being wanted was something she'd never experienced; it was a loss she'd had to accept in her life. She couldn't start looking to someone like Ares Lykaios to fill that vital void within her.

Sex was sex. Nothing more. They'd agreed on that.

The bath water was the perfect temperature and, as she sank into it, Bea acknowledged that she was a little sore. Parts of her body that had never been used made themselves known, so she winced a little.

He was watching, and a small grimace appeared on his own features in response.

'I'm fine,' she promised. And then, because he seemed genuinely worried, 'Better than fine, in fact.'

His smile was her reward. It shifted across his face, changing his features completely, so, for a moment, all she was capable of was staring. 'I'll be back.'

She was tempted to make a Terminator joke but he was gone too quickly. When Ares returned he was naked, holding two glasses filled with a pale amber liquid.

'Scotch?' She wrinkled her nose.

'You don't like it?'

'I've never tried it.'

'That seems to be the theme of the night,' he quipped, placing the glass on the edge of the bath before he stepped in, taking a seat opposite her. The tub was large—easily able to accommodate them both—yet their legs brushed and she was glad. The contact was a different sort of intimacy. She welcomed it and cherished it even as her own warnings swam through her mind. She knew she could balance the physical delight of his presence against the mental knowledge of his impermanence in her life.

Not just *his* impermanence. Everyone's. The unreliability of other people. Bea had sworn a long time ago that she'd never depend on another soul, certainly not for something as important as her happiness. She would enjoy this moment while knowing how fleeting it was. Convinced she could balance those beliefs, the germ of an idea flared in her belly.

'So, I've been thinking,' she murmured, reaching for the Scotch glass, her voice level despite the buzz of what they'd shared.

'Go on.'

His tone was cool, muted, and she hid her smile behind the glass.

'Perhaps I will stay here for a month.'

He tipped his head back and laughed, a deep noise that reached inside Bea and squeezed her tummy.

'I mean, not just because I really, really like what we just did,' she said with a lift of her shoulders.

'Of course not,' he murmured, mock serious. 'This would still be purely business.'

'Oh, absolutely. I might even have to call you Mr Lykaios from time to time,' she said, tilting her head to the side as she considered that. 'Or sir, if you'd prefer.'

He grinned, finishing his own Scotch before placing the glass on the edge of the bath and moving closer to her.

'As your self-appointed instructor in all things sexual, that does seem appropriate.'

'You mean there's more to learn?' she enquired with wide eyes.

'Oh, Beatrice, so much more. Where to start…?'

* * *

As always, he woke with a start, a sense of foreboding knotting in his gut that drew him immediately into consciousness. It didn't ease when he became aware of the warm, naked body at his side, her soft brown hair fanned across the pillow, stirring needs within him that should have been well and truly satiated by the night they'd shared.

On the streets of Athens he'd slept with one eye open, aware that danger could come at any point and that if it did it would be his responsibility to defend them both, to protect Matthaios. It was an alertness for danger that could only be eased in one way: control.

Ares didn't lose sleep about his business interests because he oversaw every single aspect of his empire. No matter was too small to escape his attention. In his personal life it was much the same.

Everything was on his terms, always.

The women he dated understood that—he made sure of it. Just as he had with Bea. He'd been crystal-clear.

Despite that, he felt a deep, dark worry that he might hurt her. He couldn't say why, but he had the strongest sense that there was something within Bea that needed protecting, a vulnerability she desperately tried to conceal, but which he nonetheless sensed.

He wouldn't hurt her.

They'd both acknowledged what this was, and he'd been open about the limitations of it. They'd even put an expiry date on her remaining with him. Surely that was some form of insurance?

Fighting a strong desire to wake her with the kind of kiss that would lead to so much more, he slid out of bed and dressed quickly, dragging on some low-slung jeans and a black shirt. If Danica woke he didn't want the crying to disturb Bea—she needed to sleep.

At the door, he took one last look at her. She was so beautiful and peaceful, so…trusting when she was asleep.

Despite the assurances he'd just given himself, the sense of foreboding was back, chewing at his gut. He pulled the door shut behind himself.

'Excuse me,' Bea apologised, stifling the fifth yawn in as many minutes.

Ellen's expression was sympathetic. 'The baby kept you awake last night?'

Heat suffused Bea's cheeks as she smiled awkwardly, looking away, infinitely preferring not to think about all the ways in which she'd been kept awake. Not by a baby, but by the sinfully sexy Ares Lykaios instead.

'Xanthia says you have a heap of experience with children.'

'I have lots of younger brothers and sisters,' the girl agreed, her round face dimpling as she smiled affectionately. 'And I have been hired as a babysitter since I was about nine years old,' she added.

'How old are you now?' Bea prompted.

'Twenty-one. I know I look younger,' Ellen laughed.

'Yes, you do,' Bea agreed, gesturing for Ellen to walk on ahead, into the lounge. Danica was set up in a playpen, lying on her tummy with a soft baby's ball in the palm of her hand.

Ellen made a little squealing sound of delight. 'Oh, she's so beautiful. May I pick her up?'

'Please,' Bea encouraged, interested to see how well Ellen handled Danica. The surge of protective instincts firing through Bea surprised her. As with the first night she'd held Danica, it was an almost maternal humming in her blood, a feeling that there was an invisible cord connecting the two of them, that she would fight to protect with her life.

Ellen spoke in Greek to the little girl, something that

was wholly appropriate but which felt like a knife being plunged into Bea's heart. She felt excluded and unwanted. Old feelings spread through her; she turned away.

It took a moment for Bea to get her own emotions under control, and to remind herself that she had a life and a real job back in London. Despite the fact that Amy had been reassuring in an email—they had an excellent team of staff who would be able to continue to work to the high standards required by the London Connection's clients while Amy, Clare and Bea were away—she still knew she needed to get back at the end of the month. There was no guarantee Matthaios would be out of rehab by then, despite what Ares hoped. If Bea could leave Danica with someone like Ellen then she'd have the peace of mind of knowing Danica was being not just looked after—but loved.

'How often can you work?'

'Every day.' Ellen smiled sweetly, rocking Danica on her hip. 'I'm between jobs at the moment, so the timing is perfect.'

'Yes.' Bea's voice caught in her throat. She coughed to cover it. 'I really need help through the day, so that I can get some work done.'

'You're a lawyer?' Ellen said curiously.

Bea nodded. 'Not the kind that goes to court though. I think it sounds more exciting than it is.'

Danica made a little noise then, and one chubby arm extended, reaching for Bea. Her heart turned over in her chest, the sense of being wanted and needed by Danica making her ache.

For a moment, Bea resisted. The longing to feel wanted was always followed by the knowledge that she wasn't—and that would happen here too. While Danica seemed dependent on Bea now, she knew that when she left Porto Heli the baby would have Ellen and Ares, and then Matthaios. Her life would continue without Bea, whereas she would always think of—and miss—the little baby who had so quickly worked her way into Bea's heart.

She wanted to resist out of a need for self-preservation, but those damned maternal instincts had her crossing the room and taking the baby from Ellen's arms. Danica put her little head on Bea's shoulder.

'Why don't I give you a tour of the house?'

An hour later, all the terms had been agreed. Ellen was going to spend several hours a day with Danica, and more if needed. She was helpful, flexible and had a kind nature. Bea told herself she was glad, even when she knew that with the admission of Ellen into the household staff, Ares's need for Bea lessened dramatically. It was a very good thing, then, that she was keeping a level head and not allowing their insane sexual chemistry to make her want more than was on offer.

CHAPTER ELEVEN

'IT'S SO BEAUTIFUL HERE.' Bea sighed appreciatively at the colours lighting up the sky—pink, purple, grey and silver, as the sun dipped closer to the horizon, preparing to draw a blanket of stars overhead. But for now it was a stunning display of dusk, her favourite time of the day, and Bea's soul drank it in.

They'd watched a week's worth of sunsets together since the first night they'd shared. By unspoken agreement, a rhythm had formed to their lives. Ares worked long days, often in his Athens office, returning after Danica was in bed. Bea worked when she could; despite Ellen's presence, she tried to limit herself mostly to Danica's nap time, so that she could be involved in the baby's life, and be sure things were running smoothly.

There was no cause for concern with Ellen. The young woman was calm and enthusiastic at the same time, an excellent companion for an energetic baby.

Bea's phone buzzing caught her attention. She reached behind her, swishing the screen to life, her pulse firing up when she saw a message from Amy.

'Bad news?' Ares's voice was deep and husky.

Bea read the message, her frown deepening.

Sorry I've been MIA. Try not to stress about what you're

seeing in the papers—I'm okay. It's nothing like last time. I'll explain everything face to face. Love you. X

She didn't have the heart to tell her friend—a PR exec— that she hadn't read a newspaper headline since she'd been in Greece.

'Not bad news, I don't think...' She shook her head, quickly googling her friend's name and gasping when she read the first headline that appeared.

Palace Scandal! History repeats itself with new Lothario-in-Chief!

'Oh, no, Amy!'
She skimmed the text, baffled by the revelation of Amy's relationship with the Prince of Vallia. Last Bea had heard, Amy was going there in a professional capacity. So what was going on? This wasn't exactly good PR for the prince. She clicked into another article, shaking her head, reminding herself that Amy's text had explicitly said she was okay. It went some of the way to assuaging Bea's worries. Besides, there was no way Amy would get involved with a guy like Luca Albizzi. Not after last time.

Nonetheless, she hit the forward button on her phone and sent the article to Clare. Speaking of MIA, she'd heard nothing from the third member of their trio, but Clare had said she'd likely be unavailable for a while, so that was hardly surprising.

Trying to ignore the *frisson* of worry, Bea brought herself back to the present, focusing on the warmth of the sun on her arms, the colours in the sky and, of course, the man in the pool.

Ares drew closer to the coping, his dark hair a wet pelt against his head. She watched the way the droplets rippled over his shoulders, admiring his tanned flesh and muscled arms.

'You're sure you won't join me?'

Her smile was wry. 'As I've told you every time you've asked, it's way too cold for swimming.'

He laughed. 'It's warm, I promise.'

On previous nights the evening had brought a chill breeze, but tonight there was more heat in the air. Though summer was still another six weeks away, the promise of its warmth surrounded them tonight.

'I'll compromise by sitting at the edge. Deal?'

He didn't say anything, simply watching her in that intense way of his as she stood, strolling towards him then sitting down. The denim miniskirt left her bare legs free to dangle in the water, the oversized tee required a pushing-up of the sleeves.

'How was work?' She reached out, ruffling his hair with her fingers, a jolt of anticipation running through her at the ease with which she could touch him, a man who had so recently appeared into her life and made her feel inadequate and powerful all at once.

His frown was infinitesimal. 'Busy,' he said, his eyes probing hers for a minute before he looked away.

Her heart skipped a beat as, for the first time in a week, she felt something akin to insecurity whisper through her. It was as though he was hiding something from her. As always, Bea was on the alert, looking for signs that a person she cared about was losing interest in her, ready to jump before she was pushed. How often she'd employed those skills with her parents—reading them intently, leaving a room before they could suggest she go and find something else to do, pretending occupation with a book so she wouldn't appear to notice the way they fawned over the twins, hanging on their every word.

'Ellen is doing well with Danica,' she said, to lay the

groundwork for that possibility. If he wanted her to go, she wouldn't put up a fight. She'd make it easy for him, and walk away with her head held high. Worse than being unwanted, she'd learned a long time ago, was losing one's pride along with it.

'Yes.' The agreement was distracted, as though something important was on his mind.

Danger signs blared and, despite her intention to stay cool, panic gripped her heart.

'In all honesty, she could probably move in, you know.' *Say it, coward*, she urged herself. Clearing her throat, she forced an over-bright smile to her face. 'You could even release me from my kidnapping early.' She let the words hover between them, the suggestion that she would be completely fine with that.

'What?' His drawn-together brows showed confusion, as though it was the last thing he was expecting her to say.

'We agreed to a month before Ellen entered into the equation, and when Danica seemed much less settled,' Bea pointed out quietly. 'She's like a different baby now. You don't really need my help any more.'

The words were a form of acid in her throat. She tried to hold his eyes, to look brave and unconcerned, but she couldn't. She focused on the water instead, blinking several times to push back an overwhelming rush of emotion.

'We agreed to a month.' The words cracked around them harshly. 'I expect people I do business with to uphold their end of a deal. Are you trying to renege on our agreement?'

It was the reassurance she craved but in the strangest possible sense. This was so much more than business... wasn't it?

Doubts and uncertainties warred within her. She had no experience with men to compare this to, no idea what she'd wanted him to say. It was an indication that he didn't want her to leave though. Shouldn't that be enough?

'I'm not reneging,' she denied and, despite her best efforts, the words were softened by hurt.

He swore in his native tongue, coming to stand between her knees, looking up at her face intently. 'Do you want to go home?' he prompted, his own expression impossible to interpret. He was evidently far better at shielding his emotions than she was hers.

Home.

It was a strange word to employ, because it spoke of a sense she'd never known in her heart. Only as Ares asked the question did Bea realise she'd never actually thought of anywhere as home.

'I will not keep you here against your will.' The words seemed cut from glass, each sharp and cold, with the power to wound. But to wound who? His voice softened. 'And I will not sever my relationship with the London Connection. You do not need to stay because you're afraid of repercussions.'

It wasn't losing his business she was afraid of now; it was losing herself.

'Did you ever intend to fire the agency?' she asked quietly, moving her gaze to his face.

'Clare has managed my interests better than I can imagine anyone else doing,' he admitted finally. 'I never let my personal feelings enter into a business decision. Having made a single mistake in two years would have been a pretty poor reason to fire her.'

Bea's heart felt strangely light. 'So you were just using Clare's absence as leverage over me?'

He lifted his fingertips from the pool, dribbling a little water over her knee. 'I use whatever tools are at my disposal to achieve what I want.'

'And what did you want?'

'To get to know you better.'

Her ears were filled with a rush of noise like a tidal wave. 'Why?'

His frown was swift; she almost missed it. 'I can't say.'

'Why not?'

'I mean I don't know,' he corrected quietly. 'You were different, somehow.'

'Different to what?'

He braced his hands on the pool coping, pushing up effortlessly and holding himself there, a feat of abdominal control that even in that moment she didn't fail to notice. 'I was fascinated by you,' he corrected, brushing her lips with his, sending arrows of need through her body, arrows that almost drove all other thoughts from her mind. 'You were a contradiction and I wanted to understand that.'

He dropped back into the pool, resting his arms over her legs.

'And do you now?'

'No,' he answered immediately. 'If anything, the more I get to know you, the less sense you make.'

Her hazel eyes flared wide, surprised by that analysis. 'I think you're looking too hard. I'm actually very simple.'

His laugh was disbelieving. 'Liar.'

She dipped her fingertips into the pool, dribbling water over his shoulder before dropping her hand to his flesh, tracing invisible circles there.

'Stay the full month,' he said quietly, his eyes probing hers. 'So that I have more opportunity to make sense of you.'

It wasn't exactly what she needed to hear—no one had ever managed to offer Bea that—but it was enough. Enough for now to stave off her basic insecurities, to make her feel that he really did want her with him. He wasn't looking for an excuse to push her away; he wasn't counting down the minutes until she could leave. And even though he had Ellen to help with Danica, he still wanted Bea to be a part of their lives. For now.

* * *

'What is that song you sing to her?' Ares asked later that same night, when Bea was almost asleep. Her eyes were heavy and it took her mind a moment to wade back from the drugging proximity of sleep. Her body felt as though it was glowing, pleasure spreading through her limbs as the way he'd made her feel earlier set her pulse racing.

She hadn't been back to the guest room since the first night they'd made love. They hadn't discussed it; this had simply evolved out of a mutual need to be together at night, a desire to hold and touch, to wake up and reach for one another, satiating themselves over and over...

'Which song?' she asked sleepily. She flicked a glance to the bedside table. It had just passed midnight. Not terribly late but, given the way they were spending their nights, she was snatching sleep wherever she could find it.

His own voice was low and deep, so that when he hummed the familiar tune to Bea it sounded somehow mystical and different. She caught her breath, unused to hearing the song from anyone else.

'It's called "Calon Lân",' she murmured, turning in the bed so she could face him, resting her head on the pillow. 'It's Welsh.'

'You speak Welsh?'

'No.' Sadness etched her smile. She'd never told another soul why she knew that song, and yet the words bubbled through her now, pulling her towards him. 'I used to hum it as a girl—just a few lines, all that I could remember. For a long time, I didn't consciously know where it had come from, nor why I sang it. My adoptive dad, Ronnie, recognised the tune and played the full song for me.'

'Where did you learn it?'

Her heart skipped a beat. A pain that was almost too raw to speak of sliced through her. But Bea was nothing if not brave; confronting pain head-on was something she'd had to do enough times to be able to face it now.

'It's the only memory I have of my birth mother,' she said quietly. 'It's not even a memory,' she corrected, 'so much as a fog. A haze. If I think on it too hard it's like trying to catch soap in the bath—slippery and impossible. I can't remember what she looked like, and I can't remember anything about my life before…before I came to live with Ronnie and Alice—' her voice was rushed '—but I know she used to sing the song to me. She must have done it often, because it's kind of imprinted inside of me. And when I sing it I can feel her arms around me. I know that sounds strange.'

He shook his head once, just enough to disabuse her of that idea. 'Memory is a funny thing.'

'Yes.' She bit down on her lip. 'When I heard Danica crying, the words just came out of me. It's always comforted me, the song, and I thought it might do the same for her.'

'It appears to work wonders.'

She nodded, pressing her palm to his chest, feeling the steady rhythm of his heartbeat.

'What happened to your birth parents?'

She realised she'd been afraid of this question. No one had ever asked it. Amy and Clare had always instinctively understood that it was a no-go area. It was an almost impossible thing to reveal, because it was like admitting to someone that you just weren't very lovable.

'They didn't want me.' The words burned their way through her heart. She clamped her lips together in an attempt to stem any more.

A crease formed between his brows as he analysed that statement. 'For what reason?'

And there he'd found the crux of the matter. She laughed uneasily, flipping onto her back and staring at the ceiling. 'I was a difficult child, I guess.'

She couldn't look at him, so didn't see his reaction.

'It's fine,' she lied. 'They did the right thing and gave me away, obviously expecting I'd end up with a family more capable of caring for me.'

The silence that fell was barbed. 'And did you?'

Another question she'd never been asked, but this time because Amy and Clare had been able to see the truth for themselves. 'I grew up with everything you could want.' Her voice had a practised tone to it—the same one she'd used whenever people had enthused about how 'lucky' she was to have rock royalty for a dad and a bona fide supermodel as a mum.

'Why do I suspect that's not true?'

Damn him! She didn't want to talk about this. 'Are you kidding? Who wouldn't want to be raised by a couple of celebrities?'

'Lots of people,' he answered simply. 'And definitely you.'

Her throat thickened with emotion.

'You hate attention,' he said gently. 'And yet, given their fame, I imagine you received more than your fair share.'

His perceptiveness knocked her off-balance, so she turned her face to his, her eyes wide.

'It was a strange way to grow up,' she agreed, careful not to reveal more than was necessary. 'They thought they couldn't have kids, so I was spoiled rotten when I first came to live with them.'

Most people would focus on that, wanting the details of just how much people like Ronnie and Alice would give their daughter. People were, in Bea's opinion, always obsessed with the minutiae of a celebrity's life—how were they like 'normal' people and in what ways did they differ?

Not Ares. He wasn't so easily diverted by the mention of fame and fortune.

'And then she fell pregnant and everything changed for

you,' he prompted, recalling their earlier conversation, on the night they'd arrived at Porto Heli.

'In many ways.' She lifted one shoulder. 'Anyway, as I said, I really don't like to talk about my family.'

'I let you get away with that once, but not again.'

She blinked, surprised.

'I want to understand you,' he reminded her. 'And I suspect this is at the root of your mystery.'

'There is no mystery,' she demurred with a quick shake of her head.

'Why did you decide to study law?'

The subject change was so swift it almost gave her whiplash.

'I was good at it.'

It was a throwaway comment but the expression on his face showed something else, as though he was sliding another piece of a puzzle into place. She angled her face, hating the sensation of being a bug beneath his microscope.

'I imagine you received a lot of praise for that,' he said thoughtfully.

Bea pulled her lips to the side. 'I don't know what that's supposed to mean.'

'You received accolades for your academic achievements?'

'I mean, I graduated with a first, so in that sense, yes.'

'And your parents? They were proud?'

The pain was as fresh as when she'd called to tell them her results and her mother had spoken over the top of her to announce that Amarie had started dating a Hollywood actor.

We think they might get engaged soon! He's so delicious, darling.

'Of course they were,' she lied.

Without even turning to look at him, she knew he didn't believe her.

'Are you someone for whom good grades came easily?' he asked.

'No.' Oh, how she hated the bitter tears that were flooding her throat. She swallowed desperately. 'I suppose I have a bent for the law—it came more easily to me than, say, mathematics did. My mind definitely works a certain way. But I studied hard, to the exclusion of everything else. I was determined to—'

He waited for her to finish the sentence.

'To do well,' she finished lamely, not wanting to admit to him that making her parents proud had indeed formed a huge part of her motivation.

'And you did,' he said gently. It wasn't praise. It wasn't congratulations. And yet hearing him say those words warmed some small part of her, so she blinked her eyes and smiled, a weak smile pulled from her soul.

'Thank you.'

He lifted a hand, running it over her hair, his eyes following the movement of his fingers. 'I used to look at people like you and think you had it all. I would jealously watch university students with their books and rucksacks, their easy lives, and wish more than anything that I could trade places. I desperately wanted to be able to study. I thought people like you had it so easy.'

'Compared to you, I did,' she murmured softly.

'I don't know if that's true.' He moved closer, his lips brushing hers. 'There are many things besides food that people starve for, *agápi mou.*'

CHAPTER TWELVE

BEA WAS BEYOND worried about Amy. The last time they'd spoken, everything had been fine. Sure, the conversation was rushed, but Bea had presumed Amy was just caught up with work. But now Amy was back in London and her first order of business had apparently been to send this email. Bea read it again, shaking her head at Amy's request: Fire me, before this scandal gets out of hand. It made no sense, and all Bea could think was that she needed to speak to Amy, to tell her she loved her and would always support her. There was no way anyone was getting fired, no matter what had happened!

'Where are you? When are you coming back?' Amy asked when Bea called to reiterate her support. But before Bea could brush the question aside and bring the focus back onto Amy's email, Amy had a text from her demanding mother and had to abruptly end the call.

Bea's placed her phone down with a growing sense of disquiet.

The following week was the first time Ares had been allowed to see his brother and the visit brought with it a maelstrom of emotion. Matthaios looked good, but still, it was impossible for Ares to shake his sense of anxiety, as though he might say or do the wrong thing and set Matthaios back in his recovery. He felt as though he must walk a mile on eggshells.

'Who's the woman in the photo?' Matthaios asked conversationally, pointing to the image of Bea on Ares's phone.

Ares's eyes were drawn to her face, the affection she felt for Danica obvious in every line of her body. From the way she cradled Danica so completely, to the look in her eyes as she stared at the baby's dimpled face.

'Just someone who's helping me care for her,' Ares hedged uncomfortably. After all, that was the primary purpose of having Bea at Porto Heli. Never mind that they'd also spent the past three weeks exploring each other's bodies and minds to the point where she was almost all he could think of.

Not that Ares would ever really let a woman have that kind of control over him. He was focused on his work, on Matthaios, and now on Danica. That was it.

'*Theós*, she looks like her mother.'

For a moment Ares thought Matt meant Bea, who bore no resemblance to Ingrid whatsoever, except, he conceded, for their slender frames. But Ingrid had been so Danish, with her white-blonde hair and sky-blue eyes. Belatedly, he understood. Matt only had eyes for Danica. He was staring at the phone so hard it was possible a hole might burst through it.

'I will ask your doctors if I'm allowed to bring her here,' Ares said firmly. 'You're doing so well, Matt. You seem like yourself again.'

Matthaios looked to his older brother, shaking his head slowly. 'Don't bring her to this place. It's bad enough that I'm here,' he muttered, dragging a hand through his hair. 'I don't mean that I don't need to be here. I know that I do. But I don't want Danica to see me like this.'

'She's barely six months old,' Ares reminded Matthaios.

'I don't think she'll mind that it's somewhat lacking in charm.'

'I'll mind,' he said.

'I think she misses you.'

'She deserves so much better.'

Ares's sigh was heavy, drawn from deep inside. He'd been reflecting on that lately—the bond between children and their parents or carers, the people put on this earth to keep them safe. For them, that had been their grandfather, and when he'd died they'd been cast out on their own, needing to fend for themselves. Their grandfather had died but the lessons he'd taught them remained. Ares knew that was where his resilience and determination had come from: mornings spent battling harsh weather and frigid temperatures, pulling ropes out of the ocean until calluses had formed across his palm, never once complaining or even remarking on the difficulties of that life.

'I think she's doing okay,' Ares commented.

'Thanks to you. Ares to the rescue, as always.'

But Matt was wrong. Ares wasn't coming to the rescue. He was simply cleaning up his own mess—fixing something that would never have been a problem in the first place if he'd done a better job of looking after Matt and Danica.

'Is she from an agency?'

Ares didn't immediately follow.

'I thought you said Cassandra was the last nanny they'd send you, after all the nannies I fired or shouted at.'

'No.' He shook his head. 'She's…a friend.'

'Oh.' Matthaios regarded the screen with more attention and now Ares wanted to flick the image away. A possessive heat ran through him. Not possessive of Beatrice so much as of what was happening between them. He wasn't prepared to discuss it; that felt like a betrayal. What they were sharing was inside a bubble, separate from time, and from their normal lives. Though they'd never agreed to keep it a secret, it just felt right.

'We've worked together. She saw how much I was struggling and offered to help out.'

'I see.'

Damn it, Ares suspected Matthaios *did* see. Having grown up so near in age and enduring most of life's adventures at each other's side, their relationship was very close, and Matthaios understood Ares better than anyone.

'Will I get to meet this friend of yours?'

'No.' The answer was swift and definitive. 'She must return to London next week. A month was all she could give Danica, I'm afraid.'

He ignored the swift stabbing sensation beneath his ribs.

'I don't know when I'll be out, Ares. Are you sure she can't stay longer?'

'Take all the time you need. Beatrice has hired a local girl who is also very good with the baby. Ellen dotes on her and will be available to help even when you return home. Someone who can ease you back into normal life.'

'And keep an eye on me, you mean?' Matt demanded sharply, briefly taking Ares back to the god-awful time shortly after Ingrid's death, when every question had led to an angry retort from his younger brother.

Matthaios winced apologetically. 'I know you mean well. I just hate...being here and having no...'

'Control,' Ares supplied, before his brother could even finish his sentence. 'I understand how you feel.' He could think of nothing worse than losing control of any situation, ever. 'What you have to realise is that in getting well you are taking control back. Control over the addiction that will chew through your life if you let it, just as it did our mother's.'

'I know that.' Matt's eyes fired with courage. 'I'm not going to mess this up, Ares.' He looked to the phone once more. 'She means too much to me.'

* * *

'You're very quiet.'

He regarded Bea over the rim of his glass. She was wearing the dress he'd chosen from the department store. He'd grabbed it simply because it had been nearby but, seeing it on her now, the colours were the perfect palette to draw out her complexion.

'Am I?' The question was designed to stall. She was right; he had been preoccupied since returning from visiting Matthaios.

'You've answered in monosyllables practically all evening.' Concern clouded her eyes. 'Is everything okay?'

He fingered the stem of his wine glass. 'I saw Matt today. My brother.' And then, as though she couldn't connect the dots. 'Danica's father.'

Her smile showed how redundant his second two statements had been. 'How is he?'

'Doing better,' Ares admitted. 'Frustrated that it's taking longer than expected to feel back to full health.'

'What do the doctors say?'

'That he should take as long as he needs, but that he's showing very promising signs for a meaningful recovery. It's never a smooth journey, though. It will require lifelong vigilance, so now it's about arming him with the tools to recognise when he's at risk of relapsing, as well as how to surround himself with people who are good for him.'

'What was Danica's mother like?'

Ares's smile came easily. 'An excellent influence. He adored her, and she didn't let him get away with anything. I abhor the idea of soulmates,' he said with an unintended shudder, 'but in this case I would willingly make an exception.'

'Are you so sceptical about love?' she asked, and although he knew she was determined to get back to her life in London he felt a natural throb of concern enter his bloodstream. This was the longest he'd ever spent with a woman. Ares always, without fail, left before things could get beyond the first flush of sexual chemistry. He had no interest in growing dependent on anyone, and even less in being needed.

If this time had proved anything, though, it was that he was stronger than he'd thought. Three weeks with Bea had flown by and while they'd been thoroughly enjoyable, he had no difficulty in accepting their affair was almost at an end. Oh, he'd miss her, but just in a physical way, and that wouldn't last long, surely.

'Love is fine,' he said with a careful smile. 'For Matthaios it was necessary. Ingrid changed him and even though her death destroyed a part of him, he is still a better man for having loved her.'

'But it's not for you,' she pushed, her own expression giving frustratingly little away.

'Love requires commitment and I have always preferred to be alone.'

'Why?'

'This, coming from you?'

Her grimace might have been an attempt at a smile.

'My career is my life,' she said.

He understood her drive and determination. He had always been motivated by a similar need to achieve.

'As a child, I knew that Matthaios's life was inextricably linked to mine. His success was mine to encourage. His failures landed at my feet. When my grandfather died, he left just the two of us, and Matt became dependent in a way that has haunted me ever since. I've let him down too many times, Beatrice.'

'I'm sure he wouldn't share your assessment.'

'Be that as it may, it's how I feel. I would never want anyone else to depend on me. Not a woman, not a child. No one.'

She reached for her own drink, sipping it slowly, her eyes showing she was lost in thought.

He couldn't say why, but he wanted her to understand. 'Dependence is…difficult,' he said with a shake of his head. 'My mother…' Was he really going to go down this path?

'Yes?'

His eyes locked on hers on a sigh of frustration. 'I couldn't help her. I loved her—I was just a kid and she was my mother—but it didn't matter what I said or did.'

Beatrice was frowning. 'What was she like?'

'Fun.' His grimace showed pain. 'When she was around, at least. She was full of energy some of the time, taking us to the playground at midnight or sneaking us in to see a movie, spontaneous and—' He sought the word.

'Erratic?' she supplied gently.

'Yes. Exactly. I realise now that this "spontaneous" fun usually coincided with her benders. Then the darkness would come—days of her being in bed, unable or unwilling to move. Sick, shouting at us to be quiet.'

'And so you took care of her?'

'As much as she'd let me.' He shrugged.

'And Matthaios?'

'Yes. I cared for him too. Someone had to feed him.'

Bea's eyes were filled with sympathy. He looked away, firming his jaw.

'So you can see why I'm sceptical about the whole idea of being needed by anyone. It's not healthy. I hate it.'

Bea's soft exhalation of breath eventually drew his gaze back.

'Anyone else might say that sounds kind of lonely,' she observed eventually.

Something strengthened in his chest. 'But not you?'

She shook her head slowly. 'No. Not me.'

For himself, he understood the decision, but for Bea, something inside Ares cracked apart a little. There was something completely unacceptable about the way she'd walled herself off from life and the experience of companionship.

He reached across the table, putting his hand on hers. 'I don't get seriously involved with the women I date, Beatrice, because I abhor the idea of relationships and all the emotional expectations that come from them. But I *do* date. I enjoy the company of women, I enjoy sex and intimacy. I appreciate the importance of human connection, even when I know I have my limits.'

Her smile was wry. 'I don't think that's any better than the way I live my life.'

'So when you leave here, is it your intention to go back to the way things were before? Avoiding men, avoiding dating, hiding yourself in unflattering outfits lest someone actually recognises that you're a sensual, attractive woman?'

Her cheeks turned a vibrant pink, her lips parting indignantly. 'That's not—' She clamped her lips down on the denial. 'That's none of your business.'

He laced their fingers together, squeezing her hand. 'You deserve better than the life you're living.'

She pulled her hand away. 'I like my life.'

He didn't need to say anything to challenge her. His look communicated his scepticism just fine. She huffed and stood, pacing towards the pool. As the evenings had grown warmer they'd taken to eating out here. Beatrice, Ares had learned, loved sunsets, her affinity with this time of day something he'd subconsciously begun to crave. He'd made sure he was home in time to enjoy them with her—or, rather, to enjoy her enchantment as the sky dressed itself in a different outfit each evening. Tonight had been cloudless, so the sky had filled with a gentle gradient, fading from purple at the horizon to gold and peach. The ocean took on tones to match, a steely turquoise in the lessening light.

He pushed his own chair back. Nothing he'd said had

been wrong, but upsetting Bea was intolerable. He prowled towards her, standing at her back, his hands curving over her shoulders.

'It's your life,' he murmured gently. 'And in less than a week you'll get back to it. I don't like to think of you leading it alone—even when, selfishly, a part of me never wants you to get involved with any other man.'

He felt her sharp intake of breath and laughed. 'Don't worry. I'm not suggesting that we continue this. It's pure male ego.'

She exhaled slowly. 'What if…'

The words were so soft he barely caught them. 'Yes?'

She turned in the circle of his arms, her eyes looking deep into his own, stirring something in his soul. 'What if, after this week's over, we still…see each other?' The muscles of her throat bunched delicately. 'From time to time,' she added quickly.

It was like being split apart by the stroke on an anvil.

There was danger here. Danger in the way Beatrice provoked him, spoke to him, pushed him—danger in the sweet little noises she made when they slept together, danger in the fact that he'd already spent more time with her than he had with any other woman. If maintaining control was the most important thing in his life, then Bea represented a very real threat to that.

He ground his teeth together, mentally distancing himself. 'That's not possible.'

He saw the hurt in her eyes briefly before she let them drift shut, her lashes forming two dark velvet fans against her cheeks. 'Why not?'

'Because it would just be prolonging the inevitable. I won't let you waste your life like that.'

'It's my life,' she pointed out defiantly.

'And my conscience to live with.' He regarded her

warily, hating that she was trying to move the parameters of their safe agreement.

She turned away from him abruptly so he had no idea of her reaction to those words.

He had to drive his point home. 'Bea, I like sex. I like it a lot. These last few weeks have been...better than I could have imagined. But we both knew it would end.'

Silence grew thick between them. When she spoke, her voice was stiff like iron, but quieter than the whispering wind, so he had to lean closer to catch the words.

'This isn't a protestation of love. I'm just saying we could—casually—see each other when I'm back in London. If you want to.'

Why did he hate that even more? Why did he want to shout that a no-strings relationship like that wasn't good enough for her?

It was a double standard; if she wanted to limit herself to that kind of relationship—just as he did—then that was her choice.

But Bea was different to him.

Where Ares had grown hard and ruthless out of habit and necessity, Bea was soft and sweet, vulnerable beneath a thin outer layer that imitated coldness. She wasn't cold though, and she wasn't someone who was suited to live her life alone. She was just too scared to let herself love anyone.

He clamped his jaw, turning her gently and catching her hands, lifting them to his chest. She didn't quite meet his eyes.

'I want to enjoy the time we have left, and then I want you to leave my home and never look back. Don't think about me, don't think about Danica. Go home and start your life over—only promise me that you'll keep an open mind about companionship. You deserve better than to keep pushing everyone away, *agápi mou.*'

* * *

Pain was slashing through her. A pain that was familiar and intense.

He didn't want her.

He didn't want her.

The words kept circling through her brain, prickly and sharp, so she had to bite back a groan. Her insides were awash with acid but Bea wouldn't let him see her pain. Just like she'd learned to hide it from her parents, and from everyone else, she hid it from Ares now, flicking him a careless smile even as something inside her was shattering into a thousand pieces.

He didn't want her.

'I'll grant you most of what you've asked for,' she said gently.

He was very still and that stillness was all the confirmation she needed. He'd never want her. No one would.

'I won't think about you when I leave…' the words caught in her throat a little '…but Danica will always have a place in here.' She pulled her hand free and pressed it to her heart. 'I can't promise I won't think of her often.'

It wasn't just sunset that Bea loved; it was sunrise too. The bookends of the day that broke across the sky, rendering it with a sense of magic and newness, the promise of a new dawn and new hope.

The next morning she pushed back the sheets of Ares's bed and crept out silently, steeling herself to recognise that this was almost over. Soon there would be no more waking up beside him, no more pressing back against his naked body, teasing him with her proximity, silently pleading with him to make love to her again. There was only a handful of nights left to enjoy Ares, and then she'd never see him again. Because he didn't want her.

The sand was cold beneath her feet, and damp from the

receding waves' kiss. She walked slowly at first, her arms wrapped across her chest, her eyes on the distant stars in the sky, each dwindling by the second, losing their sparkle as light permeated their backdrop.

Her first thought should have been of Danica. The little girl who'd lost her mother, and in some ways her father too, who'd been sent to live with an uncle who'd outsourced her care because he didn't know how to accommodate her in his life and heart. The little girl who had calmed at the first sign of real love and understanding. Her first thought should have been of the baby, but it wasn't. Though she would miss Danica like an absent limb, her feelings for Ares were so much more complex.

She could admit how she felt about Danica. She could understand every single emotion she had for the baby. The sense of affection, of protectiveness, her amusement at the little faces Danica pulled—everything there made sense.

She felt, Bea supposed, as one was meant to when confronted with an adorable, helpless, dependent, sweet infant. She loved her.

It was simple and made sense, whereas everything she felt for Ares was a Dumpster fire of doubt. Physically, she understood what she wanted. He was gorgeous and he made her feel as though she were floating. She could never have counted how many orgasms they'd shared, but that wasn't the whole story. This was more than just sex. It was the way his leg brushed hers beneath the dinner table each evening, the way he held her vice-like, clamped to his chest as he slept, as though he needed to exhale and inhale with the same rhythm she did. It was the way he reached for her hand when they walked, or watched her as she did something as banal as making coffee. It was the way she'd felt that first morning when she'd seen him holding Danica and a wound in her heart had started to stitch back together.

But beyond the physical it was all so murky and un-certain.

She knew she didn't want to do as he'd suggested the night before. She didn't want to walk away from him and forget he existed. She didn't want to live without him in her life.

The realisation made her gasp. She stopped walking, shocked into an inability to put even one foot in front of the other. It shouldn't have surprised her so much; wasn't that what she'd been suggesting last night? Hadn't she tried to find a way to maintain some form of relationship with Ares?

And he'd shut her down. Pushed her away. Oh, he'd done it so well, so beautifully, so *kindly*, as though he really cared about hurting her feelings, but the root cause had been the same. He wanted her to leave at the agreed upon time. He wanted her to leave and never contact him again.

He wanted her out of his life.

Her fist lifted and pressed against her mouth, blocking the sob that was welling in her chest.

Everything Bea had ever read about adoption had spoken of the total unwavering love and commitment an adoptive parent felt for their adopted child—the fact that most wouldn't make the distinction between biological and adopted. That hadn't been the case for her. Not only had her adoptive parents acted as though they regretted bringing her into their lives, her mother had frequently said as much. Not in so many words—Alice was too delicate for that—but she'd made it abundantly clear how she felt.

Like the time a photographer from a glossy magazine had come to the house to take photos to accompany an article they were featuring, and Alice had sent Bea to the study, suggesting it would be better with 'just the real fam-ily'. She'd been thirteen years old, home from school for a brief holiday, and the phrase hadn't made sense at first, then it had filtered into her brain like a thunderstorm at its peak, screeching and whirling with the force of a tornado. She'd gone to her room and cried, but out of those tears a determination had formed. She'd sworn she'd never let Alice hurt her again.

Oh, that hadn't been possible. Though Bea tried to be hard-hearted, she wasn't. Naturally she was soft and loving, and every insult and exclusion from the only people she thought of as family lashed her like a whip at her spine.

It wasn't only their cruelty that had cut her, though. It was their volatility. When Alice had wanted the world to see her as a compassionate, altruistic doyenne of charitable acts, she'd brought out Bea for everyone to see, disregarding Bea's natural dislike for cameras and attention. At those times Alice appeared to dote on Bea, and Bea, so starved for affection and warmth, had lapped it up, craving more, wondering what she'd done to deserve the sudden spurt of affection. It would dissipate just as abruptly as it had emerged, Bea packed off back to boarding school, and weeks would pass without a call or text message from her parents.

Her spirit broke so many times over the years, she thought it had been destroyed beyond repair.

She thought she'd got to the point where she would never again run the risk of being hurt. She'd pulled right back from her adoptive parents, deciding that she could play her part at Christmastime, visiting them for lunch and then speaking to Ronnie and Alice as equals—the less she expected of them, the better things went.

She'd grown out of wanting their love, and she'd told herself she'd never want *anyone's* love again. It was too dangerous, too likely to lead to emotional carnage, and God knew she'd suffered enough of that in her lifetime.

She sank down onto the sand; it was cold beneath her

bottom. Staring out to sea, a wall of fear surrounded her, as vast as the ocean beyond this bay.

Despite everything they'd done to her, Bea loved her parents. She'd tried not to, but love wasn't something you could choose to feel or avoid. Love was as non-optional as breathing. And somewhere since meeting him, probably the night he'd stormed into the office, so cranky and unlike anyone she'd ever known before, Bea had fallen head over heels in love with Ares.

It was a disaster.

She knew without a shadow of a doubt that he would never love her back. And she knew intimately the pain that came from loving and not having that love returned.

If he felt anything for her whatsoever, he would have accepted her suggestion that they find a way to continue seeing one another, even after she went back to London. He hadn't. He didn't love her and that meant one thing and one thing only.

Bea had to escape.

CHAPTER THIRTEEN

HIS ARMS AROUND her waist were almost too perfect to bear. She allowed herself the weakness of sinking back into him just for a moment, one last sublime second of physical closeness, one last moment in which she could pretend that everything was just as it should be, before shattering the illusion with the truth.

Her heart stuttered in her chest, the enormity of what she was about to do dragging on her like a stone.

You could stay, a little voice in her head taunted. Stay for the rest of the week, enjoy the intimacy he was willing to offer, gather the crumbs of his affection for Afterwards, when he was no longer a part of her life and she needed to line her heart space with as many gold dust recollections as she possibly could.

At what cost?

Another sob welled in her chest and she pulled away from him, moving towards the corner of the kitchen, her palms pressed to the counter, her spine straight as she rallied every iota of strength she possessed. Fortunately, Bea had a lot of experience with difficult goodbyes, and even more with heartbreak.

'Beatrice?'

God, she loved how he used her full name. He was the only person who did, and the way he said it, with his accent, spiced with desire…

She swallowed, turning around and forcing her eyes to meet and hold his. She saw the speculation in them, and then the concern.

'Something's wrong.'

She'd asked Ellen to take Danica for a walk in the pram, having given the little baby a tight squeeze and a kiss on the tip of her nose, her heart breaking with the abundance of affection she felt for a child she had known for less than a month. So much for never wanting children! Never wanting to fall in love! What a fool she'd been to think she could dictate such basic human emotions.

'What is it?' He crossed the room, catching her hands in his, lifting them between them as he'd done the night before. It was a strange and fitting gesture, bridging their hearts in some way.

A thousand words swirled through her brain but she struggled to pluck the right assortment to form a sentence that would explain the realisation she'd had, and why that meant she had to leave immediately.

'When I graduated from university my parents sent their personal assistant to take photographs and give me a gift,' she said softly, recalling the delicate diamond bracelet in the turquoise box. 'The assistant was as awkward about it as I was devastated. He took the photos, gave me the gift and left as quickly as he could.' Her throat felt as though it were closing in on itself. 'I was so angry, Ares. It was a simple graduation ceremony only an hour's drive from their house, and they couldn't even make it. They didn't want to.'

He frowned, nodding slowly, though the reason for Bea divulging this obviously made little sense to him.

'My life has been filled with this horrible feeling of loving people who'll never love me back. Of knowing that nothing I do will ever make them proud, or even really make them aware that I exist. They supported me financially—they gave me anything I wanted materially—but they had, and still have, no idea who I really am. And yet I love them, because they're the closest thing to parents I've got.'

Her eyes swept shut as so many memories and hurts battered her, swelling within her, demanding to be shared.

'I know what it feels like to live in a void of uncertainty. Loving and not having that love returned is a horrible way to live, so I swore I'd never risk it. Why would anyone love me, anyway?'

His hands squeezed hers. 'Stop that. You know what an incredible woman you are. Any man would be lucky to have you.'

'Don't.' The word whipped between them, fierce and furious. 'Don't lie to me. Don't placate me with empty words.'

Surprise etched its way across his features.

'You say that but, as I've learned, words are cheap. It's easy to say one thing when you feel exactly the opposite.'

Something like proud defiance lit his eyes. 'I never say what I don't feel.'

'But you don't love me,' she challenged him.

His features grew taut, his lips tight.

'You say any man would be lucky to have me, but you don't want me. Are you not "any man"?'

'Beatrice...' He said her name like a plea, and her gut ached because this was all too familiar. How often she'd been made to feel guilty for complaining. Oh, not recently, but as a young girl, before she'd learned to accept the reality of her situation, when she'd still thought there could be an explanation for the inequities of her parents' treatment of her versus the twins, she'd argued for her cause, only to be made to feel as though she were being overly dramatic.

'Don't gaslight me,' she snapped, earning herself a look of complete shock.

He pulled his hands away, lifting his palms to her. 'I'm not. I'm simply trying to understand—'

He didn't finish the sentence. His brows drew together as he scanned her face, as though he might find answers there.

'What I suggested last night, about us seeing each other again after this week—it wasn't just because I enjoy having sex with you. I like being with you. I like spending time with you and getting to know you.' She shook her head with frustration. 'No, not getting to know you. I feel like on a soul-deep level I know everything there is to know about you. I feel like if it's possible that one person could be designed to fit perfectly with another person, then you're *my* person.'

His jaw shifted as though he were grinding his teeth together; he said nothing.

Bravely, she pushed on, her voice soft now, thick with emotion. 'I lied to you last night, Ares, but only because I've been lying to myself. It turns out I gave you my heart the first night we met, and I want you to keep it for ever.' She only became aware that a tear had slid down her cheek when it landed on her wrist.

'I can't believe this.' The words were short, his own emotions colouring the sentence so it emerged with obvious disappointment. 'I was so clear—'

'I know you were,' she agreed, a part of her withering at his clear-cut condemnation of how foolish she was being. 'But did you really think that would be enough?'

His eyes flared wide and something sparked in her chest. Hurting him felt good. What was wrong with her? How could she want to hurt the man she loved?

Because he was hurting her, and she was so tired of that. So tired of being hurt and ignored by the people she loved.

'Did you think that telling me I couldn't love you would mean a damned thing when you *invited* me, every single night we spent together, to do exactly that? Your words told me not to care but your body made it impossible not to.'

'That's just sex,' he said, but his voice was uneasy, guilt evident in every line of his face.

'Wow.' Now it was Bea's turn to feel pain—more pain than she'd known. 'Just sex. Good to know.'

'Beatrice, that isn't what I meant.'

'I thought you didn't say things you don't mean.'

He compressed his lips. 'Stop trying to trap me. I'm attempting to explain—'

'But that's just words again,' she interrupted, panic making her voice high-pitched. 'You say I can't love you, but do you even stop and think about whether or not you love me too?'

He wore a dismissive mask, his eyes glittering grey. 'I do not need to think about it.'

Her chest ached. Tears caused her throat to sting. 'So you don't love me.'

A muscle flexed near his jaw. 'I've said this from the first night.'

'Yes, yes,' she groaned. 'You did. But that was almost a month ago. Do you really still feel that way?'

He stared at her for several seconds and then nodded. 'Yes. It's exactly how I feel.'

He was being so clear and emphatic. Only a fool would continue this conversation when it could result in just one thing: more hurt. More rejection. Yet still she stood there, allowing the screws to be tightened, a glutton, apparently, for punishment.

'I came here wanting to hate you for kidnapping me, and then I saw you with Danica and I saw you with me and everything changed. I fell so completely in love with you, Ares.'

'Stop.' He shook his head. 'Stop saying that, Beatrice. It's a betrayal of everything we agreed. I don't want your love. I don't want you to need me. For God's sake, I don't want anything from you—got it?'

His outburst surprised them both. His words were so much more certain than she'd expected. She'd hoped for a hint of doubt. For a sign that on some level he might be torn, or starting to comprehend his true feelings. But this was adamant and determined. No one who felt even a hint of love could speak like that.

She angled her face away from him, the enormity of their situation and her error, first in loving him and second in telling him, spreading through her.

'Hurting you is the very last thing I wanted.'

She nodded slowly. 'Then why are you?'

'Do I have an alternative?'

She looked deep into his eyes, trying to fathom his meaning.

'I don't love you, Beatrice. Should I lie to you, just to avoid making you cry?'

Even now, his words were so cutting. Devastation wrapped around her. It wasn't only from what he was inflicting on her; it was the culmination of every feeling of worthlessness she'd ever known.

He cupped her cheek so gently that it was a lie in and of itself. His touch spoke of such tenderness and affection, yet he didn't feel those things for her.

'I don't love you, but not because you're unlovable, *agápi mou.*'

She dipped her eyes downwards, focusing on the floor between them, fresh pain scoring her heart. 'Then why not?'

She felt his gaze burning the top of her head and waited for an answer, an explanation, anything he could offer that would lessen the sting of this rejection.

'Because I'm not capable of it. And because it's not what I want.'

You're not what I want. So simple. So final.

She blinked rapidly, trying to clear her eyes of tears and

her brain of the tangle of emotions. 'I have to get out of here.' It was a whispered resolution at first. Then stronger. 'I have to go home.' Home? What a farce.

'Yes.' His agreement was the final straw. She spun away from him just in time; her sob escaped with enough warning to muffle it completely. 'I'll have my jet fuelled up.'

'No.' It was an immediate visceral reaction. 'Not your jet.' She swallowed furiously. 'If you can just get me to Athens, I'll organise my own flight home.'

'Beatrice, be sensible. I have a plane on standby. It's no trouble.'

'No.' She shook her head to underscore how serious she was. Everything about his private jet would only remind her of him. She couldn't do it. 'I want to do this myself. Please.'

His eyes warred with hers. She felt he was about to argue and held her breath, reserving her energy for exactly that. But, to her surprise, he dipped his head in agreement. 'When would you like to leave?'

'I'm ready now.'

His eyes glittered, something like rejection in them, and a fierce dismissal of that, but again he nodded. 'I'll get Danica so that you can say goodbye.'

'I've already done that. Ellen's taken her for a walk.' Heat flushed her cheeks. 'I didn't want them to overhear our conversation.'

His eyes narrowed and she felt ice run the length of her spine. 'You've thought of everything,' he remarked with stony reserve.

'Don't you dare make me the bad guy here.'

He stared at her, something tightening in his features before he sighed. 'I'm not. I'm well aware that title is completely mine.'

She could only stare at him, her heart in tatters at her feet, her soul withering deep inside her.

'Meet me on the roof when you're ready. I'll be waiting.'

* * *

It was an unconscious echo of the words he'd said on the day they'd gone shopping. So much had happened since then, he hadn't consciously evoked that time. But he'd thought of it again as he'd waited by the helicopter, watching her walk towards him holding only a garment bag which contained, he presumed, her ballgown. She brought no other bag, none of the clothes she'd accumulated whilst staying here.

He was both glad and sorry. Sorry because it showed how deeply he'd wounded her that Bea wasn't even able to take her own clothes, and glad because these physical items would serve as some kind of reminder of her. So that when he woke up at night and wondered if it had all been a dream, he'd see the clothes and know that, no, for a little while, he'd had Beatrice in his life.

And he could have her for longer, he argued with himself as she approached. All he had to do was ask her to be patient. To let him see if he could love her.

But he knew the answer already.

This wasn't about whether he could love Beatrice; it was about whether he wanted her to love him. To depend on him. To rely on him for her happiness and safety. There had been someone relying on him since he was a young boy, and without fail he'd let them down. His mother, his brother, now Danica—he hadn't even been able to hire appropriate staff to care for her. The idea of Bea depending on him, only to realise what a terrible idea that was…to see her life turn to ashes as he failed her in some vital way?

No.

He couldn't bear that.

He'd let her go and, despite what she might think now, she'd get over him. She'd move on and because of the experience they'd shared she'd be more open to love with the right sort of man next time.

'Armandos will take you to the airport,' he said when

she was almost level with him. 'Unless you would like me to come with you?'

She bristled visibly, moving her head to the side. 'I'd prefer to go alone.' Her smile was brittle. 'Thank you.'

Ever polite, he thought with a harsh twist in his gut.

'Beatrice?' He had no idea what he was going to say, but he knew it didn't feel right to let her leave like this.

'Thank you for everything. With Danica.'

Her eyes shifted to his shoulder. 'I loved spending time with her.' Her lower lip wobbled and he moved quickly, opening the door to the helicopter, understanding the small kindness he could show her now. She just wanted to escape. Trapping her here to talk was further proof of his inability to be the man she needed.

'Let me know when you're back in London,' he requested. 'So I know you arrived there safely.'

She grimaced. 'I'll be fine, Ares. You can start forgetting about me right now.'

What could he say to that? He'd practically boasted to her about that being the wise thing to do. He couldn't deny it now, or she might read something into it. But as the helicopter lifted off, becoming a distant, gleaming speck of black against an azure blue sky, he knew he'd never forget Bea, and strangely he was glad of that.

Bea was in a fog. She managed, somehow, to buy herself a ticket on the next plane leaving for London, and to contemplate sending Amy a quick text to let her know she'd be home soon. Except Bea didn't want to see Amy or Clare. For the first time in her adult life, Bea truly felt that she didn't want to talk to her best friends. Not about this. She simply needed to be alone.

Amy would know within seconds that something serious had happened, and Bea couldn't lie to one of her best friends. She had to be stronger before they had that conversation.

If Amy had been a less worthy friend it would have been possible to presume she'd be too wrapped up in her own life to notice anything amiss with Bea. But Amy was loyal, kind and compassionate and she'd likely take one look at Bea and realise that her heart had been shattered. Hell, she'd probably insist the London Connection drop Ares as a client after this, and Bea knew they couldn't afford that. She had to heal a bit before she saw either Amy or Clare again, knowing their loyal streaks would be invoked. No one was expecting her back in London for a few more days. She'd sneak home to her apartment and lie low, just until she was ready to drag her brave face back into place.

Decision made, she went through Security and waited near the boarding gate, trying not to think about Ares, about Danica, and about how much she was already missing them both.

It was a stunning sunset. All the colours streaked across the sky, the deepest oranges and reds with a shimmer of gold, purple glowing from behind the scant covering of silvery clouds. Ares stared at it and felt a gut-punch of sorrow. He was sorry that Bea wasn't with him; she'd have loved it. Sorry that they weren't going to see another sunset together.

Sorry that he'd hurt her so badly.

Sorry that he'd never see her again.

Just horribly, regrettably sorry.

She never texted or called to let him know she'd arrived in London but, given the lack of news about a plane crash or the kidnapping of a twenty-nine-year-old executive, he had to presume she'd made it there and chosen not to contact him. A wise decision, but he yearned to hear something from her. Just to know she was okay.

* * *

As a child, his grandfather had told him often that 'time heals all wounds', and Ares had generally felt there was truth in that. But the more time that separated him from Bea, the worse he felt. Danica was unsettled and, two days after Bea left, Ellen moved into a guest room so she could be available to help around the clock.

Ares took that as an opportunity to leave Porto Heli, where everything, everyone and everywhere, reminded him of Bea. He needed to get away from her, any way he could.

CHAPTER FOURTEEN

'OH, MY GOD.' She stared at the rapidly spreading stain of milky coffee against a broad chest, her heart in her throat as her eyes lifted higher to ascertain that, yes, somehow, surely in an alternative universe, Beatrice Jones had once again managed to spill her coffee all over Ares Lykaios's chest.

It made no sense. Her brain struggled to translate what she was seeing. She'd barely slept since returning from Athens four days earlier. She was living on a strange combination of Netflix and coffee from the coffee chain beneath her apartment. She didn't even have to order now; when the baristas saw her walk in they began to prepare her drink, so all she had to do was tap her credit card and grab it when it was ready.

And in the case of this, coffee number four for the day, slam it into the chest of the only man she'd ever loved.

'I swear I put on the lid.' But the fact that it had burst open the instant she'd bumped into him might make him beg to differ.

Oh, God. She looked terrible. She couldn't remember the last time she'd showered. Her hair was scraped back into a ponytail, her shirt had a stain on the sleeve and she'd abandoned make-up for the sheen of takeaway noodle fumes.

'Beatrice.' He growled her name from somewhere deep in his throat and goosebumps ran across her skin; her stomach flipped. She looked at her watch for no logical reason except that time would tether her—she hoped—to reality. It was almost five in the afternoon. Of what day?

'What are you doing here?'

Of all the questions running through her brain, that was uppermost.

'I came to see you.'

Obviously. Why else would he be in this exact part of London? 'Is it Danica?' she asked quickly, concern for the little girl momentarily eclipsing anything else.

He flinched. 'Danica is fine. She's…at home with Ellen.' His lips were a grim smudge on his face.

'Oh. I'm glad.'

'May I come in?' He gestured to the security door to her building.

Bea stared at it, panic gripping her heart. She shook her head instinctively.

'Just for a moment.' There was something so imperative and commanding in his tone that Bea found herself sighing and moving towards it. She could control this situation. And she could definitely control how much she let him see of her pain. She had pride and she would use it to strengthen her resolve until he finally left. At the same time, she acknowledged that she desperately wanted him to stay. Seeing him under any circumstances was better than not, and oh, how hungry she was for the sight of him, the feel of him.

'How did you find out where I live?'

'It wasn't difficult.'

Of course it wasn't difficult for someone like Ares Lykaios. Somewhere during the time they'd spent together in Greece, she'd come to see him as a mere mortal, simply a man she'd fallen in love with, but he wasn't anything so pedestrian as that. He was powerful and could do whatever the hell he wanted.

She buzzed open the security door then gestured to the

door at the top of the stairs, a shiny black with a golden number four emblazoned on it.

'There are two apartments downstairs,' she explained as she averted her gaze from him, knowing she couldn't watch as he walked up the stairs or desire would undo every effort she was making to hold onto her pride. 'But no apartment number three. I've always wondered if the original builders thought it was unlucky or something.' She clamped her lips together, aware she was filling the nervous silence with babble and hating herself for that.

At the door of her apartment she hesitated, her eyes darting to his before returning to the lock.

'Two minutes,' he commanded, and when she still didn't move he reached out and took the extended key from her fingertips and inserted it, pushing the door open with an expression that was inscrutable.

Bea's heart was in her throat, emotions running rampant. She wasn't prepared for this. She'd wondered if she'd ever see him again, but had presumed that she'd at least have time to brace for that, to prepare herself for the mental hurdle of being near him once more.

This was *hard*.

She fought ingrained good manners, pointing to a chair without offering him a drink. Despite the dark patch spreading over his shirt, she refused to do anything to accommodate him. She'd had enough of being trampled. Enough of putting her heart out there and having it unceremoniously refused.

Bea's apartment had a large open-plan kitchen and lounge area. She kicked off her shoes then padded into the all-white kitchen, depositing the almost empty coffee cup into the sink and washing her hands before slipping a pod into her own machine. The muscle memory of the task was reassuring and somewhat calming; his eyes on her as she did something so simple was not. The machine whirred as dark coffee began to run into the mug.

When she turned around, he was staring at her intently and her breath slammed through her. She wanted to stamp her foot and she realised her temper was running away from her. How dared he come here with no warning, looking so damned perfect? As though nothing in the world was bothering him. As though his life was continuing completely as normal.

'What are you doing here?' Pride be damned. The words were a husky groan, a plea for him to disappear again so she could continue getting over him.

His lips compressed. The coffee machine stopped whirring.

'I can't sleep.'

She stared at him, the words making no sense.

'Then you should go see a doctor. See if they'll prescribe you something.'

'It wouldn't help.'

'I'm sure it would.'

He shook his head. 'Every time I close my eyes I see your face on that last morning in Greece. I see the way you looked at me when you told me you loved me and I didn't say it back, and I feel as though something is being twisted in my chest, the blade of a dagger, I don't know. And then I'm wide awake again. I just…need to know that you're okay. That's all.'

Her heart stuttered. She turned away with the pretence of reaching for her coffee, cradling it in her hands, taking a perverse pleasure in denying him the same courtesy. It was childish, yet she didn't care.

'I'm fine.' Pride came to her rescue. She'd begged him to love her once. She wouldn't do it again.

He nodded slowly, his eyes scanning her face.

Please go. She couldn't handle this much longer.

'Fine.' He dragged a hand through his hair. 'Good.' He frowned. 'I'm…glad.'

He turned towards the door and took two steps in that direction then made a deep noise of frustration, pivoting to face her. His eyes pinned her to the spot, his features a mask of something she couldn't fathom. He stared at her long and hard, so the air between them became thick with unspoken words, and then he swore, a dark, throaty curse in his native Greek, a word that reverberated around her kitchen again and again.

'Damn it, Beatrice. I can't do this.'

She wasn't capable of speaking.

'I can't be the man you want me to be. Do you have any idea how much I want to give you what you want?' He strode towards her and she braced for that as best she could, but it wasn't enough. She wasn't prepared to be so close she could see the flecks of silver in his grey eyes, breathe in the scent of his alpine cologne, mingled with her spilled coffee.

'It's not that I don't love you.'

She almost choked on her breath.

'It's that I don't want you to love me. I need you to stop. Tell me you made a mistake and that you were wrong. I can't bear to think of you feeling that way about me.'

He waited, staring at her, his chest feeling as though it had been cracked in two. His eyes pleaded with her to give him what he needed. He couldn't live in a world where Beatrice loved him. The thought of disappointing her, of letting her down in some vital way, was the worst thing he could contemplate.

Hell, he'd already let her down. He could see the hurt in her face even now, days after that disastrous conversation.

She wasn't okay.

And he didn't know how to make her okay.

'There was no mistake.' She blinked at him, as though just realising something. 'And there are no regrets.' He was unprepared for her hand lightly brushing his chest, the flatness of her palm against his heart, as though she couldn't resist feeling him there. 'I'll always love you and, even though that hurts like hell right now, I'm grateful. I never thought I'd fall in love.' Her lips twisted in a poor imitation of a smile. 'I wouldn't trade the experience of falling in love with you for anything. The time we spent together was honestly the best weeks of my life.'

Her words rang with courage. He closed his eyes against it, wondering at the way the world was shifting beneath his feet, old certainties seeming to erode in the face of her determination.

'Don't you see, Ares? You're off the hook; don't beat yourself up with guilt here. You don't have to love me back. Just spending that time together was a gift.' She sniffed and he fixed his eyes on her face in time to see a single teardrop fall from the corner of one of her beautiful, expressive eyes. 'I'm not okay right now, but I will be. The pain will fade, and then I'll just have those memories. Good memories, almost all of them.'

Her heart was open to him, beautiful and forgiving, if only he'd get over his own fears and accept it. But life had made him cautious. Her heart might not have been broken, in spite of what she'd been through, but he feared his was.

And yet she was being so brave! What must it have taken Bea to face her feelings? To confide the truth of them to him. Didn't she deserve as much in return?

He ground his teeth together, his stomach unsteady as he tried to find words without overthinking them.

'I've never known anyone like you. I'd planned to fly out of London after my meeting with Clare, you know. I wasn't meant to remain here, but then I met you and you suggested I come back the next day, and I invented every excuse in the world just to see you again. You bewitched me from the start.'

Her eyes were wide but awash with disbelief. 'You were unimpressed.'

'No, I was…fascinated. Why do you think I demanded you accompany me to the ball?'

'So you wouldn't arrive alone,' she reminded him. 'So the media wouldn't get a photo of you appearing solo.'

'I go to events on my own all the time. My ego isn't so fragile, Beatrice, that I can't handle being photographed without a glamorous woman on my arm. No, it was never that.'

'So why then?' she pressed, removing her hand from his chest and curling it around her coffee cup again. She sipped it, dropping her gaze from his, pushing him away a little. He could feel that she wanted to keep him at a distance and sought to close it.

'I just wanted to be with you. I wanted to sleep with you.' He threw the words at her, needing her to understand that he was *that* kind of man. Someone who liked to seduce women he barely knew and then move on.

No mess. No emotional confusion.

'And if Cassandra hadn't quit, we would have had sex and you'd have forgotten me a week later?'

Despite what he'd thought a moment ago, he contradicted himself with a shake of his head. 'I don't think so. You were already so far under my skin, *agápi mou*. When I look back at the way I spoke to you that night, the way I threatened you—I was terrified of losing you. I'll never forget what you said to me: that if I'd simply asked, you'd have stayed. I'd never known anyone like you before. So kind and good and compassionate. So full of love, Bea, you were aching to give it.'

Her sob was almost silent, wrenched from deep within her chest.

'You loved Danica instantly and I wanted to be a part of it.' He grimaced, the full truth of his actions spread out before him. 'Do you remember what you said, the morning you left Greece? You told me I made you fall in love with me, and you're right. Not consciously, but I was so self-ish. It wasn't enough for me to have your body. I wanted all of you, everything you had to give, and that included your heart.'

She shook her head frantically. 'Don't. I can't—'

He didn't know what she was going to say, but he was getting so close to understanding his own actions. He lifted a finger to her lips, silencing her as he searched for what he'd felt and why.

'Nothing good has ever come from loving me.'

Her eyes swirled with contradictions, but she stayed quiet.

'I've loved you since that first night we met, I think, but I have no idea how to love you. I have no idea how to be a man who deserves you and, *Theós*, you deserve so much. I am being selfish again, coming here, telling you this, when the best thing for you would be if I had just let you walk away.'

Her sob was softer this time, and then she was leaning forward, pressing her forehead to his chest, her gentle sobs filling him with emotions he couldn't comprehend.

After a moment she pulled back to look up at him, shaking her head slowly. 'You're such an idiot.'

He lifted his brows.

'How do you not see yourself as you really are? How can you be so disillusioned?'

He frowned.

'You keep thinking that you let people down, but I see the opposite. I see a boy who had to parent his mother, and raise his brother. Even now, as a man in his thirties, you're picking up after Matthaios. You are good and kind and honourable, and I've got news for you, Ares.'

He waited.

'You're full of love to give as well. I watched you with Danica and saw the way you felt about her, your big, beautiful heart exploding with a need to protect her and care for her. You want to know how to be the man I deserve?'

His lips parted on a roughly expelled breath.

'By doing this! Exactly what you're doing right now. You came here today and you told me the truth about how you feel, even though that's kind of terrifying. Love isn't just an isolated emotion. It's held up by so many others! Trust and respect, kindness, humour, intention. I trust you to do the right thing by me—and that doesn't mean I'll never get hurt again. It doesn't mean you can protect me from anything bad ever happening in my life. It means that, whatever happens, I want to go through it with you.'

'But what if—'

'What if—what?' she interrupted quietly. 'Life is full of "what-ifs". The only one that matters right now is this: what if you walk out of here today and we never see each other again? Will you be able to live with *that*?'

Everything inside him froze. He stared at her, revulsion barrelling through him. 'Absolutely not.'

Her little laugh was tremulous but happy.

He groaned as realisation finally settled around his heart.

'You're right. I'm an idiot. I can't—won't—live without you. My first instinct that night was to kidnap you, take you to my home and keep you there as long as I could, and it was the right one. Please come home again, Bea. I love you.'

Her heart exploded, the word 'home' exactly what she'd been ruminating on for days. How Porto Heli had become a part of her soul without her realising it, all because of the man who lived there.

She didn't hesitate; there was no need. Bea didn't have a single doubt in her mind as to where she was meant to be, and with whom.

'I will,' she agreed, smiling up at him, her heart full. 'But not right away.' She laced their fingers together. 'I have to break it to the girls that I'm moving to Greece…'

'Oh.' He nodded. 'Then we can live here. I don't care.'

Bea laughed. 'I do. I want to come home.' The word cracked with emotion, and his expression grew serious, wondrous. 'Give me a week, okay?'

A lot changed in a week. Beatrice wasn't the only one whose life had taken an unexpected shift—Amy and Clare had revelations of their own, and excitement about their futures overlapped with frantic business meetings and staff hiring, rearranging the corporate structure to ensure the London Connection could continue to grow even with the best friends living in different cities around the world.

Of one thing they were certain: their commitment to the business—and their loyalty and love for one another—would never change, no matter how far apart they were geographically. They were friends, sisters of the heart, and always would be.

EPILOGUE

'IT'S A PLEASURE to meet you.' Matthaios smiled as he drew Bea into a warm hug, kissing her on both cheeks before releasing her. His exuberance was understandable. After several weeks in the rehab facility he was clean and sober and completely committed to living a sober life. Between them, Danica squawked, lifting her hands towards Matthaios, and at the same time the little girl burst into tears, shaking with the force of her emotions.

'Aw, she's so happy to see you.' Bea's own eyes sparkled with emotion as Matthaios clutched Danica to his chest.

He spoke in Greek, low and soft, smiling as he hugged Danica as though he'd never let her go. Ares came to stand beside Bea, his arm around her waist drawing her close so that she fitted at his side perfectly. He was warm and he was home. She was home.

'She can't stop crying,' Matthaios said anxiously, without taking his eyes off the baby's face.

'She's just a little overwhelmed,' Bea reassured him. 'She has no other way to express how she's feeling, so she cries. They're happy tears, I promise.'

He nodded, kissing Danica's head, brushing their cheeks together. 'I've missed you too, little one.' He lifted his eyes to Beatrice's face, then sideways to Ares. 'Thank you both. I promise I won't let her down again.'

'I believe you.' Ares nodded. 'But we're always here for you, any time you need us.'

Bea smiled warmly, underscoring Ares's sentiments.

Later, when Danica was settled for her afternoon nap, Matthaios held a coffee cup in his hands, staring out at the idyllic ocean view. The day was warm, the water still, so Ares was already planning an evening swim with Bea, who'd gone to get changed.

'It's serious between the two of you?'

Ares turned to his brother, nodding. 'What do you think?'

Matthaios's grin was knowing. 'I think you're besotted and I'm glad. I've never seen you like this before.'

'I've never been like this before,' he said with a lift of his shoulders. 'I love her.'

'I can see that.'

Saying it felt right—and having Matthaios's quick acceptance meant everything to Ares. 'What I said before, Matt, I'm here for you. Whatever you need.'

'I appreciate that, but I've already needed you more than enough. It's time for you to live your life without worrying about me.'

'I'm not worried,' he said truthfully. 'I'm proud. Facing your demons is hard, and you've done it twice. I think you're a superhero. But even superheroes come unstuck sometimes, and if that ever happens you know I've got your back.'

Matthaios nodded, sipping his coffee. 'I know, but this time is different. I feel different. And I'm not going to risk hurting Danica ever again. I'm not going to be like Mamá.'

Ares thought about that—their mother's repeated benders, her hangovers, her disappearance.

'I'm keen to get on with my life. Get back to work. I have to be someone Ingrid would have been proud of—I owe that to her.'

'Yes,' Ares agreed, because he finally understood what it meant to love someone with all your heart, and how that love changed you. 'You do, Matt.'

'Excuse me.' Ares turned at Ellen's interruption. Matt's eyes glanced over at the young woman. 'Bea said you wanted to be told when Danica was awake. It's her bath time.'

'And you are?' Matt prompted, standing, his manner assessing.

'This is Ellen,' Ares explained, getting to his feet. 'I told you about her.'

'I remember.' Matt extended a hand. 'Thanks for everything you've done. I appreciate it.'

'It's been my pleasure. Danica's adorable. I will be very, very sorry to see her go.'

As the two of them disappeared into the house, Ares stayed on the balcony, staring out to sea. Life was full of unexpected twists, and he could never have foreseen this. A chance meeting, an inconvenient scheduling mishap in the midst of one of the most stressful weeks of his life, had led to him finding the woman of his dreams. It was a piece of good fortune he feared he didn't deserve, but one that he knew he'd live the rest of his life being grateful for.

The sun was low in the sky but the water was still warm, lapping against Bea's sides. She clung to Ares, her legs around his waist, her arms at his neck, and she smiled because she was happy, as she'd been more often than not since coming to live with him.

Her parents had shown more than a passing interest in them as a couple, though Bea suspected that was because there was something newsworthy in her relationship with a man like Ares Lykaios, rather than being genuinely happy for her. She made a mental note to be on the lookout for pesky paparazzi, who would, no doubt, be sent by her mother, hoping for pictures to grace the pages of the tabloids. Even the thought of that couldn't dull Bea's happiness.

'They seemed so good together,' she said, thinking about Matthaios and Danica. 'He was really comfortable with her.'

'I noticed that too. I'm glad.'

'He knows he can stay with us as long as he wants, doesn't he?'

Ares nodded. 'He's keen to get back to Athens, to resume his life. His own business has been looked after by his chief financial officer, but that cannot go on for ever.'

'Let me guess. He shares your control freak gene?' she teased, kissing the tip of Ares's nose.

'I hope that's not a complaint, Beatrice Jones?'

'Absolutely not.' She blinked at him with wide-eyed innocence. 'I happen to like it when you take control.'

'I'm glad to hear it.' He emphasised his point by kicking back a little in the water, so that it was too deep for Bea to stand. She kept her legs wrapped around his waist, perfectly safe and utterly content.

'You know, when we first met, I remember you telling me that you had no intention of getting married.'

Bea tilted her head to the side, the throwaway comment one she had no recollection of making. 'Did I?'

'At the time, I paid it little attention. I thought I felt the same way.'

Her stomach lurched. 'And you don't?'

He shook his head slowly, his eyes boring into hers. 'No. Meeting you made me realise I feel the complete opposite.'

Bea's heart skipped a beat.

'I have been wondering if there's anything I might say or do to change your mind,' he said, running his hands down her back.

She sank her teeth into her lower lip, the man she loved staring at her so intently. 'To what end?'

'So that we can stand in front of our friends and family and agree to spend the rest of our lives together. What do you think?'

'Are you proposing to me?'

'Yes.' The simple response rang with determination and she laughed because she suspected he would do or say whatever it took to assure himself of her agreement. And, while her heart was already saying yes, she couldn't resist the chance to tease him a little.

'It would require a new contract,' she murmured, but her eyes showed her delight.

'Indeed.' He nodded. 'I wouldn't have expected anything less. What terms this time?'

'Hmm.' She tapped her fingers on his shoulder thoughtfully. 'Coffee in bed every morning?'

'Done. What else?'

'A lifetime of happiness?'

'And togetherness,' he tacked on.

'As little time spent with my family as possible.'

His laugh was gruff. 'Just every second Christmas.'

'Excellent. And lots of time with Danica and Matthaios.'

'And Clare and Amy.' He nodded.

She stared at him, her heart skipping a beat.

'And one day children of our own?' he suggested carefully, as though he was surprised to find himself wanting that.

Bea felt the same—it was something she'd ruled out for so long, but now she knew what she wanted, and it was more than a life with Ares. It was a life with him and a family too, children who would grow up surrounded by their love. 'Definitely.' Her voice cracked a little. 'You know, I've spent all my life feeling unwanted, and like I didn't belong anywhere.' She shook her head wistfully. 'I just didn't realise that the place I was meant to be, and the man I was meant to be with, weren't in my life yet.'

'I've been waiting for you,' he agreed quietly, 'and I didn't realise it either.'

A powerful look of understanding passed between them.

'I'm taking this as a yes,' he said as he dropped his head to hers.

'Oh, it's a yes,' she sighed, kissing him slowly. 'In fact, it's a thousand of them, and then some.'

The sunset was spectacular once again that evening, but neither of them noticed the colours in the sky. That didn't matter, though. There was a lifetime of sunsets awaiting them—every evening for the rest of their lives.

Two years later...

'You didn't have to come. I know how busy you are!' Bea fussed, reaching a hand out to Luca and Amy, smiling from ear to ear. Ares had never seen anyone so beautiful as his wife in that moment. Her face was still pink from her exertions, her hair pulled up into a loose ponytail, and all he could think was that he wanted to photograph her like this, so he could always remember her vital, incredible strength.

'As if I'd miss it,' Amy squawked.

'As if she'd let me,' Luca joked, but he showed he wasn't serious by bending down and kissing Bea's cheek before extending a hand to Ares. They shook like old friends—appropriate, given that they'd become very good friends in the intervening years, even working together on a wind turbine plant in South Africa.

'This is for you.' Amy held out an enormous box of Bea's favourite chocolate truffles. 'I know, they're probably the last thing you can think of right now, but later tonight you might want some spoiling.'

Tears sprang to Bea's eyes—a hazard of her current emotional state. 'Thanks, Ames. They're perfect.'

'I wanted to get the bear,' Luca said with mock disappointment.

Amy rolled her expressive eyes. '"The bear" is a six-foot-tall bright blue teddy bear that would take up half of this room. Trust me, take the chocolate.'

'Oh…erm… I think we've got all the bears we need,' Bea said with a crinkled nose.

'Where is he? Where's my godson?' Clare swept into the room, all fabulous glossy brown hair and glittering blue eyes.

'*Our* godson,' Amy corrected, hugging Clare tight. Dev entered a step behind Clare.

'He's over here,' Ares said, turning to the little bundle who was sleeping, swaddled up, in a small crib to the side of Bea's bed. His heart jerked at the sight of their infant, and a love so powerful he felt as though it might swallow him burst through him.

'Lemme see, lemme see!' Clare clapped her hands together, her heels clipping across the linoleum floor. 'Oh, my goodness, he's utterly perfect, Bea. You did good, Mamá.'

Bea relaxed back against the pillows, her eyes heavy, her smile permanent.

'He is very handsome,' Dev remarked, shaking Ares's hand. 'Must get that from his mother.'

Ares laughed. 'I hope he gets just about everything from her. If he does, then our son will be perfection itself.'

Clare and Amy shared an amused look, but Bea only had eyes for her husband.

'I ran into the twins downstairs,' Clare said, moving closer to Bea.

'Which twins?'

'Your sisters,' Clare prompted.

'Oh.' Bea's eyes skittered to Ares's. 'Mum must have told them I'd gone into labour.'

'Do you want me to ask them to come back tomorrow?' Amy asked gently.

Bea thought about that, then shook her head slowly. 'Honestly, no. They're here, and that's something I never would have thought—maybe today's a day of new beginnings,' she said with the kind of optimism that could only come from the euphoria of having given birth.

'They were just ordering coffee when we passed them, so I'd say you've got some time before they visit.'

'I'll tell them not to stay long,' Ares said, coming to place a hand on Bea's shoulder. 'You must be exhausted, and you've already had Matt here.'

'It *has* been a rather busy morning,' Bea said, but she didn't mind. Seeing Danica with her little cousin had been so heart-warming. She loved their son with all her heart, but Danica would always hold a very special place in her affections. She continued to spend as much time with her niece as possible, and knew she always would.

'On that note, we should let you have some rest,' Amy offered.

'Oh, no, please don't go,' Bea complained. 'I haven't seen you both in weeks!'

Amy nodded. 'We'll come back tomorrow.'

'And stay for lunch?'

Clare wrinkled her nose. 'Only if we can bring it. Hospital food is—'

'Totally gross,' Bea agreed. 'Deal. Dim sum?'

'Done.'

A moment later they were gone, and in the precious moments that followed, Bea allowed herself to feel completely, utterly at peace. Her heart was full and her future bright.

'I love you,' she said to her husband as her eyes drifted shut.

'And I love you.' Ares kissed her head then returned to the sleeping baby's side, his eyes trained on the infant their love had created. For so long, he'd lived in fear of being depended on by anyone, and now he could think of no greater honour than this—being needed and valued by two people as precious as his wife and child. He considered himself a very lucky man indeed.

* * * * *

MILLS & BOON

Coming next month

HIS BILLION-DOLLAR TAKEOVER TEMPTATION
Emmy Grayson

"Mr. Cabrera?"

The husky feminine voice slid over his senses and sent a flash of heat over his skin. He took another deliberate sip of his wine before turning his attention to the second woman who had invaded his space this evening.

Her.

The blonde woman he'd locked eyes with before Alejandro's arrival now stood before him. The neckline of her dark blue gown plunged down in a V to the silver ribbon wrapped around her slender waist. From there the dress flowed into a long, billowing skirt that reminded Adrian of the waters of the Mediterranean before a storm.

His eyes drifted back up to her face in a slow, deliberate perusal. Lush silver-blonde curls enhanced her delicate features. Violet eyes stared back at him, and her caramel-colored lips were set in a firm line.

"Yes," he finally responded, his voice cool, showing that, despite the unusually intense effect she was having on him, he was still in control.

She stepped forward and held out her hand, bare except for a simple silver band on her wrist. Adrian grasped her fingers, pleasantly surprised by her firm grip.

"My name is Everleigh Bradford. Congratulations on your Merlot. It's exquisite."

"Thank you." He arched a brow. "While your compliments are appreciated, was it necessary for you to ignore the 'Balcony Closed' sign and invade my privacy?"

Everleigh's chin came up and her eyes flashed with stubborn fire. "Yes."

Intriguing... There were plenty of men who would have cringed at the slightest hint of his disapproval. But not this woman. She stood her ground, shoulders thrown back, lips now set in a determined line.

"You're a busy man, Mr. Cabrera. I need to speak with you on an urgent matter. I'm sorry for breaking the rules, but it was necessary for me to have a moment alone with you."

Her honesty was refreshing. A night with someone as bold and beautiful as Everleigh would more than make up for his past few months of celibacy.

He infused his smile with sensuality as he raked his gaze up and down her slim form once more, this time letting his appreciation for her body show. "I would greatly enjoy a moment alone with you."

Everleigh's cheeks flushed pink. The blush caught Adrian unawares. Was she an innocent or just playing a role? Much as it would disappoint him, she wouldn't be the first to go to such lengths to catch his attention.

"This has nothing to do with sex, Mr. Cabrera."

"Adrian."

Her lips parted. "I... Excuse me?"

"Please call me Adrian."

Those beautifully shaded violet eyes narrowed. "This is a business discussion, Mr. Cabrera. First names are for friends and family."

"We could become friends, Everleigh."

What was wrong with him? He never teased a woman like this. He complimented, touched, seduced... But with this woman he just couldn't help himself.

Perhaps it was the blush. Yes, that had to be it. The delicate coloring that even now crept down her throat toward the rising slopes of her breasts...

"We will never be friends, Mr. Cabrera," Everleigh snapped. "I'm here to discuss your proposed purchase of Fox Vineyards."

"Then let's talk."

Continue reading
HIS BILLION-DOLLAR TAKEOVER TEMPTATION
Emmy Grayson

Available next month
www.millsandboon.co.uk

COMING SOON!

We really hope you enjoyed reading this book.
If you're looking for more romance, be sure to
head to the shops when new books are
available on

Thursday 13th May

MILLS & BOON

THE HEART OF ROMANCE

A ROMANCE FOR EVERY READER

MODERN

Prepare to be swept off your feet by sophisticated, sexy and seductive heroes, in some of the world's most glamourous and romantic locations, where power and passion collide.

HISTORICAL

Escape with historical heroes from time gone by. Whether your passion is for wicked Regency Rakes, muscled Vikings or rugged Highlanders, awaken the romance of the past.

MEDICAL

Set your pulse racing with dedicated, delectable doctors in the high-pressure world of medicine, where emotions run high and passion, comfort and love are the best medicine.

True Love

Celebrate true love with tender stories of heartfelt romance, from the rush of falling in love to the joy a new baby can bring, and a focus on the emotional heart of a relationship.

Desire

Indulge in secrets and scandal, intense drama and plenty of sizzling hot action with powerful and passionate heroes who have it all: wealth, status, good looks…everything but the right woman.

HEROES

Experience all the excitement of a gripping thriller, with an intense romance at its heart. Resourceful, true-to-life women and strong, fearless men face danger and desire - a killer combination!

To see which titles are coming soon, please visit

millsandboon.co.uk/nextmonth